CW01572511

THE CROFT'S IN
THE AMERICA'S

THE CROFT'S IN THE AMERICA'S

The second in the series of stories
Involving Lord Croft and his wife, Janet
This time in and around the islands of the Caribbean

RICHARD ROGERS

Copyright © 2012 by Richard Rogers.

ISBN: Softcover   978-1-4797-2244-0
             Ebook   978-1-4797-2245-7

All rights reserved. No part of this book may be reproduced or transmitted in any form or by any means, electronic or mechanical, including photocopying, recording, or by any information storage and retrieval system, without permission in writing from the copyright owner.

This is a work of fiction. Names, characters, places and incidents either are the product of the author's imagination or are used fictitiously, and any resemblance to any actual persons, living or dead, events, or locales is entirely coincidental.

This book was printed in the United States of America.

To order additional copies of this book, contact:
Xlibris Corporation
0-800-644-6988
www.Xlibrispublishing.co.uk
Orders@Xlibrispublishing.co.uk
304660

Dedication

To my wife for her patience and support during the long hours she spent
alone whilst this book was written

Apologies

Once again I confirm that this book is a figment of the author's imagination
and is not based on any character I have ever met; nor are any of the
organisations mentioned in this book based on any information I have
received during my research and bear no relationship to anyone, or any
society, organisation, present or past, any customs or other government
officials, or any law enforcement officer whatsoever.

Introduction

Lady Janet Croft had been married to Lord Croft for a few years; she had met him as a young man when she had still been married to her first husband. Janet, by her own confession, had been very promiscuous during her three years at university, afterwards she had married her first husband, a much older man, in the hope he would be a steadying influence on her. She had remained faithful to him until she found he was in a homosexual relationship; after the initial shock of what she had witnessed, she stayed with him, but had taken to sleeping separately for almost a year. One night, after she and her husband's protégé, Roy Croft, had carried her inebriated husband up to bed, she had confided in him her husband's darkest secret. She had seemed so overwrought that Roy had put his arm around her and comforted her; one thing had led to another and finally she had encouraged him to make love to her. She quickly realised that the young man was innocent and totally inexperienced. Janet, however, had taken a liking to him, an attraction which had, over a period of time, developed into an infatuation. During this period, she coached him in the art of seduction, emphasising the techniques of 'how to satisfy a woman's needs in every way'. Roy Croft had absorbed her teaching and had become a skilful lover, making him popular with many women. Although Janet knew he had become quite a Lothario before and after their marriage, she never knew, however, just how many women he had seduced, or indeed the fact that he had fathered several children by them.

At the point where this book begins, Roy and Janet have two children—a boy, Sean, aged two, and a girl, Sheenagh, aged nine months; they had lived throughout their marriage in a castle, in the south-west of Ireland, with its own harbour. Roy Croft's success in the world of business had first gained him a knighthood, and after the successful completion of a large military contract, he had been awarded a seat in the House of Lords by a grateful government. Having once achieved the peak of his career, he had grown restless, his job ceased to give him satisfaction. Deciding he needed more challenge, he had put his boat up for charter, and after being drawn into crime by the IRA, his converted wartime MTB had several refits, and the upper structure now resembled a Sunseeker 75 with a flying bridge. However, that's where the resemblance ended. The internal specifications were not up to the luxury of the Sunseeker range of boats for several reasons; the boat had a top speed of over sixty knots and had two hidden torpedo tubes as well as well-hidden armaments such as rocket launchers, Sam7 missile launchers, machine guns, and handguns hidden in secret compartments. Roy had used the boat for gunrunning and drug trafficking to help the Irish cause in general, and also for transportation of terrorists to and from training camps in North Africa. His involvement had grown to a point where he had actually committed murder and finally realised he was now a criminal himself. The IRA had taken him on to the inner committee; as a result, he had become an extremely wealthy man, and when it looked as though the authorities were closing in on him, he planned to move to the Americas until things cooled down.

The decision to move to the West Indies was made after one of the British Secret Services had begun to take an interest in the activities of the local branch of the IRA and in Lord Croft in particular. The one-year lease of the castle had been taken by MI5 or MI6, which of the two had not been discovered; but the occupant, Agent Stella, had confessed to Lord Croft that the reason for taking up the lease was to try and discover what part he, as a Lord of the realm, was playing in a reactivated once 'defunct' unit of the IRA. They had searched the castle, but, thanks to the skill of the architect Gordon O'Leary and the workforce provided by Lord Croft's friend Charlie Drake, nothing incriminating had been found.

The story commences as the couple, having let the castle, proceed to move to the West Indies. Janet and the children preceded Roy and taken up temporary residence in the Sandpiper—a hotel in Barbados, whilst Roy set out on his journey from the west coast of Ireland down the coast of Spain to North Africa before turning west to Brazil and then northwards to the West Indies, where he planned to meet up with his wife, Lady Janet Croft, and their children. His crew of three consisted of Elian, his skipper; Fiona, his cook and general factotum; and Gael, a slim twenty-year-old trained terrorist with a muscle structure most trained athletes would die for; in addition, she was fully proficient in all types of weaponry. All three of his crew were not only well chosen for their skills but were also part of his ever-growing list of mistresses.

During his time serving the IRA, Lord Croft, Roy, had in the line of duty to the cause had sunk a European naval gunboat with all hands and killed a man cold-bloodedly. He had aided the cover-up of other crimes carried out on behalf of the IRA, including summary execution of a proven traitor to the cause. He believed that he had sunk as low into criminality as it was possible to go, but read on . . .

Chapter 1

Lady Croft, Janet to her friends, arrived in Bridgetown, Barbados, with her children's nanny, Morag, and her two children, her son Sean, aged two, and her daughter Sheenagh, aged nine months. Lord Croft, Roy, had booked them in a luxury suite at the prestigious Sandpiper hotel whilst he brought their converted MTB across from Ireland. The accommodation at the hotel was superb with every facility possible, and for the first two days, the family lived in the lap of extreme luxury. Janet had been looking forward to a spell in the Caribbean sun and spending time on the beach with the children; in reality, she had quickly grown bored. She was missing Roy already, and if the truths were known, a few pangs of jealousy were creeping into her thoughts. Janet had always given Roy his freedom where women were concerned believing that peace and harmony were better than constant arguments, and he had taken advantage of every opportunity. She was aware he was aboard his cruiser with three young women, none of whom were averse to sharing Roy's bed. She, on the other hand, could only look forward to sleeping alone, and although Morag helped with the children, life in the hotel soon became tiring.

Janet had grown accustomed to living in a large castle where she could disappear whilst leaving the domestics to cope with domestic drudgery, here there seemed no space, nowhere for her to hide, and she had no friends on the island. To Lady Croft, what had seemed as an idyllic break had become a chore. Janet was feeling low, neglected, and unloved. When, out of the blue, she received a phone call from a Dr Michael Crosby, one of her many lovers from her university days. Immediately, Janet recognised the voice, from the strong deep tones, as that of Michael; she listened in awe as he began.

"Janet, is it really you? I have phoned almost every hotel in town since Carl, whom I had not heard from for simply ages, rang me last night and informed me you were staying in Bridgetown. I had no idea you were married and you are now Lady Croft. You certainly seem to have made good since the old days."

Lady Croft's mind went back to that day in Ireland when Carl and his young wife had come to the castle to look at it with a view to lease it for a year, whilst Carl did a year's sabbatical on the flora and fauna of the west coast of Ireland. Whist she had been showing him the extensive grounds, he had made himself known; recognition had hardly registered when she had felt him pull her towards him in a passionate embrace. Returning to the castle, Janet had been unable to resist the temptation, the chance to feel young, glamorous, and desirable to other men had been too strong. She had let Carl seduce her in her own lounge whilst her husband, Lord Croft, was busy showing Carl's wife, Camilla, around the extensive living quarters of the castle.

Janet recalled that she had been wildly enthusiastic just as she had been as a young student; the pleasure, however, had been cut short when her sexual indiscretion had been discovered, first by Roy, her husband, and then by Camilla, Carl's wife. There had been an argument and the young couple had left. Roy had been saddened by the event, but he could not really raise any objection to her uncharacteristic behaviour as he had never regarded monogamy as part of his marriage—a fact that Janet had always been familiar with, as she had not only taught him the skills but had also openly encouraged his permissiveness. Janet, who had never broken her marriage vows since marrying Roy, had always resolved to be a faithful wife, content with Roy as a husband despite his many mistresses. Carl had flattered her, overwhelming her with his complimentary remarks, and she had delighted in the attention she received from him. Janet had never considered following Roy's example, but what with sudden appearance of Carl in Ireland and now a call from Michael, here in Barbados, her world had suddenly seemed to take on a new perspective. She had never considered anyone else, but the sudden appearance of two acquaintances from the past, both showing her so much attention, simply turned her head. Janet remembered Michael as one of her ardent followers at university, losing track of him after he received his Ph.D. in Marine Biology; he had disappeared into the wilds of the West Indies to study marine life there.

The strong but soft Irish lilt of Michael's voice snapped her out of her trip down memory lane as he asked her,

"Janet, I would love to see you again. Would you care to spend a day with me aboard *Petra*, my research boat? I came across from St Lucia, especially to try to see you."

"What research?" Janet asked trying to hide the excitement in her voice as her heart pounded in her chest.

"I am currently carrying out a research on some of the unique marine life on the tiny outcrops to the south of the island."

Janet's heart fluttered; she felt her youth returning. First, it had been Carl and now, Michael; it was like a dream. Janet readily agreed without a second thought as to the inevitable outcome of such a renewal of their earlier liaison that Michael had suggested.

"Look, I'll come over to your hotel this evening. I'll book a room for the night, if that's OK by you? We could have dinner together, and we could leave for the boat early in the morning. I understand you have a young family. Will you be able to arrange someone to look after them?"

The children were obviously not invited, and warning bells should have sounded in Lady Croft's ears, but this seemed the golden opportunity to break out of the boredom of life alone in the hotel; male company was what she needed.

"Being wealthy has its compensations, Michael. I have a nanny to look after the children. I'd be delighted to have dinner with you. It will be just like old times. I'm sure Morag will have the children tomorrow. I'll expect you this evening, say seven for seven thirty. I'll see you in the hotel bar."

Janet was thrilled to be going out with her old friend and lover; summoning Morag, she informed her, in a bubbly and girlish voice,

"Morag, I've been invited out for dinner and a day with an old friend on his boat tomorrow. I know you will manage whilst I'm away, but if you need any assistance with the children for any reason, I'm informed the hotel offers a full nanny service. It appears all the staff are fully trained for any emergency."

"When can I expect you to return, your Ladyship?" Morag asked. "I will have to tell the children something, they will miss you?"

"Oh, I'm only planning to be away for the day," Janet responded, but the exuberant excitement showed through in her voice.

Morag was curious but said nothing at the time.

Once Morag had left the room to return to her charges, Janet looked out her skimpiest bikini, the one which had ties at the side of both top and bottom. She intended to sunbathe whilst on Michael's research boat, and tan lines were not going to be the order of the day. After the children had been bathed and put to bed, Janet spent time deciding on the most suitable dress for the evening, then enjoyed the care she put into her make-up before she went down to join Dr Crosby for dinner. Wondering if he would have changed over the years, she need not have feared, for she recognised him immediately, noting how he had matured; not only did he have a wonderfully natural tan but also the older Michael had grown far more handsome than she remembered him. Just being with him, and remembering how things between them had once been, made her feel free of the boredom and chores of just hanging around with the children. She could feel her needs grow as they sat and talked of their days at university. Janet remembered that Michael had always been a thoughtful lover, albeit very demanding at the height of their relationship. She remembered at university they had at times made love several times in a day. Talking in the vista of the handsome man across the table, she wondered if he still had the same stamina.

"Did you ever marry, Michael, or are you still a bachelor?" Janet asked. Michael raised his eyebrows enquiringly at the question, and then shaking his head, he replied,

"Apart from the occasional local girl, my sex life is like the Sahara. I am," he said, "married to my research."

They reminisced about old times as they sat drinking their aperitifs before going into the dining room for dinner. During the meal, Michael was attentive and, like Carl had done, showered her with compliments about her appearance and that she did not look like a woman with two children.

Once the meal was over and they had leisurely drunk a couple of bottles of wine, they danced to the music of Caribbean steel band. Michael held her close during the slower dances, and she did not need to be told she still attracted him, that much was quite obvious. They laughed and talked with the ease of old lovers, as the evening passed with Janet becoming more relaxed than she had been for days. When it grew late, Michael asked,

"Do you need to get back to your family or do you have time for a nightcap? I have a well-stocked bar in my room."

Janet knew where it was leading; her heart was pounding with expectation and excitement when she readily accepted his offer. Michael's bedroom was much smaller than the suite she and Morag occupied with the children, but he had a king-size bed. She wondered if he had requested it in particular. Janet sat on the chair by the window and watched as her companion switched on the portable radio by the bedside. Michael looked at her smiling in *that* special way she remembered from long ago as he inserted a CD he had taken from within his briefcase. Janet wondered casually if he had brought several and had chosen one according to her mood. If so, she was not disappointed as the CD he chose was one of a slow dance music that had been popular when they were both at university. They began to dance together; Michael, now not overlooked by anyone else, held Janet tightly against him, his fingers gently caressing her exposed back and shoulders. She made no sign of resistance when she felt his other hand casually moving up to her breast; she pressed herself against him as she would have done in days gone by.

Janet gave herself up to Michael's gentle entreaties; she was soon lost in a feeling of total surrender influenced by the gentle lull of his soft kisses. Lost in her excitement, she gave scant thought of Roy or the children as she allowed herself to meld to the soft caress of her older but handsome lover. She vaguely gave a thought to Roy, for, to her, it seemed that over the last few months, somehow, their lovemaking had lost some of its wild intensity. However, Michael did not have the skills of her husband, leaving her unfulfilled; she forgave him, putting his failure to satisfy her down to his somewhat monastic existence. Despite the enjoyment of the evening, Janet kept asking herself, why was she doing this? Was it trying to recapture her youth or was it just that she needed a change? Had she grown tired of her monogamous marriage and the humdrum of being a mother of two children?

Janet and Michael lay in each other's arms for some time before she saw the time; then she reluctantly got off the bed and walked slowly into the shower. Janet dressed, and the reunited lovers kissed; Michael kept entreating her to stay for what remained of the night, seeming somewhat disappointed at her refusal.
"I'll need to get back for the children," Janet replied, adding, "I will need to see them before we leave tomorrow. You will have to be satisfied until then, Michael. You were always so impetuous and demanding, if I recollect correctly."
"I'll see you in the morning, my darling," he replied, barely able to hide the disappointment in his voice.

Janet was up early the following day; as usual, she supervised breakfast before departing for her day aboard the research boat *Petra*, leaving Morag to watch over the children. Joining Michael in the foyer, she was driven to the jetty where the boat was moored. Janet was like an excited schoolgirl, away from the supervision of her parents for the first time, and after boarding the large vessel, they headed out to sea where Janet relaxed luxuriating in the sun-kissed warmth of the Caribbean sun. Janet had no interest in watching

Michael at the wheel and spent much of the time lying naked on the foredeck, something she would never do when the children were around. Janet smiled to herself, imagining how much Morag would have been shocked to the core seeing her naked. Michael headed to a quiet cove off one of the islands. It was a delightful spot hidden from view with a stretch of white sand and palm trees; it was like something out of a dream. Janet gave herself to Michael's entreaties unhesitatingly, and they made love out in the open, on the deck, and on the sandy shore shielded from prying eyes. It was an idyllic situation; Janet was far from the worries and cares of family life, transported back through time; as if intoxicated by Michael's very presence, she felt joy and happiness radiate through her from their being together.

The mood, however, was broken when the ship's radio bleeped, and after Michael had answered, his disposition seemed to change. They sat and drank, and it was late afternoon when they berthed back at the quayside. Much to Janet's surprise, Michael asked,

"You may wonder who called me on the radio. Well, it was a friend with an invitation, and as a result of that call, I have a question for you, Janet. Would you like to join me for dinner tonight with the British High Commissioner at the Official Residence?"

This was just what Janet had wanted, a chance to meet people from her own level, a chance to make friends, and she knew that an invitation to the High Commission would give her the golden opportunity to achieve this. She threw her arms around his neck and kissed him as she replied with a mixture of joy tinged with annoyance at such short notice, for she wanted to look her best for the occasion,

"I'd love to join you, Michael. I had no idea you moved in such illustrious circles. I just wish you had given me more time. I've got to do my hair and make myself presentable. Is it formal or casual?" Janet asked.

Janet's mind, already forgetting about the enjoyment of the day, was worrying what she was going to wear, how could she get her hairdresser to fit her in at such short notice, and what was her skin going to look like after a day in the sun. Michael's response, however, brought a smile to Janet's lips.

"I don't think they would mind if you appeared at the table naked."

"Why would they want to look at my body? Janet asked. I've had two children and the stretch marks show."

"I don't think anyone would notice," Michael said gallantly.

Janet spoke wistfully, remembering how fresh and soft her skin had been when she was at university.

"Flattery will get you everywhere, Michael, but when I look in the mirror, I realise my age is beginning to show. I'm getting to be an old woman."

Michael responded quickly, perhaps too quickly,

"I really don't think so. I think you look stunning!"

However, the compliment was lost as Janet had already left the vehicle and was racing up to the suite to prepare for the dinner party at the residence of the British High Commissioner. With hardly a word to Morag or the children, other than a quick "Hi", Janet showered, washing away any signs of her indiscretions from her sun-soaked body; as she dried herself, she looked into the mirror admiring her tanned skin, thinking to herself that she had a well-kept and trim figure even after having two children. Despite the stretch marks she had mentioned to Michael, she had to admit to herself as she indulged herself in the pleasure of the reflection in the mirror. There was no sag in her breasts, her waist was still slender, and her hips tapered down her well-shaped legs. *'Stop admiring yourself,'* she mouthed to herself. The hairdresser had closed for the evening. She cursed under her breath before muttering,

"You have a lot of work in front of you, my girl, if you are to make your hair beautiful for tonight."

Janet emerged from her bedroom looking like a beauty queen prepared to take the first prize; she looked good and she knew it.

"Oh, Mommy," Sean said, "you look very beautiful. Are you going to see Daddy?"

Janet, with a twinge of guilt in her voice, replied,

"No, darling, Daddy is still on his way by sea, it's a long way, and he won't be here for another week yet. I am going to dinner with an old friend from university."

Sean looked puzzled.

"Does Daddy know him?" he asked innocently.

"No, darling, but I must go or I'll be late."

She kissed the inquisitive youngster and her daughter, Sheenagh, before going out to meet Michael. Morag looked worried as she saw Lady Janet sweep out of the door, looking more like a teenager going out on a hot date than Lady Croft, the wife of an English Lord. Morag then bathed the children before putting them to bed and ordering herself dinner. She sat down in front of the television; after pouring herself a drink, she made herself comfortable and watched a movie on the in-house hotel movie channel.

Janet went down to reception and walked through to the bar where Michael sat waiting for her. Michael took a deep breath when he saw her; she looked absolutely gorgeous. Janet's hair was perfectly coiffured; her make-up had been lightly applied over the tan of her skin and the short black dress showed her figure at its best. The dress showed just the right amount of cleavage to show promise, but not enough to be tarty or obviously flaunty, perfectly highlighting Janet's firm breasts. Michael had found it hard to believe they were real when she had been naked on the boat, although they had been bigger than he remembered at college; there was no hint of sag despite the fact that she had two children. The dress finished mid-thigh and showed her perfectly shaped thighs which tapered down to well-proportioned calves and trim ankles. As she got closer, he could see the sling-back court shoe setting off her well-shaped ankles. Michael knew he would be the talk of the whole of the expatriate community, with Lady Janet Croft on his arm. What he could not understand, however, was why his recently acquired friend Mark, an aide at the British High Commission, had asked him to dine at the residency and why he had specifically asked him to invite Lady Croft as his guest.

They arrived at the residency, a colonial-style building with well laid out gardens and lawns; they were received by the fastidiously dressed butler, who announced them as Dr Michael Crosby accompanied by Lady Janet Croft; they were shown into a well-stocked bar where they were welcomed by British High Commissioner, Sir Martin Claiborne; together with his much younger wife, Lady Jayne Claiborne; along with Sir Anthony Martin; his wife, June; and their seventeen-year-old daughter, Alison; who looked terribly gauche with braces on her teeth and thick glasses; finally, there was Michael's friend Mark. Janet noted mentally that he was extremely handsome and several years younger than Michael, and she wondered how such a young man had risen to be a consular aide so quickly. The pre-dinner conversation was light and the cocktails flowed freely. The dinner gong sounded, and Janet found herself seated opposite Michael and between Sir Anthony and the handsome young aide, Mark. The dinner conversation was mainly about the life on the islands, the possible dates when the next ball was to be held, and at which Embassy or Consul the affair would be hosted. Janet felt these British expatriates led very shallow lives. They withdrew into the drawing room for brandies and coffees; all but Mark and Janet began to smoke, cigars for the men and cigarillos for the women. The atmosphere became thick with cloying smoke, making Janet cough a little as she moved closer towards the French windows. Janet thought nothing of it when the handsome and debonair Mark suggested they step into the garden; his excuse was that the smoke was becoming a little more than a trifle uncomfortable.

Janet had been wondering how she could get this young man to herself for a while to find a little more about him. Now it seemed as though the perfect opportunity had finally presented itself. Janet allowed him to take her arm as they walked out into the tropical garden; there was just a hint of a chill in the air as they moved through the grounds, making their way towards the headland overlooking the sea. Janet shivered, and Mark took off his jacket and placed it around her shoulders. Mark then steered her towards a tree enclosed area sheltered from view of the house. When they had entered the sheltered area, she could smell the soft fragrances of the night-blooming jasmine and several other tropical fragrances that she could not readily identify. The wafts of these sensual bouquets together with the backdrop of the pale glow of the moon and the trees sheltering them from the slight chill on the breeze set the scene, as she felt Mark turn her towards him and heard him say,

"Lady Croft, I hope I have not been getting the wrong messages all night, but I have to say you look delightful this evening. I feel I must offer you my excuses for being too forward, but I cannot resist the temptation to give you a kiss."

If Janet was expecting a polite kiss on the cheek, she was somewhat taken aback, but at the same time flattered by the younger man's attention. Mark pulled her against him, and she felt his lips close over her own; her mouth opened and she felt his tongue move in between her parted lips and dance lightly and gently over her tongue. He pressed his body against her as his arms enfolded her in what she could only term as a passionate embrace. The kiss became more passionate and Janet felt herself mould against the handsome young man recognising the fact that he was very aroused. Mark however took it as an act of compliancy and a willingness to go further; his hand moved upwards cupping her breast as he thrust his hips forward. *Oh my God,* Janet thought to herself, *this is going far too quickly. This has not happened to me since college.* But in her present frame of mind, wanting to get back to those earlier times in her life, she did nothing to show Mark any resistance. Once again Janet relaxed and allowed nature to take its course.

Mark was enthused, he considered himself an expert in the art of seduction and things moved quickly, far quicker than he had anticipated. Mark moved quickly, but not too fast to alarm or move too quickly despite Janet's apparent eagerness. Janet, on the other hand, was still amazed at how quickly things had moved forward; they had only been in the wooded grotto for not much more than a few minutes and she was giving herself unreservedly to this young handsome stranger. Time stood still as she acknowledged Mark's apparent skills at seduction and lovemaking. Janet was, for the second time in a day, transported to a time when she was carefree and unrestrained by the ties of marriage. She felt twenty years old, and completely divorced from reality.

All too soon the madness was over; Mark's breathing, like hers, took a few minutes to return to normal, but there was no embarrassment inflected in his voice as he muttered softly,
"Oh my God! Lady Croft, or can I now call you Janet? How did that happen so quickly? I just could not seem to hold anything back. I hope you are well protected as I have a reputation for being very fertile."
"My husband must be the most fertile man in the world," Janet replied with a smile, "so I'm always protected. I never ever miss a pill, or he would get me pregnant every time we made love."

Mark, riding the slight on his boastful inference to his own fertility, enquired, trying not to sound too inquisitive or that he was well aware he was still on the high seas,
"Where is this husband of yours tonight? I would like to meet him."
"Oh, he's bringing our ocean-going cruiser across from Ireland for us to tour the Caribbean Islands." Janet replied, searching for her clothes and making herself as presentable as she could. "The children are too young to make that long trip, so I came on ahead."
Mark's reply sounded corny, even to Janet who had rearranged her clothing and was trying to tidy up her hair.
"How very fortunate for me!" He said, "Can I ask if you would care to join me for lunch at my bungalow tomorrow? I will have a car collect you from the hotel"

Mark checked that he was once again presentable before straightening his tie; then retrieving his jacket from the tree trunk, he placed it once more around Janet's shoulders. They headed back towards the house, and Mark showed Janet the way to the bathroom, and he waited patiently whilst she completed the task she had started in the secluded coppice. Janet carefully reapplied her simple make-up and tidied her hair, so that, apart from a faint flush, which thankfully was partly hidden by her tan, when she reappeared, she looked as though nothing untoward had happened.

They returned to the dining room, and Janet complimented Lady Jayne Claiborne on her garden,

"What a lovely garden you have, Lady Claiborne! I would love to see it sometime during the daylight. The wonderful smells of the evening flowering plants would indicate you personally enjoy the garden."

Lady Jayne was delighted; Janet could not have given her a better compliment if she had planned it.

"Oh, call me Jayne, please, and I'll call you Janet. These titles are all very well but a little cumbersome amongst friends, don't you agree? Thank you so much for the compliment, but I merely plan and supervise. The gardeners do all the hard work for me, it makes gardening such a pleasure. I would love to have you over soon," she said, adding, "I understand you are staying at the Sandpiper with your children."

"Yes," Janet said, thinking how well-informed the Commissioner's wife was about her guests. "I'm in the King Suite."

"I'll arrange for you to come early next week." Lady Jayne quickly responded, "I will ring you tomorrow to arrange the visit. Hopefully, your husband, Lord Croft, will be here then, and you must both come with the children."

Lady Jayne pulled Janet to one side and continued,

"Janet, I should have warned you about Mark. He always considers himself a bit of a ladies' man. I hope he behaved himself out there in the garden. Just watch out for him, won't you? He can be a bit of a cad at times. Even I have had to call a halt to his unsolicited attentions on a number of occasions when his behaviour got a little out of hand. If I was to mention it to my husband, he would have the cad sent back to London immediately. Although between you and me, I have to admit he is such a handsome man to have at these sorts of evenings. Don't you think so, Janet?"

Janet, who remembering how quickly things had moved in the seclusion of the garden, could only nod in agreement.

When the evening gradually drew to a close and the party broke up, it was Michael who drove Lady Croft back to the hotel and to his bitter disappointment, for he had no way of knowing what had happened in the garden that evening. Janet excused herself from going up to his room for a nightcap by saying,

"I'm just too tired, Michael, but don't take it the wrong way. It's been a long day, and I enjoyed time we had together on the boat, and this evening topped the day off beautifully."

Michael was going off to St Lucia early the next morning, so he kissed her, his embrace spoke more than words, and as he broke the kiss, he whispered huskily,

"I hope we can meet again over the weekend when I plan to return to Barbados from St Lucia."

Janet nodded and gave him as smile as she went up to the suite, leaving Michael to console himself at the all-night cocktail lounge. Arriving in the luxury suite, Janet shook Morag, who had fallen asleep on the couch in front of the television, before she went through to the shower, letting her clothes fall as she went. There, for the second time in twenty-four hours, Janet carefully erased all traces of her adulterous indiscretions before going to bed; where, due to her exertions and the effects of alcohol, she slept soundly until the next morning.

Chapter 2

Lord Croft had set out with his all-female crew of three after handing the keys over to Stella, who, with her supposed husband, would be the tenants of his castle in the south-west of Ireland for the next year. Although he was quite aware she was an agent of the Irish branch of some security section of either MI5 or MI6, who wanted to discover all they could about his connection with the IRA, Lord Croft had delayed his departure whilst the agency had done a thorough search of the castle and discovered nothing. Roy knew this was due in the main to the fact that he had successfully utilised the services of his architect and friend, Gordon O'Leary, who together with Roy's building contractor friend, Charlie Drake, had contrived to disguise the entrance to his secret storeroom and wartime armoury. Feeling satisfied that he was at least above suspicion for the time being, together with his crew of three, he pointed the prow of the cruiser in a southerly direction. The cruiser, a converted Second World War MTB, after extensive refitting, externally resembled one of the Sunseeker ranges of luxury cruisers, except that with turbocharged diesels, Roy's cruiser could achieve over sixty knots. The redesigned boat had a range, at normal cruising speed, in excess of 3,000 miles, and that was without the temporary fuel tank, on inflatable rubber floats, which would be towed behind the cruiser for the crossing.

Lord Croft's crew consisted of his skipper Elian, aged around twenty-five, who with a full master's certificate had sailing skills beyond her years; both gained whilst spending her teens and later years on fishing boats off the west coast of Ireland, where storms were the natural order of the day. Elian was Roy's most trusted crew member; she could handle a machine gun and side arms as she had done on several occasions during the time the two of them had spent running arms, drugs, and trainee terrorists for the IRA.

The second crew member, Fiona, was Elian's younger sister, aged twenty-two, and had just seemed to become one of the crew; she acted as cook and cleaner aboard the craft; she could also handle a side arm, trained by Gael, and the local members of the IRA. She was besotted with Roy, knowing he was married, and she could never be anything other than his mistress. Nevertheless, she gave herself to him whenever an opportunity arose. As a result, she had already had an abortion, in England, with Elian's help and guidance, much against her better judgement, when she had found Roy had unwittingly made her pregnant some months before. Abortion was a mortal sin, and she had resolved never to go through such a thing again. Fiona was determined that if she got pregnant in future, she would carry her child to term, even though she was not married. She had always been free with sex in her youth, but since she had met Lord Croft, she kept herself exclusively for him; she only wished he felt the same way, but, alas, it would never be so.

Gael, the third and the final member of Roy's crew, was a bit of a misnomer. She was skinny and flat-chested, but she was muscular and was strong as an ox. She had been trained as a terrorist, by the IRA, in North Africa, and Roy had met her on one of his trips to North Africa carrying trainee terrorists. On the first occasion they had met, due to circumstance that threw them together, they had made love in his cabin; their attraction for each other had continued when Roy collected her and her companions after their extensive terrorist training, even though her head had been shaved at the time, but at Roy's request, she had since let her hair grow; she now had a cropped hairstyle, which would slowly grow longer as time went by. She was only eighteen, but her bedroom skills excited Roy; she had recently missed her period, but pushed the possibility of pregnancy to the back of her mind. Her terrorist training had been in all range of weapons: RPGs, Sam7s, heavy and light machine guns, and side arms. Her self-defence skills were well above average and had been known to bring men, well over six foot and three times her weight, to their knees. She was the boat's general handy person and was also in charge of the armoury aboard the cruiser.

The cruiser's wide range of weaponry had originally been inherited from the armoury situated in the underground store under the castle, which had previously been a secret base during the Second World War. When Lord Croft had acquired the castle, the boat, a wartime MTB, had been on chocks protected by 'duck oil' in the boathouse, still fully equipped with torpedoes, deck guns, and heavy machine guns and the ability to drop depth charges. Since the boats refit, Roy had retained the boat's two torpedo tubes, now hidden from the prying eyes by the new superstructure; the deck guns had been replaced with two hand-held rocket grenade launchers and two hand-held Sam7 launchers, together with missile-lock radar. The launchers were in a specially designed locker in the bowels of the hull, together with machine guns, side arms, and ammunition for all the weapons carried aboard; in addition, they carried anti-missile rockets loaded with chaff instead of explosive warheads, in case of missile attack on the boat. The armaments had been donated by the IRA during the period Lord Croft had been engaged in their operations. The cruiser was further equipped with secret compartments for carrying drugs, and recently, Elian had discovered a compartment built into the wall of the main cabin; this hidden compartment was left over from the boat's wartime clandestine operations when it had been used for carrying large amounts of forged British and European notes left over from the war.

The cruiser headed south towards Spain; Roy and his crew planned to stop off for the first night at the port of A Coruña, one of the ports they had used during their runs to and from North Africa. There they were to meet up with Fergus, a replacement skipper who Roy had trained to take over the drug dealings at sea, whilst he was off to the West Indies. The boat Fergus operated was registered in the name of a company with Lord Croft as one of its directors, and the boat was normally berthed at Cobh, near Cork. The reason for the meeting was due to Fergus being delayed on his last drug collection and Roy needed to check that everything had been OK. Having satisfied himself that all was well, they were heading down the coast when the newscast on the radio in the main cabin announced the discovery of a man's body; the report claimed it had apparently been washed up close to the port of A Coruña. The newscaster reported that the man had been shot, 'execution style', with a pistol to the back of the head. As the fish had eaten most of his flesh, it would be difficult for the authorities to identify the body. Investigators were trying to ascertain how long the body had been in the water. From the initial examination, it was believed that body could have been left over from Second World War—the body could have been well protected, trapped in a wreck off the coast. The press release had indicated that the body had been buried at sea, and the use of ammunition boxes from the Second World War weighing the body down seemed to reinforce that theory.

However, Lord Croft knew it was the body of the man he had executed, IRA style, for raping Kerry, whilst four other terrorist trainees had held her down. Roy had reacted instinctively and had simply walked up behind Kevan and shot him, leaving Gael and the other four to clean up the mess and to dispose of the body. They body had been stripped, wrapped in the soiled bed linen and canvas, before being tied to several wartime ammunition boxes to make it sink. Gael had instructed the four terrorists to dump it overboard when they had been thirty miles off the Spanish coast. Apparently the corpse, according to the radio report, had been snagged by a deep-sea fishing net and brought to the surface. Roy walked up to the flying bridge where Elian had control of the boat and told her to keep going, explaining the reason. He instructed her to make for the Portuguese estuary leading into Setúbal, where he would try and get a berth for the night. Roy went below using the ship's radio to communicate with the port; he secured an overnight berth. They anchored the cruiser; whilst Roy and Elian secured the boat for the night, Fiona prepared their evening meal and Gael cleaned and oiled the weaponry below. Elian pulled Roy closer to her, her face showing signs of concern, and said,

"Roy, I'm worried that the body might be identified and traced back to Ireland. If that happens, there is a possibility it could be traced back to you and the IRA."

Roy's reply put her somewhat at ease.

"I understand your concern, Elian, but it is unlikely. You know how, though, Gael is. She informed me that before disposing of the body, she removed Kevan's teeth with pliers, and by this time, the fish would have eaten most of the soft tissues from the body. So any remains of the flesh on his fingers would be too far gone to leave any identifying prints. With the wartime ammunition boxes, the report was already assuming the corpse may have been a wartime victim who had somehow been protected and finally been washed out of a sunken wartime vessel and decomposed rapidly. Identification will depend how much flesh, if any, had been left after the fish had finished."

Fiona called out from the galley,

"Food's ready!"

The four of them sat down and ate supper. Elian, being the skipper, had organised a rota for sleeping with Roy on the journey to the West Indies, electing herself to take the first night. Leaving Fiona to clear away and Gael to lock the armoury, Elian and Roy went into the stateroom. To Roy, it felt strange having Elian arrange a rota for the three of them to take turns to sleep with him; he had always preferred to take things as they came, the formality felt awkward. It was almost as though he were married to the three of them; it all felt a bit too prearranged. They undressed like any married couple would do and climbed into bed. They lay under the bedclothes naked with their bodies touching; Roy turned and put his arms around Elian, planting gentle kisses on her face and neck. His kisses felt like tiny electric shocks to Elian, who had waited all day for this moment; she lay back completely at ease, surrendering entirely to Roy's control. They made love for what seemed like hours, both partners totally oblivious to the unmistakable sound of their lovemaking, as it travelled though the hull, clearly audible to the other two crew members, both envious of Elian lying in Roy's bed.

They soon fell asleep in each other's arms, only awaking as the early morning light flooded through the porthole into the stateroom. They stirred, and Elian encouraged Roy to make love to her again. This time the awkwardness of the previous night's prearranged rota seemed less important as they relaxed and made the most of their time together. It was still early, and afterwards they dozed, wanting to rest as long as they could before heading further south. Roy woke to the soft caress of Elian's fingers along his face and neck; he hoped she was not asking him for more. He wanted to be in a reasonable state when he arrived in the West Indies. *God, he thought, if the other two react as Elian, for the rest of the voyage, I shall be worn out when I get to Barbados;* Elian felt his mouth as it covered hers, but their passion was spent and the kiss lingered, but went no further. She pushed Roy away and whispered,

"As much as I would like you to make love to me again, Roy, I don't think in reality it's possible. We have a long way to go, so conserve your energy. There's plenty of time. We don't want you to kill yourself. Save something for another day. I was just showing you my appreciation, not encouraging you to make love to me. Now I suggest we get up, shower, and show our faces."

Roy reluctantly agreed; he knew he was spent for the time being: he needed to recoup; heaven only knew how he would cope if every night was going to be a repeat of the last.

Eventually standing up, Elian walked towards the tiny heads to shower, opened the shower door, and turned on the water; as soon as it was warm, she stepped inside. The water ran over her, washing the perspiration and traces of their night's activities from her satiated body. It was time to get under way; they had a long way to go. She walked out of the shower; she could see that Roy was still considering pulling her back into bed, but she dodged his grip, but there was no way she could take any more this morning. Grabbing her robe, she opened the door and slipped quietly into her own cabin to dress in fresh clothes and ready for breakfast. Gael was still asleep in her cabin, but Fiona was in the galley, making breakfast for all of them. Roy sauntered into the galley seeing Fiona bending down; she was getting something from the lower cupboard. He had still been in the mood for more sexual pleasure and was tempted, but knowing his limitations, he resisted the temptation to move in close behind the attractive young woman. He simply ran his hand over her buttocks; she turned, startled by the sudden touch. The noise behind him made him start. He felt like a child caught with his hand in the cookie jar. It was Elian.

"Oh God, Roy, are you never satisfied? Having spent half the night with me, I find you with your hands on my sister's backside. You are truly incorrigible! It's a good job she is on the three-monthly contraceptive injections, the same as I am, or I'm sure you would have got both of us pregnant during this trip. If you check the rota, you will see that it's not really Fiona's day. It's Gael's."

Roy grinned as he pulled his hand away from the firm rounded cheeks of Fiona's backside.

"Well, I'll not disappoint her as you well know."

He lifted Fiona's short skirt and playfully slapped her bottom. Fiona grinned and, to her sister, whispered,

"Spoilsport, Elian! If you had not disturbed us, anything could have happened."

Elian grinned and followed Roy into the dining area and sat down.

They breakfasted, and when Gael joined them, Roy thought she looked tired, but her mood and her looks brightened as the day progressed and they headed further south. Taking the opportunity, they refuelled at Tangiers before heading further south and anchoring some twenty miles off the west coast of Africa, using a sea anchor; Elian would be on the first watch while Fiona would take the second. They were well away from the coast; having been the intended victims of West African pirates before, they were taking no chances. Roy had already opened the gun locker and had put the rocket launchers in the lounge. Gael had helped bring up the munitions; being reassured that everything was ready in case of an attack, Gael strolled into the stateroom and stripped off her clothes, dropping them casually on to the floor. As Roy came through the door, she was already in his bed. Roy was easily coerced into making love by this muscular young woman, her energy seemed endless, and it was considerably later when they lay beside each other whilst until their breathing slowly returned to normal. Gael casually left Roy in bed, glancing back at her lover with a self-satisfied look on her face. As she walked towards the heads, totally oblivious to her nudity, she whispered,

"Roy, you are something else. I hope you can continue managing to satisfy all three of us on this voyage. I have to admit you have the power to excite me more than anyone I know. If you're not careful, and take it easy, you could arrive in Barbados a shadow of your former self."

"As much as I would like to keep up with the three of you, I don't think it's going to be possible. I have to save something for my dear wife. She would be angry if I could not perform my marital duties when I arrive. Although, Janet is very understanding about my extramarital activities, even she has her limits."

Walking out of the small shower, Gael whispered to Roy as he embraced her, "Now, Roy, don't start again. We need some sleep if we are heading out across the Atlantic in the morning."

Roy pulled her to him and kissed her on the mouth. She felt him lift her up and carry her back to the bed. They lay with their arms around each other, and it was some time before Gael realised Roy had fallen asleep. She lay back feeling exhausted, but somehow too tired, sleep seemed to evade her for some reason. She had a premonition that something was going to happen. At this moment in time, Gael was oblivious to the fact that she had been impregnated some weeks before and would be carrying Roy's child for the next eight and a half months. She lay still with Roy's arm around her; it felt comforting as she listened to the silence of the night, the quietness only disturbed by the lapping of the water against the sides of the hull.

Suddenly she heard another sound; it was something out of the ordinary, strange, and unexpected, and at the same moment, Roy flipped his eyes open. Both people instantly alert, sat up trying to pinpoint the origin of the sound, drawing upon memories in their endeavour to identify it. Then they heard Elian call out the challenge,

"Ahoy there! Who are you and what do you want? Identify yourselves."

Roy sat up, ready for the worst; Gael, as always instantly alert, her tiredness forgotten in an instant; they swung out of bed, still naked. The two of them ran into the lounge grabbing weapons as they rushed up the companionway. Roy threw himself flat on the deck, giving Gael a clear view over the side of the boat. The night was dark and eerily silent, apart from the creak of timbers and the sound of water; silence hung around them like a cloak. There was no answer to Elian's challenge, but the sound of water lapping against the hull of another boat close by was unmistakable. Fiona, clad only in a T-shirt, poked her head up out of the lower deck; she had a Sterling automatic rifle gripped in her hands. Gael slipped out of the cabin door on to the deck, keeping her naked body as low as she could; she moved silently forward, pointing the rocket launcher in the direction of the sound. Elian heard Roy give a low whistle from below, and she hit the start button just as Roy cut the lines to the rigged sea anchor. As soon as Elian felt the cruiser free from the anchor's restraint, she pushed the throttle forward and switched on the searchlights.

There before them and to starboard was a wrecked yacht; she was adrift, the mast was down, and there were signs of a fight; bullet marks had torn through the sides of the cabin and the bridge, and in the glare of the spotlight they could see, even from that distance, that its instruments had been smashed beyond repair. Elian closed the throttles, but kept the motor running. She knew only too well that it could be a trap. As there were no signs of life aboard the stricken craft, Roy called to Elian,
"Circle the hull, giving her a wide berth and be wary. Whoever did this could be lying in wait for us. Don't approach the hull until I get back. I'm feeling a little exposed. I need to go below and put on a pair of shorts."
Roy slipped below and pulled on a pair of shorts, then buckled on his waist holster complete with its side arm, before going back on deck; Gael had no such qualms about her nudity. She stood naked, still pointing the grenade launcher in the direction of the yacht. She was just as comfortable with or without clothes; her combat training had taught her not to stand down until she was given the all-clear, regardless of the circumstances.

They circled the disabled yacht; Gael handed Roy the rocket launcher grabbing his machine gun.
"Keep me covered," she whispered.
Jumping the narrowing gap between the two vessels, she was as sprightly as a gazelle, her naked body recovering from the jump as though it had been just a step. She called out, challenging the night like a sentry on guard duty, a pretty one at that, standing like a nubile statue, but she remained as alert as a cat stalking a mouse.
"Is there anyone aboard? We have you covered with grenades and machine guns."

She fired a burst of bullets in the air to prove her point. There was a stunning silence after the sound of gunfire had died away across the empty sea; only the creaking of the disabled ship could be heard. Suddenly Roy saw Gael cock her head to one side as if she had heard something; Roy gripped his weapon in readiness for trouble, signalling to Elian to be ready to move away fast. The two boats were now almost touching, and Roy laid the grenade launcher on the deck, then pulled his side arm from his waist holster, and jumped aboard the wrecked yacht. Gael pointed below and, laying aside the machine gun, took Roy's 9mm Beretta; then lithely and, with catlike stealth, she moved into the ruined stairway leading below. Roy heard her voice. It did not sound challenging but supportive, as she whispered to an unknown person below,

"It's all right. You're safe. You can come out. We are friends."

"Fiona, throw me that hand lamp," Roy called out.
Reacting instantly to the order, Fiona tossed the torch she was holding to Roy, who reached out and deftly caught it. Switching it on, he shone the light into the cabin below. From a cupboard under the companionway, a blonde head appeared, staring unbelievably at the naked figure of Gael, as she stood with her pistol in her hand. To assure whoever was emerging that she was a friend, Gael dropped the clip and ejected the bullet in the chamber, before she dropped the empty weapon on the cushions in the cabin. Then bending forward, she helped the blonde-haired figure out of the cramped space and assisted her to stand. The figure appeared stiff, weary, and cramped from being tucked up in the confines of the small cupboard for some time.

"Is there anyone else aboard?" Gael asked the trembling figure.
Gael put her arms around the hunched figure to prevent whoever she had discovered from sinking down on to her knees. The young woman shook her head sadly and whispered softly, the voice trailing off,

"No, they are all dead."

Gael half-carried the figure up the ruined gangway of the half-submerged yacht; Roy laid down the machine gun and helped the shocked young woman up on to the deck. The young woman stared at him open-mouthed, appearing to be in a state of shock as she was still supported by Gael; she watched as Roy and Fiona secured the yacht to the side of the cruiser. Then Gael, helped by Fiona, transferred the hapless figure across on to the deck of the cruiser. The young woman seemed startled and confused; she was shaking with fear and shock as Fiona grabbed her hand. Gael asked for the torch and to the amazement of all, still naked, she began a methodical search of the yacht. Finding some clothing in one of the cabins, she pulled on a T-shirt, which was much too big, and a pair of shorts, which more or less fitted her. Finding no one else aboard, she recovered the Beretta and the clip, which she slid into the handle, and re-cocked the weapon. Gael was not one for taking any chances. Then she climbed back up onto the yacht's deck, and Roy grabbed her as she leapt across on to the cruiser's deck.

Going cautiously below, they saw Fiona giving the young woman, who appeared to be of similar height and age, the rescued items from the yacht and a cup of sweet tea. Instructing Fiona to put the newcomer into the stateroom, Roy went back on to deck, leaving Gael to assist below. The first signs of a new dawn were beginning to appear, and taking advantage of the half-light, Roy went aboard the yacht to recover any belongings he could find; they wanted to be away before full daylight, just in case whoever had done this came back. There was little or nothing to be found, except a holdall in the cupboard the young woman had emerged from. All the supplies had been taken and all the instruments ripped out or smashed. The radio had been ripped out of its place, leaving the torn wiring exposed and rendering any means of communication useless. Taking a closer look around, Roy could see what looked like blood on the foredeck and on the base of the mast. There was little else of value left on board the yacht and as it could be a danger to any vessel, Roy made the decision, went below, and opened the seacocks. The water began to flood the lower deck; Roy jumped back on to the cruiser and cast off the securing lines. Then after giving the signal to Elian, they slowly widened the gap between the two vessels, and once clear, she pushed open the throttle and headed west. Roy went below and, entering the stateroom, sat beside the other two and listened as the nameless young woman began to tell her story.

She introduced herself simply as Madeleine.
"Thank you all for saving me," she began, "I can explain how I came to be on board and alone; it began after I had been backpacking. I met up with Clive Barnard and his brother Simon, the owners of the yacht, in Tangiers. I had had a couple of run-ins with a bunch of the locals. I was in trouble when Clive stepped in and rescued me from what could easily have ended in me being raped or worse. Naturally, when he and his

brother offered to give me a ride on their yacht, back up into Portugal, I was only too grateful to accept."

Seeing Madeleine tremble as she spoke, Roy poured her a large brandy and let her sip the spirit, pausing for it to take effect and sooth her shattered nerves. When she had stopped trembling, Madeleine continued,

"We had been no more than two hours out of port when we were approached by a launch, and as it came closer, fortunately for me, Simon told me to stay below. Then, out of the blue, the launch called for us to heave too, and when Clive refused, they put a burst of machine-gun fire across the yacht's bows. Clive had wanted to make a fight of it despite the odds being against them. They only had a handgun between the two of them," Madeleine said to emphasise their predicament.

Then after pausing for a moment, she continued with her tale.

"Simon stood by the galley door and whispered to me to get below and hide under the stairs with my holdall so that no trace of my presence would be found on board. I climbed into the cramped space, covering myself with a blanket, and lay quiet, too, frightened to breathe, let alone say a word. I heard the men from the other boat come aboard and start smashing everything in sight and Simon," Madeleine whispered, a shudder running through her as she recalled the moment. "Well, I'm not sure who it was, either Simon or Clive had protested. He tried to tell the men who had boarded that there was nothing valuable on board. The next thing was; I heard someone give a cry, followed by several shots, after which it went quiet. I never saw either of them again. I lay still, covered in that blanket, afraid to move a muscle as the boat was searched and various items taken. I was sure they would find the cupboard under the stairs, but thank God, they didn't. I'm sure I would have been shot if they had found me. I had enough of that kind of threat when I was ashore. I knew only too well what I could expect if they found me."

Madeleine began trembling again as she took another sip of brandy from the glass in her hand. Fiona comforted her by putting her arm around her. Roy, understanding her grief and fear, whispered,

"Hush now and rest. Tell us the rest when you feel better."

"No, let me finish my story. I will feel better when I told you everything. I heard the launch move away, and the sound of heavy machine-gun fire followed. I heard the cracking sound as the mast broke. The boat healed over, and I was fearful that it would capsize and sink, but luckily, the mast must have broken off completely and eventually the yacht righted itself again. I lay in that cupboard for twenty-four hours, afraid to come out in case the pirates, or whoever they were, came back. It was only when I heard a woman's voice that I found the strength to call out. I have to admit that I was not so sure I had done the right thing when I saw," she pointed to Gael, "your naked, muscular body, carrying a gun in your hand. I was frightened, and I only relaxed when I saw you unload the weapon and bend to help me out of that cramped space."

Elian, curious to know what was going on below, locked the steering and set the throttle to just keep the boat under way. After ensuring they were well clear of the main shipping lanes, she came down to see what the fuss was all about. Roy took control using the lower cabin controls, and they got under way once more. Madeleine showered and dressed in her shorts and a clean top. Roy saw that she was remarkably pretty; her blonde hair, now washed, hung down her shoulders; she was about five feet four inches tall, slender, and very pleasing to the eye; his imagination ran riot as he tried to imagine how she would look naked on his bed. He quickly put the thought out of his mind; as she had been traumatised and shocked, he would leave her for a couple of days to recover and would find more out about her. Once she had slept for a few hours, the crew moved her into one of the smaller cabins, after showing her the heads and where everything was situated. They told her they would hand her over to a passing ship, if she wanted, or she could accompany them on their way to Barbados. Madeleine gave a cry of relief,

"What a coincidence! My parents live in Barbados, and I have been attending university in England. After qualifying, I chose to do a year's backpacking before I returned to the West Indies. I would love to come with you. I'll help out where I can, but I'll be going home."
They ate supper, and Madeleine was still puzzled as to the arrangements on board, but she said nothing as none of the women wore a wedding ring. She knew Elian was the skipper, but that was all she had deduced, and it was a mystery that would be solved in time. She had no intention of being too inquisitive. When they had offered to take her with them, her curiosity could wait.

Roy was on watch as they ate supper, and Fiona took Roy his main meal and sat watching him eat, and when he had finished, she said,

"It's going to be cramped with Madeleine on board. It has rather upset the arrangements, hasn't it? I'm pleased because the rota Elian had set seemed rather sterile to me. I prefer to make love to you when the opportunity arises, not on a strict rotational basis. It makes things seem sterile and awkward."

She jumped up on the cupboard, beside the wheel, that served as a plotting table, and pulled Roy towards her, kissing him with a rising passion.

"Like now," she whispered.

Quickly, Roy locked the wheel setting the autopilot, then, after looking around and satisfying himself no one else was about, took advantage of the opportunity offered to him. It was difficult up there as anyone could walk up from below at any minute. Both of them knew it had to be quick; sometime later Roy moved away, and Fiona quickly rearranged her clothing before collecting Roy's plate. She kissed her lover on the lips, then, with a broad smile on her face and a feeling of satisfaction, went below to wash up and clear away.

Chapter 3

Lady Croft spent the morning playing on the beach with the children, giving Morag a well-earned break. Just before lunch, Morag came down to collect the children and give Janet time to shower the salt, suncream, and sand off her body before changing for her lunch appointment. Much to Morag's disapproval, Lady Croft dressed in a bikini and a beach robe. In Morag's eyes, that was no way for a married woman to be going out for lunch. Janet had dressed in that manner as the lunch was to be casual, with only Mark and herself present at the bungalow pool. Janet reminisced in her mind about the pleasures the young man had bestowed on her the previous evening and was looking forward to an intimate lunch for two. The consulate driver arrived to collect Lady Croft, and after the short drive, he dropped her at the entrance to Mark's consular provided bungalow. Janet walked up to the front door and rang the bell. She did not really know what to expect, but when Mark opened the door to greet her, she kissed him on the cheek, and, in response, Mark slid his arms around her waist and whispered,

"Hi, Lady Croft, I must confess I had my doubts about you actually coming, but now that you are here, I have to admit you look good enough to eat."

Janet glowed with self-esteem and smiled as she followed him into the kitchen where she saw that Mark, or one of the consulate's catering staff, had been busy; a wide variety of salads and cold meats and smoked salmon lay on the kitchen surfaces and a bottle of champagne was opened, with two more on ice. As Mark picked up the open bottle, he enquired,

"Lady Croft?"

"It's Janet remember," she quickly corrected him.

"Janet," Mark corrected himself, "do you want to eat now or later?"

"Later," she replied. "Where's the pool?"

Mark pointed the way and poured two glasses of champagne as Janet walked out to the pool deck, where she calmly slipped off her terry robe, and casually pulled the ties to her bikini top and bottom and dived naked into the pool, letting the cool water wash away the tiredness of the morning she had spent with the children. Mark arrived seconds later and, placing the glasses on the glass-topped poolside table, followed her example. Dropping his shorts, he dived in the cool waters of the pool, bobbing up beside her with a grin that showed his intentions. Mark reached out and, placing his arm around her shoulders, kissed her on the mouth, pulling her towards him and pressing his chest against the fullness of her breasts.

"Down, tiger," Janet whispered throatily.

It was still late morning, but from the way Mark was reacting to her naked body, pressing so intimately against his, she could see where this would lead. The kiss deepened and Janet relaxed, raising no objection as his hands freely moved over her. She was elated and felt far younger than her years; seeing her naked, even with the visible signs of having two children, this handsome young man desired her. Janet was missing the comfort of having Roy around, he was still far away at sea, and being highly frustrated, she was easily aroused. She closed her legs behind Mark's back and drew him close; in a matter of minutes, Mark had moved her along to the broad steps of the pool.

"God, Mark, you're eager," she whispered.

Janet felt herself lifted from the pool and, then closing her eyes, gave herself up to the lustful feelings engulfing her. She enjoyed being cosseted and caressed by the skilful lover she remembered from the previous evening. It hardly seemed to matter that it was broad daylight, and they had not even had lunch. All too soon Janet felt her responses begin to quicken. God, she couldn't remember when she had last felt so lustful, or her arousal raise this quickly; she put it down to the youthful energy of the man seemingly so eager to satisfy her every whim.

"Oh, Mark, slow down, there's no rush." She cried out.

The energy of youth knows no bounds, and Janet's words of warning were ineffectual as Mark continued his desires unabated; eventually, and somewhat breathless, they parted, and Mark lifted her up from the stone surface of the poolside and placed her gently on one of the recliners protected from the burning sun's rays by the shade of a large umbrella. Mark handed her a towel before he sauntered casually back towards the kitchen as Janet closed her eyes and relaxed.

Mark had been gone sometime; when she heard him return, he handed her a fresh glass of champagne, and they lay lazily sipping the contents, the bubbles somehow tantalising Janet's nose. It was strange. Soon afterwards, Janet felt a little heady from the effects of the drink; that in itself was somewhat unusual for her; she put it down to the fact that she had not eaten. Janet felt relaxed enjoying being alone with Mark, the handsome and virile young man she had only met the previous evening. The feeling of total freedom seemed to float through her whole being; there was no thought of her husband; she was like a teenager. She was totally uninhibited by their nudity or the fact she had made love to a virtual stranger before lunch; she felt so decadent. Suddenly Janet sat up, somewhat startled at the sound of male voices coming towards them from within the house.

"Oh God, Mark, you said there was only going to be the two of us, and I'm lying here naked."

Mark smiled. Janet was somewhat taken aback as she recognised that the smile this time was not with a pleasure, but it was almost with a grin of triumph, and although worried by the sudden turn of events, she was not to know that it was to hide what he had planned all along. What he had experienced earlier with the exciting woman beside him was an added bonus, he had not expected.

"Don't worry," he said, "it's only my staff from the High Commission. They certainly won't mind your nakedness, if you don't."

Three men around Mark's age walked on to the pool deck wearing only swimming shorts, and on seeing Mark and Janet lying naked, they pulled off their shorts and dived naked into the pool. Janet could only watch them aghast, her mouth hung open in surprise as the three of them climbed out of the pool; they may well have been his staff, but it was obvious what they had in mind as they crowded around her. As Mark introduced each of them to her, each one stooped down and gave her a kiss; it seemed bizarre. Mark got up and brought Janet another glass of champagne; Janet, who felt as though she needed some Dutch courage, drank it and asked for another. Mark fetched her yet another glass, and when she drank, the headiness had increased and felt different; she could not explain the feeling, but she became more relaxed, her concerns about being alone naked and vulnerable diminished; she, for some unknown reason, suddenly felt completely uninhibited in the presence of the four men lying naked near her despite the fact that each one began to pass lewd and suggestive comments about her; they were not, in the slightest, perturbed or embarrassed by her presence.

Inwardly, Janet felt that she should leave, but she seemed to have no strength in her limbs. Mark walked over to the wall opposite and opened a small door just above head height. Janet looked at him, but she could not make out what he was doing. The only thing puzzling Janet was the fact that, for some unknown reason, she was gradually becoming more and more aroused as the three men continued talking and describing in detail how they would like to make love to her; the talk was becoming bolder and more explicit with each passing minute. Mark came back and began to touch her in places reserved for more private and intimate moments, and Janet felt she was open and on display for all to see.

Uncomfortable with the way things were developing, Janet did not want to do this in front of the others, but found that she had no will to stop Mark touching her so intimately. She could not find the will to resist, and her muscles seemed unable to obey what her mind wanted them to do; she fought to move, but she felt totally at the mercy of her now ardent admirers. Moments later, she watched Mark leave her lying exposed before the three visitors and go to a small control box on the wall of the house. Then he returned and, to her horror, made love to her in front of the others quite blatantly and without holding anything back. Normally, Janet would have been horrified at the very thought of such a thing happening to her in front of other men, but she seemed unable to put up any resistance. The look on Mark's face was grim; there was no sign of the tenderness he had displayed the previous evening or earlier when she had arrived; now his face was contorted with a lust she did not recognise. Time stood still as each man took their turn, as one by one had unprotected sex with her as if it were an everyday occurrence. Janet's mind did not seem to understand how she was letting this happen. She tried hard to object, but she seemed almost in a daze, incapable of stopping the inevitability of it all.

Janet's mind blotted out the coarse remarks and the lewd comments; Janet had no idea how long the depravity continued as her body was subjected to one gross act of rape after another. Finally, Janet thankfully lost consciousness, and when she woke, it was dark. She was lying naked by the hotel pool with a curious security guard staring down at her. She pulled her robe, which lay beside her, about her nakedness and the evidence of her afternoon of debauchery clearly visible on her body. The startled and shaken guard ran for the night manager, who upon seeing her so stressed and in such a state of distress called a doctor and helped her up to her room. Janet felt very uncomfortable, ashamed, and embarrassed being found in such a state in a public place. She had no doubt that if it had not been for her title; she would have been arrested as a common whore and would have spent the night in downtown jail. Janet waited until she was alone with the hotel doctor, and she demanded that he take a blood test. The doctor sympathised and examined her. He said to her in hushed tones,

"You seem to have survived your ordeal well, Lady Croft. There does not appear to be any internal damage. Are you in pain, would you like me to hospitalise you and do a more thorough examination although there's no bleeding or evidence of an internal tear?"

Lady Janet Croft was in pain, both physically and mentally; the shame of what had happened slowly dawned on her. She was grateful when the doctor gave her some painkillers. As the effect took over, she relaxed a little and asked him to take a semen sample and send it to the lab for a DNA test. He looked concerned and asked if he should call the police, and she nodded. Tears began to run down her cheeks as she fully became aware that her nightmare had turned in to a reality.

"Yes, please," she whispered.

Janet, still shaking with shame and the growing anger within her, could feel the tears of humiliation and remorse welling up and streaming down her face. She thought to herself, *How this could have happened to me? In all my years of freedom of sex, I had never been the victim of rape. How could Mark have done this to me? He must have given me a drug.* Whilst she waited for the police, the telephone rang. Janet reached out; in her confused state of mind, she hoped it would be Roy.

The shock of recognition filled her mind with hate as she realised it was Mark; she cursed and screamed into the telephone. Unable to stop the flow of screams and violent curses, Mark blew a whistle very hard and loud close to the mouthpiece. The shrill sound of the whistle shocked Janet, instantly cutting off her curses. She could not believe how cold and calculative Mark's voice was, as he instructed her to switch on the television and turn over to Channel 93. Fortunately, the doctor had left the room, and Janet reached for the remote and switched over to the channel. The picture, although grainy, was clearly of her making love to Carl in her own lounge at the castle in Ireland. *How was that possible?* She asked herself. Then the image of her on the deck of the *Petra* making love with Michael came into view, followed by a scene of her making love to Mark in the garden of the High Commissioner's residency, and then followed, as if this was not sufficient proof of her shameful adultery, the pictures of what could only be described as an orgy with four men. Janet sat dumbfounded staring at the pictures, the last scenes sending shivers of revulsion down her spine. The harsh sound of Mark's voice snapped her out of her horrified daze.

"If you don't want these pictures distributed and shown on every channel on the *in-house* television, then when the police arrive, you will tell them you made a mistake and you were not raped but partook in the orgy willingly, but regretted it later and claimed you had been raped."
Janet, who never normally swore, said vehemently,
"Why have you done this to me, you bastard?"
The answer she got shook her to the core, leaving her at her wits' end, and no nearer the reason for what she was being shown on the screen before her.
"You will find out all in good time. Now do as I say or what I have threatened and worse will happen and you will be unable to prevent the consequences, Lady Croft. I'm sure your husband would not be impressed with your behaviour, would he? Don't think you can agree to my demands and then make a formal complaint. I shall know the moment the police arrive and believe me, I shall hear every word."
The phone went dead. Janet had a hollow feeling in the pit of her stomach as she stood under the shower and washed the horrors from her bruised body, revelling in letting the water cleanse her and ease the pain from her soiled torso. Janet wrapped herself in the terry towelling robe the hotel provided its guests and sat down to await the arrival of the police, her mind unable to take in how Mark had been able to obtain pictures from the castle, Michael's boat, the residency, and finally, the apparent orgy at the Bungalow. It had to be some kind of conspiracy, but by whom and why, she could not begin to comprehend.

The police arrived, and when the inspector came into the room with the hotel doctor, he looked at the wide staring eyes and the white face of Lady Croft. The inspector's face was kind and gentle as he took out his notebook. He turned to the doctor and asked softly,
"Is it all right to question her Ladyship, she looks to be in a state of shock?"
The doctor stepped forward, and he could see Lady Croft seemed, if it was possible, more shocked than when he had left to call the inspector.
"Has anything happened, Lady Croft?" the doctor asked; his voice soft and full of empathy.

Lady Croft shook her head and, to the doctor's surprise and the inspector's astonishment, did as she had been instructed by Mark, being careful to use his exact words.

The police inspector looked closely at Janet; he looked at the doctor enquiringly, before speaking,
"Lady Croft, are you sure about this?" He asked not quite understanding her change of mind.
Knowing what the consequences would be if she did not say 'yes', she nodded sadly.
"Has anyone threatened you since the doctor left?" The police inspector asked, "If so, that in itself is a serious crime. It would not be the first time this has happened in Barbados." He then added, "If you change your mind, you should ring me on my cell phone. Don't call me from the hotel, either, use your own cell phone or a public phone well away from the hotel."
Shaking his head in despair and after explaining that if she did not report what had happened as a crime, he was helpless to prevent it happening to another woman, he left the hotel.

The following morning, the doctor rang the suite. Janet feared what he was about to tell her. *Had she been infected with some disease?* Janet was somewhat relieved when the doctor replied in the negative, but she was still abhorred when he informed her that the lab had found traces of the drug Rohypnol in her blood.
"What is Rohypnol," Janet asked, "what does it do?"
"It is used as a date-rape drug, rendering you incapable of any resistance and unable to prevent what happened to you. Do you want me to inform the inspector?"
"I dare not," she whispered. "No, do not inform the inspector. Will you just let me have the result of the blood work and the other tests?"
The doctor tried to make her change her mind, but eventually, he reluctantly agreed not to contact the inspector.

For the next week, Janet did not leave the hotel; she played with the children on the small private beach allocated to the suite. Time allowed her mind and body to heal, but the memories of what she had watched on the television screen at the hotel would stay with her for months. As promised, the High Commissioner's wife invited her to come to the residency for morning tea and asked if her husband had arrived yet. Janet agreed to go but said softly, not wanting the children or Morag to overhear her,

"I would love to come, but only if that aide, Mark, is not anywhere near me. I never want to see or be in his company again."

Somewhat taken aback by the request, Lady Claiborne informed her,

"I'm sorry, Lady Croft, if that cad has upset you in anyway. I'm pleased to tell you that Mark and his whole team have been recalled to England urgently, so he will no longer be a part of our staff, a situation all the women at the embassy will be grateful for." Lady Jayne Claiborne said with some vehemence, knowing well she was breaking the code of silence reserved for all diplomatic staff.

Janet finally plucked up the courage as she realised that staying cooped up with the children and Morag would do nothing to shake her out of the depression she had begun to sink into, and with some considerable effort, she went to have tea with Lady Jayne and a few of her friends. The morning passed pleasantly enough, but Janet was pleased when the small group of society ladies broke up to go home. Janet sat and waited as instructed whilst the High Commissioner's wife saw the other guests leave. Lady Croft seemed to have lost a lot of her confidence, and Lady Jayne was concerned, especially as Janet had said she did not want to meet Mark. Lady Jayne would speak to her husband about Mark and tell him how the disreputable young man had pulled her into an embrace and tried to kiss her in the garden just after he had arrived. The two women sat and talked, forming a friendship that would last for many years. Once the ice was broken and they had discussed her family, Janet was surprised when her host told her she had heard what had happened, explaining that the community was small and, in her capacity as the High Commissioner's wife, it was her duty to keep her ears and eyes wide open. Before Janet left, Lady Jayne whispered in all sincerity that if she could help in any way, she would be pleased to do so; in the meantime, she would set aside an afternoon for Janet to bring her children and her husband for tea when he arrived. Janet returned to the hotel where she would stay until her husband, Roy, finally appeared with the cruiser. She tried in vain to contact him, but he was still out of range, and she would have to wait until he contacted her.

Lady Janet had decided she would tell Roy the full story as soon as he arrived; Oh God, she would have to tell him how she had given herself freely despite the promises she had made to him. She would have to disclose that they, whoever 'they' were, had pictures of her sexual encounter with Carl at the castle, as she thought she realised that whoever had done this to her, had planned it for a long time. They had pictures of her having sex with Michael on the boat, and they even had infra-red pictures of her with Mark in the residency garden. She shuddered at how the pictures at the bungalow showed her to be complacent in having wild uninhibited sex with four men, but despite appearances, the use of the date-rape drug made it rape. It was a very elaborate set-up even for blackmail. *Just what was it all about?* She wondered. *Could it be something to do with Roy's work with the IRA*, but she realised that these men must work for the British government to be able to have access to the British High Commission here in Barbados. Her whole world seemed to collapse in on her; she hoped Roy would be here soon as he would know what to do.

The following day, the hotel reception rang Janet's suite to say that a Lady Jayne Claiborne was here to see her, asking if was it convenient for her Ladyship to come up to the suite? Janet considered for a moment and said,

"Will you send her up immediately?"

Lady Claiborne asked Janet to call her Jayne and asked if there was anything she could do to help. Janet recognised something was worrying her visitor; it was obviously more than just a concern over what had happened to her.

As they spoke, it became clear that Lady Claiborne was very upset. Janet could see that Jayne had tears in her eyes and suddenly it all came tumbling out.

"Oh God, Lady Croft; I'm sorry, Janet," she said, tears coursing down her face. "I'm sorry to burden you with my problems; you have enough of your own at the moment, but I feel I can't discuss it with Sir Martin as he's too distraught. It appears that we have lost track of Martin's daughter Madeleine. She is my stepdaughter. She was born to Martin's first wife. In fact, there is not that much age difference between us. It seems that, after all her father's concerns and warnings of the dangers involved, it appears that she has gone to Europe backpacking, and no one has heard from her for more than a week."

Janet tried to calm the distraught woman; to Janet, it seemed as though Lady Claiborne felt in some way that Madeleine's disappearance had something to do with her, even though that was both impractical and impossible.

"I feel Madeleine may not have wanted to hurry home after finishing at university," Lady Jayne continued, "because she and I do not get on together. She has never really accepted me marrying Sir Martin."
Janet put her arm around the disconsolate woman and held her, giving soft words of support but letting Lady Jayne weep until she could cry no more.

When Lady Jayne finally calmed down and recovered her sense of decorum, she apologised for her senseless behaviour.
"I'm sorry, Janet. Please forgive my unforgivable behaviour. I came to console you, not burden you with my worries."
Janet, still holding Lady Jayne, assured her she had sympathy when it came to troubles in the family. To try and restore her credibility, Lady Jayne asked Janet,
"Tell me, Janet, but if you do not want to, I shall fully understand. Tell me, was that awful experience when you suffered that unforgivable attack on your person, did it have anything to do with Mark?"
The look on Janet's face answered her question.
"I thought so. He left so soon after it happened." Lady Jayne said, "I never really liked Mark from the day he had arrived, but it takes all sorts to be in the diplomatic service as we cannot like everyone. I have enquired around, and it appears none of the established staff had liked him. Mark and his team of three had been overbearing and cocky." She added, "He and his team were on station for only such a short time, something to do with an assignment, but I never discovered what it was, and thank goodness, they've now left, to go back to England."

Janet remembered Roy finding a radio tracking device stuck to the bottom of his boat when she had discussed the possibility of actually going to go to the West Indies. It was about the same time, it appeared from what Jane had said, that Mark had arrived in Barbados. *Could it have been a coincidence?* She did not think so after what had happened to her. The British Secret Service (MI5 or MI6) must be following her husband for some reason. What could he have been involved in? Janet asked herself. She only wished she had paid more attention to his business charters for the IRA. She hoped he was not too involved; however, from the lifestyle they lived at the castle and his ability to take a year off gave her some indication that he was extremely well paid. Janet wondered if she should tell Lady Jayne, she could not yet get out of the habit of thinking of her by that name, about Roy's charters and his links to the IRA, but she just shook her head and said,

"I can't bring myself to discuss it at the moment. Perhaps when I have spoken to my husband, I may be able to talk about what happened, but it's too soon at the moment. Let's change the subject, and you tell me about your stepdaughter."

"Madeleine has always been a bit of a rebel," Lady Jayne began, "ever since my marriage to Sir Martin. It was always obvious the young woman missed her mother, who had died after surviving a plane crash some years before."

Lady Jayne fished in her handbag and produced a picture of a pretty blonde woman being presented with her degree at university, and handing it to Janet, she added,

"We had wanted her to return to Barbados with us, but she had refused saying that she had been cooped up in the university for three years and had studied hard, much to the detriment of her social life, which had enabled her to achieve a first-class honours degree. She told her father she needed to broaden her outlook, and as she was over twenty-one, she was able to decide what she wanted to do. She informed her father that it was not as if she had to ask his permission and that she was going to go backpacking for a year in Europe and North Africa. Nothing her father said would change her mind, so we reluctantly had to fly back here without her. Sir Martin had made her promise that she would contact him at least once a week to let him know she was all right. Sir Martin is so worried. She's over a week overdue since she sent the last message. The last thing he heard from her was that she was crossing over to Tangiers. Nothing has been heard of her since, although Martin hired a private detective to try and trace her."

Janet looked shocked.

"I do hope she is all right." Janet said fully understanding the way Lady Jayne felt. "It must be a terrible worry for you, and here you are concerning yourself about my troubles, which seem small, against the dangers your stepdaughter could be in."

The two women in their mutual need for consolation in the time of their troubles went out to join Morag and the children on the private beach; that moment seemed to be the catalyst for the beginning of a close friendship between the two women who seemed to have so much empathy between them. Lady Jayne, who had fallen in love with the Croft's children, said,

"Janet, you must bring them to the Residency. I have been trying to persuade Sir Martin that we should start a family." She went on sadly, "Sir Martin is much older than me, and he feels it would be too much of a burden for him to start a new family at his time of life."

Lady Jayne confided in Janet that she was working on him, and although she had not discussed it with her husband, she had already stopped taking any precautions against getting pregnant, but so far nothing had happened. She could only conclude that Sir Martin had a very low sperm count, added to the fact that he was almost sixty. The two women lunched together in the beach restaurant, and the friendship was cemented over a bottle of expensive champagne. They parted arranging to meet again in two days' time.

The following day, Janet spent with Morag and the children on the private beach. Morag was a little shocked when Janet had stripped off to get an all-over tan; she was not used to seeing Janet nude, but had to admit to herself that her mistress still had an excellent figure; she looked like a model. The day went well, and Morag had not seen Janet so happy since they arrived. The terrible, depressive mood that had come over her when she had been discovered by the hotel pool naked seemed to have lifted ever since that nice Lady Claiborne had been to visit her.

Lady Jayne arrived again, the following morning, but her mood was more sombre than ever, and she looked very worried; Janet asked her if she had heard from her stepdaughter. Lady Jayne, whom Janet had considered a strong-willed person, broke down and cried. Janet put her arms around her as the tears coursed down Lady Jayne's cheeks.

"Oh, Janet," she cried, "the detective agency contacted Martin and told him she was last seen boarding a yacht in Tangiers with two well-to-do English men. They set sail and the yacht is overdue at its next destined port of call. I'm worried something bad may have happened. The agency did say that modern-day pirates had been active in the area of late."

Janet did her best to comfort the distraught woman, who was grateful for Janet's concern. The action served to strengthen the bond of friendship between the two women, even more. Janet just wished Roy would contact her soon. The children had spent the morning with Morag, who was, for the first time, wearing a swimsuit she had bought at the hotel shop instead of that awful black dress. The children loved it. When Morag rolled in the sand with them, they were very happy, innocent of their mother's worries, but eagerly awaiting the arrival of their daddy.

Chapter 4

Roy stood at the helm of his cruiser, feeling the strain a little; he had been at the wheel for eight hours not only keeping the craft on their intended course but also watching the radar constantly alert for any sign of an approaching craft. The weather was good and visibility was excellent, but there was a fairly heavy swell on the sea, and wishing to conserve fuel, Roy had kept the cruiser at the most economical speed. It would normally have been easy to just switch over to autopilot, but with a heavy cross swell, it had not been possible, and his shoulders ached as did his legs and thighs. He was only too happy when he saw Elian appear up the companionway to relieve him. It had been jointly decided that eight hours on and eight hours off would be the best way for them to handle the crossing, and only if the weather turned stormy, they would need both at the wheel. They were now some eighty miles off the coast, but still within the range of trouble. They were all beginning to relax after the event with the yacht *Commander's Choice*; the likelihood of contact with the pirates was becoming less and less of a worry. Roy was worried about the yacht, which by now would have been reported missing. The radio, along with the transponder, had been smashed by the pirates. Someone, somewhere, would be worried about its whereabouts, and as yet, Roy had had no opportunity to report what had happened to the yacht. They were still not on the main shipping lanes, where they could contact a ship and inform them that they had rescued one of the yacht's passengers. Roy knew someone, somewhere, would be worried about the crew, not without due cause.

Roy accepted the kiss on the cheek from his skipper and they exchanged pleasantries. Elian had just taken the wheel when, out of the corner of her eye, she noticed, several blips appear on the radar screen; they were too small to be much bigger than their own cruiser. What struck her as strange was that there were three craft, all of which appeared to be heading in their direction. She drew Roy's attention to three craft approaching from different directions. They were on the very edge of the radar screen, but strangely, all three appeared to be converging on their position at the same speed. Roy looked closer.

"That's strange, Elian, what do you think?" Roy asked.

"Trouble," Elian replied. "After the sinking of the *Commander's Choice*, I don't want to become another statistic at Lloyd's."

They waited several minutes to see if any of the distant vessels changed course; none of them did. Making up his mind that they could present a problem, Roy ran down to alert the others of the impending risk, adding that they may have an imminent and serious problem ahead. Roy, not wishing to overly alarm his new passenger, asked Madeleine to stay below. She watched in awe as Gael brought up the weapons from below, her mouth opened in surprise when she saw the rocket launchers and machine guns together with side arms.

"Are you expecting a war?" she asked Gael.

Turning to her, and seeing the look of shock and worry once again return to Madeleine's face, Gael retorted,

"If it's the pirates who attacked you, we may well have a war on our hands and we could well be fighting for our lives. Don't just bloody well stand there, give me a hand." Then, as an afterthought, she demanded, "Can you shoot?"

"I was a university champion at skeet shooting." Madeleine replied somewhat eagerly,

"That's fine," Gael replied, her voice clearly showing signs of exasperation, "but clay plates are not in the habit of shooting back. Do you think you could handle a situation as serious as this?"

Gael handed Madeleine a Sterling automatic rifle. Madeleine took the strange weapon in her hand, and Gael rapidly explained the safety mechanism, the single and automatic selections, and how to load and unload the clips. Madeleine brought the gun up, her hand near the trigger.

"Christ, girl, watch where you're pointing that bloody thing. We don't want casualties or holes in the boat from friendly fire, now do we?"

"Sorry, Gael, I didn't think. It's a strange weapon for me to handle."

Gael looked skywards in despair.

"Stay below," Gael told her. "We don't want casualties if we can help it. Shoot out of the portholes in the lower cabin if you need to."

Gael ran up the companionway, placing one rocket grenade launcher on the flying bridge and one in the lower wheelhouse; machine guns were put in strategic places on the decks, and everyone was given side arms and spare clips. Elian had been calling on the radio using the open channel, but none of the approaching blips had responded.

"Shall I get the Sam7s and the surface-to-surface missiles?" Gael asked Roy gravely. "We don't want to give them the advantage of getting too close; if we let them we could be taking fire from three sides."
Roy nodded and asked Elian if any of the three craft, now closing on them rapidly, had responded to their signals. Elian shook her head and called out,

"Three unidentified craft, approximately two miles out, still converging on us and closing, I suggest we change our course or you open fire."
"Call once more," Roy snapped, not wishing to fire on friendly boats.
Elian called again. There was no response!

"No response! Approaching craft now one and a half miles and closing," Elian called back.
Gael suddenly appeared with the Sam7shoulder launcher, and Roy loaded the tube from behind her, and Elian saw what was happening and reacted immediately: she reached down and switched on the missile lock radar and called the approaching craft once more.

"Still no response," Elian called. This message was immediately followed by, "Missile locked on target."

Gael checked behind her shoulder to make sure Roy was clear, and somewhat grim-faced, he gave the signal; Gael launched the first missile unhesitatingly. The missile whooshed out of the tube and hurtled some ten feet above the water towards its target. Elian watched to see if the nearest and targeted approaching vessel should break the silence of the radio and make its intentions friendly, her finger ready to press on the *abort* button. There was no such response, and in the distance, through the binoculars, Roy saw the nearest of the rapidly approaching craft explode, sending men and guns high into the air. Roy muttered,

"Good shot, Gael. We've got one of the bastards' dead centre."
The other two came on seemingly undeterred. Gael nodded to Roy to load the second missile. Roy loaded it and cleared the area.

"Missile-lock on!" Elian shouted,
Not waiting for Roy's signal this time, Gael fired the second missile in the general direction of one of the approaching craft just as shells from the two approaching boats started to spatter well short of Roy's cruiser. The second craft, much nearer this time, erupted in a blast that deafened them all. The missile struck just at the waterline, sending men and guns together with debris, churning upwards in a maelstrom of smoke, fire, men, and pieces of the destroyed craft.

"Cut loose the towline to the fuel tank!" Elian shouted to Fiona, who was on the lower deck with a machine gun in her hand, ready to fire back if the pirates came closer.

Fiona raced to carry out the instruction. She released the capstan drive and the line unwound rapidly. As soon as the line went slack behind them, Fiona gave the thumbs up. Elian opened up the throttles, sending the cruiser up onto its plane racing across the water away from the rapidly approaching craft which was still firing heavy machine-gun bullets in their general direction; none had yet come within striking range. The boat was built along the lines of Roy's cruiser and was presumably fitted with twin-turbo diesel engines that had obviously been modified, but apparently, despite these changes, it was still not as fast as Roy's cruiser. Through the binoculars, Roy could see the approaching craft had no marking or registration and had been fitted with heavy machine guns on the main and on the aft decks. The forward gun was firing in their direction, and they were just outside the range; spurts of water were getting too close for comfort.

Madeleine's head appeared at the companionway as she yelled at the top of her voice,
"That's the boat that attacked the yacht. They are the killers."
Roy consulted with Elian and Gael and decided they would destroy the last pirate rather than try to outrun them.
"Did you load the torpedoes before we set sail?" Roy asked Gael.
"Yes," she replied, "but they are not armed."
"What about the missiles?" Roy asked her again.

Gael, knowing her complement of ammunition in the armoury, answered without hesitation,
"We have six more active missiles and two airburst anti-missile chaff for deployment in our defence."
"We'll load another missile," he told her.
Gael ran below and brought up another missile They loaded it and saw that the boat giving chase had seen the missile being loaded and had turned away, intending to leave the scene. Roy ordered Elian to turn and give chase; the last thing they wanted was for the pirates to follow them under cover of darkness and attack when they least expected it. Elian turned and opened the throttles, giving the cruiser a speed in excess of sixty knots. Roy asked Gael to arm the torpedoes. Gael went below and reappeared saying that the

torpedoes were armed and ready. Roy went down to the lower cabin and selected the switch left over from the wartime panel, and the torpedo doors set either side of the hull slid silently open. The fleeing pirates saw they were being chased and began to fire from the rear heavy machine gun. The shells of the Vickers gun were closer than Roy had thought, and water in front of the cruiser was being splattered with the shells being fired at them. Elian began taking evasive action; Gael came down and informed Roy that the range for the torpedoes was set at 2,000 yards and were set to explode on contact.

Elian knew the torpedo doors had opened from the red-light indicator on the panel and accordingly she took a wide turn until they had a broadside view of the pirate craft. Roy waited until the range was right and deployed one of the two torpedoes. The sleek length of death shot out in the direction of the pirate vessel, the wartime torpedo sent a trail of bubbles behind it. The cruiser either saw the torpedo launched or they had excellent radar facilities aboard and were attempting to evade the approaching steel fish. Roy raced back up on deck with Gael; she picked up the missile launcher, and Elian switched on the missile lock. The missile was set to 'heat seek', and Elian called out,

"Missile lock on."

Gael released the missile as the pirate vessel tried in vain to evade contact with the nearing torpedo; they almost made it, but it took the fleeing craft astern. The resulting explosion took away the rear transom, rudder, and screws as flames shot skywards and the vessel lost way immediately; just as the missile picked up the heat from the explosion of the torpedo and it slammed into the back of the disabled pirate vessel, fragmenting the fibre glass hull, a second explosion almost immediately indicated the fuel tank had been breached; no one aboard stood a chance. As the smoke cleared, the sea was covered with fragments of wood and fibreglass, but of the pirate crew, there was no sign. Roy gave any survivors no quarter; he waved Elian on. Elian, as practical as ever, retraced their course; until she located the floating tank, she went alongside, and Gael, using a boat hook, secured the line and re-hitched it to the rear capstan. Then Elian resumed their original course once more.

Madeleine and Fiona came up from below. Fiona was visibly shaken while Madeleine was white-faced.

"My God," Madeleine said, "what kind of cruiser is this? It's better fitted out than a naval patrol boat. Are you by any chance British Secret Service or are you pirates yourselves?"

It was not without some misgivings that Madeleine allowed Roy to take her below; he first gave her a large glass of Irish whisky and then took her through the door and sat her on the bed in the stateroom. She was trembling slightly, and Roy sat down beside her, put his arm on her shoulder in what he considered was in a fatherly fashion, and began to tell her the story of how he acquired his MTB. Madeleine sat open-mouthed as Roy continued his story. He omitted all reference to the IRA, his drug and gunrunning activities; Roy told her they had acquired the rockets from an undisclosed source after he had removed the wartime deck guns and had redesigned the boat. He explained to Madeleine that this was not the first time he had tangled with pirates, but these were the best equipped he had come across so far.

The whisky had given Madeleine a flush to her face and neck; the effects had somewhat mollified how she felt about the information, and the whisky had been quite smooth to the taste. Madeleine could not deny that she was definitely feeling better, and looking up at Roy, she politely asked if she could have another. Roy poured her another glass, and this time he poured one for himself. He went on to tell her he has set up a private charter business, which had proved successful and very lucrative, and he was on his way to the Caribbean to meet his wife and children.

"But the crew?" she asked incredulously, "I have heard you make love to them; how does your wife feel about you being alone at sea with your all-female crew?"

Roy began to explain how he had met Janet, how she had taught him everything she knew about sex, how they had finally married and under what circumstances, and how his wife had said she would never stand in his way with his relationships with other women, provided he always had time for her when she needed him. Madeleine sat gaping at Roy, thinking to herself, *this good-looking man must really be something in bed*. She proffered her glass, and Roy poured her another generous helping. Noticing not for the first time that the flush rising up her neck and into her face had deepened, he presumed it was from the effects of the alcohol, and soon after taking another sip from her third glass of whisky, she began to lean against him in a completely relaxed manner.

Roy wondered if he should make a move on this nubile and very attractive blonde-haired young woman he and his crew had rescued from death by drowning, or worse, starvation. He knew nothing about her, apart from the fact that her parents lived in Barbados. He took a chance and asked her about her boyfriends at university. The whisky was taking effect and any inhibitions she might have harboured in front of this rugged, seafaring stranger had long since been liberated.

"Oh, there were one or two," she said cautiously, "but nothing serious." Taking another gulp from her full glass, Madeleine plucked up her courage, sat up, and put her arms around Roy's neck; she said,

"Thank you so much for rescuing me from almost certain death, twice now. How can a girl thank you under such traumatic circumstances?"

Even as the last word left her mouth, she turned her face upwards and pulled him down before she kissed him softly on the lips.

Roy took pride in his seductive art; it was just too good an opportunity to resist satisfying another woman's need, and it was sometime later when he went to the heads and washed away all signs of their lovemaking. He took his time dressing, taking more than a lingering look at the figure of the latest addition to his ever-increasing list of mistresses. He never understood why women were attracted to him; perhaps it was some kind of animal magnetism, pheromones; whatever it was, he hoped it would continue for many years to come. Madeleine felt languid after her sexual experience with Lord Croft, her latest love. Sir Martin, her father, would be disgusted with her if he knew. However, she had no qualms as her father had married that 'Jayne' woman who had been his secretarial assistant when her mother had died; she had been disgusted with her father for marrying a woman not much older than herself. Snapping out of her thoughts, Madeleine sat up, and as she dressed, she lazily said, almost to herself,

"My goodness, Lord Croft, it's no wonder they all let you make love to them. I never felt so good after sex in my life. You even put my college professor to shame. What is it about men like you that seem to draw women to you like a magnet?"

Roy only half-heard what she said, and realising she really required no answer to her hypothetical question; he let the door close behind him.

Roy walked into the galley where Fiona was preparing the evening meal; she turned to look at Roy and smiling, as she noticed the young woman slip out of the main cabin and into her own, she whispered with a hint of jealousy,

"It sounded as though you enjoyed young Madeleine's favours, your Lordship; from the look on her face, when she passed the galley a few moments ago, I'd say she enjoyed it too." Adding casually, "Dinner will be about half an hour."

Roy smiled but gave Fiona no reply as he walked up to the flying bridge where Elian was at the wheel and Gael was sitting on the upper deck, cleaning and oiling the weaponry they had used earlier. Elian said,

"From the noises coming from below, Roy, I would say my schedule and rota have gone for a loop. We shall just have to see how things work out. Madeleine appears to be yet another of your conquests. I just hope she's on the pill; knowing you, if she's not, she'll be pregnant before she gets home."

Looking up at Elian's comment, Gael swallowed hard. She was conscious of the fact that she still had not started her period, and she was now really late; in fact, her next period was almost due. Even though she had taken her pill regularly, she still couldn't understand why she missed her monthly periods, but she had not taken her gastro-enteritis into consideration when her pill would not have been absorbed. She was the youngest woman on board and had really no idea what she should do; she was an expert in munitions and keeping fit, but pregnancy was something she'd never expected or indeed knew anything about. Her mother had never explained things to her; she had taken it upon herself to go across the border to get a supply of contraceptive pills when she had learned she was going abroad for training. All she knew was that if she took a pill a day it would prevent pregnancy; she had never remotely considered the possibility that they could ever fail.

Madeleine shared the main cabin with Roy, again that night, much to the annoyance, if not anger, of the rest of the crew. It was always the same: whenever Roy took a new mistress, the others had to take a respite until the novelty wore off. It was sometime later when Roy went up to relieve Elian, who had done far more than her supposed eight-hour shift. Roy walked up behind Elian, who stood at the wheel, and tapped her on the shoulder, and half-turning, she gave him a look of admonishment.

"I have to hand it to you. You certainly seem to have been captivated by our newest arrival, and she seems to have stood the course well. It was very late when the noise from your cabin finally stopped."

Then in a jocular tone of voice, she added,

"I've told you before, if you keep up that pace, you will be no good to Janet when you get to Barbados. You'll have worn yourself out. Now please take over. I need some well-earned rest. Oh, and if young Madeleine is coming all the way to Barbados with us, it would be better to get her to help out with the chores and make life easier all the way around. If the rest of us have to work, then so should she."

Having made her point about an extra pair of hands to relieve the crew, Elian went below for some well-earned sleep. They were now in the main shipping lanes, and Roy kept a close watch on the radar screen, avoiding close contact with the huge vessels cutting their way through the ocean. He spotted an American freighter and called the vessel on the radio. The efficient radio operator asked him to identify himself, which he did, giving his name as Lord Croft aboard the cruiser *Spirit of the Isle* out of Tralee. Roy explained to him that they were not equipped with satellite radio and requested the operator to pass on a message; the operator agreed and asked what the message was. Roy told him to pass a message on to the authorities that they had rescued a woman passenger from the yacht *Commander's Choice* which had been attacked and sunk by pirates off the coast of North Africa. The yacht had been registered in England and the two crew members had been killed by their attackers. He sent for Madeleine and asked her, who she wanted to be notified of her rescue. Roy went weak at the knees when she said,

"The British High Commission in Barbados? My father is the High Commissioner, Sir Martin Claiborne. Please inform him that I am safe and we should be arriving," then looking enquiringly at Roy who indicated three, she continued, "in three or four days' time."

Madeleine handed the microphone back to Roy, who, having given the man on the receiving end of the two-way call all of his details, asked the radio man to pass a message to his wife staying in the Sandpiper hotel on Barbados. The radio operator keen to assist said,

"Lord Croft, I can do better than that. If you have the telephone number, I'll willingly patch you through by radio telephone."

Roy gave the hotel number, and the hotel reception answered. Roy asked the receptionist to put the call through to the King Suite, and Janet answered.

When she heard Roy's voice, Janet burst into tears, much to Roy's concern.

"Are you all right? Are the children well?" He queried, somewhat alarmed.

"Yes," Janet answered, "but I have so much to tell you. When will you arrive?"

"In three or four days," Roy confirmed, "that is if the weather holds. You know how fickle that can be. Do you think you could do us a favour? Can you phone the High Commission to inform them that I have the High Commissioner's daughter safely on board after rescuing her from a sinking yacht?"

Roy did not quite understand when Janet said,

"Oh my God! Roy, Lady Jayne is right here. Speak to her yourself."

Another woman's voice, identifying herself as Lady Jayne Claiborne, came on the crackly line.

"What is that about Madeleine?" she asked. "Is she safe, Lord Croft?"

"I'll let you speak to her yourself, Lady Claiborne." He gave the microphone to an unbelieving stepdaughter.

"Hello, Jayne, I'm safe and well. Please tell Daddy not to worry. I'll be home in three or four days' time, and I'll tell you all about it then."

Lady Jayne was ecstatic and wanted to know more, but Roy shook his head as he felt the ship's operator had been more than generous already.

They flashed the radio link and thanked the ship's operator for his help; the operator replied,

"You're a long way from home, Lord Croft, so go safe. The weather forecast looks good for the next few days. Have a safe journey and good luck."

Madeleine hugged Roy and thanked him for letting her speak to her stepmother, who she had never really got on with. Madeleine went on babbling about her stepmother not being much older than herself and she had hated it when her daddy had told her he was marrying a much younger woman. Madeleine had loved her mother and had hated the fact that her father had replaced her.

"My father had the audacity to tell me that Jayne would be more of a companion for me than a mother, if and when anything happened to him. Jayne always hoped things would work out between us in time, but it's been difficult, to say the least," Madeleine said, unable to hide the vehemence in her voice.

Madeleine had to admit to herself that Jayne had certainly sounded relieved to hear her voice and had obviously been worried that something had happened to her; perhaps she had misjudged her new stepmother and the reasons she had for marrying her father. She was still deep in thought as she went below.

Chapter 5

To give the vessel more speed and shorten the time to get to Barbados, Elian, with the help of Roy, pumped the fuel from the floating fuel tank, and after it had been completed, they deflated the floats and let the fabric tank sink. The cruiser, released from the drag of the tank, could now cruise at a higher speed and be more fuel efficient, but even then it still took Roy and his crew three days to reach the Island of Barbados via the island of Fernando de Noronha, Part of the archipelago of Pernambuco, up past French Guiana, then north, past Trinidad and Tobago, continuing to Bridgetown in Barbados at which stage both Roy and Elian were tired of handling the cruiser. At the higher speed, more concentration was necessary, and both of them were feeling the strain. Roy was not only mentally tired, but his constant sexual activity had also helped to drain his strength; he would need a rest when he reached the hotel. When they were within range, they radioed ahead and the hotel gave Roy permission to anchor off the hotel beach, informing him they would, as part of their service, have customs and immigration available to meet them, a service the hotel offered to their wealthier clients.

Gael by this time was desperate to see a doctor to confirm if she was pregnant, but she was still undecided what to do about the baby if the test results turned out to be positive. Not knowing how she would get to see a doctor ashore, Gael confided in Elian, who was shaken by the news, admonishing her for not being more careful. Initially, Gael was determined to have the child, but Elian persuaded her to take a break and go to London to have the abortion, after explaining the difficulties that she would have to undergo if she wanted to complete the voyage. Elian had also told her she was far too young to be having a baby around and had a full life ahead of her with plenty of opportunity to have babies when they were planned. Gael had finally agreed she would do as Elian had suggested if the doctor confirmed her pregnancy. The customs and immigration check went without a hitch. Roy was sure that the presence of the British High Commissioner and his wife may have had something to do with the lack of formalities. Janet was there to welcome Roy and his crew as the cruiser's tender pulled up to the beach; Janet threw her arms around Roy's neck and hugged him close to her. Rooms were arranged for the crew, and Madeleine kissed Roy goodbye. Much to Sir Martin's surprise, it was more than just a friendly peck on the cheek. She held Roy close to her and whispered in his ear,

"Just don't go far, I'm planning to come and see you tomorrow. I'll ring and make the arrangements."

The children were so pleased to see their daddy, and the next couple of hours were spent with the children on the beach. As the afternoon drew to a close, Morag gave the excited, but tired, children their supper and put them to bed. To their delight, Roy read them a goodnight story and finally went into the shower to get cleaned up. Roy took his hip flask from his pocket and took a pull of potcheen, a potion prepared by Cathleen, one of his staff back in Ireland, which, although prepared from some secret recipe of her mother's, had a similar effect to Viagra. Roy had seen that look in Janet's eyes before; he knew what was expected of him. Janet joined him, hungry for his touch, but still wracked with guilt and worry, she was determined to make love to him before she broke the news of her own sexual indiscretions and her rape and abuse in the hands of Mark and his staff. Janet used all her knowledge and skills, letting the water in the oversized shower cascade over both of them, and she began to wash Roy's body; the potcheen had its effect, and much to Roy's delight and surprise, the attention he got both in the shower and in bed were reminiscent of earlier times. When they made love, Janet was full of energy, constantly demanding, and finally, Roy collapsed beside her.

Janet sat up and opened a bottle of champagne she had ordered and poured the bubbly liquid into the glasses and handed one to Roy, as he sat up surprised at the way she coaxed him to join her. It was unusual for Janet; she was not usually so ready to drink, especially so soon after making love. Taking the glass, he looked closely into her eyes and saw she was a little distant, and he recognised that she needed to tell him something.

"What on earth's wrong?" Roy asked her. "We have just experienced a wonderful loving reunion, and far from celebrating with the champagne, I have the distinct feeling you are troubled and need to talk. Tell me, what's wrong?"

Janet burst into tears. This was not the Janet he was used to; she was usually confident and strong. Roy put his arms around her, endeavouring to comfort her; he was completely overwhelmed by her sudden change of mood.

"Oh God! I'm so sorry, Roy. I don't know what made me do it. I don't know what in the world came over me."

The words tumbled out of her trembling lips; the champagne meant as a toast was pushed aside, forgotten for the moment. Janet burst into tears, reminding Roy of the first time he had comforted her prior to the first time they had made love whilst her first husband lay in an alcoholic stupor upstairs. He poured her a drink of whisky and sat back down beside her, holding her until her racking sobs quietened.

"Nothing can be that bad. Come on; tell me, what is worrying you? I've not seen you like this since Tom, your first husband, passed away. I know it's not the children. They seem happy and well-adjusted to life on the islands. I can tell you are not sick, so tell me, what's wrong?" Roy asked, concern and worry sweeping over him like a black cloud.

Janet pulled herself together and began to tell her story.

"You are fully aware that I made love to Carl back at the castle in Ireland." Seeing the look of concern cross Roy's face, she hurriedly prevented his interjection by continuing, "Now don't interrupt me until I've finished. Well, I have to confess far from feeling guilty about the episode. I have to confess that I enjoyed it. It reminded me of the time I was at university and had lots of free love and sex. I suppose, it brought back memories of my younger days before the children."

Roy feared the worst. *Had she found someone else?* He well remembered that he had opened the door and had seen her with Carl back in Ireland, but that was behind them, and he had never blamed her. His mind a whirl of possibilities; as he thought to himself. *Why is she so upset about something that happened then?* Roy's anxious thoughts were interrupted as Janet continued,

"Well, he rang me a couple of days later," she whispered as she hesitated, as if not quite knowing how to proceed, "and he told me that Michael, another of my ex-lovers from my university days, was in the Caribbean doing marine research. Carl told me he would get Michael, now Doctor Crosby, would you believe, to ring me when I arrived. I felt good about the prospect of seeing Michael again, so I did not object. Then not long after I had arrived, Michael rang me and invited me to dinner; I felt like a schoolgirl again going out on a date, which my parents would not have approved of. To cut a long story short, we had dinner, and he made love to me in his room afterwards, and I agreed to go out on his research boat the next day. I lay naked on his boat, and we made love several times again."

Seeing the look of concern cross Roy's face, she quickly reassured him, "I don't mean love in the sense that we love each other. There was no love involved. It was just enjoyable sex, just as we had done when he was with me at university. I'm sorry to admit it, but it felt wonderful. He was very persuasive, and we had unprotected sex several times during the day."
Roy's mind went blank. *The bastard's got her pregnant,* he thought to himself. Janet then began to weep again. Roy told her to drink some of her Scotch, and he patiently waited for her to confess that she was having Michael's child. To his surprise, she continued her story; once again, he had misjudged her motives.
"When we got back to shore, out of the blue, he suddenly asked me to go with him to the High Commissioner's Residence for dinner. I was surprised as he had not mentioned it earlier, but I accepted his invitation, and when we arrived, I was introduced to Sir Martin Claiborne and his wife, Jayne. I'll tell you all about her after I have unfolded my sorry tale. Another couple, I forget their names, were there with their daughter, and the other guest was a handsome man named Mark. I never knew his last name. After dinner, everyone smoked except Mark and I. He could see how the smoke was having an adverse effect on me and kindly offered to show me around the grounds whilst the party finished their cigars."

"I was on top of the world. Here I was a married woman, with two children, and he was a young man paying me compliments and offering to walk in the garden under a tropical moon. It sounded so romantic. I'd had several drinks, not that I am offering that as an excuse, but I let him seduce me in a secluded wooded grotto, in the grounds of the residency. I have to admit he certainly knew just how to take advantage of the situation and seduce a lonely woman. We had sexual intercourse under the stars. I know it sounds sordid, but at the time it felt so romantic."
Roy winced at the thought of yet another man having sex with his wife, and from what he could deduce from the speed at which it had happened, he too would have probably done so, totally unprotected.
"Oh, my darling, I admit that he was such a good lover. I let him make love to me again before we left the seclusion of the grotto, and I was in seventh heaven. I was the belle of the ball, and this handsome young stranger had just made a wild and passionate love to me. As he walked me

back to the house, he invited me to lunch at his house the following day. I accepted."

Janet paused momentarily to judge Roy reactions; then quickly continued with her tale of woe.

"I was picked up the following day by a consular car and driven to Mark's bungalow. We swam naked, and I know it was wrong of me, but I let him have sex with me again. Then not long afterwards, unannounced and seemingly totally out of the blue, some of his friends arrived, and when I objected, he simply laughed it off and gave me a drink. From that moment on, I had no control. I knew what was happening around me, but I had no power to stop it. I was helpless to prevent them, and during the rest of the day, each and every one of them raped me. I must have lost consciousness, for when I woke, they had dumped me, naked, by the hotel pool, for anyone to see. Fortunately, it was quite late, and the pool area was quiet. It was a security guard that found me and raised the alarm. The hotel manager and his staff were very understanding and helped me to my suite and called a doctor. The doctor took samples of my blood and the semen. Later, he told me I had been given the date-rape drug Rohypnol and that the samples of semen he had taken from me, apart from confirming that I had had multiple partners, was apparently useless for DNA purposes."

Roy was fuming, but he said nothing; he waited for her to finish.

"The worst is yet to come," she said.

Her eyes watching Roy's face contort with worry and concern as she waited for Roy to explode; she held up her finger and touched his lips, preventing him from interrupting her confession. Roy could not imagine any worst news. *Was she pregnant with one of her so-called rapists? No,* he thought; he could never accept that. He remained silent, his blood boiling with anger as he listened to the sorry tale of atrocities his wife had suffered.

"Mark rang me before the police arrived and told me to tune in to one of the channels on the hotel television. I almost died. There were movie pictures of me having sex in the castle with Carl, then pictures of me having sex on Michael's boat, followed by infrared pictures of my sexual encounter with Mark in the grounds of the Residency and finally pictures of my apparent orgy with four men." Tears flowed freely as she struggled to continue, "I asked him why he had done this to me. He simply laughed, saying if I told the police what had happened, he would show the pictures to every room and on every channel in the hotel. Oh God! Roy, I'm so ashamed I had no idea why this man had done such a thing. It must have taken a lot of planning to get pictures from all those places. He also said, I would find out why he had done this later, but I have never heard from him since. Lady Jayne, the High Commissioner's wife, said that Mark and his three cronies had been recalled back to London the day after they had raped me."

Roy knew he could never be angry with his wife for her infidelity. After all, she had always been so understanding, putting up with his own extramarital relationships with almost every woman he had ever come in contact with; she had even witnessed him having sex with several of them. But rape was a crime; Roy could not, and would not, accept, no matter what the circumstances were. He paced the room constantly, reassuring her he was not angry with her, and although he did not approve of her sexual activities during his absence, he accepted them. Janet went on to her knees saying,

"Oh God! Darling, I just don't know what came over me. I just had this mad fling. Believe me, it won't happen again."

Roy raised her to her feet and kissed her tenderly, his voice calm and full of understanding as he whispered,

"Janet, you know I love you like no other woman I have ever met. I can never condemn you for what I have been guilty of myself, but let me assure you, if it's the last thing I do in my life, I will get to the bottom of this abhorrent attack and rape. It's one crime I can never forgive anyone for committing."

They went back to bed, and Roy held his wife in his arms all night long and, at her request, made gentle, tender love to her the following morning, before they showered and went to have breakfast with the children. After breakfast, Roy spoke quietly to Janet, saying,

"I want you to tell Lady Jayne about your rape. I don't care what else you tell her, or indeed how you were persuaded to accept the lunch invitation to Mark's house, when you have told her it was Mark and his staff who perpetrated the violent rape. I want you to ask her to come and talk to me. I understand that she and Madeleine are coming over for lunch today. When lunch is over, take her somewhere quiet and talk to her. Don't come back with her afterwards. Madeleine and I will come and find you."

Janet, glad he had not berated her for her stupidity, nodded acquiescingly, inwardly glad of his understanding.

Lady Jayne and Madeleine arrived at the suite, and although there was little to distinguish the pair by age, their dress code made them seem aeons apart. Lady Jayne wore stylish, expensive, but conservative clothes, whereas Madeleine wore clothes to draw attention to her youth and beauty. Lady Jayne wore an expensive designer lightweight suit that must have set Sir Martin back a pretty penny, and Madeleine wore a smart blouse, cut fairly low and worn loose at the waist, complemented by a short pleated skirt in the latest fashion, in use by the younger set on the island. Roy had ordered lunch to be served on the patio overlooking the beach. They ate a leisurely lunch with a couple of bottles of wine. When they had drunk coffee, Roy, realising from the signals he had received during lunch that Madeleine had dressed provocatively for his benefit, watched as Janet and Lady Jayne left, leaving him alone with Madeleine.

Madeleine was totally captivated by Roy; she had to thank him for saving her life; in all probability, *captivated* was not a strong enough term, *obsessed* would have been nearer the mark. It was as though she had a schoolgirl crush on the man, for both his standing in her psyche as well as his sexuality. She simply could not resist his charm, and she made it obvious to him. As soon as they were alone, she put her arms around him and unashamedly kissed him and drew him closer to her. Roy knew it was wrong to take advantage of the overzealous young woman, but he had never been able to resist the chance of sex with anyone young, attractive, and, above all, vulnerable.

"Oh God! Roy, make love to me. I have missed you so much," Madeleine whispered, totally unashamed that she was offering herself to an older man.

Roy took his hip flask from his pocket and drank Cathleen's brew. He felt the spirit warm as it went down his throat, and shortly afterwards, Roy felt its Viagral effect. *Oh God,* Madeleine thought to herself, *I just can't resist this man. What on earth would my father say if he could see me now? He would disown me;* but she seemed in the grip of something more powerful than her conscience, as she responded to his Lordship's sexual prowess. The sex was euphoric, and when it was finally over, the lovers gradually came down from their exhilaration and lay against each other, totally spent. Neither of them had heard the door open whilst they had been engaged in the wild and unreserved act of making love. Lady Jayne had stood open-mouthed at the sight before her eyes. Her stepdaughter was making love to Lady Janet's husband.

It was the first time in her life Lady Jayne had ever witnessed anyone making love. She could not bear to think of it just as having sex; in her state of shock, she had steadied herself against the door, suddenly aware that the erotic view of the couple, who were obviously totally oblivious to her presence, was unbelievably affecting her own desires. Witnessing the whole episode had a profound effect on Lady Jayne; it had shaken her to the very core. She thought the whole scene was disgusting as she let the door silently close. What she could not explain, however, was how the sight had affected her. She was horrified when she realised she was highly aroused by what she had just witnessed.

Lady Jayne walked away, unable to explain the effects of what she had witnessed, she had not felt so aroused before and wondered if she should tell Lady Janet; but after what the poor woman had already suffered at the hands of Mark, she felt it was better to be discrete and let matter lie for the time being. It was out of a feeling of decorum that she gave her stepdaughter some time before she dared return, and even then she knocked discretely before entering. When she entered, it came as no surprise; Lord Croft and Madeleine were calmly sitting and drinking wine as though nothing untoward had happened between them. She joined them at their invitation for a glass of wine before they all went in search of Janet, to say goodbye, before they left for the Residence. Roy thanked Lady Jayne for the luncheon invite for him and the family the following day, drawing Lady Jayne aside, telling her he needed to speak to her after lunch on a personal matter.
"Of course, Lord Croft," Lady Jayne replied politely. "You know anything my husband or I can do for you will be a pleasure after you so kindly saved our daughter's life from those pirates. If you prefer privacy, we can discuss the matter in my private office."
Jayne felt she owed him that for the safe return of Madeleine, even though he was obviously being rewarded by Madeleine in a very different way; she only hoped the silly young fool was on the pill. She reminded herself to ask her stepdaughter before Lord Croft and his family arrived the next morning.

Roy, Janet, the two children, and Morag arrived at the Residence the following day to be met by Sir Martin, who shook hands with Roy as though they were long-lost brothers, informing him that he would forever be in his debt, and anything he could do for him in any way, he would go out of his way to help. Lunch was a family affair with Lady Jayne helping with the children, like a second mother. Madeleine caught Roy's eye, and she pointed him to the garden. Roy excused himself and walked into the magnificently laid out garden, which could have easily been an English country house apart from the tropical feel of the plants. Roy saw Madeleine beckoning him towards a tree-lined grotto; this he thought must be where Mark had seduced his wife; the spot was perfect, out of sight of the house, a wide low wooden seat with no back stood in the centre, and thick bushes and trees surrounded the central area. Roy entered the secret place, and as he turned, Madeleine threw her arms around his neck and covered his lips with kisses. Her ardour was infectious and urgent as only a young woman's crush can be; Roy offered a token resistance, but her youth and vitality won. The sun, the sky, and the gentle breeze were the only witnesses to their hectic and hurried sexual encounter.

"Oh, Roy, that was better than ever," Madeleine murmured softly.

They lay there for some time before they parted, quickly rearranging their clothing; they both looked calm and relaxed; the only sign of their frenzied sexual activity, minutes before, was a healthy flush showing in Madeleine's face. They walked slowly back to the house. Janet glanced up at Madeleine's rosy complexion and Roy's relaxed way of walking; she knew immediately that the couple had been sexually active. She said nothing and allowed Madeleine to take Sheenagh from Lady Jayne so that Roy could go into the office and discuss with Lady Jayne the urgent and private business Roy needed her to help with.

The office was quite large, and acting in a formal manner, Lady Jayne sat behind the desk and Roy sat in front of her. Lady Jayne looked at him and asked,

"Lord Croft, I am listening. Janet told me what that cad Mark had done. I have no explanation for his unbelievable behaviour. All I can do at this stage is to apologise. I will certainly ask Sir Martin to disclose his disgraceful behaviour to his superiors."

Then she looked up and asked,

"Now what was it you wanted me to do for you? You know both Sir Martin and I are forever in your debt."

Lord Croft spoke quietly but with a grim determination in his voice,

"As you have just confirmed, you are well aware of what happened to Janet at that rogue Mark's house, are you not?"

Lady Jayne nodded to confirm that she did indeed know in great detail what had happened.

"Well, I would like you to get me copies of a photograph of each and every one of the rapists and a name and, if possible, an address for Mark and the others."

Lady Jayne pondered for a while, and an outrageous plan came into her head. It was so outrageous that she felt a flush run up from her very core to her hairline.

Roy saw the flush and thought she was angry that he had dared to request her to obtain confidential information; but before he could say anything, Lady Jayne began to speak,

"What I am about to say in answer to your request must be kept strictly between the two of us, do I have your word?"

Roy nodded, wondering what she was about to say. She continued to speak to him in the same hushed tones. Roy could not understand why she spoke so softly, but then she began to explain,

"When Sir Martin's first wife became so ill after the plane crash, I was working as his personal aide and used to arrange his meetings, deal with all his correspondence, personal and business, so I was privy to the seriousness of her condition. Sir Martin asked me to help by taking over from his wife as hostess for all the receptions. I was to be available to receive foreign dignitaries and welcome visitors, both when he was present as well as away. This continued for almost a year after his wife died. Then one day, he called me into his office and told me how grateful he was for all the help I had been. Then as if in the way of an apology for what he was about to propose, he informed me that foreign office were pressing him to either marry again or relinquish his position to a married man."

"He apologised," she added, "informing me that he understood that he was more than thirty years my senior and had a daughter only a few years younger than myself, and then he broke the bombshell. Completely out of the blue, he asked me if I would become his wife. He explained that his sexual drive was not high, and if I did not want sex to be part of the arrangement, he would understand perfectly. I was not in love with the man, but I had grown to respect him. I sat and considered his proposal of marriage and realised the benefits it would bring, so I accepted. It was a marriage of convenience, not a love match."

She dropped her voice even lower as she continued seemingly embarrassed by what she had to tell him.

"We did consummate the marriage, and excuse me for giving you information not normally divulged, but you will understand in a minute. We usually make love once a month. Sex with Martin is a simple affair; it's quick and unexciting, and when it's over, he simply rolls over and goes to sleep, believing he has done his duty."

Roy sat there listening to lady Jayne divulge secrets that should only be shared between Sir Martin and herself, wondering where this conversation was leading and what it had to do with his request for information. Lady Jayne paused for Roy to digest what she had told him. Then she began again,

"I have spent some considerable time with your wife and family over the last few weeks and have come to the conclusion that I would like a child of my own. I have never taken or tried to avoid a family and nothing has ever happened. I have visited several gynaecologists who assured me that I am perfectly normal and there is no reason why I should not conceive. Therefore, the only conclusion I can come to is that Sir Martin has become either completely infertile or has a very low sperm count. You, on the other hand, according to Janet, have a very high sperm count. What I am proposing therefore is that in return for the information you want, I will expect you to father my child."

Seeing the shocked look on Roy's face, she went on to say,

"I do not mean you would have the ignominy of going to a clinic and donating sperm. I want you to make love to me." Lady Jayne paused to let her suggestion sink in and added quickly, "It would be on my conditions and over the seven days of my ovulation."

"I will encourage Sir Martin, who goes away on Monday morning to London, to make love to me over the weekend, before he leaves, so that he would believe, should I conceive, that the child was his. You would simply have sex with me every day he is away. There will be no intimacy other than the simple act of making love. I simply require you to do the deed. It will be straight sex and nothing else. I am quite aware of your sexual activities with Madeleine, but if you agree to carry out our bargain, I will not inform her father of what I know. Now do you agree? If you do, I will have copies of the files, you wish to see, at the end of our first sexual liaison on Monday next."

Roy sat totally amazed at Lady Jayne's proposal; it was outrageous, but he needed the information on Janet's attackers urgently, and he needed it by

Monday. Under the circumstances, he felt he had little or no choice he had to agree to Lady Jayne's shameful and indecent proposal. He had to admit he looked on her in a completely new light, realising she was almost as attractive as her stepdaughter. The thought of making love to her put her in a different category, and he was looking forward to breaching the defences of a woman he had considered to be unavailable. He walked out of the office with a smile on his face and a new spring in his step.

Chapter 6

When Roy arrived back at the hotel, Janet went with Morag to get the children bathed and ready for bed, leaving Roy alone. He took advantage of the time and rang to Ireland. He needed to speak to Sam Delaney, the head of the IRA group he had worked with prior to leaving Ireland, and he needed to speak to him urgently. It was Kate Delaney who took the call, saying that Sam was away, but she would get Sam to ring him on the secure cell phone within the next half an hour. Roy rang Elian's room and asked her to go out to the cruiser and bring the private cell phone back to him as quickly as she could. Once she had delivered it, she asked if everything was all right. Roy simply nodded and said,

"Thanks, Elian, everything is fine for the moment. I'll call you later, if I need you."

Roy sat down and waited for what seemed an age. It was almost an hour later when the call came through. After the usual pleasantries had been exchanged, Roy told Sam the story of how Janet had been doped, with the use of Rohypnol, raped, and videotaped, and threatened with exposure together with the veiled hidden threat of something more sinister. Roy informed Sam that from what he could gather about the methods and the involvement of people at the British High Commission, he believed it was the work of one of the British Secret Service, either MI5 or MI6. He added,

"Sam, I believe it is some sort of plot to blackmail me into giving up information that would lead back to you, and the committee, in an attempt to discover what our activities are. They obviously believe you are still an active cell, but are at a loss to know how and why. I have made arrangements with a local source to get me details of the men involved, photographs, and as much detail as can be obtained."

Sam Delaney listened in silence; when Roy had finished, Sam took a deep breath and asked.

"Who is your source, Roy? Can you rely on its integrity? Above all, can your source be trusted not to disclose to whom and why they handed it over?"

Roy thought carefully before replying. He did not want to disclose his source to Sam, so he just said,

"I can vouch personally for the source, and as far as integrity is concerned, the person in question would have far more to lose than us by disclosing who or why the information had been passed."

"OK, send me the photographs and as much detail as possible, I'll use my connections at this end to track them down and find the current whereabouts of the perpetrators," Sam said, his anger controlled.

He would do anything necessary to track down Janet's attackers; he needed to know the reason for such atrocious and unacceptable behaviour.

Roy emphasised that no action should be taken by Sam or any of his group; it would be Roy's decision to take whatever action he wanted. With the rape of Roy's wife, Sam concurred that Roy himself could have the pleasure of taking whatever action he wanted to take, although Sam emphasised that he would help in any way he could, but that unless requested he would not interfere. They rang off. Roy spent the weekend with Janet and the children; Janet was pleased to have Roy's complete attention day and night, and she enjoyed the benefit of her husband's undivided attention; he was considerate in their lovemaking, and she was happy that he had not condemned her for being such a gullible fool.

Monday came and the call came from Lady Jayne; she had the information that Roy was expecting; he needed the information badly to enable Sam to track and trace the instigators of Janet's ordeal. Lady Jayne asked Roy to be at her residence at two o'clock sharp. He wondered if she really wanted him to go through with the arrangement or whether she had come to her senses. He hoped the latter, but if so, what would she do about the information he wanted so desperately? Roy was hopeful that the information would still be forthcoming, and the call suggested she would be willing to give him at least a copy of the files. Roy explained to Janet that Lady Jayne was helping him to track down Mark and his cronies and would be back later. Lord Croft arrived at the residence and was shown into the drawing room to wait. A member of the residency staff offered Lord Croft a drink, and when the large tumbler of whisky had been served, Roy sat quietly waiting for Lady Jayne to arrive. He had just tossed the last of the whisky back when she appeared and motioned him to follow her. She preceded him up the broad staircase, and they arrived at one of the doors leading off the main corridor. Lady Jayne opened the door, and they went into an anteroom. Roy felt uncomfortable but was determined to go through with the arrangement come what may. When she disappeared into the bedroom, Roy realised that Lady Jayne was actually going to go through with her plan, and he was a little perplexed as to why she had asked him to wait. He heard her call softly; he opened the door and entered the darkened room.

What happened in there was something Roy would always remember; Lady Jayne had been shy, and she lay under the covers, braced and stiff with embarrassment, but by the time, what for her had been a necessary chore to get Lord Croft to impregnate her, had ended with Lady Jayne's sexual awakening. When what had begun as a duty was over, it had become a lustful joy that Lady Jayne had never thought possible. Roy rose up from the bed, and as he walked towards the bathroom to shower before dressing, he was surprised when she turned towards him and said, her voice husky with sexual satisfaction,

"Today I have come to understand what Madeleine sees in you. I feel a different woman, and for the first time in my life, I've actually enjoyed sex. There is a first time for everything. Now that I have broken my marriage vows, albeit for what I consider to be a good enough reason, I may as well go all the way and follow up with another first. Roy, you may not believe this, but this will be the first time I've ever showered with anyone else," adding as she joined him. "It makes me feel so decadent and wicked."

Roy was surprised as her soft hands traced over his firm muscular body as if she was seeing a man for the first time. It was difficult to break away, but Roy felt they had been alone too long, and the staff may well jump to conclusions that could be embarrassing for both of them. After they had dressed, Lady Jayne was elated her body felt wonderful. She had a distinctive glow running through her; she smiled at her new lover and mouthed the words,

"Thank you."

As the two of them descended the broad staircase, Roy wondered if she intended to keep her end of the bargain; he need not have feared in that respect. Lady Jayne was a woman who kept her word if not her marriage vows. She showed him into a small room and rang for a maid, and whilst the maid stood waiting, Lady Jayne asked him to have tea whilst she got the documents he had so richly deserved. Roy declined tea, and when Lady Jayne returned with a thick envelope, he was drinking a glass of malt whisky. She had a smile of contentment on her face as she sat, and after the maid had poured the prepared brew, she sat drinking the aromatic tea.

When the maid had left them, she spoke emphasising the bargain they had made between them.

"I shall be expecting you again tomorrow," she said, speaking in a quiet voice, "and for the next five days after that." She then added with a smile, "I never imagined getting pregnant could be so pleasurable."

When Roy got back to the hotel and opened the thick brown envelope, it contained copies of the personnel files of all four men with several photographs of each. Roy rang down to reception and asked if they had any facilities for copying. A porter came to the suite and escorted him to the office facilities available for business guests; it contained photocopiers, fax machines, PCs, and almost anything a business guest could require. Not wishing to be compromised by having a copy on the PC hard drive, Roy photocopied the documents in full colour and sent Sam copies of the files by courier; he knew that, by the following day, Sam would be busy tracking the perpetrators through his contacts.

The next few days were pleasurable for both participants, with Lady Jayne eagerly awaiting Roy to arrive and make love to her. To Lord Croft, however, it was a bargain. There was no love involved. It was an arrangement. That was the only way Roy could describe how he felt; they had struck a bargain, and both participants were duty-bound to see it through. On the Sunday morning, the last day before Sir Martin's return and the last day of the arrangement with Lady Jayne; it was Madeleine, who rang Janet and said,

"Hello, Janet," and after the usual greeting had been exchanged between them, she said, "Jayne asked me to invite you and the children for lunch at the official residence. Would you come early as I would like to spend some time with you and the children, before lunch is served?"

They arrived, and Roy was surprised when Madeleine pulled him aside and, in a stage whisper that everyone could hear, said,

"Lord Croft, I need help with a project I'm trying to write about my experiences before and after I was attacked, and me not being a boating person, there are some technical details I would like you to explain."

Roy turned to Janet, who just smiled, and Roy followed Madeleine up the main staircase.

"Make love to me," Madeleine said casually once they were in her private room.

He knew that time was short that he had to go down and have lunch with the family before they missed him, and then he had to fulfil his contract with her stepmother. He thanked the instinct that had made him bring a hip flask with Cathleen's potcheen; today he would probably need it. Roy knew he could not afford to take his time; it has to be quick. Shortly after both had satisfied their carnal appetite, Roy stood and, using the en suite facilities, refreshed himself, as did Madeleine.

"We have to go down to lunch," he said. "Otherwise, someone will come up and see where we are. I think your stepmother already believes we are having a relationship, and I suspect Janet has already guessed I'm up to my old tricks."

They dressed and arrived downstairs just as the lunch was served.

Lunch was a leisurely affair, and it was a couple of hours later when Lady Jayne asked Roy to go to the office as she had something to show him. Once outside the dining room, she pulled him upstairs. This time she did not take him to one of the guest rooms but into her own bedroom. Today she wanted their tryst to be memorable, and for some reason, she did not disclose she wanted it to happen in her marital bed. Lady Jayne revelled in this new experience, and she let Roy, for that was how she now addressed him, make love to her for what, according to their contract, was to be the last time. Afterwards, they showered, resisting the urge to touch each other, for now the bargain was complete. They went downstairs to join Madeleine and the family, and as they entered the room, Janet looked at Lady Jayne and knew instantly that Roy had had been up to his usual indiscretions. Lady Jayne's high flush and new confident walk told Janet all she needed to know. How Roy could make love to her newly found friend when he had already, as far as she knew, made love to Madeleine, her stepdaughter before lunch? *The randy sod,* she thought to herself, *he is getting worse; much worse, and his sexual appetite seems to be growing. Now that he is over thirty-five, when would he ever calm down?* Roy saw the signs in Janet's eyes, and he was aware she knew what he had been up to; she could read him like a book, and all that Roy knew was that he had done more than he should; he would suffer the pangs of overindulgence for some time. He tapped the hip flask in his pocket to check he had not left it in Lady Jayne's marital bedroom just in case.

Returning to the hotel later, Roy saw the desk clerk waving a message. The note simply read: *The four are in Dublin and their assignment will last for a few days. I will phone at eight o'clock your time.* Roy looked at his watch; it was seven thirty. He would get the call on his private untraceable cell. The call came through as Janet was putting the children to bed. Roy took the call, and Sam's voice repeated the message saying,

"Roy, if my information is correct and I have no reason to doubt its credibility, it is understood the team will be undertaking a surveillance job for about a week. I am led to understand it is a 24/7 assignment, so the four of them should always be at or near this location." He spoke quietly as though he might be overheard when he gave Roy the details. "Do you want a sniper? If so, ring this number in Dublin. His name is Padraig, and he will be expecting your call. Good luck!"

The line went dead. Roy rang and booked the first flight to Shannon with a connection to Cork; he would need to pick up a hire car, something unobtrusive, and then collect whatever he needed to carry out his planned operation, from the underground workshop at the castle. Thank God he had had Gordon leave that secret entrance to the armoury far from the castle itself. When Janet came, she asked him to kiss the children goodnight. Having done that, she put them to bed, and when she returned, Roy broke the news that he had to leave for Ireland on urgent business on the first available flight the following morning.

Janet's face registered her disappointment,

"Oh, Roy, why now? We are supposed to be on holiday," she said. "We can't use the boat, because Fiona and Gael are in London and you're going to Ireland."

Then as if realising she would be without him for some time, she pulled him close to her and whispered,

"Let's not waste another minute. I am in need of what you so generously give to young Madeleine, and I really cannot believe that you also had sex with Lady Jayne. How on earth did you manage to penetrate her defences? I thought she would be more than able to resist your charms."

Then looking puzzled, she whispered,

"I must have taught you better than I had imagined. You're really incorrigible."

When they finally went to bed, she asked Roy what he had poured himself from the hip flask.

"Just a drop of the good stuff I keep for myself," he answered with a smile.

They made love before falling asleep; Janet slept well, but Roy was fitful, the problems of what he planned to do constantly revolving around in his head.

Roy slept for two hours before getting up and leaving to catch the flight to Shannon. He was only too aware he had done too much; his ache from his groin hurt like the very devil, and he was glad of the rest. He slept through the long flight, waking just before touchdown. When the short internal flight to Cork landed, Roy picked up his hire car using a false name and address that Sam had made used in booking. No questions were asked; no licence was requested. Roy told the clerk he would require the vehicle for two weeks; paying for the vehicle in cash and leaving a cash deposit to cover the excess in case of an accident, he drove out of the airport heading towards the castle.

Chapter 7

It was late afternoon when Roy arrived at the secret entrance to the underground armoury, situated as it was, two floors below the boathouse. He searched for the key he had hidden in the dry stone wall nearby and swung open the heavily reinforced door. He wiped away the thick cobwebs, which indicated that no one had entered this dark and secret domain. Using the torch, which he had brought from the car, he swept the walls near the entrance until he found the switch. Reaching inside, he switched on the lights, which gave a dim light from the old-fashioned bulkhead fittings set in the concrete ceiling above. Roy walked slowly along the dimly lit long underground passage still reminiscent of Second World War; the damp walls gave off an eerie glow from the phosphorescence of the chemicals in the soil. The ground was uneven and difficult to move, walk over, where, over the years, the brick flooring had lifted on the damp peat soil. He arrived at the bulkhead door separating the armoury from the open area used for general storage, and then using the correct code, he heard the lock give a satisfactory click. Silently thanking the engineers who built the entrance all those years ago, Roy pushed the steel bar upwards; hearing the concealed bolts release, he swung the thick steel door open on its huge hinges. The racks of weapons and ammunition stood out starkly like shapes from a different time in the dim light coming from the open door, leaving shadows of gloom deeper within the unlit depths. With the main power off, the exterior source was the only illumination available, and strange shapes were cast from the dim exterior lighting. Roy stepped inside and snapped on the switch to the main power board, the sudden glare of light momentarily blinding him.

Then after letting his eyes accustom themselves to the glare, he began moving swiftly along the racks; he selected three 9ml semi-automatic Berettas, a rifle with night scope, a Sterling machine gun, two packets of C4 (a gift from the IRA), the wartime C3 had proved too brittle and had broken into brittle blocks too unstable to use, a timer, detonators, and a couple of hand grenades. He quickly stripped the rifle and the Sterling machine gun and paced the whole lot, including ammunition into two flat;

sponge-lined steel boxes with a limpet type of magnet set inside the base of each. Then using a small trolley, Roy wheeled the two boxes, not without difficulty, back along the long, uneven floor of the corridor, and from there, he transferred them to the car. He pulled the carpet out of the boot and attached the two boxes to the metal supports at the rear of the back seat; then he replaced the carpet. He stood back to check, and he was pleased to see the area looked almost unchanged. It would take an expert, much more skilled than the average policeman, to spot that the boot was shorter by a few inches, especially at a roadblock. He returned the trolley to its place, switched of the mains power, and relocked the munitions bulkhead door before retracing his steps along the passage once more. He switched off the overhead lights, locked the door, and returned the key to its hiding place.

It was getting late, and Roy decided he would take a chance and visit the castle; he knew it was risky; the Secret Service may have found their way into the workshop, but he knew they had not found the munitions. He had to know if it was still safe for him to be in the area. Marion, alias Stella Francis, the British secret agent, who had been placed in the castle, would no doubt be the first to break the news. Roy drove up to the front door and rang the bell. A camera above the door, a recent addition, Roy noted, lit up with a faint green glow of its LED, and Stella Francis's voice said,

"Oh, it's you, Lord Croft. What can I do for you?"

"I was in the area," Roy replied, "and wondered if you would mind if I dropped by."

The latch on the front door clicked open and the heavy door swung open by an unseen mechanism. *Another addition,* he thought to himself, and the voice of Marion, sounding at least an octave higher, said,

"Of course you can. Please come inside."

Roy entered the hallway, and the door behind him automatically closed, and he walked through to the lounge where Marion sat with a large tumbler of Irish whisky in her hand, saying,

"I thought you might like this. Are you on your own?"

When Roy nodded in admission, her whole countenance changed; her smile became a grin.

"Oh, good show! We can have a little fun. By the way," she said a twinkle in her eye, "the last time we had sex, you bugger, you got me pregnant, and when my real husband found out he was going to be a father, he could not believe it and was as happy as a dog with two tails. Now the silly bugger won't touch me, just in case he harms the baby. So you find me somewhat frustrated. I hope you can take the pace."

Roy knew what to expect; as he took the glass in his hand, he bent down and kissed her on the lips.

"Oh God! Roy, I remember you so well," she whispered.

It was Marion who took the initiative, and Roy pushed her away.

"Steady on, old girl," he whispered. "Let me get comfortable. I haven't finished my drink yet."

Apologising, Stella moved along to allow Roy to sit beside her.

"I'm sorry, but I feel so frustrated, and you gave me so much pleasure last time I just could not help myself. Come, sit beside me, and tell me, why you're here."

"Before I do that, have your forensic boys found or manufactured any evidence against me. Am I a wanted man?"

"Of course not. If they had found anything, there would have been an International Warrant issued for your arrest. You would have been picked up as soon as you landed. You know that, as well as I do."

Roy put on a serious face and, looking Marion in the eyes, said calmly,

"I am going to put in a strong complaint with the Law Lords that the agency have harassed me with no evidence whatsoever and have persecuted me and my family."

"Oh God, No! What now!" Marion exclaimed. "What's that silly bugger in London been doing? He seems to have a personal vendetta against anyone with any connections to the IRA. He has become totally irrational since the Good Friday Agreement."

"You mean to tell me you are not aware of the attack on my family? Suffice it to say it happened, and we have positive proof of who the culprits were."

"Christ," Marion said, "that will put the bloody cat amongst the pigeons. There'll be hell to pay."

"Let's leave it at that, shall we? I'll have another drink if I may, and then perhaps we can get back to where we were. Are you really pregnant?"

"Oh, without a doubt, Thanks to you," she retorted quickly.

"How do you know it's mine? It could easily have been your husband's, couldn't it?"

"Believe me, it's yours. I know," she replied, the twinkle glistening in her eyes as she reached out for him.

Roy helped her to her feet, and she pulled him through the door up to the bedroom she usually shared with her husband.

"Where's your husband?" Roy asked, not wishing to be caught with another man's wife; he enjoyed the sex but was usually wary of being caught in flagrante delicto. "At what time you expect him back?"

"He's at a conference in London, or so he tells me. I shall not see eye nor hair of him until the weekend. We have all the time in the world to enjoy the carnal pleasures that I know, only too well, you are all too familiar with."

They rose from her marital bed sometime later to go down to the kitchen for a cold supper before retiring and resuming their sexual frolics, and it was the early hours of the morning when they fell into a sexually induced sleep.

Roy woke early and showered quickly and dressed before a bleary eyed Marion, who had woken as she heard him moving about the room, opening her eyes wider said, disappointment showing in her face,

"Oh, dressed already!"

"Yes," he said, "I have to go to England for an appointment, and it's almost as quick to drive as it is to fly these days."

She sat up, climbed out of bed, before pulling on her robe, and offered to make him breakfast.

"Where are all the staff?" Roy enquired.

"I like to sleep late, so I insist the staff don't arrive until eight."

"Don't spoil them for when I return, will you? Thanks for the offer to cook for me, but I'll get breakfast on the road. I have to be on the mainland for a meeting later this evening, and I can't be late. I hope to see you again soon."

Roy went over and kissed her on the forehead and hurried away. Marion watched the bedroom door close behind him and flopped back on to the bed, still tired, and she was asleep again long before Roy had got to his car.

Roy was not going to England, as he had told Marion; he was heading for Dublin, where he was to deal with his wife's four rapists; he could not wait to get his revenge. Rape was a crime he utterly detested, and he was incensed even more as it had been perpetrated against his own wife. He would have to drive all the way; there was no way he could take the hidden boxes on the plane. On the way, he rang Gordon and said he would be in town for a couple of days, asked if he would like to join him for supper.

As usual Gordon would not hear of Lord Croft, his and Megan's friend, staying in a hotel.

"You must come and stay in our new home," he said. "Megan would love to see you. She often asks if I have heard from you. There's plenty of room. Megan is pregnant again, and her sister Mona is staying with us for a while. I'm sure she will be more than happy with your company. Her husband is away on business."

Roy accepted the offer and asked for directions to Gordon and Megan's new home.

Pulling the hire car over to the side of the road, Roy wrote down the directions carefully. When he finally arrived in Dublin, he followed the directions and found himself in a very upmarket part of the city; he was very impressed. *Gordon's practice must be doing very well,* Roy thought. *He certainly must have landed some big contracts since he did the work on the castle.* He reminded himself to ask him about it. Roy stopped outside the double gates and spoke over the intercom. Megan recognised the voice and the gates opened, and Roy drove up the drive and pulled up outside a large Victorian house. *Very imposing,* he thought to himself as he stepped out of the hire car on to the broad gravel path leading up to a portico covering a stout wooden door.

Megan opened the door and hugged him as well as she could, being well into the third trimester of her pregnancy, before giving him a kiss on the cheek, whispering so that no one would hear,

"You did it again, didn't you? You oversexed, darling, but I've missed you. I'm glad you're here. I'll take you through to meet Mona, my sister. She is staying with us whilst her husband is in Ireland on business."

Roy followed her into a large reception room furnished with period-style furniture. Megan looked at her sister and said,

"Mona, this is Lord Croft. You must have heard me speak of him."

Mona looked up from the magazine in her lap with what could only be called a smirk.

"Why, yes, of course, you've spoken of him often, Megan. I'm intrigued and very pleased to meet you, Lord Croft."

She stood and ignored Roy's outstretched hand and hugged him, giving him a polite kiss on the cheek.

"I've been waiting to meet you since Gordon announced you would be staying over, Lord Croft. Megan has told me a lot about you."

"It's Roy, and it's all good, I hope?" Roy retorted.

"Depends what you define as good, I suppose," Mona said, looking across at Megan with a grin.

Roy's initial reaction to the woman before him was shock; Mona was the very image of Megan when he had first made her acquaintance, before she had borne any of his children. Roy realised that the attraction that had happened between Megan and him was there once again. Mona's and Roy's pheromones clicked; there was an immediate chemical attraction between them. Mona sensed the same feelings as her body reacted to the pheromones that Roy was unconsciously sending in her direction. *So this was the man Megan had told her about?* Mona thought to herself; she could well understand how her sister had fallen for him; he was a very good-looking man. Mona felt herself blush as she took his hand. The crimson flush rose from the visible swell of her cleavage and seemed to rise to the roots of her red hair. Roy took the proffered hand; it was like a bolt of electricity running between them; both of them felt the instant attraction. Stepping back as Megan approached, he accepted the large Irish whisky, and as Roy took the glass, Megan, with a sly grin on her face, said,

"You two get to know each other whilst I go through and see how dinner is cooking. Oh, and Mona, show Roy up to his room when he's finished his drink. He's in the room next to yours."

Roy walked towards the fireplace and looked at the framed photograph of Megan, Gordon, Mona, and, No! It couldn't be, could it? The photograph had a man with a very familiar face, but the likeness was undeniable. Yes, it was someone that Roy recognised almost immediately from the files Lady Jayne had given him. Standing next to Mona with his arm around her was none other than Mark, the man who had drugged his wife before he and his three agents had raped her unmercifully. He felt his anger rise just by looking at the face before him.

"Who's the man in the picture?" Roy asked as casually as he could, desperately trying to hide his rising anger.

"That's Mark, my husband," replied Mona in a disinterested voice. "If you could call him that as I've seen less of him since we've been married than I ever did before."

Roy could hardly believe his luck. He had wanted to track him down, and here he was talking to the man's wife, Megan's sister. He instantly began to plan how he could get retribution for Mark's unforgivable behaviour in more ways than one. Mona was a very attractive woman; at that precise moment, he decided with a grim determination to return the compliment; he had no intention of raping the woman, but he intended to do his utmost to have an intimate sexual relationship with her by whatever means he could.

"Why do you say that?" Roy asked. "I think Gordon told me that you haven't been married that long."

Mona answered with a great deal of tension in her voice; she was obviously angry with her husband, for abandoning her once again for work, he would tell her nothing about; all the secrecy seemed so out of date these days, and she suspected there was more to his absences than he ever told her.

"Only a few months," Mona replied, "but he has been away more than he has been at home. It's the business he's in, something to do with security. That's why I'm in Ireland. He had to come to Dublin on a surveillance job with his three subordinates. They are on a 24/7 stake out of a nightclub, something to do with the IRA or the Mafia for all I care. He's left me here whilst he is somewhere in Dublin, and he says he can't spend any time with me. He only got back from Barbados recently, and he couldn't or wouldn't tell me anything about that trip either. I wonder if he loves me at all. If he did, he would tell his bosses he has a wife at home who he needs to spend a little time with, instead of all this secrecy about his job. When we got married, he never warned me that he would be away from home so often."

Roy appraised the woman in front of him, her attitude was almost anger, but under that anger was a sense of frustration. He picked up her susceptibility, her need to be flattered and cosseted was very apparent. He would wait for the right moment to make his move on her; he hoped she would be as pliant and accessible as Megan had been the first time they had met; only time would tell.

"I cannot believe your husband of only a few months could leave an attractive woman alone whilst he spends time abroad. I can well understand how it must affect you. It shows a distinct lack off appreciation for needs of such a lovely young bride. I'll never understand young men these days. They seem to take so many things for granted and wonder why their wives seek their much-needed love and attention elsewhere."

Roy noticed the flush on Mona's face deepen as she looked at him in a new light. *Here is a man,* she thought to herself, *who understands the feelings and needs of a woman. Why can't Mark be more like him?* Lord Croft tossed back the last of his whisky, and Mona said, the anger replaced by huskiness he had not heard in her voice earlier,

"If you've finished your drink, Lord Croft, I'll show you up to your room," and with a toss of her red hair, she proceeded to head for the door.

Picking up his overnight bag, Roy followed her up the stairs, her calves and ankles moved tantalisingly before his eyes. When they arrived at the top, a broad passage led to several bedrooms. Arriving at the door to the bedroom next to hers, Mona pushed it open. Roy expected Mona to leave him to unpack. However, Mona walked in front of him into the bedroom and, turning to face him, put her arms around his neck and kissed him on the mouth.

"Tell me," she asked, "is everything Megan has told me about you true?" Roy felt her press her lips against his own, to his surprise her lips parted, her tongue snaked in between his lips and their tongues duelled and danced. To Roy, this seemed to be the perfect opportunity for his vengeful retribution; he wondered how far Mona would be prepared to let her anger overcome her natural defences, after all, Mark had seduced his wife, and here Mona, Mark's wife, was apparently offering herself up to Roy almost like a sacrificial lamb. Roy was a man with a more than an adequate but healthy sexual drive, and his response to this unexpected situation was too good an opportunity to miss.

Roy slid his arms around Mona's waist and pulled her close to him. She pressed her hips forward as if in surrender. The rising passion between them seemed to deepen just as it had with Megan, all those years ago. Roy took the seemingly offered opportunity; he knew he could end with a sharp slap on the face, but all the signs were for an easy seduction of a neglected wife. Throwing caution to the wind, Roy ran his hand over the swell of her breast. Mona gasped and whispered throatily,

"Oh, Lord Croft, I don't think we should be doing this. I'm a married woman."

"It's Roy," he corrected her.

"Roy, Megan was so right when she told me you were a forceful man always ready to make love to an attractive woman. It seems to be weeks since Mark touched me. I keep telling him a woman also has needs, but he just laughs and tells me I can wait. He tells me a woman appreciates it more when she is kept waiting, but sometimes a woman's needs must come first."

Roy pushed Mona back, and they fell in a heap on the bed; it was almost a repeat of when he had taken Megan for the first time. Mona seemed to be more than compliant; she seemed incapable of resisting his advances; she seemed to be carried along in an almost dreamlike state as she surrendered to the skills and caresses of a man who knew how to take seduction to a new level. Mona had been feeling neglected and lonely without her husband beside her, and now this handsome Lord Croft, a man her sister had told her so much about, was making love to her, and it was exciting her beyond her expectations, and she let herself go throwing any reservation she may have had to the wind.

The passion passed and Mona looked into Roy's eyes in an uncomprehending manner. She could not understand what had happened; she had let Lord Croft, a man she had met only a couple of hours earlier, to make love to her, in her sister's home, and to her concern, he had not used any form of protection. Megan had been right: the man had some sort of animal magnetism about him; she had been unable to resist. Even as these thoughts raced through her mind, the realisation of what she had done struck home.

"Oh God! What have I done?" she asked him. "I just could not help myself. I got to the point where I just had to let you make love to me. It's Mark's own fault. He should be here when I need him." Then as if that, somehow explained her adulterous behaviour, she said calmly, "Oh Lord, I know it's wrong, it's a mortal sin, but I have to admit I feel so much better now. I pray that the priest will give me absolution at confession."

She pushed Roy up, and he rolled aside. She began to sit up; she looked down at the stranger beside, knowing in her mind that, for some reason, this act of blatant adultery, which she acknowledged to herself that she would have to confess to her priest, would not be the last time she let him make love to her. She had an inner glow she had never experienced with Mark, and it felt wonderful despite the fact that she knew it was a sin before her God.

"I must go," Mona said to him. "I have to clean up."

Grabbing her clothes, she moved quickly and disappeared into the bathroom and emerged shortly afterwards, looking somewhat refreshed with a new tinge of colour to her cheeks.

"I'll see you downstairs," she whispered, kissing Roy on the cheek. "I haven't a clue what Megan will think. I seem to have been up here for ages." Then, as an afterthought, with a wry smile, as she left him to unpack, she added, "I do hope you'll be staying a few days."

Roy had preparations to make; he dialled Fiona's number and asked how things were going, and Fiona's reply after her initial greeting startled him.

"Gael has decided to have the baby and put it up for adoption. She says if it was God's will for her to have this child against all odds, she could not bring herself to kill it. Gael says she's already killed men, and she can't bring herself to kill her baby."

Roy expressed his concern, but he told Fiona to tell Gael that he respected her decision. Then he told Fiona what he wanted her to do.

"I need you both in Dublin," he said. "I will book the tickets and make reservations for you both in at the Gresham. Pick up the tickets at the terminal. I'll make the ticket open for the first available flight after you get to the airport. Get a flight and let me know when you are at the hotel. Tell Gael, baby or not, I have serious work for her to do."

"Yes, sir, I'll do that. We'll go to the airport and pick up the tickets as soon as we are packed," Fiona replied instinctively.

Roy smiled at her ready compliance; she acted without question, something he admired about all of his staff. Roy rang the airlines and the hotel to make the bookings, instructing them where to send the confirmation of the bookings, before showering and dressing. Once Roy was dressed, he took out his digital camera and set it up with a clear view of the bed and slipped the remote under his pillow. Ensuring that everything was in place for his plan to succeed, he went downstairs where Gordon and Mona were waiting for him, and he accepted the drink Gordon had poured for him.

"I understand you've met Mona already," Gordon said.

Gordon had been somewhat surprised to see Roy give his sister-in-law, Mona, the slightest peck on the cheek.

"Oh yes, you could say that," Roy said with a broad smile on his face.

Megan entered and informed everyone that the dinner was ready. They went into a large dining room and sat down. An Irish woman of about fifty came in with the soup, and Megan introduced her as Mary the housekeeper who was helping her with the children and the house.

The meal was, as always, very good, and after the dinner, they all sat down in the lounge and had a few drinks. Roy asked Gordon how the business was doing, and Gordon replied,

"Oh, do you remember when you came and I was having problems with one of my clients?"

Roy nodded; he remembered it very well; he had got Megan pregnant in Gordon's marital bed on that very occasion.

"Well, there was a problem involved with the project manager. He was using inferior materials for a construction job, making the foundations well below spec and I spotted it. If the building had been allowed to proceed, it could well have become unstable, and God only knows what would have been the consequences. The job was for the Irish government, and they were so grateful for me informing them, and, in the end, saving millions of euros and the possible loss of life that I was awarded the *most preferred architect* status, and now I get almost all Irish government contracts. The practice has grown to one of the biggest in Ireland, and I am doing very well out of it. The way Megan keeps getting pregnant. It's a good job. I have got a good practice. I need the money just to know I can educate the children and bring them up in a decent manner. Every time I sleep with her, she seems to get pregnant again."

Roy smiled to himself; all of Gordon's children, Megan had told him, were Roy's. Lord Croft had to admit it had been a pleasure to make love to her on each and every occasion; many times, whilst Gordon had been close by, at her own home and at the castle.

Mona retired apparently to go to the kitchen or to the bathroom, and as she did, so did Roy. He said he needed to go up to his room for a few minutes and would be back down shortly. He raced upstairs and caught up with Mona; Roy caught her arm and pulled her into his room. Almost as soon as she entered, Mona grabbed him and kissed him ardently, saying she wished she could stay in his room with him, but it would look odd if she did not sleep in her own room. Mona's lust sprang up; she wanted him now, but the household was still awake; someone would surely hear them; she had been highly aroused at the thought of letting him make love to her again all through dinner. She needed him so badly; he had awakened her sexuality as no one had ever done before, and she whispered,

"I will come into your room when everyone is asleep."

Roy was determined to make love to her again, and although she promised she would come to his room later, she could come to her senses and change her mind. The opportunity may not arise again; she was in his room now, and he was not going to wait, if he wanted to carry out his plan it had to be accomplished quickly; he had to make love to her whilst she was in her present mood.

Mona could feel his urgent need; she knew her own need was rising like a storm deep within her; she gave a soft moan, knowing she would not be able to resist his entreaties for long. Mona, between her desire and her moans, said,

"No, Roy, we do not have time. When the house is quiet and everyone is asleep, I will come to you."

Roy knew he would not let her go as it had to be now. He scooped her up into his arms and carried her to the bed. Mona had a wild look about her as she felt herself unable to resist him, whatever the cost.

"Oh God! Roy, not now," she protested, "Oh God, but it feels so good."

Her protests became less obvious as Roy embraced her.

"Oh God! We can't do it now. Megan is still about. She will come to see where I am. She will surely hear us."

Feeling that fate was against her, Mona felt herself relax; she knew it was useless to put up a fight, and she lay back giving herself up to the inevitable.

Mona's passion overcame her protests, and she seemed unable to resist Lord Croft, who, by her sister's own confession, was the father of at least one of her children. The madness continued and just as Mona felt them, both shuddered, though a mutual climax. They suddenly heard footsteps along the corridor. Megan was calling,

"Mona, where are you? Your hot milk drink is going cold."

Roy rolled aside as he struggled to rearrange his clothing. Mona struggled to her feet as she kicked her underwear under the nearest chair and tidied up her own appearance and touched her hair back into place, unable to do anything about the flushed appearance of her face and neck.

"I'll have to go. I'll try and see you later."

Roy nodded, waiting until Mona had left the room before switching off the remote; his plan was going better than he could have hoped, and he was enjoying the pleasure of making love to Mark's attractive and compliant wife, as an additional bonus.

Roy went down and chatted with Gordon, and Roy asked,

"Tell me, Gordon, with all this work you are getting, when we return to Ireland, will you have time to rectify the changes we made to the castle, the ones you made before we left for the Caribbean?"

Gordon assured Roy that he would always have time to do work for him.

"The castle work," he added, "was the turning point in my life. It brought me luck, both business-wise and family-wise. It seemed to be the pivotal point in my whole life as my business thrived, and even Megan fell pregnant. It all seemed to happen when you came into our lives. I shall always be grateful to you. It was you who brought me prosperity and a new sense of family and belonging as well," he said, pointing to the house. "The business speaks for itself."

They sat and drank for another hour before Gordon said,
"I'm sorry to break up our little session, Roy, but I need to get some sleep. I have to leave early tomorrow."
"You are right, Gordon," Roy agreed and, after checking his watch, added, "I had no idea it was so late. I also have my work to do tomorrow."
With that, the two of them retired up to bed, and arriving at his room, Roy was disappointed' he had expected Mona to be waiting for him. He undressed and lay on the bed. Mona had lain awake until she thought everyone would be asleep. She had heard Roy come upstairs a little while before, and creeping out of her bed, she tiptoed across the room and slipped off her nightie before wrapping her robe around her nudity. Then listening carefully to ensure everyone was asleep, she opened the door and slipped quietly into the hallway. She tapped the door quietly and entered Roy's room cautiously. To her delight, in the glow of the bedside lamp, she could see that Roy was waiting for her. Mona slid the robe from her shoulders and climbed on the bed. This time there was no hurry, and after a long and pleasurable session of unhurried and enjoyable sex, they both fell asleep in each other's arms, but not before Roy had used the remote to stop the camera.

Roy had been asleep for about two hours when he woke to find Mona sprawled totally naked on his bed; he switched on the camera to show her still in his bed as the light streamed into the room. Resisting the temptation to make love to her again, he shook her awake. Mona was startled to see it was morning. She rose wearily and pulled her robe about her and kissed Roy; she walked slowly to the door and, listening to make sure no one was about, opened it and hurried back to her own bedroom. She showered and sprawled across the bed naked and fell into a deep sleep. Megan found her later that morning and knew instinctively that Roy had made love to her sister and that explained why he had been so bright at the breakfast table. He had a new conquest to his name; she smiled, wondering if her sister had been wise enough to take some kind of preventive measure to avoid pregnancy, despite the fact that, as a good Catholic, it was against the churches directives; if not Megan was only too aware of the risk, her sister was putting herself in. Megan knew only too well to her own detriment that her children were proof enough of that; she was only too aware how fertile Lord Croft was, and to her knowledge, he never took any precautions; if her sister was not on the pill, Mona had confided in Megan that Mark was the only one who was cautious; he had, she had said, never had sex with her without being very careful not to get her pregnant. Megan shook her head; it was not for her to worry. Who knew how things would turn out, only time would tell?

Chapter 8

When Megan came back downstairs, Roy was on the phone, arranging to meet someone in Dublin at the Gresham hotel in an hour's time. He kissed her on the cheek, and Megan whispered with a twinkle in her eyes,

"I see that poor Mona is tired out this morning. You are such a wicked man, but as you can see, I'm not going to be much good to you this trip, now am I?" she said, pointing to her bulging tummy. "I don't have too much longer to go."

Roy went upstairs and slipped quietly into Mona's room. He could hear her in the bathroom, and opening her handbag, he pulled out her purse and took out her driving licence and quickly made a note of her home address. He put everything back and slipped out of the room, unseen. On his way to the Gresham Hotel, Roy rang Sam.

"Can you get one of your contacts in London to go to this address?" He gave him the details. "I want them to search for any files, DVDs, or videos or anything similar. It is imperative that I get my hands on them, and warn your contact that if he discovers them, it would be very inadvisable to view the contents," he emphasised.

Sam understood and, when Roy told him that he believed Mark and his team were watching either an IRA or Mafia connection in Dublin over the next few days; Sam asked if he needed any help. Roy responded that he had Fiona and Gael and was convinced that would be quite sufficient for what he had in mind. They rang off.

Roy arrived at the Gresham, and after checking at the reception that both Gael and Fiona had arrived, he used the lift to reach to their floor and knocked on the door of the room where they were staying. He was greeted by Fiona and Gael, and after the usual greetings had been exchanged, he drew them to one side and gave them details of what he wanted them to do. He went down to the car and brought up the two boxes from the boot. Gael checked the equipment and saw that the night scope was the one she liked using; it was the one with long range and very accurate sightings. Roy pulled the disk from the camera and, using his laptop, made a copy. He returned the disk to the camera; he had not quite finished with it yet. They had a meal, and Fiona went into the town to get a box of surgical gloves from the chemist, and when she had returned, Roy took out the envelope containing the photographs of the four-man team.

"Study these photographs. Memorise them carefully. I want you to go out on to the streets in the area around the club and try to spot any of these four men. You may see one or two of them together. The others will be keeping surveillance on whoever they have targeted. Be very careful. They are armed and dangerous and will stop at nothing to achieve their goal, to get pictures of whatever or whoever they have been instructed to compromise."

Gael nodded, fully aware of the dangers of the operation Lord Croft was undertaking. After studying the pictures carefully, committing them to her memory, she left to follow Roy's instructions.

Then Roy looked at Fiona; she looked as attractive as ever, but after the night with Mona, he could resist the temptation; there were more important things to do. Roy went over to the dressing table to finalise his plans. It was two hours later, when Gael returned, she had spotted one of the men going into a block of flats opposite the club and had seen one of the windows on the third floor glint as the man inside had been using either a telescope or binoculars to study the comings and goings at the front entrance of the club. Roy asked her to point out the building on the street map. Roy requested Gael to prepare the explosives, and he and Fiona then left together to carefully study and note the watcher's movements.

It was Roy who spotted the car, with Mark at the wheel and another of the four in the passenger seat; as it pulled in at the kerb, the two men got out and entered the building. Roy nodded, and Fiona quickly followed the two men into the block of flats. They were standing by the lift when she came in through the door; the two men looked up but not recognising her as a threat they took little notice of her. The lift opened with a hiss of steel sliding along its guides, and the two men stood aside as Fiona entered, and once all three were in the lift, Mark pressed the third-floor button, and Fiona pressed the fourth. The two men got out, and Fiona rode up to the fourth floor before riding the lift back down to ground and confirming that they had got off at the floor where Gael had seen the curtain move. Roy waited for about five minutes, noting the time, as two other men, Roy recognised from the photographs, emerged from the building and climbed into the car to drive away. Roy returned to the hotel after requesting Fiona to monitor how often they changed shift. Meanwhile, back at the Gresham, Gael had completed preparing the explosives; both were neatly packaged with the detonator and timing device, both having a magnetic pad to enable them to be attached to any steel surface.

Gael looked up as Roy entered the room. She seemed relaxed despite the fact that the explosives she was handling were sufficient to destroy a good part of the hotel. Roy, after admiring the workmanship, said gravely,
"Gael, you never cease to amaze me. These look as professional as any I have ever seen. Now go to the flats and find Fiona. She will point out the car. Avoid being seen. Then at the earliest opportunity, I want you to attach both devices under the car, one below the driver's seat and one under the petrol tank."
Gael acknowledged that she understood, and when Roy held out his hand, she dropped the remote control, which would start the timing device into the outstretched palm. Before she left, Roy handed her two of the Berettas and the sniper rifle packed in its bag.
"I want you to keep one of the 9mls with you at all times and to give one to Fiona, just in case either of you are spotted. You know what to do under those circumstances? Shoot first and get the hell out of there. We can always set something up later. The last thing I would want is for that team to get hold of either of you. You know Fiona is not as well trained as you, so keep her in your sight at all times and keep me informed when the explosives are in place, and phone me if anything out of the ordinary should happen whilst I'm away."

Satisfied she understood her instructions fully, Roy then returned to Gordon's house in time for the evening meal. It was just after they had eaten that Roy excused himself to answer his cell. It was Gael.
"The explosives are in place," she said, "and Mark has taken a dark-haired woman up to the flat. She seemed a little unsteady on her feet as though drugged or drunk, but she put up no struggle," she added. "The woman appeared to be more than willing to go with him. A short time afterwards, I saw them go upstairs; there had been a commotion at the club. Several tough-looking characters had appeared asking everyone if they had seen a dark-haired woman. The description they gave matched the lady who had been with Mark."
It sounded to Roy as though Mark had taken someone up to the flat under the influence of Rohypnol, if so, he would have to move quickly.

Sam picked up the phone as soon as it rang, almost as though he had been expecting the call and as soon as Roy recognised the voice he spoke quickly.

"Sam, I'm at the location you gave me. Who owns the club on the corner opposite?" Roy asked.

"I thought you knew, Roy. It belongs to Michael O'Reilly, one of the committee members, and it's run by his wife. You must have seen him often at our meetings."

Roy explained what was happening, but requested that whoever Sam wanted to inform, it was imperative that they did nothing for the moment; he had plans in place and did not want anything to upset them. Roy could hear the doubt in Sam's voice; he knew he would only be too anxious to warn Michael of the danger his wife was in.

"Sam, please ask Michael not to do anything stupid, although it's not good news. I am convinced other than the risk of the possibility her having sex with the four men present, no other harm would befall his wife. If Michael goes in there with all guns blazing, he will upset my plans and could well get his wife killed and get us all arrested by the police."

After a moment's pause, Sam reluctantly agreed to do nothing.

Changing the subject, Sam informed Roy,

"The London address, you gave me, has been searched and several DVDs were discovered in a safe in the property."

Before Roy could respond, Sam added quickly,

"Before you ask, Roy, I can verify that the operatives who carried out the search are trusted men I've used many times before, and they have assured me that they had no idea what was recorded on them. The package containing the DVDs is being couriered to the Gresham hotel, as we speak, marked for the attention of Fiona."

Roy went back into the lounge and apologised to Gordon and his family for his having to leave them again so soon, explaining that it could not be helped as the business was urgent and he would be back later, but he had no idea how late he would be. Gordon went with him to the door and gave him a key.

"I know it must be urgent for you to go out at this time of night for a meeting," he said. "Just take this in case we are all in bed when you get back."

Roy thanked him and drove quickly to the block of flats; when he arrived, he checked that the Uzi machine gun was concealed in the boot; he knew Gael had the silenced snipers rifle dismantled in the large bag she kept with her at all times. Arriving at the club, Roy quickly sized up the situation, then gave his instructions,

"Gael, I want you to get to the top of the building housing the club. I'm sure you will find that you have a perfect view of the flat window where they are entertaining Mrs O'Reilly. I'll leave you to guess what entertaining means. If I'm right, I believe it entails the use of Rohypnol, the date-rape drug."

Roy saw Gael flinch; she knew exactly what would be happening in the bedroom of that flat. She hated the thought of rape as much as Roy did, and she looked at Roy questioningly. Roy told her that he wanted her to take out one or even two of the occupants when he gave her the OK on the cell phone she carried with her. She nodded grimly, and asking the burly man on the door the way to the artists changing room, she entered the club, unchallenged. It explained why she was carrying a bag with her. As soon as the opportunity arose, Gael slipped out of the dressing room up the back fire escape on to the roof. Gael knelt down and unzipped the bag, and with the skill and speed she had learned during her training, she assembled the rifle and screwed the silencer in place. She took up her position and lay still, hidden from sight, waiting for the signal.

Looking through the night scope, Gael could see the curtains were not drawn tightly; she observed the four men apparently waiting to take it in turns to rape the drugged woman, who seemed only too willing to take them on, under the influence of drug. Gael had never come across the date-rape drug before and had not been aware of its effects before Roy had explained, and what she witnessed made her very angry. She had been instructed by Roy not to shoot Mark, if she could help it, as he wanted to deal with him personally. Roy and Fiona made their way up to the third floor. It had not been difficult to identify the room they wanted; the position of the lighted window had been the clue. They waited outside the door; Fiona watched as Roy selected Gael's cell from his list of contacts and pressed the call button to give his signal; two of the men were standing by the open window, half-concealed by the drapes. Both men appeared to be naked and were casually smoking; Gael could make out their faces through the powerful scope, neither of them was Mark. She took aim and, in short succession, downed both men; the other two were busy and did not even hear their companions give any sound as they silently collapsed, their lifeless bodies slumped half out of the window.

Roy charged against the door, and Mark, who busy engaged in what he did best, was naked with the hapless woman beneath him, whilst the fourth man was calmly filming every aspect of the incident. The sound of the door bursting open stopped Mark in his tracks; before Roy could stop her, Fiona pushed past him and unhesitatingly aimed the silenced 9mm weapon at the cameraman and pulled the trigger twice in rapid succession. *A double tap! Gael must have taught her that*, thought Roy in the split second before he struck the back of Mark's head with the butt of his Beretta.

Mark gave a gasp of surprise as he slumped down on to the dark-haired woman beneath him; Fiona went back and closed the flat door whilst Roy pulled the unconscious Mark off the woman who had slipped into a drug-induced deep comatose sleep. Roy, helped by Fiona, dressed the unconscious Mark before taking him down in the lift and putting him in passenger seat of the Agency car parked outside; his hands and feet were securely tied, and Roy taped a piece of tape across his mouth. The tape was some which Roy had taken from the hotel, after Gael had prepared the explosives. Then after putting a hat half over Mark's face to conceal the tape and once they were satisfied it looked as though he was asleep, they both went back upstairs. Roy needed to collect the camera and dress the woman who lay back totally naked, completely unaware of the mayhem that had happened around her. Fiona cleaned her up, and Roy pulled the dead agents from the window, where they had slumped down, and then helped by Roy, she dressed Mrs O'Reilly; Carrying her between them they took her downstairs, where unobserved they put her into Roy's hire car. All this had taken less than ten minutes, and they were joined by Gael, who grinned at the fact that she had downed both her victims without either of them making a sound. Roy instructed Gael to drive the unconscious woman to the hotel and put her to bed and return for him at a location to be arranged and told Gael when she received his call she was to leave Fiona with the drugged woman in case she woke up.

Roy, with the unconscious Mark still in the passenger seat of the agency's car, drove the vehicle out of the city heading towards an isolated spot out on the main road to the west coast. When clear of the city limits and well out in the rural area of the road; Roy looked for the isolated side road he had pinpointed on the map and brought the car to a halt in one of the passing places on the narrow road. Roy checked whether Mark's hands and feet were secure and waited for him to wake up. It was some time before Mark slowly gained consciousness, finding himself gag-bound and with a throbbing headache, a dry mouth filled with a ball of material preventing him from making a sound and a piece of tape across his mouth. His vision slowly cleared, and seeing who his captor was, he began to struggle; quickly realising he was securely tied, he stared defiantly into the face of Lord Croft. Roy ripped the tape from Mark's face causing him to wince with pain, and then he pulled the wad of cloth from his mouth. Mark gasped for air and his mouth formed into a cruel sneer as he muttered looking towards Roy,

"You'll pay dearly for this, Lord Croft, you bloody idiot. Do you know who I am?"

Roy pushed the ball of cloth back between Mark's lips, avoiding the snapping teeth, and said, not without some conviction in his voice,

"I know exactly who you are, Mark Beddows. I know where you live, what you do to the wives of the men under your surveillance, and who you are married to. Your wife's name is Mona, and she is staying with her sister Megan at her family home in Dublin."

Mark, unable to move, stared wide-eyed at the man holding him captive. For the first time in his life, he felt a chill of fear run down his spine.

Roy watched with some pleasure as he saw the fear run across his captives face, then he continued,

"First, I am going to show you a DVD I have made. When you have seen it, you will know how other men feel when you show them what you have done to their wives."

Roy turned on the camera and opened the viewer, enabling Mark to see the images displayed. Mark stared unbelieving as he saw his wife enter his Lordship's bedroom. He saw him make love to her, staggered that to all appearances she was not under the influence of any drug. It was only too apparent that she had been only too willing to give herself freely and voluntarily to Lord Croft's sexual advances; her only outward concern was that someone might hear them. Mark could not believe that she had let Lord Croft make love to her like that; he could see that from the pictures displayed so vividly before his eyes that Lord Croft had worn no protection; he felt sick as he witnessed his wife having unprotected sex with the man sitting beside him, the look on his Lordship's face was the cruellest smile he had ever seen on any man.

Seeing the look on Mark's face gave Roy much pleasure and once again he pulled the gag aside and pulled out the ball of cloth allowing his prisoner to speak.

"You bastard," Mark said, "somehow, you must have drugged her."
Roy put the cloth and gag back and let the picture continue. Mark saw his Lordship lie naked on the bed. Mark blinked, his eyes opened wide as he saw his wife enter the room of her own accord and let Roy Croft make love to her again, totally without any apparent restraint. Then he continued to watch again, aghast, when she went into the bedroom on a different occasion, his eyes following Mona's every move as she slipped off her robe and climbed willingly into Roy's bed.

Mark was beside himself; the images were too much for him to bear; he tried to close his eyes from the scene before him.

"Stop! Enough! I can't bear to watch anymore," he cried. "You must have forced her to do those things. She is not that sort of woman. What kind of man are you? You devil!"
God, he could not believe what he had been watching as his heart sank; now he knew exactly what other men felt when he showed them the recordings of their wives. But Mark had seen with his own eyes that Lord Croft had not drugged his wife; she had gone to bed with him as a willing participant. Mona had not been drugged; she had done what Mark had witnessed of her own volition, which made the act of adultery far worse.

"OK, Lord bloody Croft, you bastard. You've proved your point. What now?"

Roy did not answer the question; he simply re-gagged the man and began to wipe the vehicle down carefully until every inch was swabbed, leaving no trace of any finger marks on any part of the vehicle. Mark's fear grew, beads of sweat formed on his brow as he realised the only thing Lord Croft could do to prevent Mark from betraying what he had witnessed to his superiors; he would have done the same thing in his position. He knew then that he would never see the light of day again. Roy set the camera up on the dashboard so that Mark could see his wife's infidelity once again, and he rang Gael, telling her where to pick him up. Roy, using a pair of surgical gloves, drove the car off the road until it was completely hidden from the road in a field by a busy quarry that blasted rocks throughout the day and night. He showed Mark the remote control and let him see Roy deliberately set the timer, but he did not let him see how long he had before the device would explode. Mark would have to sit and know he was going to die but not how long he had before he would stand before his God and pay for his sins.

"It will be a test of your courage, Mark. You can sit here and wait for the seconds to tick by, or you can press the detonator and cut your torturous last hours or minutes of your life short. It's entirely up to you. Either way I shall have the pleasure in the knowledge that my wife's rape has been avenged. I hope you join the other three of your comrades in hell."

Mark's eyes were wide open; he struggled wildly to try to escape, knowing full well that it was hopeless, as the knots were tied by a man who was a seaman and knew ropes and knots only too well. After retrieving the camera, Roy closed the car door and walked quietly away, leaving the man, who had raped his wife, terrorised, knowing that he would soon die but not the exact moment of his death. Gael picked him up, and they heard the dull thud as the vehicle exploded, sending Mark to join his fellow secret agents wherever they were destined to be. Roy was satisfied as he had achieved his revenge. When Roy drove Gael back to the hotel, it was very late. He asked Gael and Fiona to let the committee member's wife, come out of her drug-induced stupor, when she had regained full consciousness, they were to tell her that the men who had raped her had been dealt with and to give her the copy of the disk containing all the details of her ordeal, and say that she must decide if her husband should know or not. The knowledge that they had been killed was all she had to know. After that had been done, they were both instructed to return to London and from there fly to the Caribbean and wait for Roy to arrive. He merely told them as he still had unfinished business to complete.

Roy returned to the O'Leary household in the early hours of the morning; he was somewhat surprised to see Gordon waiting up for him.

"Sorry, it's so late, Gordon, but I did not expect you to wait up for me."

"I began to worry about you, Roy," Gordon said, handing him a glass of whisky. "I knew you had a key, but you did not know your way around from the kitchen, and I didn't want you to disturb the whole house when you got back."

"The business associates I was with insisted on taking me to some club. I'm sure you know the sort, and they insisted that we all stayed until the show finished," Roy lied to cover his tracks; if Gordon was ever questioned, he would have an alibi.

"I know about those clubs," Gordon said, smiling. "I only hope you got out with your honour intact. Some of those places can be very rough indeed," he said with a wry smile on his face.

The two men had another drink before Roy climbed the stairs and climbed quietly into bed beside a sleeping Mona; he would enjoy the next few days, making love to Mona taking her well past the date of her ovulation as Roy intended to enjoy his revenge, extracting the most from the situation. He never could resist a little pleasure mixed with business.

When Roy visited the Gresham the following day to settle his account and see if Fiona and Gael were off to Barbados, he viewed the DVDs that had been delivered. He was not surprised to see several of the committee member's wives on screen, but as far as he could see, each and every disk was the original taken from the camera and it gave Roy great pleasure to destroy each one after he had watched them. After all, he chuckled to himself; he never knew when such information may come in handy. When Roy finally decided it was almost time to leave Ireland, the headlines were full of details of a triple murder, the bodies of three men which had had been found naked each having been shot in a flat in the centre of Dublin had not yet been identified. The police were mystified; it was a killing reminiscent of the old days something they had not witnessed since the Good Friday Agreement. A few days later, the newspapers carried details of another death: the burnt-out wreck of a car had been found by a passing cyclist; the car had apparently been carrying explosives and had, according to the Irish police, exploded as it had gone off the road. The explosion had been so great that there was insufficient remains left of the occupant to make any easy identification possible. Forensics, the broadcast had said, were still trying to put together the pieces, but the debris had been scattered over a wide area, and no one had heard anything suspicious due to the fact that a quarry had been blasting in the area at the same time.

The day came when Roy had to leave for the Caribbean, and a tearful Mona, who had now given up trying to hide her liaison with Roy, begged him to stay a little longer on the last night they would ever have together. Roy was determined to make this last time as memorable for her as he could. Mona confessed that she had heard nothing from her husband Mark since he had dropped her at Megan's. She had no idea that he was dead at

Roy's hands. To Mona, the last few days had seemed like a dream come true; she had enjoyed her adulterous liaison with Lord Croft, but now the truth was it was time for him to leave. Mona realised she had to come back to reality, and the pangs of guilt began to overpower her thoughts. Megan had warned her that this moment would come; she had told her Roy was happily married, but he was a true philanderer and a Lothario of note. Now that moment of truth had arrived this was their last night together, in the morning he was going away, Mona had enjoyed that last night, but as daylight streamed into her bedroom, she wondered if she would ever see him again. Hopefully, she could keep her infidelity from Mark, who would never understand why she had been led astray by the likes of Lord Croft. Deep down, despite the guilt, she felt happy in the knowledge that she had repaid her husband for neglecting her. The last few days would always be a reminder of what she had missed. It would be a time to remind her that she had married the wrong man. Mona made up her mind she would remain with her sister for a few more days, then, whether Mark contacted her or not, she would return home to London to wait for her own errant husband's return. She knew she could stay with Megan for as long as she liked, but she needed her own space. It would be some time before she would hear that she was a widow, but that would only come to light sometime after she had received confirmation that she was pregnant with Lord Croft's child.

Chapter 9

Roy had to return the weapons back to the castle prior to returning the hire car; this time, however, he decided against revisiting Marion at the castle as it would confirm he had been in Ireland at the time Mark and his underlings had been killed. Instead, he went to see Sam Delaney and informed him how he had tied up the loose ends, after disposing of Mark and his cell. Sam was delighted to hear the finer details of the attack on the nefarious group of British secret agents. He took Roy through to the study and pulled out a sheaf of newspaper cuttings referring to the deaths. The newspapers carrying the story gave details of the three men found shot in a flat in Dublin. The police had no idea who perpetrated the violent crime, and it had not been reported that the men were British agents. Sam's contacts, however, had informed him that the three men had been identified and their bodies were being flown back to England in secret.

MI5 or MI6 neither apparently had any idea what the group was doing in Ireland, nor apparently had they any idea who had been responsible for their deaths, and consequently, the whole matter had been quietly laid to rest. The word was that the body in the car had been unidentified, and it was rumoured that the wreckage of the car had been shipped to London, a sure indication that they believed it could belong to their missing agent. Sam smiled as he said,

"My contacts told me a detailed investigation has begun to get to the bottom of things. No arrests have been made, and it appears that the group have been on some unauthorised clandestine operations known only to their section head. A person who incidentally, it has been confirmed, have been temporarily relieved of his post pending the outcome of the investigation."

The two men re-joined Kate in the lounge; she looked well; her pregnancy was advancing well, and Sam was as proud as a man could be, and he seemed genuinely pleased to become a father, especially as the doctors had said it was going to be a boy.

Kate embraced Roy, kissing him on the cheek and he could tell that she was bursting to tell him her latest news.

"Oh, Roy, I thought I should tell you that I had a call from Lady Blanchester. She rang to tell me her latest news. Would you believe, it at her time of life, it's been confirmed that she is going to have a baby. His Lordship was not too happy to begin with, but he has finally accepted that his wife would not have an abortion."

Kate looked closely at Roy, who made no sign that he knew anything about Lady Blanchester's current state of health.

"That sea voyage I took her Ladyship and her daughter Karen on up the coast of Ireland must have done her the world of good," Roy said.

Kate smiled and nodded her head in agreement.

The following day, Roy flew back to the Caribbean to see Janet, his wife; she hugged him and made him promise he would not go away again during their holiday, and they packed the boat to start a tour of the Caribbean Islands; after all, it was what they had come for. It was Gael who had broken the news to Janet that she was going to have a baby, but she absolutely refused to name the father. She had indicated that when the baby was born, she intended to put it up for adoption. Janet had sat down and spoken to her like a mother, finally persuading her to wait until after the birth and make up her mind. Janet explained to her that when the time came, she could well change her mind, once she had held the child in her arms. Janet pointed out that she was very young, and, really at nineteen, she would have every right to change her mind. Roy; Janet; Sean and Sheenagh, their two children; Gael, Elian, and Fiona, the Roy's all-female crew; and Morag, the children's nanny, set out for a magical tour of the islands. They were going to sail south as far as Trinidad and Tobago and then just visit St Lucia and the rest of the islands over the next few months before deciding if they should go back to Ireland or not. That was the plan; no one had given any thought as to what would really happen.

The Croft family and their crew visited the islands of Trinidad and Tobago, and everyone soon had a tan, even Roy had started to walk about without his shirt; His sex life with Janet and the children aboard was somewhat restricted, but he enjoyed having the family together for a change. Life had seemed too perfect. When they had landed at St Lucia, Roy had gone ashore. Roy had early that morning received a call from a stranger, claiming to be a friend of Sam Delaney, inviting him out for a drink; curious, Roy had accepted the offer. Resulting from that meeting, Roy had been invited out to dinner with the possibility that a business deal could be in the offing. Roy had gone to the small hotel to be met by several dark-haired, olive-skinned men who, it turned out to be, were Italians, all of whom claimed they knew Sam personally, and Sam had recommended that they meet up with Roy to discuss certain business proposals.

Roy had been wary at first, quietly refusing to have anything to do with their business proposals, informing them that he was enjoying a family holiday and would not consider any charters whilst he was in the Caribbean. The mood of the meeting changed quickly; the group around the table persisted with their offer, not wanting to take 'no' for an answer. When they could see that Lord Croft was determined not to do business with them, the offer became a threat, with the group conveying to Roy that it would be in his best interests to do a number of trips to and from Colombia and Cuba. There was certain cargo that needed to be moved without attracting the attention of the authorities, and from what Sam had told them, it seemed Lord Croft was the best man for the job. Roy could see from the attitude of the group that there was little room for manoeuvre, and reluctantly, finally, he agreed that he would do the job, provided he could find somewhere for his wife and family to stay whilst he was away on one of their illicit runs, explaining he had never involved them in his business and had no intention of doing so now or at any time in the future.

The group agreed and informed Lord Croft that he should not be concerned himself about finding accommodation; they would find him a house on one of the islands that they could guarantee his wife would fall in love with. When the arrangements were in place, they would contact him again; in the meantime, he should enjoy himself with his family. Over the next few weeks, the family group toured island after island; it was an idyllic time enjoyed by everyone aboard. Until that was, before they arrived at the island of Mustique, one of the Grenadine Islands; there Roy was contacted and told to take his wife to view a property, introducing the idea they should rent a house for a while to give them all a rest from the constant worry of the children aboard the ocean going craft and allow the youngsters more freedom. Roy supposedly contacted an agent, and as a result, Janet was shown a palatial colonial-style building that she fell in love with immediately. The island setting was unique with the palms and the tropical plants running down to the sandy beach being an idyllic playground for the children. The small town nearby was called Bay Town, and amongst its other attractions, the town had a small restaurant named after and run by a man named Basil. The restaurant was famous for its BBQs and occasional entertainment; the night Roy, Janet, and the crew visited they had a Swedish magician who had been fairly good and got Janet and Elian to participate in his performance. Janet had been thrilled; Roy never knew if the whole thing had been contrived or not, but it was there that she had met one or two of the other residents on the island. They seemed so friendly, telling her about the social life they had and the constant parties within the small island community. It all seemed to be a paradise, too good to be true. There was a supply boat that called by every week. Janet could not believe it when she learned they could rent the place for six months. The house had several wings and a host of domestic staff who would make her life so easy.

Janet was so taken with the house that she was eager for Roy to take the lease for the six months; she appealed to him to let them stay,
"Oh, Roy, it would be delightful for the children. I would not have to constantly worry about them falling overboard. I could invite a few friends from home to come over for a short stay. I could invite Kate Delaney, your mother, and her companion, what was her name? You know the Indian girl who came to the christening, oh yes, I think her name was Shilpa, or something like that."
Roy replied knowing he would be away for quite some time,
"Darling, if you wish, you can invite anyone you want to, but Kate is pregnant, and she will be far too advanced in her pregnancy to come, so she will not be able to visit."
Janet, as the group had planned, was ecstatic; she wanted to stay on the island, and when Roy, apparently, reluctantly agreed to her having her way, Janet was beside herself, and it was settled they would take a six-month lease, which, for some reason she could not fathom out, had been offered to them at a ridiculously low rent.

Once they had settled in, Roy broke the news that he had been referred by Sam to some people for charter work and, as life on the small island bored him, had decided to take up the charter, and it would mean he would be away for several weeks at a time, but the money offered was excellent.
"I'll have words to say to Sam when we meet him again," Janet said indignantly, "but I understand how you feel. You always seem to want to do something, and you never want to just lie back and relax. I'll be fine. I've already sent for some friends to come and keep me company. Your

mother and her young Indian companion have agreed to visit, and I'm expecting to hear anytime when they are due to arrive."

Roy got the crew together and told them they were back in business, and put the question to Elian, did she think Gael was up to it, as she was now showing signs of her pregnancy. Elian looked pensive before she replied,

"Oh, I think we can manage somehow. I'll show Gael the handling side of the boat, and it's time she had more experience as a skipper, if in return Gael instructs Fiona and myself in the weaponry and armaments. That way we could manage without having to recruit anyone else."

It was agreed, and Roy contacted the group of Italians saying that they would need an isolated atoll with a quiet and unobserved cove where he could retrain his crew and arrange to re-equip the cruiser with torpedoes, Sam7 rockets, and general ammunition. The next three weeks saw Fiona and Elian become experts in the use of the boats armaments; both Fiona and Elian had a natural affinity for the work. The speed at which the two women accepted the training and the accuracy of both became something the Italians found hard to believe; they admitted to Roy that they rarely used women in their operations, but were pleasantly surprised with the results of Roy and Gael's training methods.

The cruiser was finally battle-ready and fully rearmed, including a torpedo from a disused ordinance depot the Italians had discovered; the crew headed back to the harbour and spent a few days ashore with Janet and the children. Gael had taken the cruiser inshore navigating the reefs with a skill that even Elian had to admit was excellent. Her understanding of the radar equipment and depth finders had been excellent and her navigation skills proved to be first class. The Italians paid a visit and handed Roy over ten million dollars in cash to pay for the cocaine, informing Roy that if anything happened to the money, he would never see his wife and family again. The oldest man, whom Roy understood was the head of the family, added,

"Even though you came so highly recommended by a trusted friend, you, Lord Croft, will still have to prove yourself to our satisfaction. Let me emphasise once and for all that if for any reason you should fail in this mission, not only your own life and that of your family and crew would also be forfeit, but also the life of the man and his family whose recommendation we accepted."

Roy nodded grimly; he understood only too well what the consequences would be and would speak severely to Sam about this whole set-up when, hopefully, he returned to Ireland. After they had left, Elian opened the wall in Fiona's cabin and hid the money where she had found the counterfeit wartime cash. When the door had been closed, no amount of tapping or searching would disclose the secret hiding place; the original had been designed by experts. The only reason Elian had stumbled upon it was when she was trying to remove the blood stains from the rapist Roy had executed.

Roy had impressed on others that he had always considered that his team were the best; now he had to prove it all over again. They had retrained and honed their skills as any efficient team should be capable of; there was no animosity when they were at sea, and all three seemed to share Roy's attentions without any obvious problems of jealousy occurring. Roy's life aboard on the surface was idyllic.

The time came for them to leave on their first charter on the American side of the Atlantic. Janet and the children came down to the quayside to see them off; Janet kissed Roy goodbye and whispered,

"Dear God, be careful, my darling. I have a bad feeling about this trip. Please be extra vigilant. I would hate to lose you to a bunch of South American bandits or pirates."

They finally set sail for Colombia; the actual pickup point, as usual, would only be sent when they were off the Colombian coast. Roy, unbeknown to Janet, still had business to settle in St Lucia; he needed to know how Michael became involved in the set-up of his wife. They pulled into Marigot Bay on the west of the island, and Gael, being pregnant, was sent to try and locate Michael and his boat. Most islanders had only one thought about the unmarried marine biologist; the islanders were inclined to believe that one of Dr Crosby's casual girlfriends had returned after conceiving his love child; they were all guilty of having mistresses of their own; it was an established custom on the island and try as she may; Gael could not get them to help locate him.

Gael gave up with them in exasperation, and when she tried the Diamond Botanical Gardens and Research Centre, telling them she had studied with him at university and was on a holiday with a few friends on the island; she seemed to have more luck; she was told that Michael was doing research on the tiny atolls to the south of the island and pointed out the area on a wall map. Roy set out for the atolls and, using the cruisers superior speed, had soon covered the majority of the area. They had not seen any sign of Dr

Crosby or his boat when Gael suddenly spotted Michael's research vessel anchored off the southernmost point of a tiny outcrop of the reef. Roy held his breath as Elian and Gael edged though the rock-strewn waters using the depth finder and sonar to the fullest extent. Finally, they anchored beside the smaller vessel and waited. Michael came up from the depths, and after climbing aboard the research launch, he ranted and raved demanding an explanation. Roy called the crew to one side and told them to wait for him but to be ready for a quick getaway if things turned nasty. Roy stepped aboard, and the two men went into the cabin. Michael, still angered by the intrusion into his beloved territory, spoke sharply,

"Don't you realise you have entered a restricted area reserved purely for the study of a recently discovered marine colony, and by blundering in with a huge powerboat, such as the one you're using, you will have had disastrous results. The large area you have disturbed could take weeks, if not months to recover."

Roy understood the man's commitment to his work and apologised,

"I'm sorry, Dr Crosby, for any damage I may have caused, but I can assure you what I have to discuss is of far more importance to me than any study of marine life."

Michael spluttered and went red in the face; he was so angry he could have strangled Roy.

"I'll have you know," Dr Cosby said. "I have spent my life in these waters studying the strange marine developments. It's my life's work."

Roy could see he was getting nowhere, and he needed to settle the matter quickly. He drew out the 9ml from the holster tucked into the back of his belt and fired once into the air through the cabin door. The deafening silence that followed was instantaneous.

Having stopped Michael's incessant babbling, Roy spoke very quietly and with a look that made the now terrified man keep silent.

"I want to know," Roy said, "how you came to know that Lady Janet Croft, my wife, was in the Sandpiper hotel. Don't try to deny the fact. I know everything that went on. I only need to know how and why." Roy continued, "She is a free agent, and if she chooses to let you make love to her that is her business, and I have no objection to that. What I need to have confirmed to me is, first who told you she was there and who told you to take her to dinner at the High Commissioner's residence? Believe me, I am angry enough to kill if necessary, and I want the answer from you now."

Michael knew he was in trouble and said falteringly,

"I was at university with Janet, and when a mutual friend rang me from Ireland and told me if I wanted to see her again she would be at one of the hotels from a certain date. I had to see her again. I rang every hotel until I found that she was staying at the Sandpiper."

In fear and trepidation of any reprisals Lord Croft may do to him, Michael went on cautiously,

"The two of us, Janet and I, had a wonderful sexual relationship at university, and I just wanted to know if the attraction was still there. Love never entered into our relationship, it was just sex."

"Who rang you?" Roy interjected; his anger flared at Michael's attempt at pleasantries.

"An old mutual friend; Dr Francis; Carl Francis, he rang me to tell he had bumped into Janet in Ireland, and she had been more than compliant in taking up where they had left off. He was pretty cocky, and he told me she was, I'm sorry to say this but you wanted the truth, just as good in the sack, if not better than when she had been at varsity."

Roy cringed at the news but held his temper.

"What was your relationship with this Carl Francis?"

"We were just good friends at university," Michael answered. "He went into botany, and I went into marine biology, after qualifying."

"Was there anything else?" Roy asked.

Michael could see where this was going and knew he had better be frank.

"Well, on one occasion, he asked me if I was interested in joining one of the government agencies as a sleeper agent. Carl told me at the time the money was excellent for just being trained and I would do nothing until they asked me. He said they may never ask me, but the retainer would be paid for the rest of my life." Michael, now fearing for his life, went on to say, "I was a student at the time and needed every penny I could get my hands on. I agreed. The training was a bit of a laugh, all cloak-and-dagger stuff, and after which I was supposed to have signed a copy of the official secrets act and theoretically I could be jailed for life for telling you all this."

Roy had heard about MI5 or MI6 sleepers, recruited during their time at university, but he had never believed it until now.

"What did they tell you to do?" Roy asked the man standing meekly before him; the fight seemed to have gone out of him, and he had lost all his aggression.

"I was to try and seduce her, and if I was successful, I was to invite her on to my boat for the day. I suppose she was just looking to try and get some of her youthful days back. I'm sorry again to tell you, but we both had a wonderful time. Both of us were momentarily transported back to times gone by, and it was almost as if we had gone back in time. In a physical sense, I mean. I think someone must have been watching us make love on the deck because as we pulled into the harbour, a strange call came through instructing me to invite her to the High Commissioner's residence for dinner. I had never been there before in my life and was a bit overwhelmed at the chance to go. The voice gave the code word Carl had used and simply instructed me to say that a friend, called Mark, had invited us, and I was to introduce her to him as an old friend."

Roy's face was like thunder at the audacity of the British Secret Service especially as Marion had confirmed they had no evidence against him.
"So you simply followed the orders?"
Michael was now trembling.
"What is this all about anyway?" he asked.
"All in good time, my friend," Roy muttered. "What happened then?"
Michael almost whispered his response,
"I introduced her to Mark, telling her he was an old and trusted friend, as I had been told to do. That was supposedly the end of my task. I was to keep out of it from then on, apart from returning Janet to the hotel, if required, at the end of the evening. After the meal, you know how these things are, everyone including the women in the higher society smoke cigars or cigarillos. With everyone smoking, the air was blue with thick cigar smoke. I had told Mark that Janet hated smoke; as a result, he invited her out into the garden. I have no idea what took place outside. I was not privy to that. I only know that when I drove her back to the hotel Janet was tired and that was the last time I saw her, and that is the truth. I swear."

Roy could see how Michael had been used by the secret service agency and felt sorry for him.
"I should just inform you that Mark and his cronies invited Janet out for lunch the following day and gave her Rohypnol and raped her for the entire afternoon, partly due to your co-operation and information."
Michael was aghast.
"Oh my God, I had no idea. Is she OK? They did not hurt her in any serious way not that rape in itself is not serious, but I hope there was no

permanent damage, physically or mentally. I could not live with myself if that had happened. Janet was always a good friend to me. I promise I will never say a word about this visit to a living soul. I am so ashamed at being used by Carl of all people. I will never talk to him or that Mark fellow ever again."

Roy said quietly, mainly to cover his tracks if anyone ever enquired.

"If Mark or Carl ever contact you again, speak to them, but contact me on this number and tell me exactly what either of them tells you to do. Do not under any circumstances tell him you know about Janet's rape or that I have been to see you. If you can get a contact number where you can get in touch with either of them, as we are staying in the Caribbean for some time, I have no doubt one or the other will want you to do something else for the agency. But be warned. I can kill you far easier than they can, and I'm a lot closer."

Roy swung himself up to the cruiser and backed the seventy-three-foot vessel slowly and quietly away from the marine research vessel, trying not to do more damage than they could help. A very subdued Michael waved Roy off; he was a very worried man, and he hoped that Carl would not contact him again, but in the back of his mind, he knew it was inevitable.

Roy signalled for Gael to take them out to sea; their destination after wasting so much time with Michael would have to be the Venezuelan island of Blanquilla, where they would spend the night in readiness to be off the Colombian coast the following evening as planned. The authorities on Blanquilla gave Roy no end of problems; they wanted to know why he was there and where he had come from and what was his destination and seemed utterly unconvinced that he was holidaying with three women, one of whom was obviously pregnant. They finally left them alone, but Roy had a distinct feeling he had not heard the last of them. Fiona prepared the meal; the idea of going ashore after the long argument with the port officials was shelved until they reached the island of Aruba or Curaçao; these were Netherlands territories, and Roy hoped the reception would be better. Roy and Elian went to bed late that night after checking the weapons were securely hidden from any inspection and secure in the knowledge that the money hidden in the wall would not be found unless the cruiser was broken up.

They retired to the stateroom and as they lay in bed. Roy had his arm around Elian as she whispered,

"Oh, Roy, please make love to me. I have a bad feeling, and I'm worried that this trip is not going to run smoothly at all."

Roy, who was still angry at the way they had been treated by the overzealous officials, was eager to have the chance to put his anger aside. Elian held him close and whispered,

"I never thought they would go. I don't know why, but their presence sent shudders down my spine. I just need to know you are there for me. I just need you to comfort me. Please make love to me."

Roy was as usual only too pleased to comply with his skipper's request and put the concerns he felt about the trip to the back of his mind. He too had a bad feeling, but he hoped he would be able to deal with whatever was sent to try them. The next morning it was an early start. Elian went up top to prepare for an early departure, and Roy, as usual, was hungry after a night with Elian and went looking for breakfast. It was still very early, and Fiona had not dressed; she was wearing her T-shirt, which barely covered her decency; as Roy walked into the galley, Fiona bent to get a dish from the cupboard below. Roy groaned lustfully as he gazed upon the sight before his eyes. He walked up behind the half-clad Fiona, putting his arms around her. Seeing Fiona half-turn and give him a nod and a smile in reply, Roy was certain he would be able to make love to her there and then. When they heard a sound from above, they separated as they heard footsteps descending the companionway.

"Is breakfast ready or are you two too busy to want any food?" Gael's voice quipped,

"I'll bring it out now, Gael. It's ready," a red-faced Fiona called back.

Roy shook his head as things were definitely not going his way; perhaps it was an omen of things to come.

The trip to Columbia went smoothly enough with everyone vigilantly on the lookout for patrols, especially along the coast of Venezuela. They had kept well out to sea far beyond the twelve-mile limit, not that it seemed to matter in any way to the patrol boats. Roy had been warned the Venezuelans knew no boundaries. At the appointed time, Lord Croft and his crew met with the fishing boat off the coast at the co-ordinates given, just off the Colombian coast near the Pta Espada close to the Gulf of Venezuela. There was no conversation between the parties only a look of mutual distrust, as the soft packages were loaded one by one aboard the cruiser. The surly Colombian skipper, aboard the fishing boat, kept eyeing up the three female crew members with avarice, but he made no move on them apart from touching them inappropriately as the packets were handed from one vessel to the other. Finally, the transfer was complete and the drugs hidden below. Roy handed the money over and the two boats parted. Whilst Elian took the cruiser back into deep water, the crew swabbed the decks and the companionways with chemicals to remove the faintest traces of drugs that may have escaped from the packages even the sniffer dogs would not be able to pick up, when they had finished, the strong smell of chemicals saw to that.

Roy had been specifically instructed by the charter group not to head directly from the pickup point to Cuba, but to retrace his steps back towards Blanquilla Island, in an attempt to confuse the satellite systems. If the two converging boats had been spotted by the DEA, (Drug Enforcement Agency) any attempt to head directly for Cuba would have raised alarms and patrol boats would have been dispatched to intercept at the earliest convenience. Keeping well out to sea, Elian, under Roy's watchful eye, headed back in the general direction of Trinidad, intending to play the tourist and anchor off one of the smaller islands where diving was a popular pastime. Arriving without seeing any of the patrols, Elian found an area free of any other visitors; they anchored just offshore. At Roy's suggestion, they spent the break in their schedule, relaxing all day in the sandy beaches and enjoying the diving. Both Elian and Gael had become expert divers, and Roy spent most the day below the tropical waters, whilst Fiona stayed aboard keeping watch out for any suspicious boats, and on their return, Fiona cooked supper from the fish the others had speared. Roy produced a bottle of excellent white wine and shared it between them. Fiona, having been the one to do the day shift, was the one to share Roy's bed that night, whilst Gael and Elian shared the watch. Breakfast was early as they had a long trip ahead of them to Cuba. Elian joined Roy and Fiona below for breakfast, the intention being for it to be a leisurely affair, giving Gael the opportunity to take the wheel for the first part of the journey.

Roy felt the cruiser move out from its anchorage and head out to sea; they had finished the food when Gael called out in alarm,
"You'd better come up here quickly, Roy. We have visitors, and it does not look good. They came out of nowhere, like some kind of apparition."
With no time to race up the companionway, Roy turned to look in the direction of the sound of a powerful engine. It was a Venezuelan-patrol boat. It had appeared from behind a small tree-covered island and had

obviously been waiting for them. Armed officers stood on the deck. Roy and his crew had no time to grab their arms and protect themselves. Under the threat of being shot, they had no alternative but to comply with the orders called out on a megaphone, and with great reluctance they stopped the engines and waited for the Venezuelan captain to board. In broken English, he declared,

"This is a restricted area. You have no right to be here."

Roy indicated to his crew to remain quiet as the captain continued,

"I am coming aboard to search your vessel. Any move on your part to resist will result in one of you being shot, do you understand?"

As the captain and three of his officers boarded, he pointed to Roy and commanded his officers to secure him. Two of the boarding party grabbed Roy's arms and, using handcuffs, they secured him to the railings. With two of the patrol ships company keeping the three women covered, the other two men proceeded to search the vessel, and after an hour's fruitless search, they found nothing. The scowling captain was disappointed at finding no contraband and, obviously, was not satisfied.

"Why are you here?" he demanded, and added as if noticing the three attractive crew members for the first time. "With such a pretty crew, secure them all."

Roy watched helplessly as the three women were secured and strip-searched by the officers. They spared no opportunity to take full advantage of the situation as they fondled and touched the three women, and Roy could see the look of expectation in the officers' faces, and it was obvious this was not the first time such a situation had occurred with women aboard boarded vessels. The captain pointed to Fiona and said,

"This one is mine. You can share the others."

Roy was incensed as the captain laid Fiona on the deck and, using hit brute force, raped her in front of the others, taking her with the crudity and insensibility of a dog mating with a bitch. Roy's heart went out to her as he heard Fiona cry out in pain.

Roy turned in the direction of the other two, his anger boiling up inside him like bile as the bitterness of hatred rose in his throat as he watched the animalistic display of uncontrolled lust. Another officer from the patrol boat jumped aboard, and the four of them began to drag Elian and the pregnant Gael down onto the deck and ripped off what little clothing the strip-search had left behind them; they unceremoniously raped them without any fear of the consequences or reprisals of their action. As Roy had feared, this was obviously not the first time the boarding party had done this, and he realised they would be lucky to get away with their lives. Roy struggled in vain, the steel of the handcuffs cutting deeply into his wrists. Gael would under normal circumstances have been able to fight off her attackers, but with her hands cuffed behind her back and afraid she might damage the baby, she lay back and let them have their way. The ordeal was finally over, and Gael was lying on the deck, still conscious but bleeding badly. Elian was lying nearby, unconscious, and Fiona had fared little better, lay sprawled where the captain and his first officer had left her.

The violent orgy was finally over, and the captain, now once again dressed in his uniform, ordered his crew off the cruiser and said to Lord Croft, his voice filled with contempt,

"Now let that be a lesson to you. Don't try to enter Venezuelan restricted waters again." He added, "Let me give you one final warning, if you ever mention this to anyone, you will be arrested for illegal entry into restricted waters and spend a few years in a Venezuelan jail, where the prison guards will use you and your crew for pure pleasure."

Once aboard their patrol boat, the Venezuelan crew cast off, leaving Roy and his vanquished and unconscious crew handcuffed and adrift on the open sea.

Roy knew from his study of the maps and tidal information of the area that, in these waters, there were many hidden reefs, and if the boat floundered, they would be lost without trace. Gael lay whimpering as excruciating pains coursed through her; she was bleeding badly from the misuse of her body during the contemptuous rape by the four officers and finally by the captain. Roy called her, and she moaned as she opened her eyes.

"How are the others?" Roy asked her.

Gael cast her eyes over the prone figures and muttered, her face contorted as she was obviously in great pain,

"They are both out cold! I just hope those bastards rot in hell." She grimaced.

"Can you stand?" Roy asked her tentatively.

Gael nodded, but Roy could see she was in agony as she began to drag herself unsteadily to her feet.

"Can you get the bolt cutter to remove these cuffs?" he asked.

Gael gritted her teeth; she knew the danger they were in, adrift in these waters, so close to the reefs they had explored the previous day. It was no good; she was in far too much pain to walk. Roy could see the agony in her face, as she clutched her stomach and sank back to the deck. Gael was never one to give in to anything, and ignoring the agony tearing through her body, it was with a grim determination she set her mind to be oblivious to the racking pains; she gradually dragged herself to the deck locker. The combination lock was out of her reach, and with an effort that drained her of energy, she put her back against the door and gradually pushed herself upright.

Roy watched her with a new admiration as Gael strove to conquer her pain; it was with great difficulty she half-turned and, using her cuffed hands behind her, slowly turned the dial waiting for the click as each number dropped another tumbler into its place. Roy heard the faint click as the lock sprang open, and she grabbed the sill and, with a supreme effort, dragged herself half into the locker. Roy, seething with anger, sympathised with her predicament; he knew from the pain reflected on her face that she was suffering agonising pain. Gael, with her hands behind wedged half in and half out of the tight space, unable to look where to find what she wanted, reached inside the locker searching and gave a cry of relief when she felt the bolt cutters in her hand. Gael then sank back to the deck and, with the cutters gripped in her fingers, she slowly and painfully dragged her body to Roy and, unable to hold back the agony, pulled herself to her feet, letting out a scream as the action sent racking pains up into her uterine cavity. Standing as erect as she could and with the bolt cutters held behind her, knowing if she let them fall, they would drop into the sea and the boat and its crew would be lost, dashed onto the reef nearby.

With a strength summoned up from her deepest reserves, Gael gripped the cutters and, with a cry of agony or triumph Roy never knew, cut through the chain, securing Roy's cuffs to the ship's rail and unable to do any more, she collapsed in a heap. Roy was still cuffed, at the wrists, but the chain between them hung down and his hands were free. He knelt beside Gael's unconscious form, knowing how much she had suffered in the effort to release him and lifted her gently, carrying her down to the cabin below. She needed urgent medical attention; it was obvious that from the amount of blood loss that she was losing the baby. Roy raced back up on deck and checked the depth finder; they were all right for the moment, but the current was dragging them towards a rocky outcrop some 200 metres or so away. He knew the crew needed his attention, but at that moment, in order to preserve all their lives, the safety of the boat had to take precedence.

Roy raced up to the upper deck, but the keys for the ignition had been taken by the Venezuelans. He knew without the engine power he would not be able to drop anchor; Roy raced back to the steps and pulled the spare anchor from the chain locker and, securing it to one of the lengths of rope, coiled on the deck; then he lashed it to one of the capstan drives and tossed it overboard. The anchor dragged through the sandy bottom as the boat drifted in the current towards the rocks. Roy dived down to the lower controls and searched for the spare keys; after several minutes he found them; then he put the key into the ignition on the lower deck dashboard, turned it, and punched the start button, praying that the boarding party had not disabled the starter. Thankfully, they had not had the presence of mind to do that; they had been far more interested in the physical abuse of Roy's crew; Roy gave a sigh of relief as with a deep-throated roar the engines sprang to life. Roy switched on the lower instruments as the depth finder and sonar came to life. They were almost on the rocks. Roy manoeuvred the craft, slowly edging the vessel away from the jagged razor-sharp edge of the reef.

The anchor he had thrown overboard was now hindering his attempts to move further away from the reef. Roy heard a moan from above and shouted,
"Fiona, Elian, whoever that is I can hear, either cut the rope or pull up the anchor on the port side."
There was no answer, but Roy heard the sound of the rope coming over the side, as the rope wrapped around the windlass, and the sound of the boat moving through the water in the direction of the anchor. Suddenly the anchor pulled free from the sand and banged against the side of the boat; they were free. Roy moved the boat out of danger; Elian, who had heard him call, had done as he had asked and staggered to join him in the lower cabin; the effort had been too great that she collapsed outside the door. Then a pale-looking Fiona, who had slowly regained her senses, climbed down the companionway, obviously in pain, and she looked at Gael, who was losing blood, and tears began to run down her face.
"Hold the wheel," Roy said a little too sharply. "I must see how Elian is." Elian had been torn and was also bleeding quite badly, and Roy helped her down to the cabin. He relieved Fiona, asking her to go and attend to

the others. There was no hospital on the island, and he knew he had to get help; he opened the throttles wide as the cruiser leapt forward, and Roy headed for Curaçao at full speed. It would take several hours to cover the 200 miles or so by which time Gael, who had already lost the baby, would be in a desperate situation; Roy knew more than likely that she could lose her life.

Fiona, to Roy's amazement, had managed to stem the bleeding using pressure with the heel of her hands pressed down on Gael's uterus and elevating her feet; she explained to Roy that she knew how to do that from her mother, having been an unofficial midwife in the village when she had been a child. Fiona explained that she needed to increase Gael's blood pressure by raising her feet above the level of the heart, but I need a drug to help and several pints of blood as soon as possible. Elian had stood open-mouthed as she had watched Fiona work on the hapless Gael. Roy called to her to take the wheel and went to see what they had in the medicine store below. All Roy could see that, may be of some use in such unexpected circumstance, was a giving set and some out-of-date saline solution. Roy got on the new radio and broadcast an SOS. The call was answered by a cruise liner which was only thirty miles away. The radio operator asked what the trouble was, and when Roy explained, a call went out for the ship's doctor. When the doctor came on the line and had listened to Fiona as she related the problem, he informed her that regrettably the saline was too old to be used safely. Fiona went back to her patient, and Roy took over the radio; the doctor asked if it was possible to get Gael to the ship. Roy checked the distance between the two vessels and estimated it would take them half an hour or so to make the trip. The doctor concerned for the woman's life told Roy he would request the captain to turn in the direction Roy was approaching from and that would reduce the time for the journey.

The two vessels converged and all three crew members were taken aboard. Fiona, who was well enough but still in pain after treatment, returned to the cruiser. Roy let her bandage his wrists, and they followed the cruise liner to the port of Willemstad on the isle of Curaçao. It was the best equipped hospital in the area. The ship's company were very co-operative, and when the two seriously injured women had been admitted to the hospital, Roy reported the incident to the port authorities. The officer in charge was sympathetic and said that they were sorry, but apart from registering a complaint with the Venezuelan authorities, there was nothing they could do to rectify the matter. It was not the first report they had had about such instances. This, however, was one of the worst attacks they had ever seen. Both women would recover, but they would need to stay in hospital for a few days and would need to undergo an AID's test as well as being tested for other sexually transmitted diseases, and it would be at least a week before they would be well enough to set sail. Roy, realising he would be late for the rendezvous, rang the emergency number he had been given by the Mafia, the group who had chartered the boat, and explained the problems; they understood his predicament, but they were not very sympathetic.

"Is the cargo intact?" they asked. Then his contact added, "We will reschedule the delivery for two weeks' time, but it is imperative you do not miss this second deadline, whatever the circumstances; you know the consequences of failure."

The tone of voice indicated that they were impatient; the cargo was needed to meet the demands. When Roy had completed the call, he spoke to Janet on the telephone relating what had taken place; she was shocked at the news and asked when he would be back. Roy said,

"We should be away for approximately one month, but I'll try and keep in touch."

Janet expressed her sympathy for Gael and the loss of the baby and worried about the safety of them all; she reluctantly rang off.

Roy was so furious he could not wait to get to sea. Roy decided, despite the threats to his own life and that of his crew, that he would, if possible, delay their departure to Cuba for a few days to search for that bloody rogue patrol boat. The crew decided that they would teach the captain a lesson that they were not to be taken for granted, a lesson he would never forget in a hurry. As it happened, the stay at the hospital for Gael was longer than expected, and Roy knew his revenge would have to wait for the time being. At last, they had the all clear, and Roy set out with three sexually traumatised crew members. They turned north towards Cuba and made the delivery as arranged. To everyone's surprise, including Roy's, a cargo of purified cocaine was loaded aboard the cruiser with written instructions from his employers. The note simply read:

To make up for lost time, and as a result we have to make changes in order to meet our delivery quotas. Lord Croft, you will therefore be required to make an additional run to the Florida Keys, for which you will be suitably rewarded. The time and location of delivery will be given by radio.

This was a job that had not been part of the original contract. The orders had come from the top, and Roy knew that they were ruthless bunch; with his wife and family on the island of Mustique under their watchful eye and susceptible to attack, he had little choice but to comply with their request.

Roy and Elian studied the route they would take and used every ruse in the book to successfully dodge the American patrols; the whole crew knew that the US coastguard cutters were constantly on the lookout for drug smugglers. In making the rescheduled delivery, Roy had to call on his own and Elian's skills using every ruse in their acquired knowledge to successfully avoid contact with the American vigilant patrols; only constant use of the extensive equipment aboard and regular changes of course enabled them to achieve their destination. Roy was only too relieved when he was able to hand the cargo, worth in excess of a hundred million dollars street value, to several cigarette boats which would make the final run to various points along the coast. Once the task had been completed, it was as though a huge weight had been lifted from Lord Croft's shoulders. Just to get the cargo off his boat in such well-patrolled waters was an achievement; Roy breathed a sigh of relief when he instructed Elian to head south.

Chapter 10

Roy had been well paid for his extra journey, but he had kept in touch with Janet regularly, and now he was on his way back, he broke the news to her that he had an urgent business in Blanquilla. He told her it was personal, and she could expect him back soon, but not before he had settled a score. Janet knew what he meant to do and her heart sank. He intended to take on the patrol boat; Janet had no idea how well equipped for just such a task Roy's cruiser was, and although she said nothing to Roy's mother, Shilpa, or the children, she in her heart of hearts did not expect to see Roy alive again. Roy's mother asked her several times what was wrong, but the tearful Janet could not or would not say. Roy's aging mother put her daughter-in-law's sadness down to the worry about the unwarranted attack on Roy's cruiser and the unfortunate loss of Gael's baby; what else could she be so sad about, as she was situated in the lap of luxury on this idyllic tropical paradise? How was she to know what danger her son was putting himself and his crew into or whether any of them would survive?

The determination of Lord Croft and his crew to seek retribution meant they had to constantly train, daily honing up their fitness and firing skills until they were like a military battle-ready team, at the peak of fitness. All three of the women had acquired long, slim knives, and all of them, every spare minute, could be seen with an oilstone honing them to a razor sharpness, woe betide anyone who tried to attack any of them in future. The knives never left their possession, asleep or awake. They were ready to take on the rogue crew at any given time. They knew the patrol boat call sign and the number painted on the side, but apart from the name Rodriguez, the captain, they knew nothing about the rest of the crew. They headed towards the Venezuelan coast, carefully avoiding the shipping lanes; they wanted no warning of their presence being sent before them. They approached island of Blanquilla from the north, rounding the eastern side of the island and then turned west. They were now on the same heading as they had been on the previous occasion, prior to the attack. This time they were ready. Gael was up on the flying deck; she had side arms and a heavy calibre rifle with scope sights and a grenade launcher on the floor beside her; Fiona was laying on the deck in a bikini with a side arm and a Sterling automatic machine gun under the towel lying beside her; Elian was in the lower cabin armed with a grenade launcher, a Sterling machine gun with several magazines, and a side arm at her belt. They approached the spot, and as they had predicted, a patrol boat appeared from the reef, exactly as on the previous occasion; only this was not the same patrol boat. They hailed Roy to stop, and the captain, armed, walked towards the rail of his ship. Roy asked,

"Excuse me, Captain; I was wondering if you knew the whereabouts of Captain Rodriguez. This young woman," he pointed to Fiona, "wanted to speak to him. I believe she has something to give him."

"No, Señor," the captain of the patrol boat replied, "but if you will put up your hands, I can see the pretty one will do for me, Captain Ferdinand, what she has for Captain Rodriguez she can give to me. Is that not so?"

Resigned to the fact, from the sudden intake of breath from the flying deck, that a fight was inevitable, Roy raised his hands and heard the distinctive sound of a heavy calibre bullet slipping into the breach of a rifle. The captain smiled as the leer of lust on his face clearly depicted what he had in mind; as his men stood behind him, side arms drawn, he prepared to jump aboard. The evil glint deepened as he addressed the bikini-clad Fiona.

"Hi, pretty one, show me what have present you have for me."

That was as far as he got. Roy heard the 'phut' of a silenced round being fired; he felt the wind from the round as it whistled past his head; the captain who was midway between the two vessels initially had a look of surprise on his face when his nose and mouth seemed to somehow close in on itself and the back of his head exploded sending a red stain against the wheelhouse behind him. He just seemed to crumple, and Roy threw himself to the deck as the three women opened fire with the machine guns. The armed officers were not expecting the withering fire, and they hardly got a round off. Silence followed, and there was just the tinkle of cooling metal, and Roy turned saying, with a weary grimace on his face,

"That was a little premature, ladies. Sadly, I have to inform you it was the wrong crew."

Gael shrugged her shoulders and replied, a little too cocky for Roy's liking,

"Lord Croft," she said, addressing him formally as if to emphasise her point, "after what the captain said about Fiona, it was clear what was going to happen. They are all seemingly tarred with the same fucking brush."

Roy jumped aboard the patrol boat, and all were dead, even the radio operator had been shot before he had managed to send off a message; the radio was still switched off. Taking out his side arm, Roy directed the weapon at the radio and fired three times, sending his shots into the GPS transponder, terminating its ability to send out the position of the vessel to the Venezuelan satellite system. Roy threw a rope to Elian and asked her to attach it to the cruiser's stern. Roy steered the patrol boat as it was towed out to deeper water several miles out to sea. Roy, helped by an unrepentant Gael, dragged the bodies below to the deck and locked them all in the captain's cabin; it was little more than a windowless cupboard really, but it would prevent the bodies floating to the surface and being washed up on some beach. Then they went below and opened the seacocks. The lower deck soon started to flood as Roy and Gael jumped on to the cruiser's deck, and they moved away, watching the patrol boat slowly settle and finally it sank beneath the waves. They powered up and went to St George's on the island of Grenada. They anchored and went ashore. They found a restaurant near the quayside, where they discussed the fact they had unwittingly killed the wrong crew; it was agreed to stay for a few days before going back to see if Rodriguez and his crew returned. That being decided, they had a good supper and a couple of bottles of wine to celebrate before returning aboard.

Roy retired and went to bed; he had not been asleep long when the sound of the cabin door opening woke him. There, in the dim light, he could see Fiona; she stood looking at him; he asked,

"Whatever is the matter, Fiona, what's wrong?"

Fiona stood stock still as though trying to make up her mind what to do next. She had heard Roy ask her the question; she stood silent, unable to speak for the moment. She felt so ashamed of her body after it had been violated by the Venezuelan captain and his crew; she knew that she had had to overcome that feeling in an attempt to find answers to several as yet unanswered questions, so that her life could go forward. She felt her face flush with embarrassment; when seeing him look startled, tears began to trickle down her cheeks. At last, she spoke quietly, almost a whisper. Roy strained to hear the words.

"Do you still think I'm attractive after those men raped me?" she asked. "I'm so ashamed of my body. I feel it must have been my fault they did that to me. I must have provoked them, and again, today, that man would have violated me if he had half a chance."

Roy spread his arms in a gesture of loving care, seeing the lines of distress lighten as he watched silently. Fiona reached down and gripped the hem of her oversized T-shirt, raising it above her head, leaving her standing in just a pair of flimsy panties. She stood looking like a silver statue bathed in the moonlight as it shone through the porthole, the silver rays catching her breasts, making them appear almost metallic and unyielding. It had been days since Roy had made love to any of his crew members; walking silently past the seemingly transfixed figure, Opening the door he checked that the other two were asleep; there was no sign of anyone. Turning around, Roy was in time to see Fiona half-turn in his direction; by this time he could see she was completely naked. He wondered where she was concealing the all-important knife that never seemed to leave the possession of all three crew members since the rape had occurred, when he saw the bright glint of the razor-sharp blade on the table beside the door. Roy glanced back at the statuesque Fiona; her body was in perfect shape, and there were no signs of the ugly bruises that had appeared after Rodriguez and his men had raped her. Roy felt ashamed, for even though he knew the trauma that Fiona had gone through, he was aware of his own growing need.

Fiona slid silently under the covers and held back the sheet in such a manner to leave no doubt in Roy's mind she wanted him to join her. Accepting her invitation, Roy slid into bed beside her. Roy made no move as he lay still almost afraid to let his skin touch hers. He was aware of her hesitation and was afraid to make any sort of contact for fear of breaking her already weakening determination as he saw the ripple of slight tremors of fear run through her. Roy had to speak to break the awkwardness of the moment, and he began to whisper softly, care and understanding in his gentle enquiries.

"Fiona, why have you come to me, if you are so afraid? Are you sure this is really what you want? I'm quite happy to be more than patient to help you over this trauma. If you need more time, I shall not press you to do anything you do not want to do."

Fiona had stumbled for words, trying to cover her embarrassment at having to stand before him naked; now that she was in his bed. Perhaps this had been a mistake, what would she feel when he touched her, would she scream, would the fear and terror return? Fiona knew she had nightmares when she even thought about sex, and here she was lying naked beside Roy, a thing she thought she could never do again. Her voice was shaking as she whispered in a trembling voice,

"I have to know if I can ever make love to anyone, ever again. I've missed you so much. If I cannot ever have the joy of your love raising me to such emotional heights, then when I have taken my revenge, I might just as well be dead."

Tears were still coursing down her cheeks as she continued,

"In my own mind, I know that all men are not like those pigs, and sex can be enjoyable and fulfilling, but the memories are still so strong that my body still resists my mental desires." Fiona said quietly, "I just need to know if the pain and horror I felt at the time of my rape is going to remain with me forever, or when someone like you makes love to me, will I be able to accept it and enjoy the intense and wonderful feelings, we, have always felt."

Fiona continued saying that although she had not been torn like Elian and Gael, and they would take longer to get over the physical injuries, she just had to get over the mental horror of being taken against her will. Roy turned to face her, seeing the way Fiona cowered away, still undecided whether she could go ahead with this. Roy understood how she felt, and he spoke softly, his manner gentle,

"I understand your worries and concerns, Fiona. If this was what you really want, I will try to be patient and gentle, but if you change your mind or at anytime you feel you want me to stop, all you have to do is ask."

Roy moved towards her putting one arm around her waist and gently pulling her towards him until their bodies touched. The moment was like a lightning bolt had hit her, and she jumped and shuddered in his arms. Once she had settled down, Roy asked tenderly,

"Are you all right, Fiona? Are you sure you want to go on with this?"

When she nodded, Roy began to make love to her with a gentleness she had never thought he was capable of. It took time and tender loving care as Fiona slowly relaxed and finally began to relish the pleasure she had always enjoyed with Roy. When it was finally over and they lay together,

"Are you all right now?" Roy whispered quietly.

Fiona hugged him and whispered back,

"Oh yes, I feel wonderful. Thank you for being so patient with me. I feel fulfilled. I feel like a human being once again instead of an animal. I just want more of you, but not now, perhaps later or maybe even tomorrow."

Roy slid from her grasp, stepped away from the bed, and went into the tiny shower; once he was refreshed, Roy dried himself, shaved, ran a comb through his hair, and dressed, leaving his somnolent night-time visitor sleep until she fully recovered from what he could only imagine as a traumatic relief from her fears. Lord Croft had a bounce to his step as he went up onto the bridge to begin what had to be another day.

The small harbour was abuzz with the news, being broadcast on every radio and television station, that a Venezuelan patrol boat had gone missing. The newscaster on the radio was heard to say,

"It appears that all contact was lost with the vessel twenty-four hour earlier, and no sighting or communication had been received since the previous check-in time. It appeared a complete mystery. There had been no reports of any storms in the area, and it was feared that the vessel may have struck a reef and sunk."

The announcer made the point that,

"At this stage, no foul play was suspected. Other patrol boats and aircraft are searching the last known area. Anyone having knowledge of the vessels whereabouts or any sightings were being requested to report to the authorities immediately. Any vessel in the area wishing to join the search would be welcome, inviting them to report to the co-ordinator of the search by radio."

After which several channels were identified as being opened for the purpose of contact. Roy called the crew together for a meeting to discuss their next move.

"We have two choices," Lord Croft said, addressing his crew. "We can either go back to the house on Mustique and lay low, or we can join the search and take the opportunity to sink the other patrol boat when it would be least expected. If we are fortunate enough to do as we plan, we can then make a run for our home base on Mustique."

The vote was unanimous; all three women wanted to get the bastards who had violated them as soon as possible. They had breakfast and cast off heading back in the direction they had come from the previous day. Roy disabled the transponder and ensured that any satellite search would not be able to pick up their radio identity and instructed Elian to change the name and registration number on the hull for a Panama registration. Contacting the co-ordinator and rendezvousing with several others, they eventually left to join the search, under the guise of a Panama-registered motor cruiser.

Roy instructed Elian to take the southern route towards the group of islands called Los Testigos and Los Frailes before turning north towards the islands of Los Hermanos. The route was well chosen; they did not see, nor were they seen by the other craft searching in the vicinity of Blanquilla, the last known place the vessel had been reported. As they approached the island of Blanquilla from the south, they heard the sound of a lone aircraft searching far to the north. Roy, using the long-range radar, spotted a boat heading their way in a hurry; using the cruiser's powerful binoculars, he could see it was a Venezuelan patrol boat, and they slowed almost to a halt and lay still in the water, dropping an anchor. As arranged, the three women wore the skimpiest bikinis and lay in different parts of the boat as though sunbathing with a towel nearby hiding their weapons. Roy sat slumped on the bridge, feigning sleep. The patrol raced towards them; Roy looked through his half-closed eyes and recognised the number and gave the signal. The three women lay in readiness. Gael lay half in and half out of the lower cabin; she took careful aim; as the vessel approached, a soft 'phut' sent the high-velocity bullet screaming towards the oncoming craft. None of the crew noticed as the radio aerial broke off as the bullet struck it, and it was whipped away in the slipstream to fall into the water behind the wake of the boat.

The captain was at the helm; he thought he recognised the cruiser as the one they had left adrift. *How the hell had it got this far south?* He wondered. *It should have hit the reef and sunk much further north.* Then he saw that the cruiser had a different registration number and, through his glasses, saw naked and beautiful women lying on the deck. He wanted to repeat his last performance, and his libido soared at the very thought. He grinned if it was as good as the last time it would be rewarding and would take their mind off the search for the lost patrol boat captained by Captain Ferdinand, his long-time friend and co-conspirator. As a result of their intentions, Captain Rodriguez instructed the radio operator not to report the sighting. He was determined to board the boat and take over command; then his mind pictured the idea that he and his crew might just be able to have a little fun and recreation. It's a pity, he thought, it was not the same boat as the previous time. After all he had enjoyed raping the pregnant one a lot.

Captain Rodriguez eased the throttle back as he approached and edged forward cautiously. There was no sign of movement. He ordered his men to secure the lines, and they jumped aboard. The rest of the search party would not miss them; they had been instructed to widen the search and had given their position some way to the east when they had spotted the cruiser lying in the water. Strange thought came for Captain Rodriguez; as the motor was running, there must be someone below. Detailing two of his men to move the unconscious woman who had not moved when he had prodded her and search below. The captain turned towards the prow where Elian lay in a heap, her arm crooked under her; she looked unconscious, her colour was too good for her to be dead. He smiled, and as he walked forward, he loosened his belt in readiness; the fact that she had not moved and could well be unconscious didn't worry him a bit. By the time he had reached Elian's prone form, he heard two grunts from the direction of the cabin. *What were those fools doing? Couldn't they move a body without his help?* His trousers were around his ankles as he turned to see what the noise was. The two idiots who had been detailed to go below were on the deck, but something was wrong with what he saw, one of them was staggering around with his hand holding a bloody wound, spurting blood from his neck, while the other one was lying under the kneeling woman, who had in turn straddled the prone form, and he could see quite plainly that she had a knife at his throat. The semi-naked figure of Fiona had the radio operator at gunpoint; he was standing aboard the patrol boat with his arms in the air and a wet patch forming around his groin; he had seen his two shipmates overcome by the apparently dead or unconscious woman, lying in the doorway. Moments later, the shocked captain saw a man's figure stand up with what appeared to be a grenade launcher pointing at the patrol boat with his finger pressed on the trigger.

Captain Rodriguez stopped dead in his tracks.

"What the . . ." was as far as he got.

When he felt a slight tug in the area of his groin, followed by the feeling of a warm wetness covering his hand and a sharp pain ran through his testes. He looked down and his penis was still in his hand but was no longer attached to his body. He screamed as the blood began to run down his legs. The long scream seemed to be the trigger; Fiona turned her head slightly for a second. But her attention was not on the patrol officer she was covering. The patrol officer's hand shot down to his holster and, in a flash, fired off a round hitting Fiona in the left shoulder. Her body snapped back as the slug hit her, but both she and Roy, up on the flying bridge, fired at the man left aboard the patrol boat almost instantaneously, one shot through the head and one through the heart. The Venezuelan radio operator was dead before his body hit the deck. Elian drove her knife up into Captain Rodriquez's groin, severing his femoral artery and snatching the knife back as the captain pitched forward. The fatally wounded captain felt fear grip him as he screamed again before hitting the deck; Elian calmly repositioned her weapon and slid the knife silently through his chest and into his heart; the prone figure gave a gasp and his feet danced a rapid tattoo on the deck, as the life left his body. Gael had cut the second man's throat even before he had time to scream or plead for his life; Roy looked incredulously at each one as all three women were covered in blood.

The bloodlust quenched, the shock set in. Fiona, clutching her shoulder, fell backwards on to the deck. Elian pushed the dead captain up off her naked body; she stood shakily to her feet, drenched in the sticky glutinous life blood of the captain. She stood looking in horror at the lifeless corpse at her feet. Gael had been trained to expect the blood and stood dragging one of the lifeless forms towards the patrol boat, leaving a trail of red ooze behind it. Seemingly with the ease of a practised soldier, she flipped the body on to the deck of the patrol boat and turning to fetch the other, whose feet were still beating out the death throes on the deck, as his life's blood ran from the severed carotid artery. Roy brushed past her and knelt beside the wounded Fiona. The bullet had been fired in haste and had gone through the fleshy portion of her upper arm but had thankfully missed the bone; she would live but bear the scar for life. Elian dragged the captain's body to the rails and, helped by Gael, tossed the dead man to lie with the other two on the patrol boat's deck; they gathered up the last body and threw that across the gap between the two boats.

Roy gathered up Fiona and carried her below; he grabbed the first-aid box; she came to and asked,
"Did we get them all?"
Roy pressed a field dressing to her wound and nodded. Suddenly there was a commotion upstairs and a scream. Roy raced up the companionway to see another patrol officer who had been below when the shooting started, and hearing the commotion, he had crept up on deck, and seeing the mayhem, he grabbed Elian, who began to choke; her air cut off by the patrolman's arm around her neck as he fired in Gael's direction. Gael had looked up

and, without any hesitation, threw her knife and made a cut along the side of Elian's face as it embedded itself in the eye socket of her attacker. The crewman screamed and loosened his grip on the blood-soaked body of Elian; the crewman was staggering about the deck, trying to pull out the knife. His eye was no longer there; aqueous solution and blood had shot out from the socket on impact. Roy, who had raced back on deck, pulled out his 9ml and was about to shoot when Gael walked between Roy and the injured man; she stepped over Elian, grabbed the man by his hair, and twisted the knife; then drawing her arm back, dragging what was left of the eye with it, she plunged the blade deep into the man's chest. He arched his back, gave a low groan, and slumped in her arms, the life gone from him forever.

The two women and Roy dragged the five men into the captain's cabin and locked the door. When they arrived back on to the deck, they stopped dead in their tracks as the low drone of an approaching plane could be heard coming from the southern part of the search area. There was no time to cut away the patrol boat and make a rush for it; they were caught red-handed. The four of them looked as if they had been working in a slaughterhouse, but it was Gael, trained just for such a moment, who reacted first; she dived across to the cruiser and yelled for Fiona to hand up the Sam7 launcher as Elian ran into the wheelhouse and switched on the radar. Gael had the loaded launcher up on her shoulder and waited until Elian called out,
    "Missile locked on."
Roy stood and watched helplessly as the trained crew took the initiative; the first missile was launched; Fiona was like lightning despite her wound; he watched as she slapped in the second missile and tapped Gael on the shoulder; Gael launched the second before the first had reached its target. Gael staggered under the second missile launch and watched as the two missiles locked on to their target. If the pilot had his radar detection system on, he never took evasive action, and the plane exploded in a duel explosive burst of flame and spiralled down into the sea.

Roy knew that the plane could well have got off a message that he was under attack, and he cut loose the patrol boat and raced up to the bridge; he backed away from the silent patrol boat and picked up the rocket launcher. There was no use trying to avoid the noise now, not after the plane had gone down, so Roy fired two RPGs into the hull of the Venezuelan patrol boat, and the result was spectacular: the boat broke in two and sank, but just as it had sunk below the water, the rear fuel tank erupted, sending showers of burning fuel and smoke high into the air, a perfect beacon for anyone to see. Roy, however, had reacted quickly; he had already opened the throttles wide almost before the sound of the second explosion had reached him. The cruiser leapt forward, and Roy held the wheel over, sending them south-west towards Los Testigos. If they could get a considerable distance from the scene of the crime quickly, they would stand a chance of hiding in one of the tree-lined coves they had seen on their outward journey. The cruiser began a race of its life; the engines roared at full throttle; the hull up on the plane skimmed across the almost still surface of the sea, and the deck vibrated from the throbbing power beneath.

Roy was relentless as he held the boat hurtling over the calm waters, the engines pushing the boat to its absolute limit; when the three women reappeared, they had washed the blood from their bodies and were wearing fresh bikinis; the only outward sign that anything differed from normal was that Fiona had a dressing tied around her upper arm. Gael pulled the hose from the locker as Elian switched on the pump, sending the powerful jet of water sweeping the deck washing the red stains from where the captain had fallen. Elian had opened the rear hose locker, taking out another hose; Fiona had switched on the rear pump, directing the flow to the hose. Elian concentrated on the entrance to the lower wheelhouse as Fiona shut the door behind her. The ugly red marks were soon washed away; they all understood the necessity, and they would have to use chemicals to remove the final bloodstains in case of any forensic investigation. Once the evidence had been washed away, Elian reduced the pressure and redirected the hose, ensuring the last of the damning evidence of their violent crime was gone to any casual observer.

They had covered almost seventy miles and had throttled back to a leisurely twenty knots when a faint drone could be heard coming from the west, the direction of the explosion. The hoses had all been tided away, lockers had been fastened, and two lilos placed on the foredeck. Fiona climbed up to the bridge, and Elian and Gael lay semi-naked, face up on the lilos. Fiona tore off the dressing, and Roy took her into his embrace, kissing her passionately. The pilot looked at the boat below; the two semi-naked beauties waved at the handsome young pilot who circled for another look, his eyes caught sight of a man, presumably the owner, he thought to himself, apparently in a passionate embrace with another half-naked beautiful woman up on the bridge. He circled for the third time taking in the unbelievable sight before thinking what it must be like to be rich enough to own such a boat and be lucky enough to have three such lovely women aboard as playthings. He moved the stick from side to side as a signal of appreciation before turning back the way he had come. *There was no way that boat and its beautiful passengers could have had anything to do with the mess south of the island of Blanquilla,* he thought to himself. That boat may be wonderful to look at, but she could never do more than thirty to forty knots at most. The cruiser below must be at least seventy to seventy-five miles from the scene of the accident, where one of his friends from his squadron and a patrol boat had apparently crashed and exploded. What really happened would only come to light when the investigators found the wreckage and took it away for appraisal of what could have caused a plane to apparently crash dive into a patrol boat.

Roy found a quiet cove, and the three crew members lay on the shore of the uninhabited tiny atoll and sunbathed for a couple of days until the heat of the wide and intensive search died down. The cruisers name and registration was restored and all traces of any blood were permanently removed; fortunately, no bullets had struck the decking or the superstructure. Fiona took advantage of her recovered sexuality spending each night with Lord Croft, the fact not unnoticed by Elian and Gael. They would, however, have to wait a whilst for their torn muscles to heal; it would be at least another two weeks before they would even contemplate the idea of making love. Meanwhile, Fiona was making the most of it, enjoying the fact that she had Roy all to herself. The traumatic times they had been through took away any thought as to when their next contraceptive injection was due.

Chapter 11

Elian lay listening to the sounds of Roy and Fiona making love in the adjacent cabin; over the last few days, they had been lying at anchor, the sound had elevated from a quiet, soft, gentle loving relationship to the restoration of the normal noisy sex, as Fiona's sexual confidence had been restored. It appeared to Elian that the little minx could not get enough of his Lordship and was making the most of every opportunity available. Elian was concerned that the level of noise Fiona was generating could not only be heard aboard the boat but by any passing vessel or anyone close by on the island. Elian's unusual spate of envy made her think that the smug little vixen seemed to have no sense of decorum, and she seemed insatiable; his Lordship should keep her under control. Elian seethed. It had been a trying few days, and after looking at the calendar, she had suddenly realised their quarterly contraceptive injection was overdue; Fiona was vulnerable, and the way she was behaving, she would be caught for sure. Elian went to the medicine chest and pulled out the morning-after pills and the prescribed injections. Elian called Fiona at the next opportunity and, after explaining the situation, gave the startled young woman a Levonelle tablet, hoping she had been in time, and the poor girl was not past her ovulation time, in which case the pill would be useless. Then she gave her the contraceptive injection that would, if she was not already impregnated, protect her for the next three months. Elian then gave herself the injection even though she had no intention of sleeping with anyone yet.

Gael refused when Elian offered her the same contraception. Gael's reply was that God had punished her for even thinking of having an abortion, by allowing those pigs to rape her and causing her to lose the baby. Gael seemed to have a bad case of religious fervour, since her attack, although how she reconciled that with the killing of the men aboard the two patrol boats and the plane was beyond Elian's comprehension. Elian suspected she was suffering from a form of post-stress disorder as Gael had in many ways withdrawn into herself and probably needed psychiatric counselling to help her overcome her fears and terrors; her sleep pattern was erratic and very disturbed, a fact that Elian could definitely vouch for, to say the least. Over the past few nights, what with Fiona next door and Gael tossing and turning, crying out as unknown terrors filled her sleeping mind, Elian has managed to get very little sleep.

Elian eventually plucked up the courage to discuss the matter with Fiona, asking her as politely as her jealous envy would allow.

"Fiona," she began, "how is it that you have managed to overcome the horrific trauma we have all suffered. How is it that whilst the very thought of a man in my bed sends shudders down my spine, I would be filled with horrors even the thought of making love to a man, and yet you have overcome your fears and have been able to let his Lordship make love to you?"

Fiona understood perfectly, and she whispered to her inquisitor, conspiratorially,

"What's wrong with you, Elian? I would have thought you, of all people, know his Lordship better than any of us? I told him how I felt, and he was the most gentle and patient man I have ever known. He told me that if I wanted him to stop or I was uncomfortable with anything he did, I only had to tell him. It took a long time, and I have to admit it was uncomfortable at first, and I was almost at the point of telling him to stop several times. I just persevered and, in the end, it paid off. I feel as at ease with him now as I have ever done in the past. The horrors of what those animals did to us will never be forgotten, but I have managed to put it behind me and get on with my life."

Elian sat and thought about what Fiona had told her for the rest of the day, and after several glasses of wine, she plucked up the courage to go into the main cabin where Roy had preceded her only minutes before. Calling his name, Elian broached the subject confiding in Roy how she felt.

"It's difficult to know where to start, Roy," Elian began. "Even though we have known each other for years, I find it almost impossible to explain how I feel. Sex frightens me after what those officers did to the three of us, and the fact that we killed them in retaliation has not made it any easier. Like Fiona, I want to get my life back and bring some sort of normality into my everyday actions. Making love to you was one of the most pleasing things in my life, before the rape. I need you to help me. I trust you completely and ask you to treat me with the care and consideration I know you are capable of."

Roy was as gentle and understanding with Elian as he had been with Fiona, and it took longer due to the fact that Elian had been torn by the rapists and was the final act was only consummated over a three night period, but the outcome was the same. The real Elian was back, and once she had overcome her darkest fears, she knew although she would have anxieties for months, she was over her initial fears, and from that point, she could heal. Elian was on the way to her recovery.

Roy was delighted that Elian was getting back to normal and it was time to return to his wife; after breakfast, he decided the time was right to head for their temporary home on island of Mustique, where Roy's all the members of family were waiting for him. Roy confessed to Elian that he was deeply concerned about Gael, who had shown no signs of any improvement, even after the rest and recuperation of the easy unfettered life on the beach. Her depression grew deeper by the day, and there was no joy in her life; the bright young woman seemed to have sunk into a deep dark place where none of them seemed to be able to reach. Roy knew that despite all he and the others had done to try and help, Gael was in urgent need of medical attention. Elian and Fiona had to a certain degree recovered from their terrible ordeal, but Gael with the loss of the baby to contend with, on top of the rape trauma, had sunk into a deep dark post-rape depression; she had reached such a state that they did not know what she would do next. She had taken to walking about on the boat dressed in only a T-shirt, and sometimes she walked about naked with her hair unkempt and lay about lethargic and totally uninterested in doing anything aboard to help the others, and even her communication with them had diminished to a disinterested grunt when she was spoken to.

Once they were back ashore on the island of Mustique, Elian explained to Gael that she would have to wear ordinary clothes, but Gael had flounced off in a huff and deliberately cut the skirts of her dresses and skirts so short that they barely covered her underwear. Her tops were either spaghetti straps or vests, and she refused, on any account, to wear a bra; it was as though she was making a statement, one which the rest of them could not understand. Elian was at a loss how to cope with her; she could sum it up in a word; Gael had completely gone off the rails and, into the bargain, had begun to act and look like a cheap whore, flaunting herself at every man she saw. It finally came to a head later, on the first night back at the house. Roy was sitting enjoying a drink with Janet, everyone else had gone up to bed, when Elian rang him. She was in tears, very unusual for Elian; she was obviously near her breaking point. She broke the news that Gael was nowhere to be found.

"Oh, Roy, I need you to help with this. I know it's your first night back, but I'm at a loss. The last thing either of us saw of her was when dressed in her usual way, flimsy top and mini-mini skirt, and from what we could understand from the staff is they had seen her heading in the direction of town. What do you think we should do?"

Roy explained the facts to Janet, who was sympathetic but was hesitant to send Roy on a wild goose chase into town to try and find Gael, and she imagined that the poor girl could be anywhere and Roy could spend half the night looking for her.

Unwilling to let Roy out of her sight on his first night back, she shook her head when Roy turned towards her questioningly; she hated the thought of him out there and tried to say logically,

"It's only ten o'clock, Roy, give it another couple of hours, and if she's not back, we will organise a search party to find her. We have to give the girl some leeway. The last thing we want to do is crowd her in her current mental state. We need to get her to the mainland to see a specialist. If Gael thinks we have no trust in her, she may get worse."

Elian lay awake listening for any sign of Gael to return; the clock had just struck midnight, and she was about to call Roy to remind him of his promise to send out a search party when she heard a sound. The noise Elian could hear sounded manic; it was neither crying nor laughing, it was a mixture of both and sounded horrific, like a demented child. Elian pulled on a robe and went to investigate. She found Gael in a terrible state; her hair was matted with something sticky, and switching on the light, Elian gave a start. Gael's head and her clothes were covered in thick, glutinous drying blood. Elian took in the sight, and in panic, she picked up the phone and dialled the main house. Roy was in bed; they were in the throes of making up for lost time, and Roy muttering some obscenity picked up the phone by the side of the bed and listened.

Janet knew something was very wrong from the look on Roy's face. Elian had stressed that the matter was extremely urgent and he must come at once. Roy knew that Elian had a good head on her shoulders and was not prone to overstress the facts; if she said it was urgent, she meant it. Janet had asked,

"What's the problem, Roy?"

At that stage, Roy was unable to tell her. Any chance of continuing their lovemaking evaporated in an instant as Roy had pulled on his shorts and a shirt before he ran to the other wing where the crew had been allocated bedrooms. Thank God they were separate from where his mother and Shilpa were housed. Roy burst into Elian's room, and there stood Gael covered in blood, the knife, still in her hand, had dried blood on the shaft and the handle. Her dress was torn and her underwear was nowhere to be seen; her breasts were covered with blood. Gale had something clutched in her other hand, but it was the vacant stare in her eyes that worried Elian. Gael was in a state of almost catatonic shock; she obviously needed urgent treatment, which was not available on the island. Words were not necessary between the shocked witnesses; they had to get her away from the island to a trauma centre as soon as possible. Elian pulled the knife from Gael's clenched hand then stripped off what was left of Gael's dress and both she and Roy could see from the bruises, which were beginning to darken, that someone had tried to force her to have sex. Gael's thighs were red and bruised; when they had opened her hand, the remains of her torn underwear dropped to the floor. It was obvious someone had taken her to be a prostitute, and when she had refused them sex, the unknown man had ripped off her underwear and tried to rape her. Roy believed she must have reacted in self-defence, and from the amount of blood, Roy knew she could well have seriously mutilated or killed her attacker. Looking at the blank stare, both Roy and Elian doubted if the police would believe the story, dressed as she had been at the time of the attack.

It needed no explanation that if the local police inspector took one look at what she had been wearing he would say she had paraded about like a whore and had asked for all she got. Roy gripped the distraught Gael by her shoulders, looking her in the face, and asked,

"Did anyone see you with the man or when you defended yourself?"
The stony face of Gael remained fixed, her eyes wide and staring, but she slowly and deliberately shook her head from side to side; she was about to scream as her eyes widened as if seeing the scene re-enacted, but Roy gently but firmly put his finger over her mouth and whispered,

"Shush, Gael, you're safe now."
The scream seemed to die in her throat, but the glazed eyes remained fixed and staring. Roy only hoped she was right; Elian took hands and led her slowly through to the shower; Gael stood silent whilst Elian washed the evidence from her blood-splattered body. When Elian returned with her, wrapped in a thick towel, Roy had to think and think fast.

"Get Fiona to help you and take Gael to the boat." Roy said.

Roy hurried back to Janet, who had fallen asleep; with no time to lose, he shook her violently.

"Janet, get up quickly. We have to move fast. It's the only thing we can do."

Janet who had fallen into a deep sleep, shook her head, trying to clear her thoughts.

"Whatever is it, Roy? Why the sudden rush?" she asked, seeing the urgency in Roy's face.

"We have to get the children ready. I need to get away. Tell the staff we are going for a cruise to another island or something, but do hurry."

Janet was so shocked at the urgency and timing of the decision that she asked,

"Why now? You have only just got back."

Roy reminded her of the trauma they had had when the women had been raped and how they had taken their revenge. Janet nodded he had already given her the gist before. Roy was in quite a state as he explained.

"Gael is suffering from a deep-seated guilt and is in a deep depression. I was so worried about her state of mind when Elian rang earlier and said she was concerned that she had gone out on her own. When Gael came back, she was covered in blood. There is a possibility that she may have killed one of the locals in self-defence. It is imperative to get her to a hospital as soon as possible before anyone could tie her in with the death or maiming of a man earlier this evening."

Hesitating for a moment, Janet knew how protective Roy was with any of his staff; he would defend them with his life if necessary, she knew all too well that it was no good arguing with him in this state of mind, as reason had gone out of the window. By lunchtime everyone was on board, and Fiona drew up the anchor and the cruiser with all its passengers put to sea. It was quite a squeeze with Roy and Janet in the stateroom, Elian in her cabin, Fiona sharing with the still wide-eyed Gael, the two children sharing a cabin with Morag, and Roy's mother and Shilpa sharing the cramped forward cabin at the very prow of the cruiser. They headed for Barbados, where they would enlist the help of the British High Commissioner, Sir Martin Claiborne, and his young wife, Lady Jayne. Roy knew he could rely on their help after saving their daughter, Madeleine, from certain death. They would need to fly Gael to Miami for treatment; since leaving the island, Gael had rallied for a while, but now she seemed to once again sink into a listless state of shock, staring blankly out over the sea with a dazed and uncomprehending look. Roy got Janet to call on the radio and asked for Lady Jayne to meet them at the docks. Lady Jayne was concerned, and when Janet gave her a brief outline of the events leading up to the poor girl's state, she promised to be there with an ambulance and a doctor who would know what to do.

They docked, and as promised, Lady Jayne was there with a doctor, who examined Gael and confirmed she was in deep shock; hearing the history of her multiple rape and the subsequent attempted rape, he confirmed she was suffering from post-traumatic stress disorder, PTSD; she was in need of urgent treatment and admission to a psychiatric facility. Roy confirmed that the cost of her treatment was of no importance. The doctor suggested Miami, but Roy who was having second thoughts about treatment in the US asked,

"I understand you know the hospitals in Miami, Doctor, but she will be amongst strangers when she recovers. If she is well enough to fly to England, I would prefer she go there, if at all possible."

Roy wanted the distance and security, knowing she would then be far away from any connection with the death on Mustique. The doctor stood pondering for a few minutes and said,

"I must admit I would have preferred Miami, but if you insist, she will need a psychiatric nurse in attendance and preferably a companion to accompany her as well on the journey."

"Fiona, you must go with her to London," Roy said firmly.

Fiona nodded her head in agreement.

"I'll do anything to help," she added. "I can be packed and ready as soon as the flight can be arranged."

The doctor, after giving Gael a sedative injection, consulted with Lady Jayne and returned after speaking on his cell phone.

"The earliest I can get a nurse and a private flight will be early in the morning. I will arrange for the unfortunate young woman to be admitted to a local hospital overnight where I can keep her under observation. She can leave early. The ambulance will take her and her travelling companion directly to the airport. If you can have all her documents in order, I'll do the rest."

Fiona offered to accompany her in the ambulance. Elian confirmed she would pack for both passengers and gather the necessary documents together. Lady Jayne insisted that Roy, Janet, Morag, and the children stay in the guest cottage for the night and would arrange for Elian, Roy's mother, and Shilpa to stay at a nearby guest house until it was decided what the next move would be. Elian insisted that she would prefer to stay on the boat. Roy offered to take his mother and Shilpa to the Sandpiper hotel, where his mother had after being woken, disturbed, and subjected to a cramped sea voyage had demanded she be put up in a five-star hotel. That Mrs Croft senior had declared was the only place she and Shilpa would stay, whilst Janet, Morag, and the children went to the residency guest house in the residency car.

Roy arrived at the hotel and carried his mother's case up to her room; she was in a state of shock herself, when she pulled her son to one side.

"Roy, I want to go back on the plane with Gael tomorrow. All this excitement and upset is proving too much for me, and I can see you have your hands full, without me being an added liability." She added, "Don't think I'm not grateful for all you have done, but I feel as though I need to rest after the trauma of the last couple of days. Please tell Janet I like to come back when everything had calmed down."

Roy's mother watched her son's face as she spoke; she could see he was worried about something and how would he manage that boat without two of his crew; she knew Janet was hopeless with boats; she had the children to worry about. After thinking about it, she suggested to Roy,

"I know you will be short-handed, and I don't want Shilpa to miss out. I'll fly to London with Fiona and make my way home from there."

Shilpa protested, but Mrs Croft had made up her mind, and she was adamant nothing Roy could say or do would change it. Roy helped Shilpa to calm his mother down; they eventually got her into bed, and Roy, under protest, finally agreed to her request.

"I'll book you on the flight, but I do not know what Janet will say when she hears what I have agreed to let you do," Roy said as he tucked his mother into bed.

When she had settled down, Roy followed Shilpa into her adjoining room.

The door had not even closed when Shilpa looked at Roy and whispered softly,

"This is the first chance I have had to be alone with you since I arrived. Oh God! You have no idea how frustrated and worried I have been all this time."

Shilpa's excitement with being alone with Roy sent adrenalin coursing through her veins. Roy who until that moment had given scant thought to sex, but the infectious mood pushed the traumatic events of the last few hours to the back of his mind. His own need rose to the surface, his embrace becoming increasingly passionate, brought on by the evocative and unfettered mood of his companion. In the next room, Roy's mother lay listening to the sound of their lovemaking. She shook her head sadly wondering how her son could be such a philanderer. She had over the years come to realise how he behaved with women; as far as she could fathom, she believed he was capable of having sex with any woman he became acquainted with. Roy's father had never been like that; she wondered where Roy's seemingly insatiable sex drive had come from. He was married to a wonderful person in Janet; they had two lovely children, but it seemed to Mrs Croft that her son belonged to a different generation; she wondered if her son's wild passions could never be assuaged. Roy's mother was still shaking her head when she heard Shilpa cry out as she reached her peek, and then, thankfully, it went quiet, and the older woman fell into a troubled sleep.

Lord Croft and his slim Indian companion lay unmoving for a few minutes before Roy slipped from her embrace; he had almost forgotten how good in bed young Shilpa was, but the lustful session had once again reawakened the memories of far-off days. Lord Croft knew only too well that his love life was by this stage so complicated. *Did I really need to complicate it anymore?* He asked himself. He would have to see how things panned out over the next few days. Just as he was leaving, Shilpa called out softly,
"When will I see you again?"
"Soon," Roy replied.
As Roy was walking through the hotel lobby, the idea his mother had given him had struck a chord. With Fiona and Gael away, he would need a crew, especially if he had to do another run to Colombia. He would speak to Elian about Madeleine and Shilpa coming on as temporary crew members.

The concierge called Roy a cab, and he was driven back towards the High Commissioner's residence, where Lady Jayne and Madeleine together with his family were patiently awaiting his return. Madeleine had heard the car and had hurried to relieve the domestic of the need to announce his arrival, and as the man left, she gave Lord Croft a kiss on the lips, a kiss that was full of promise of more to follow. Madeleine led him into the drawing room where Sir Martin, Lady Jayne, and Janet sat talking quietly. Roy was handed a drink by the ever-attentive Madeleine, and after being pressed for more information about Gael's condition, he sat down to begin his story.

"We had been chartered to go and pick up a party from the Venezuelan coast and transport them to Cuba for a holiday and a visit to the casino," Roy said tongue-in-cheek, the lie coming easily to his lips. "The charter was quite legitimate and above board, and we were returning after dropping off our passengers, and let me add, we were well out of the limits of any Venezuelan jurisdiction."

Roy could see the rage and distress on Sir Martin's face that such atrocities had been perpetrated against a British citizen who happened to be a Lord. Roy continued to explain what had happened when they had left the island of Blanquilla and the patrol boat had informed them that they had trespassed into a restricted area. Roy described how he had been handcuffed to the ship's rail and had been forced to watch the captain and his crew rape the three women until they were too tired to continue and had then cut them free to drift onto the treacherous reefs in that part of the world.

The group who had listened patiently to Lord Croft's explanation sat open-mouthed as they absorbed the facts and were struck awe and horror. Sir Martin commented,

"I had heard rumours of barbarous acts of piracy by some Venezuelan patrol boats, but this is the worst case I have heard of."

Roy waited until everyone had calmed down before continuing,

"Gael, despite her injuries, helped me to save the boat from certain destruction, but I fear the tragedy of her losing her child seems to have had such a devastating effect on her mentally." He added, "We radioed for help and were assisted by a cruise liner, which was only thirty miles away. They gave medical assistance and took Gael and Elian to the nearest port. There both crew members had to be operated on to repair the damage caused by the vicious rape carried out by the Venezuelan captain and officers. Then to crown it all, when we got back to Mustique, Gael was attacked by some hobo, and when we found her, she was in the sad state you saw her when we arrived."

Sir Martin was incensed and, if it had not been for Roy's urgent protestations he was all for relaying the details to the foreign office for an official protest to be made to the Venezuelan government. He went on to say,

"It has been reported that the Venezuelans have been having more than their fair share of problems in that area; they claim that one of their aircraft had gone down, sinking one of their patrol boats and have requested assistance from the Americans to send a team to try and discover how the accident happened, and to cap that, another of their patrol boats has apparently been lost with all hands."

He suddenly stopped speaking and looked hard at Roy.

"You would not know anything about that, would you, Lord Croft?" he enquired.

Roy shook his head.

"No," Roy lied glibly, "one incident happened before we were in the area and the other after we had left. We did see an aircraft searching, but we were too far away to turn and offer assistance, especially with a sick crew. We had to anchor for a few days to let the poor ladies recover and have a chance to settle down before returning home."

Sir Martin nodded, but he wondered; *it was all a bit of a coincidence, and Roy and his charming lady crew members all looked very fit, and, under normal circumstances, they looked as though they were more than capable of looking after themselves.* But confirmation of that thought, he would never have, despite his unfounded suspicions. Roy and Sir Martin sat discussing the various politics of the area well into the night when Sir Martin finally took his leave from his guest and retired.

Roy was deep in thought as he began to make his way towards the guest cottage when Madeleine suddenly appeared and pulled him back into the house.

"I thought you two were never going to go to bed," she whispered, "but I'm glad I have you to myself now. Come with me."

Madeleine led Roy up the stairs to her bedroom, where she quickly made it clear what was on her mind. It was very late when Roy slid into the shower; he knew better than to let Janet sense he had been with Madeleine. The house was silent around him as Roy made his way downstairs to the side door. He walked silently across the gardens and into the guest residence. Climbing the stairs quietly, he slipped into the master bedroom where he undressed and slid quietly into bed. He was careful not to disturb Janet and was asleep in seconds.

The following morning Roy was up early; Janet was sound asleep as he dressed and walked across the garden. The idea of Shilpa and Madeleine coming with him on the next charter was becoming a fixation, and he had to discuss the idea with Elian as she would have to teach the new crew how to handle whatever was thrown at them. He crossed to the main residence to be met by Lady Jayne; she smiled knowingly.

"Good morning, Roy," she said brightly. "I know you were with Madeleine last night. I heard you. Did she tell you I was pregnant? I'm sure it was that last day we were together. Sir Martin was overjoyed at the news, at first, but I think he is not so sure now. The thought of young babies and nappies at his age is a bit worrying. Come with me, I want to show you something before breakfast," and she pulled him into the office.

Lady Jane showed him a letter from MI5 surveillance division. It was marked 'Top Secret'. The gist of the message was that certain surveillance tapes in the hands of our agents who had recently been in the Bahamas had gone missing, and it asked if Sir Martin would check to see if they may have inadvertently been left behind when the team was recalled to London. The whole team apparently had disappeared under mysterious circumstances, and the writer was anxious to locate these tapes as a matter of national security. The missive ended *'Please treat this matter as most urgent'*. Lady Jayne showed Roy the reply that had been sent, on behalf of Sir Martin, indicating that no tapes or documents of any kind could be found either in the High Commission offices or the residency occupied by the agents during their brief stay on station. The final notation made Roy smile; it said,

"If we can be of any further assistance in this matter, please let Sir Martin know. Otherwise, he would consider the matter closed."

Lady Jayne put the documents back into the safe and, turning to face him, reached up and kissed him, and it was no casual kiss reserved for visitors; this was a kiss full of passion and wild promise.

"I know what I promised when I made our agreement," She whispered, "but I had no idea what I was letting myself in for. Is it too much me to ask for more, like Oliver did? I only hope I won't get the same reaction as he did from Mr Beadle."

Roy inwardly sighed; Lady Jayne had been such a prim person, not quite a maid, but very inexperienced when he had agreed to get her pregnant. He had not bargained for this. His life was getting so complicated he had to take control or he could end in serious trouble.

"Lady Jayne, you are beautiful, and the bloom of pregnancy in your cheeks makes you positively enchanting," Roy whispered, "but do you think this is wise when you have staff nearby? I think we should wait for a more appropriate time to cuckold Sir Martin, once again, don't you? Especially when he is in residence and as much as I would love to take you up on your offer. Perhaps we could try later when he is out on official business. I would not want to rush such a pleasure. I don't have much time. I have to take my mother and Gael to the airport. If I were to send her to the by official car without going with her, I would never hear the last of it from my mother or Janet."

He bent and put his arms around Lady Jayne's waist and, drawing her close, returned the kiss with a passion that had her cheeks glowing with excitement.

"Oh God," Jayne whispered, "don't keep me waiting too long, will you? I never thought I would feel like this about anyone. Hurry back, please. Oh my goodness, I sound like a lovesick teenager." The latter part of the sentence was said quietly almost to herself.

Releasing her from his grip, Lord Croft waited for Lady Jayne as she checked in the mirror on her compact; then reapplying her lipstick and touching a few curls back into place, she nodded when she was satisfied with the result. She preceded Roy out of the office and rejoined Janet and Madeleine in the breakfast room; both of them looked at the flush in Lady Jayne's cheeks, and both suspected that she had been doing more than just discussing business in the secluded confines of her official office.

The private flight to London was due out later that morning, and they all went to see the departure of Fiona, Gael, the nurse, and Roy's mother as they left. Gael had been tranquilised and had looked more relaxed as she had boarded the aircraft. When the party had left, and Lord Croft had dropped his wife back at the residency, he returned to the boat and asked Elian what she thought about his idea. To his surprise, she accepted the idea of two women joining the crew, saying,

"I'll take them on with pleasure, but only if they agree to train for two weeks with me. I would much prefer them to the island sailors. I have seen they have absolutely no discipline and seem to loll about smoking pot, what they term as *ganja*. If both of them are willing to train hard, ask them to join me tomorrow morning. It's now well after lunch and you and I have some serious catching up to do, and there's no one about to disturb us. Why do you think I opted for staying aboard?"

When Roy left the boat, he wondered how things would go if the changes he had planned in the new crew went ahead. How would Shilpa and Madeleine fit in with Elian's idea of a rota? He realised that life would be somewhat unpredictable on this trip. As he headed back, he hoped Lady Jayne was too busy with other things to want his dedicated attention that evening as he felt too drained.

He decided he would go for a walk along the beach for an hour to rest, relax, and get his strength back. It was later than he thought when he returned, he slipped into the guest house, and there was no sign of Janet. Morag came in with the children who ran and hugged their daddy before Morag hustled them off for their bath. The gong had gone when he arrived, but Madeleine, dutiful as ever, poured him a drink before they entered the dining room. They were alone as he took a drink from the generous measure she had poured him, and taking the opportunity, he asked if she would be interested in his idea of temporarily becoming one of his crew. Madeleine kissed him politely on the cheek saying,

"Roy, my father has tried to wrap me up in cotton wool since I went missing. All I can say in the circumstances is, if my father has no objections, I will be more than happy to go with you as one of your crew. I'm sure it will give us more opportunities to develop our need for each other," she giggled.

Letting him take her arm, Lord Croft, with a grin on his face, escorted her into the dining room.

They were late, and Sir Martin did not look too pleased at the delay. Roy sat at the table and, as the wine was being poured, looked at Sir Martin,

"Oh, by the way," Sir Martin, Roy said as casually as he could, "as you know two of my crew had to go to England and I could well have another charter coming up, would you mind if I took Madeleine with me on that trip? She was so helpful after we had rescued her, and she seemed so at home at sea."

Lady Jayne almost choked on her wine, but she recovered admirably, and before her surprised husband could reply,

"Oh, darling," she said to Sir Martin, "isn't that a wonderful idea? I'm sure Madeleine would enjoy that tremendously. I'm sure all that sea air would do her the world of good, don't you?"

Sir Martin looked enquiringly at his daughter and said,

"I hope there will be no repetition of the trouble on Lord Croft's last voyage. I'm sure he will steer clear of any Venezuelan patrols." Seeing Roy nod his head in agreement, he added, "Thus assured that Lord Croft will take great care of you, all I can ask is, would you like to go with his Lordship, my dear?"

Madeleine's enthusiastic response surprised everyone, including Janet.

"Oh yes, please, Daddy. I know I would enjoy that more than anything else. I just love it aboard that lovely boat. It's so stimulating."

The smile that followed left Janet in no doubt that young Madeleine was looking forward more than just the voyage as she was hoping to be the object of Roy's attentions.

Roy then turned to Shilpa and said,

"There is a place for you too, Shilpa, with Fiona away. Would you like to join us as well?"

Janet noticed the eager nod of Shilpa's head, and she wondered how he managed to cope with all three of them on board. Janet thought she would love to be a fly on the wall, just to see how her oversexed husband coped. She thought to herself, *I hope Michael comes for a visit whilst he's away. I just know now that Mark is no longer in the picture, we could get together just for old times' sake*, and she felt herself blush at the prospect. The next few days saw Lord Croft, with Lady Jayne's help; find a furnished property for Janet to occupy, whilst he was away. Lady Jayne was only too pleased to help Lord Croft in his search, and in the confines of an empty property, Roy made good his promise to Lady Jayne, much to her delight and satisfaction. It seemed providential when the Mafia family contacted him again, shortly after he had finalised a deal on one of the larger properties, asking him to do a second charter similar to the first, emphasising that it would be the last one they would need him to undertake for the time being. But they understood he would be contacted by another group situated in Colombia who were also keen on chartering the boat.

Roy was happier leaving Janet under the watchful eye of Lady Jayne; he felt she would be safer with her than returning to the island of Mustique, where the Mafia influence was high. The training and acclimatisation of his two new crew members according to Elian was going well. Madeleine was developing into a natural sailor, and surprisingly, her knowledge of mechanics was excellent; Shilpa was an excellent cook; she had quickly adjusted to the tiny galley, and its restricted space had proved no deterrent to her skills. The weaponry training would have to come later when they were out at sea, and neither Roy nor Elian knew how Shilpa would handle that; Madeleine was well aware of the armaments carried aboard as she had seen them in action before. Roy saw to it that Janet was well settled before he left with his new crew; he had left a few days earlier than planned as both of Madeleine and Shilpa had to go through the ritual of learning how to use the weapons secreted on board. Shilpa was a little shaken when Roy had taken her below to show her the hidden armoury, and she had asked in awe,

"Goodness me, Lord Croft, what line of business are you in?"

"The charter business," Roy replied then he added, "In this part of the world, chartering can and often is a very dangerous trade to be in, and we have had to fend off pirates on more than one occasion."

Roy went on to tell Shilpa in detail about how they had been boarded and his crew raped, and suddenly she became as enthused as Madeleine to have Elian teach her how to defend herself and the boat. The next week was idyllic with them anchored off the same atoll as the previous trip; except that then, he had had three traumatised women to help, while this time he had three healthy young women to contend with. Elian ensured all were fully protected from falling pregnant, and their time spent in training was supplemented with more enjoyable entertainment during the hours of darkness. It seemed to all that the few days went by far too quickly; the idyllic days ended all too soon for Roy, the crew were fully trained and ready for the long trip. Resigned to the need to complete his obligation they set out for the rendezvous point on the coast of Colombia.

Chapter 12

On this journey, Roy avoided the Venezuelan islands and headed directly for Curaçao, where they anchored for the night. There was no rush this time, and Roy felt a good night's rest would refresh them all before setting out early for the rendezvous with the fishing boat. They all felt up to the challenge as they headed out towards the co-ordinates, always keeping a watch on the radar for patrols; even as they approached the spot, they could see the fishing boat with its nets over the stern trawling. Roy looked and remarked to Elian,

"The captain of that boat is either in the wrong place or they are not paying him enough; if he has to legitimately fish to make a living."

Elian looked through the glasses as they approached and, with a broad smile, replied,

"No, he's just shrewd. He has his nets out, but, I'll bet, it's been a while since he caught any fish. There's no sign of him having caught anything recently or of his crew being in a position to receive any catch."

Roy gave the call sign, which was answered promptly; the skipper of the fishing boat signalled for Roy to come alongside, and Elian confirmed there was no sign that any fish had either been caught or been loaded aboard the fishing boat in a long time. The captain of the Colombian-registered boat signalled to his crew, and they grabbed the ropes as they were thrown; once the two boats were secure, he jumped aboard the cruiser and shook Roy's hand and offered him a cigar, which Roy politely refused.

"You like my disguise?" the captain of the fishing boat asked with a hollow laugh. "We have been warned of increased patrols in the area, and so we had to look legitimate. Now let's get this stuff aboard, and I can go back empty-handed. All the local fishermen are struggling. There's less and less fish in the area, so I won't be on my own." He laughed as he said, "But I will be smiling I'll not be the one hungry tonight."

The two crews worked hard getting the packets from the hold of the fishing boat aboard Roy's cruiser and packed them away in the hidden spaces below. The captain, typical of the men in the area, was dark and handsome with a dark moustache on his upper lip. He looked a hard case;

he smiled as Roy handed him the bag containing the money, and he put it uncounted in the small cabin on the fishing boat.

"Don't you want to check that it's all there?" Roy asked.

"Señor, if it's not," he snarled cynically, drawing his hand across his throat, "I would not want to be in your shoes. The men who buy from us have done so for many years they know us and we know them all. The only new person in this chain is you. It will all be there, I'm sure of that," he said once again giving a hollow laugh.

Roy had long since realised that in this game, you played by the rules or you were no longer a player; the Colombians were too powerful to be crossed. The dark-skinned, weather-beaten captain looked at Roy's crew. Elian, Madeleine, and Shilpa had worked hard alongside the swarthy fishermen.

"I see you have only women in your crew? They have worked well, but if the patrols catch you, would they be of any benefit other than as a distraction?" he asked Roy.

His eyes were wide open, the evil intention of his thoughts easily recognisable in his face and those of his crew as he eyed each of them; letting his gaze ride over the shape of each woman lustfully, imagining each and every one of the three lying naked on his bed. Elian spotted the stare and the inferred intention; it had not been long since she had been raped, the memory still strong in her memory; without any warning, she drew the knife from under her skirt and threw it in his direction. The captain flinched and swallowed as it embedded itself in the frame of the doorway. The weapon had missed his cheek by such a narrow margin that he had to check that he was not cut. Elian leapt aboard the fishing boat, retrieved the weapon, then, turning in his direction, put her face close to his, and whispered, almost vehemently,

"Oh, I don't think he has much to worry about there, Captain. We know how to look after each other aboard our boat."

The captain was shaken by the look on her face, and he whispered,

"I meant no harm, Señorita. Forgive my joke. It will not happen again."

The tension went out of the situation as Elian laughed and gave the captain a kiss on the cheek.

"Looks are not always what they seem, Señor," she said with a grin, "you, of all people, should remember that."

She patted him on the back and jumped back aboard the cruiser, and Roy smiled with relief. The crew aboard the Colombian fishing boat cast off, and as the gap between the two boats widened, they waved. Roy opened the throttles; before giving the trawler a wide berth, he headed back in the direction of Curaçao.

It was late when they arrived in the harbour, but the town of Willemstad was still busy; the crew had gone ashore to get fresh supplies leaving Roy alone. When they returned, Roy went ashore to stretch his legs and get a present for Janet and Sean. He wandered aimlessly from shop to shop, in a mood of expectancy. He had no idea why his mood was so strange; it was almost as if he knew something was going to happen. Then just as he was leaving one of the gift stores, he almost bumped into one of the doctors who had been on duty when he had brought Elian and Gael to the hospital for treatment. The doctor looked so surprised to see him, and when Roy asked her to join him for coffee, she readily accepted. They sat and talked for some time; she asked about his crew and was pleased to hear that Elian and Fiona had recovered but was sorry to hear that Gael was suffering from post-traumatic distress disorder. Roy told her what had happened and that he had sent her back to England for treatment. The conversation with the attractive young doctor was easy and informal, and as the evening grew later, Roy discovered that she was originally from Holland and her name was Helga. She was buoyant, talking most of the time, enjoying being in the presence of an English Lord, and it came to light that she was in the Antilles on a three-year contract which was due to finish in the next few weeks, but she informed him she had no intention of returning to Holland as she wished to remain in the Caribbean. The coffee was replaced by a locally brewed alcoholic drink, and they sat and talked for several hours. Eventually the café wanted to close and as neither felt tired, and it was Helga who invited Roy to come up to her nearby flat for a nightcap.

Roy agreed; then after arranging with the café owner, for the use of one of his staff, he had had the parcels delivered to the quayside, so he was not burdened with his purchases. He went up to a simply furnished one-roomed flat and sat on the bed whilst Helga poured him a large whisky and the same island concoction she had drunk in the café for herself. After they had consumed a number of drinks and as the hour grew very late, Helga sat beside him and began openly flirting with him. She had begun by sitting down demurely, opposite him, and sipped her drinks, but during the course of her drinking and flirting, the atmosphere had become charged with the impending and inevitable sexuality. Both of them knew what was going to happen, neither of them wanting to make the first move. Helga rose to ask if he wanted another drink, and he got up quickly saying he would get them. They collided, and, in seconds, she was in his embrace and time stood still. Roy's head dipped down towards the much shorter doctor and his lips kissed her mouth, gently but firmly, and there was no urgency in his kiss, they had what remained of the night. No one had ever made her feel like this; she never had made love to anyone on the first date, and this had not even been a date; by surrendering to Lord Croft's obvious skills, she felt a wonderful glow pervading through her whole body.

Dawn came early and Helga lay half-awake; she had broken her own rules and realised she could well live to regret it. She felt the man beside her stir, and moments later, he sat up and looked at his watch, realising it was almost morning; the crew would wonder where he had been; he sat up, trying to reconcile where he was and who he was with. He asked for the bathroom, and Helga pointed to the door. Roy showered and dressed; he apologised, saying he was sorry, but he had to leave. He told Helga he hated to leave so suddenly, but that he was on his way to Cuba on a charter. He assured her he would call in to visit her, if it were at all possible, on his return. Helga had to get to the hospital; she would have to hurry or she would also be late, or she would have loved to persuade him to stay. She had never been so emotionally satisfied in her entire life. She only knew her new-found lover as Lord Roy Croft; she had no idea where he lived or anything else about him. Roy, on the other hand, only knew her as Helga, the Dutch doctor working at the hospital on a contract.

Helga slid from under the covers and, opening her bag, found her business card pressing it in Lord Croft's hand, and only when he turned to leave, did she realise she was wearing nothing but a smile.
"Ring me when you come back," she called as he opened the door.
Roy nodded and the door closed behind him; he was gone. Helga lay on the bed; she had fallen under the spell of a very attractive Englishman; how she was ever going to reconcile the enormity of what she had done with her conscience, she had no idea; she could not decide whether she wanted to see him again or not. She looked at the time, realising she had to shower and dress and get to work, but she seemed somewhat lethargic, lost in her own thoughts. This morning, she recognised that, she would be late arriving for her clinic, which for her would be yet another first.

Roy raced down to the quayside; the crew were looking for him worried in case he had been attacked or worse had been killed. Racing up the gangway, he jumped aboard the boat and apologised for his absence, casually he told his crew that he had met an old acquaintance and had been drinking before either of them realised it had been morning. Roy had showered before leaving, and all three women knew what that usually signified; they looked at each other and shook their heads. Elian could not restrain her inquisitiveness with a smile as she enquired,

"We don't believe it was anything casual, Roy. Now where have you been all night, and knowing you as I do, I have to ask who was she?"

Roy somewhat shame-faced replied,

"I can assure you that it was a casual meeting. I bumped into Helga, the doctor who treated you and Gael at the hospital."

Elian remembered her as a short Dutch woman, who she would not have thought would have been Roy's first choice as a companion for the night; she had not seemed that sort of woman, a little too aloof, if Elian remembered correctly.

"We just sat talking," Roy explained, "drinking the local brew, and when it got to closing time, I simply accepted her invitation to go back for coffee and a nightcap."

All three crew members were indignant; Roy was shaken as all three began speaking at once asking why he had not rang to say he would not be back, informing him of their concern that something may have happened to him. In truth, all three were grateful that he had not spent the night in a brothel, where he may have got infected and subsequently he could have infected them all. They scolded him, but the whole thing was soon forgotten as they prepared to get under way heading for Cuba.

When several hours had gone by, Elian came up to relieve Roy at the wheel; she was obviously in the mood to play. Roy was not too keen to comply; he was still recovering from his night ashore with Helga. Elian seemed more insistent than usual, she had brought up his hip flask; to appease her, and after Roy had taken a drink from the flask he locked the wheel and drew her into his arms. They kissed and embraced; they were, after all, well off the normal shipping lanes and their attention was not on the unexpected change in the weather. There was a sudden gust of wind, and the boat began to pitch wildly. They broke their embrace and looked up; the sky had darkened; in minutes, storm clouds were scudding towards them from the horizon, and the swell had come up from nowhere, and white topped waves could be seen for miles. It looked as though they were in for a bad time.

"Where the hell has this come from?" Elian gasped as she said hurriedly, "There was no warning of this on the earlier forecast?" She rushed to the companionway and called back, "I'll go below and listen for the storm warning to see what we are in for."

Roy took over the control of the boat and headed into the wind, reducing the speed. Elian came up the steps with a grave look on her face.

"It's a hurricane warning," she said a look of concern on her face. "The damned thing suddenly changed direction and is heading our way. We are almost in the midpoint of our journey and have no place to hide. I've ordered Shilpa and Madeleine to batten down everything. I'll go and supervise, and you switch to the lower controls, with what's impending, it would be better for me to take over control from there. I would suggest that you batten down everything you can up here. We will have no alternative but to ride it out. I'll see you below as soon as you have finished, believe me Roy I think this storm is really going to test Granville's work."

Roy looked up, the boat was still pitching, as he switched the control to the lower wheelhouse and locked and battened down everything he could. It would be useless putting up the cover in a hurricane; it would be swept away in an instance. When Roy got below, the storm winds had risen to a howl. The main storm was still way off, but the wind's speed according to Elian's estimate was already over 100 mph. Both had the same thought that they could not outrun it, and under normal circumstances, they would not dare to ride it out, far bigger boats had perished trying that. Roy and Elian looked at each other with the knowledge that they had no alternatives; Elian crossed herself and muttered,

"May God be with us!"

The direction of the storm was the clue to safety. This storm had suddenly, and without warning, changed its course, and the shipping forecasters were predicting the course the storm would take but the behaviour of the storm was so unpredictable that they could not be certain.

The decks had to be cleared of all things that could rip free and damage the structure. The waves were now some thirty feet high. Madeleine called out as she had seen something in the waves; she pointed in the direction of the object she had seen. Elian checked and she spotted something on the radar scope, but could not make it out. It must be some wreckage carried by the wind and dumped into the sea. Elian tried in vain to manoeuvre away from whatever it was; Roy and Madeleine, who were by now both roped to prevent them being washed overboard, made their way back towards the entrance to the cabin. When suddenly, the prow dipped down into the next trough, Roy pulled Madeleine back towards the cabin door and dragged her inside. Elian had turned west and opened the throttles. The boat leapt forward towards the next crest when the wreckage, which seemed to be some kind of metal fuel tank, apparently now almost full of water, seemed to be flicked up in the air by the crest of the wave to the south. It hurtled towards them. Elian had spotted it and swung the craft around to try to avoid it, but it was too late. The tank smashed into the flying deck, taking the upper windscreen with it and wrecking the upper steering mechanism. The boat heeled over to the port side, the weight of the tank almost dragging them under; they all thanked God for his deliverance as the tank wrenched itself free and slid down into the sea.

The cruiser, free from the downward drag, righted itself and continued to run west. Roy looked up but could not see how bad the damage was. Elian spoke grimly,

"If we can maintain this speed, we can be able to stay on the fringe of the storm, provided the forecasted course does not change again. I fear that if we get in the path of the main storm, we will have no chance we will be swamped."

Shilpa looked scared; she had never been at sea in a storm, let alone a hurricane. Madeleine helped by consoling her; but even running from the storm, the seventy-three-foot cruiser was thrown about like a cork. The forecast was that the storm would turn towards Haiti, and Elian was racing in the direction of Jamaica. If the forecast was wrong, they may still have to ride out the main force of the storm.

They were grateful that they had no sails or masts to worry about, and the water was not running into the main cabin from the damaged flying deck. Roy checked that the bilge pumps were coping with the water running down the hatchway, thankful that at least the hull was still watertight. The sky grew darker; as the storm approached, they were now riding up waves towering high above them, and after cresting the top, they were plunged down into the trough sixty feet below. Everyone had life preservers on and waterproofs even though the inside of the craft was dry. The original screen fitted in the lower wheelhouse during Second World War had been incorporated in the new design and was holding against the buffeting wind. Roy heard a groan and saw part of the upper bridge ripped away. They were in big trouble and without Elian's experience, on the fishing fleet; Roy did not believe they would have any chance of survival. She handled the boat strapped to the lug points embedded in the original old MTB woodwork; the harness enabled her to stand at the wheel even though the boat was being tossed about. They battled for some five hours, still heading for Jamaica, when Elian called to them that the storm had turned and the wind had started to fall.

"Thank God, she yelled, crossing herself in the style of all Catholics, "I think we are going to make it after all," she added, looking upwards.

The battered craft finally made the calmer waters and the cruiser now much the worse for wear moved into Kingston harbour, where they would finally assess the full extent of the damage.

The front of the flying deck, including the windscreen and the steering, was smashed and the port side of the bridge had been ripped away in the wind. The main structure had held, and from what Roy could see, it looked as though the damage could be repaired by a skilled boatyard. They were miles away from Granville, and Roy was uncertain about the local boat yards' capability to carry out the repairs to the standard he required. After he had conversed with several yards, and after they had inspected the damage done to Roy's boat, each one informed him glibly that they could do the repairs without any problem. Roy was concerned about their competence to repair the cruiser and went ashore to ring Granville to ask his advice; Granville was so pleased to hear from his old friend Lord Croft, despite the circumstances under which they had parted. Roy asked about Kirsty, and Granville replied,

"I would have told you sooner had I have known where you were. Kirsty had a boy. We have called him Granville, Jr."

The pleasantries over, Roy explained his problems: how the cruiser had been damaged by some flotsam and how the storm had taken care of the rest,

"I'm sure if it had not been for your workmanship, Roy added, "We would not have survived."

"Thanks for the compliment, Roy," Granville replied. "Send photographs by email. There must be someone local who can help. I'll look at and try to assess the damage for myself, and as soon as I have looked at the evidence, I'll send you my comments and suggestions."

The following day, Granville sent detailed drawings of the repairs to be carried out. He was concerned that the locals may botch the job unless supervised carefully, and he offered to fly out and see that the work was completed correctly. Roy glad of Granville's offer agreed.

Lord Croft quickly booked the flight and rang Granville to inform him of the flight number and arranged to meet him when he arrived.

"Thanks for that, Roy," Granville said. He then added, "Oh, when Kirsty heard I was coming to the West Indies to see you, she insisted on accompanying me. She has somehow persuaded her mother to look after Granville, Jr, and she will be coming with me. How could I refuse? I will of course meet the costs of her ticket myself, and the two of us will hopefully be with you ASAP. I think she deserves the break. It will be a holiday for her."

Lord Croft rang the hotel and confirmed the double-booking.

The following evening, Granville and Kirsty arrived; Granville went down to the harbour in the evening and winced at the extensive damage to the cruiser's superstructure.

"I rang several boatyards from England," he told Roy, "and a small yard owned by an ex-navy man, who decided to move here after the Falklands, impressed me the most. I suggest we go along and see him first thing in the morning."

Roy, having flown Granville out to supervise the repairs, had no hesitation in accepting Granville's judgement. Roy took Granville and Kirsty for supper before going back to sleep aboard the damaged cruiser; there was no way he could leave the boat unsecured with all the drugs aboard. The three crew members had elected to stay aboard as well. Privacy in the badly damaged cruiser, however, was at a premium, so Roy slept alone. Roy's primary concern other than the damage was the security of his cargo and how he would be able to let any boatyard carry out the repairs without discovering the hidden lockers containing the arms and the drugs.

The day afterwards, it was early in the morning, when Roy showered and headed off to the hotel, Granville sat alone in the dining room. Roy joined him for breakfast, and they took a taxi to the boatyard. The yard was well away from the usual repair places, and from the number of boats in for repair, it did not look a very popular venue. The yachts that lay berthed were mainly wooden, and the quality of the work looked excellent. They

THE CROFT'S IN THE AMERICA'S

found 'Taffy' under a forty-foot yacht repairing the planking. He looked up and saw the two of them and asked,

"Which of you two is Granville?"

Granville identified himself and introduced Lord Croft before explaining the problem, and Taffy called a young worker and gave him instruction on how to continue. Roy was impressed by the way Taffy watched the young man's face to ensure he understood his instructions perfectly before leaving him to get on with the job in hand. They climbed into Taffy's truck and headed for the main harbour. During the journey, Roy asked Taffy something that had been bothering him from the moment he had entered the yard.

"Taffy, the yard does not seem very busy. I would have thought you would have been overwhelmed with work after that storm? From what I could see of your work, it seemed excellent to me, so what's the story?"

"I'm not trying to get rich, your Lordship," Taffy replied. "I make enough for me and my missus to get by, and I only work on wooden boats. These new plastic and fibreglass boats drive me insane. I prefer the old wooden craftsmen made hulls to this precast method of making boats. They have no soul."

Turning into the dock, Taffy saw Roy's cruiser, his eyes lit up, and he said, not trying to hide the obvious excitement in his voice,

"She's an original MTB hull, nice conversion, is that your work he asked Granville who nodded. What happened to the superstructure?" Taffy asked as an afterthought

Roy explained how the wrecked tank had appeared from nowhere in the storm and had been whipped up in the air by a freak wave and had hit the upper bridge. He added,

"We were lucky. If the tank had hit us on the lower wheelhouse, it could have sunk us for sure. On top of which, we had already lost the tender. It was ripped off the davits by the storm. If it had not been for the experience of my skipper, I'm sure we would have died out there. It was the very devil trying to keep her afloat."

Taffy, his hand cupping his chin, nodded in agreement.

"It will take a week or so, and it will be expensive. I'll have to cut back to solid timber before I can even begin," he said with a broad Welsh accent.

Granville handed him the plans he had drawn up, and Taffy looked at them carefully and nodded his head methodically as he studied the detail. Looking at Granville, he said,

"I can work with a guy like you. You know what you're about."
The three women appeared at the door of the lower wheelhouse, and Roy said,

"Let me introduce you to my crew, Elian the skipper and the two hands are Shilpa and Madeleine."

Taffy's eyes opened wide.

"The four of you brought her through the hurricane yourselves. I'm very impressed, your Lordship," he said, and looking at Roy, he whispered, "and you're a very lucky man."

Taffy did a preliminary inspection of the damage, making notes, and when he had finished, he followed up by saying,

"Well, I'll drive back with Granville here, if your Lordship will bring the boat round to the yard. I'll have rough estimates ready for when you arrive." Then he added "Let me show your skipper on the map exactly where we are."

Elian took the helm, steering the damaged craft out of the harbour, and when she saw the entrance to Taffy's boatyard, she gently eased the cruiser towards the quayside. Taffy was there to meet them; he guided them between two quays and closed the dry dock doors behind the stern.

"I'd like to see her hull if I can, to make sure there's no damage below the waterline," Taffy said.

The water slowly began to be pumped out, lowering the boat down; he stopped the pumps and directed three of his workers into the water to place the supporting chocks under the keel. The water was then pumped out, and Taffy jumped down and admired the clean line of Roy's ex-MTB.

"She's in a lovely condition," he said. "I'd never have believed it possible. They don't build them like this today."

He climbed out, and he and Roy accompanied by Granville went into the office.

Roy agreed the price and gave the go-ahead, handing Taffy a cash deposit of US$5,000. Roy asked Taffy to send the estimate to his insurers, but he told him to start. Taffy was reluctant to begin without the assessor's agreement.

"Don't worry. If they raise any objection, I'll pay for the work myself. Speed is of the essence. I have a charter in Cuba, and I'm already late."

"Be it on your head, your Lordship." Taffy nodded and said, "I'll start the work immediately, but we had better take pictures of the damage now, and as I progress, some of these assessors can be very picky to say the least, and none of them like us to start before they have had their own look over the damage. On the other hand, my Lord, if you guarantee you'll pay the bill in case of difficulties, the work will commence immediately."

Lord Croft was reluctant to leave the boat completely in the hands of Taffy and his crew, no matter how honest he appeared. Roy knew the consequences if anything happened to the cargo, the delay due to the storm was bad enough, and it was Elian who offered to stay aboard. Leaving Granville to discuss the details of how Taffy and his crew should begin, Roy took the other two to a hotel nearby and booked them in telling them to collect what they needed from the boat for about three days. He sent a cable to the address the charter group had given him in case of an emergency telling them of the delay and the reason; they were singularly unimpressed, but they were pleased that they had come out of the storm without damage to the cargo. They asked to be kept informed of the progress to reschedule another delivery date.

Seeing there was little more he could do to assist. Roy took a taxi to the hotel where he had booked Granville and Kirsty. Walking through the hotel lobby, Lord Croft made himself known and asked for Granville's room number. The receptionist rang the room and informed Kirsty that a Lord Croft was asking to see her. The receptionist put down the phone and told Lord Croft to go up to Room 336 and pointed to the lift. Roy was met at the door by Kirsty; she looked the image of when he had first seen her at the boatyard; a time before he had known she was Granville's wife. Kirsty was blonde standing about five feet six with the deepest shade of green eyes; Roy had never been able to forget their lustre. Kirsty's long blonde hair still hung below her shoulders as she walked towards him with her arms out to embrace him. Roy could not avoid staring; Kirsty's more than ample breasts were highlighted by the deep cut of her blouse, and he could only admire how quickly she had regained her figure after the birth of her child. Roy embraced her, kissing her politely on her cheek, thinking to himself, *My God, I can hardly believe it, so soon after the birth, she looks as good as ever.* Kirsty noticed his admiring glance and smiled; then like the good hostess, she had always been, she offered Roy a drink.

"Tea, coffee, or as I recall from last time, you have a preference for something stronger."

Kirsty poured Roy a large Scotch and added a single cube of ice. Roy tossed back the fiery liquid, and Kirsty offered him another.

Kirsty invited Roy to sit on the bed and, openly flirting with him, sat beside him, her hands constantly touching his arm. She pulled him towards her and embraced him again, leaving no doubt in Roy's mind that she was inviting him to make love to her. Roy had remembered how he had enjoyed making love to her the last time and was not going to turn down the offer to repeat the experience. Kirsty had been uncontrollable; she had succumbed to the wild and uninhibited sex and to Roy delight her energy had seemed boundless. Until finally the lovers, or if Roy could put it another way, the combatants, lay still, both trying to control the urgent need to breath normally. Eventually, Roy got up off the bed, which looked as though a team of rugby players had practiced on it, and Roy's and Kirsty's clothes were strewn across the room. Roy walked into the shower and turned on the spray; the warm water washed all traces of his passionate episode from his body, and he felt satiated but tired after his encounter with the wild but lusty Kirsty, who was still lying splayed on the bed. He padded across the room and dressed before kissing the prone figure as she lay supine, oblivious to her ravaged body being displayed so lewdly to her lover, her eyes still closed enjoying the wonderful feelings which had subsided, but had left a lingering feeling of pure satisfaction.

"Thank you, you wicked, lecherous man," Kirsty whispered, "but don't go too far away, will you? I may need cossetting again, if you are so inclined to help a lady in distress, before I leave this island of love."

A few minutes later, she was sound asleep. Roy called a cab and went back to his own hotel, carefully avoiding his crew as he needed a well-earned rest.

Chapter 13

A week later, to the day, Granville and his wife flew out of Jamaica bound for London. Roy's insurance company Lloyds of London having an agent in Jamaica had given the all-clear on the repairs. Roy had change from Taffy after he had settled the excess on the claim. Taffy pulled him to one side and whispered,

"I see the torpedo tubes are still fully active on the old girl. Did you know, your Lordship?"

Roy nodded, and Taffy just winked; he did not want to know the reason or what Roy did with his boat for a living, or why the hull had been modified and locked compartments had been added within the confines of the hull. In that part of the world, it was sometimes better not to know; you lived longer. Taffy watched as the rest of Lord Croft's crew arrived, his eyes watching them board as he imagined all of them naked lying on the deck under the Caribbean sun. He felt himself respond at the very thought of what he could do to them, and he hurried home to his missus; thinking to himself that *he had not felt like this, for months*. Roy topped off the fuel tanks and headed out of Kingston before turning north towards Cuba.

The last few days had been hectic at the boatyard, but Roy had taken advantage of the spell away from the worries of command as he had visited Kirsty several times whilst Granville had been supervising the work on the boat. That was now behind him as it was back to work; they had to deliver the shipment safely or the consequences would be severe for all concerned. Elian opened the throttles; as soon as the boat was out of the harbour, she headed south until she could round Portland Point, and once out past the point, she headed west and then north to South Negril Point, then on to Cuba. The boat sped north, the co-ordinates had been communicated and the rendezvous had been set. As before, Roy was to hand over the raw drugs and receive the street-ready drugs and head towards the Bahamas, a comparatively long journey from the exchange rendezvous. They were to make their east up through the Windward Passage and along the northern Cuban coast to the rendezvous with the fast cigarette boats which would take the drugs to their final destination. Their task completed, Roy was still somewhat concerned about the American naval patrols; they would not be so easy to take care of as the Venezuelan patrols had been. The journey was easy, and he was heading south past Cat Island when a US Protector Class coastguard patrol boat came into view. Roy had nothing but the arms aboard, so he hove to and waited for the eighty-seven-foot patrol boat to pull alongside. The young American captain was polite and wanted to know their destination. Roy told him the cover story that he was holidaying around the Caribbean heading down towards the Leeward Islands on the way to pick up his family in Barbados.

The US coastguard captain requested Lord Croft to allow him aboard and asked if he could inspect the ship's log. Roy, not wishing to arouse suspicion in anyway, agreed to the young American captain's request. The captain opened the log and saw that they had been caught up in the hurricane and had put in to Jamaica for repairs, and he was about to make further enquiries as to a more detailed explanation for the purpose of their trip and where they were destined for. When Madeleine decided to take matters into her own hands, she was superb, it was almost as if she had been brought up to handle just such occasions. She approached the inquisitive, admittedly handsome young captain, explaining that she was the daughter of the British High Commissioner in Barbados, informing him that her father had chartered the boat and she was on a sightseeing holiday with Lord Croft and they were making their way back home. The young US naval officer could hardly take his eyes off Madeleine as she stood wearing a tiny bikini that barely covered where it touched. Roy taking advantage of the distraction asked the young captain if he needed to search the boat. The captain shook his head and apologised for any trouble and for any inconvenience or offence he may have caused. Then addressing Lord Croft, he wished him and his crew a safe voyage home and warned them that there were several storms out in the Atlantic heading for the West Indies and they should pay strict attention to the weather forecasts, requesting them to take shelter when advised to do so. He jumped back aboard the patrol boat, and Elian breathing a sigh of relief set off south. They took his advice and stayed the night anchored in Port-de-Paix before heading down towards the Virgin Islands.

The following morning, the weather was fine, and they were making excellent progress towards the Virgin Islands with Roy at the wheel. That, however, changed suddenly when Roy felt the engine note change; thick oily smoke began pouring from one of the exhaust ports; Roy shut down the motors, and the cruiser slowed immediately, gradually coming to a halt in the light swell. Then Elian feeling the cruiser's engines falter, followed by the cruiser slowing down, hurried down to the engine bay; reappearing sometime later to meet Roy on his way down to join her. Elian's face was streaked with oil, as were her hands.

"One of the engines has a major problem. It appears that the oil pump failed lowering the oil pressure. As a result, the turbo booster on that engine has also failed and the turbo was burning off the engine's oil. The engine will need to be taken out of service, and I will have to disconnect the drive shaft for that motor. Thank God it hadn't seized or it may well have damaged the drive shafts." She said crossing herself

Roy continued on his way below to lend a hand, and when the job was complete and they had cleaned up, Elian went back up to the upper controls and restarted the engines. There was thankfully no smoke coming from the remaining engines, but there was a noticeable drop in the power of the cruiser. They continued on their way at a slower pace on the reduced power deciding to head for Tortola, one of the British Virgin Islands.

Lord Croft contacted the port authorities and was allocated a berth in the 'Joma' Marina. After anchoring, Roy and the crew cleared customs and immigration and made enquiries about repairs, but it was obvious that although they could possibly get some spares for the older-type engines, there was no chance of locating a replacement engine or the latest type of turbocharger that had been fitted so recently. Roy made the decision that Elian would have to leave for Ireland, gain access to the workshop, where several new engines and a spare turbo booster were in the stockroom. Roy suggested that she arrange for a local trucking firm to collect the items from the castle and arrange to airfreight the engine and spare turbo before returning, Roy would arrange for a local mechanical engineer to assist with the refitting and testing of the replacement parts. Elian agreed, and her flight was booked for the following day, and later, as Roy climbed into bed, it was Elian that came to join him. She was due to leave for Ireland the following morning with Shilpa, who was to accompany her to Shannon before flying on to once again take up her duties as companion to Roy's mother. When Roy woke, both Shilpa and Elian had long since left, and as he turned to see who lay beside him, he was not surprised to find it was Madeleine.

A few days later, Elian rang from London and informed Roy that Shilpa had safely arrived at his mother's and had reported that the older woman was well. Elian informed Roy that she had been to visit the psychiatric hospital and that Gael was responding slowly to the treatment. The doctors had told her it would be months rather than weeks before she recovered and that Fiona was going along with Elian to arrange to ship the engine and turbo before they both returned to the Caribbean to repair the cruiser. Roy would soon have his full crew complement again and they would be able to return to his wife. Roy knew that would be a few days after the arrival of the new engine, and even though Madeleine was ensuring he was not short of company, in more ways than one, but despite having Madeleine on hand, Lord Croft missed his wife and was looking forward to seeing her and his two children once again.

Elian and Fiona arrived at the castle; the engines were situated at the rear of the boathouse, still accessible from above ground. They arranged with Stella that the transport would be arriving to pick up the spare engine and turbo the following day. Elian was surprised to see that Stella was pregnant, but made no comment; she would mention it to Roy on her return. The castle, it seemed to Elian, was a place where women got pregnant easily; she had no idea that the child Stella was carrying was in all probability Roy's; even if she had known, she would have accepted it as the normal, for Roy was very not only a Lothario but was also very fertile. Stella asked them to stay overnight, but both girls had family in the area and politely refused preferring to stay with family, but both said they would return the following day to supervise the loading and shipping of the spares. Once the engine and the turbo charger were consigned by airfreight to the Virgin Islands, the two women arranged to travel back to Barbados to see how Janet and the children were, prior to returning to the Virgin Islands to get the repairs under way and joining Roy and Madeleine.

Chapter 14

After Roy had left to go on what was ostensibly the last charter for the American connection, Janet had spent a considerable amount of time with her friend Lady Jayne; they went everywhere together, and the children loved their new aunty. Janet, however, grew restless after a time; Roy seemed to have been gone forever, and she knew his needs were being attended to by his crew; her needs, however, were driving her wild with frustration. Lady Jayne had confirmed that she was pregnant, and as time went by, to Lady Croft's dismay, there was still no sign of her wayward husband. Janet grew more and more frustrated, lying on the beach one morning with Morag watching over the children; it was therefore a pleasant relief when Michael, one of her ex-lovers from university, phoned to tell her that he was in port for a few days asking if they could meet and have dinner. Janet was thrilled to be able to meet Michael again, and she knew it was wrong, but her hormones were in control. Even though she had told Roy she would never have another extramarital affair, but she missed Roy so much; it had been weeks since she had had any male attention and, into the bargain, she was bored with her new relaxed way of life. Janet craved the attentions of a man, and she knew that Michael would cosset and flatter her, and she told him she would be delighted to go out to dinner with him that very evening.

Dr Michael Crosby had booked a room at the hotel in anticipation of a love tryst with Janet; whilst she had spent most of the afternoon preparing for her evening out, her hair had been done at the best salon in town, and she had bought a new dress, especially for the occasion. Her new underwear, she had to admit to herself, was a little racy to say the least. Finally, she was ready, and even Morag was surprised at how attractive she looked as she made her way to the door; she jokingly asked,

"If I did not know better, madam, I would ask who's the lucky man?"

Janet felt flattered by Morag's remark, it confirmed the way she felt about herself; Janet knew she looked good and meant to seduce Dr Michael. Rather than confide in the children's nanny, no matter how friendly they had become, she had just smiled.

"Oh, it's no one special." Janet replied, "I'm just meeting an old friend for dinner."

Although Morag had no real proof, Lady Croft's appearance belied her statement, Morag was no fool; if a woman dressed up like that, there had to be a man involved.

Arriving at the hotel, Michael had kissed Janet politely on the cheek, before they went through to the bar for a pre-dinner drink. Michael was so attentive, and he apologised for any upset he may have caused from their previous meeting, saying that Mark had forced him to do as he did and he had no explanation for what he and his buddies had done to her or indeed any explanation as to why they had done it. After several drinks, they went into the dining room, and Janet felt like a young woman again as she was once again transported back in time to her wild days at university. Any thoughts of her husband, Roy were forgotten as the compliments and attention continued to flow as Michael proceeded with his seduction of this rejuvenated and beautiful woman. Michael was unmarried, and the last time they had been together he had enjoyed making love to Janet, both in his hotel room and naked on the deck of his research boat. He thought to himself as the evening wore on that things were going well, and after they had swallowed their coffee, Michael invited Janet up to his room.

Once Michael had entered the room, he invited Janet to sit down whilst he got a couple of drinks from the bar; they enjoyed another drink, and Janet was feeling at that stage that the alcohol was having a wonderful effect on her; she was fully relaxed and had got to the stage where she wanted Michael to make a move on her. Michael was sitting on the only chair in the room, and Janet was sitting on his bed; she thought nothing of it when he moved over to the bed and sat beside her. Michael felt confident as he continued his with his determined seduction.

"I know I've told you several times how good you look in that dress, but I can't get over it. You look better than ever. I know it's some years since we were at university together, but the intervening years have matured you like a good wine." He whispered in Janet's ear,

Janet was thrilled at his attentions, knowing flattery would get him everywhere; she missed Roy, and although her husband was such a wonderful lover, he rarely told her how beautiful she was these days. Roy, like most husbands, just seemed to take her for granted.

Janet knew in her own mind that Michael had not changed, and even at university, he had been a charmer and she'd let herself swim in the wonderful feeling of being wanted. One thing led to another, far from having to take the initiative she had just given herself wholeheartedly when Michael had made his move. Janet just let it happen; she made no excuses, not even to herself as she felt herself raised to the very pinnacle of her erotic desires. When finally they lay still, the euphoria and moment of her intense climax had passed. Janet pushed the breathless Michael up off her; she walked into the shower before towelling herself dry and dressing; she spent time over her appearance until she once again looked as presentable as when she had arrived. A disappointed Michael, who had half-expected Janet to stay the night with him, was still lying on the bed as she blew him a kiss and went down to the car park to drive herself home.

The next few days saw the two of them together several times, each time ending with Michael making love to her. Janet had no qualms about her infidelity. She knew Roy would be having the time of his life with three women at his disposal, not to mention anyone else he might meet and seduce; he was, after all, what she had made him, and he was not only an excellent lover but his staying power was something other men only dreamed about. Michael explained that he was going out on a research trip for a week and would love her to come with him; could she make arrangements to join him? Janet remembered the last time she had been aboard with him, they had spent the whole day naked on the deck making love whenever the mood took them and with that firmly entrenched in her mind she said that she would see what she could do. When she got back, she knew in her own mind that the sex with Michael, far from satisfying her sexual needs, had raised her desires, and her needs seemed greater than ever. She asked herself, *Oh, why couldn't Roy be back? He has been away so long;* the odd message she had had, apart from letting her know he was alive, had done nothing to tell her when he would be back, this added to this latest problem with the engine could only delay his return for even longer. Janet rang Lady Jayne and asked her if she would be happy to keep an eye on the children as she was going to take a few days holiday with an old friend.

Lady Croft then broke the news of her departure to Morag, arranging for her to look after the children whilst she was away, telling her that Lady Jayne would be there if she needed anything and would come round every day to help her with entertaining them. Morag, as usual, agreed, but could not help wondering if Lord Croft knew of her holiday. *Young people today,* she thought to herself, *have no morals.* She was only glad that sort of thing was far behind her. The following morning, Janet kissed the children goodbye and drove to the docks, where she climbed aboard the research vessel and Michael cast off. As soon as they were out of sight of land, the two of them were naked, and Janet knew the next time she would wear clothes would be when she returned to the harbour in a week's time; her whole body tingled with the prospect of a whole week of illicit sex with her lover. After lying on the deck and soaking up the sun, Michael headed out to sea. Janet lay basking naked in the sun, as well as intending to enjoy the sex with Michael she intended to end the week with an all-over tan. The trip to his island of research took the whole day, and Janet was feeling so frustrated she decided to go into the galley and prepare something to eat; she had only just got to the galley and finished putting water in the coffee pot when almost without warning she felt the soft warmth of Michael's body approach from behind her. Janet was enthused as she felt Michael's hands sliding along the outside of her hips. He moved in closer to her; she could feel his breath on her neck.

"So your husband is away and chooses his crew rather than making love to his wife." Michael whispered in her ear, "I must confess knowing how she must be feeling I would desperately like to make love to his wife. Do you think she would mind?"
Janet half-turned and, with a look that gave nothing but encouragement, smiled and reached up their lips meeting and she surrendered to his passionate embrace; the week was starting as she had planned.

Janet had no idea who he had to account to for his research, but for the rest of the week they did little but make love on every part of the boat and in every conceivable position. Janet enjoyed it, but in her own mind she knew she would never leave Roy; one thing she did know was that if he continued to leave her alone; she would seriously have to consider the possibility of taking lovers whenever she could, her body was coming alive again and she knew she needed satisfaction from whoever was available. As she sat with these thoughts going through her mind, she was mindful that if she ever had sex outside marriage in the future it would be the responsible thing to do not to have unprotected sex. Janet hoped Roy was being careful and being responsible in the same way, but in reality she knew it was wishful thinking on her part. The week was over far too quickly and as they pulled into the harbour Janet helped Michael tie up at the quayside and gave her lover a final kiss and a hug as she climbed into the car and headed back to the house and her children her latest wild fling was over for the time being.

Arriving back at the house, Janet was surprised to see Fiona and Elian; with a hollow feeling in her stomach, she asked them anxiously,
"Where's Roy? Is he with you?"
Janet breathed a sigh of relief and was somewhat reassured to know he was still on the Virgin Islands, waiting for spares; in order that the cruiser could be repaired and he could return home. The two visitors explained that Fiona had been with Gael in England and how Gael's slow progress towards her recovery had begun. They went into detail about the trip, but intentionally omitted the violent clashes with the patrol boats. Elian told Janet how one of the turbo boosters had failed and how she had been sent to Ireland to get a replacement engine and turbo charger, which was being flown to the Virgin Islands as they spoke. Janet listened; realising that Roy had been alone aboard the cruiser with Madeleine.
"Is Madeleine all right?" Janet asked.
Thinking to herself that her philandering husband would have spent the last week making love with young Madeleine almost as often as she had made love to Michael, and any guilt complex she may have entertained quickly faded from her mind.

Morag, Fiona, Elian, and Janet spent the afternoon on the beach with the children, who were overjoyed at seeing their mother again. Elian and Fiona could not help but see how happy Janet was, and the all-over tan told its own story. Morag told them later that she had been away for a week with her old friend on a research trip; she suspected that it was Michael. The three of them seeing the joy and radiance in Janet's face knew exactly what sort of research she had been up to, but none of them would mention it to Roy despite their allegiance to his Lordship. Both Fiona and Elian knew Roy was always available to any of them at any time, and they did not blame Janet for reciprocating. The following day, they said goodbye and caught the island hopper to make their way onto the Virgin Islands to get the new motor fitted to the cruiser.

Chapter 15

Roy had enjoyed the sweet favours of Madeleine after Elian and Shilpa had left; then as the end of the week drew near, he knew he would have to find a proficient engineer to fit the new motor and turbo. It would be impossible for Elian to do it on her own; they had no workshop available nor did they have the required lifting gear with them. Roy made his way to the harbour master's office and asked Graham Peterson, the resident harbour master, if he could recommend a skilful and proficient engineer to carry out the work. Graham Peterson enquired what type of work his Lordship wanted to be carried out on the cruiser, and when Roy explained just what was needed; Graham Peterson pulled open a drawer in his filing cabinet and began to peruse the contents. At last, he looked up and said,

"If she and her crew are available, you cannot go wrong with Consuela Marias." Graham explained, "Consuela and her late husband always ran the best engineering and fitting shop on the island. When her husband was killed in an accident, she was wrought with grief. She closed the workshop and became almost a recluse. I would think she must be running short of money by now, perhaps her insurance pay-out is running dry. For whatever reason, she has now got her crew back together and is endeavouring to make the business work again. The local fishermen are an odd lot, they seem reluctant to put their trust fully in a woman engineer, even though she was far more qualified than her husband had ever been. Consequently, Mrs Marias has found getting her business back up and running has proved to be a slow process."

Roy asked before he made use of the phone and called the number on the document; he was surprised by the soft tones of the voice who answered, announcing that it was Consuela Marias speaking. Roy asked politely if he could make an appointment to see her to give her a commission to fit a new engine and turbocharger to his cruiser. She asked for his name and was quite taken aback when he replied, "Lord Croft."

"Which is your boat?" she asked.

"It's the wooden cruiser *Spirit of the Isle* in the harbour." He replied

"I've seen her. She's a beautiful boat. Come and see me as soon as you wish. I would love to see how you have converted an old MTB to look that good, Lord Croft."

Roy made the appointment for the afternoon at three o'clock. He then thanked Graham for the introduction and made his way back to the boat. Roy walked up the gangplank and could hear noises below; he kicked off his shoes and made his way down into the lower cabin. He could hear moans and wondered if Madeleine was in trouble, but for some reason he could not understand, he did not call out. As he made his way below the noises got louder and more defined; he padded softly through the lounge, and as he got closer to Madeleine's cabin, he could see the door was ajar. The sight almost took his breath away; Madeleine was lying on the bed and a man, wearing an American uniform with his trousers around his ankles, was making love to her. Madeleine was obviously enjoying the attention from the way she was co-operating, and not wishing to cause her any embarrassment, Roy moved away. The sound continued for some time rising to a long moan before subsiding and silence once again ruled.

Roy slipped out of the lounge up on to the deck; he put on his shoes and made his way back along the wharf. He sat, and after about fifteen minutes, he walked back down to the cruiser, ensuring that anyone aboard would hear him coming. Madeleine met Roy in the lounge and introduced him to Chuck, none other than the young captain of the US coastguard patrol boat who had challenged them off Cat Island several days before. Roy shook his proffered hand and asked,

"What brings you to the Virgin Islands?"

"News travels fast in these waters, Sir. I heard you had engine trouble, and I just took the opportunity to take a few days R & R, shore leave to see if I might meet young Madeleine again. I hope you do not mind my coming aboard whilst you were away?"

Roy shook his head; he had no hold over Madeleine, and if she wanted to grant her favours to the American, who was he to object.

"Lord Croft," Chuck began casually, "I saw Madeleine as I walked along the quayside, and she asked me aboard, and we sat and talked for a long time, and it seems we had a lot in common and neither of us realised how quickly time had passed."

Roy looked at Chuck, who was young and handsome; he could easily see how Madeleine could fall for his rugged looks and his smooth charm, but the young man must have something to have got young Madeleine into bed so quickly, and he was determined to try and ask her what it was when they were next alone and the opportunity presented itself. Chuck, eager to take advantage of the young woman beside him once again, asked,

"Lord Croft, would you have any objections if I called by later to take Madeleine out for a meal this evening?"

Roy was in no position to object; after all, Madeleine was a free agent, and consequently he was in no position to raise any objection. The young man kissed Madeleine on the cheek and said in a charming voice with his soft American drawl,

"I'll pick you up at around eight o'clock, Madeleine, if that's OK by you?"

He shook Roy's hand once again, saying,

"It was nice meeting you again, Sir. I hope the repairs will not take too long and won't prove to be too costly."

Then saluting Lord Croft, he climbed the companionway and left without a backward glance. Roy knowing that the young man had just seduced Madeleine could not help but admire the bravado and calmness of youth.

"I'm going to see an engineer to help with the repairs, Roy informed Madeleine, "and I only came back to say I may be back late."

Madeleine, still flushed with her recent tryst with Chuck, nodded in acknowledgement of Roy's comment and added with a smile,

"To tell you the truth, Roy, I may be back late myself."

Roy changed and called a taxi to take him to the boatyard and engineering works, belonging to the young widow, Consuela Marias. Roy stepped out of the taxi and was surprised to see a woman in her late twenties or early thirties standing in front of the office waiting for him. Consuela looked unbelievably attractive; she was a dark, brown-skinned woman from the Dominican Republic. She stood five feet two inches, with the biggest, most captivating brown eyes imaginable, and she had very long dark black hair, large firm breasts, and from what he could see below her skirt, she appeared to have well-shaped legs. Roy knew it was obvious, but he could not help but stare; when she broke the silence and introduced herself. Roy answered,

"I'm Lord Croft, but you must call me Roy. The title is a little cumbersome at the best of times. I'm so very pleased to meet you, Mrs Marias."

"It's Consuela, Roy. Nobody has called me Mrs Marias since my husband was killed."

"I'm sorry to hear of your loss, Consuela," Roy said, genuinely sorry for her husband's untimely death.

Waving her hand to prevent him going further, she invited him into the office.

Roy followed her inside; his eyes could not help but openly admire the tight round buttocks as they moved rhythmically in front of him. When she turned to face him, their eyes met, and Roy knew in an instance that there was every possibility she would be another conquest, to add to his long list, before he left to return to the boat. As usual he could not put his finger on why, but there was an instant affinity between them. Roy watched as Consuela obviously felt the same way, and there was no way she could conceal the first flush of arousal as it began to run up from her breasts to the dark line of her hair. Hoping to hide the sudden and inexplicable rise in her hormone level, she pointed to a chair in front of her desk and sat down.

"Now, Lord Croft, I'm sorry, Roy, what's this problem you are having with your boat?" Consuela asked.

Roy told her how the engine had failed on their way south and how they had taken the engine out of service to continue the journey, and he added that that the new engine and turbo would be arriving the following day and needed someone to fit it. Consuela asked more questions, but both of them knew there was something in the air besides work. She rose from behind the desk and asked Roy if he would like a drink. Hearing his reply, she poured him a generous measure of Scotch and poured herself a stiff glass of tequila. Walking towards him with the glasses in her hand, Roy rose to take his. The drinks were placed on the desk, and in seconds, she was in his arms. Unable to resist the temptation, Consuela half-turned and their lips melded together, Roy's lips pressed against the soft thick lips of the dark-skinned woman in a long smouldering kiss deepening as both felt their passions rise to the surface. Consuela's lips felt full and somewhat spongy as she opened her mouth, and Roy's tongue slid inside, finding her soft pliable tongue as it moved over his. The kiss seemed to go on forever, whilst each pair of hands explored the other. Consuela suddenly broke away, and she pushed Roy back; the chair behind him caught him just beneath the knees, and as his knee joints gave way he began to fall backwards. Roy reached out to steady himself as he fell back on to the chair, his hands clutching at Consuela and dragging her towards him, and suddenly she was sitting on Roy's lap. Before either could move, their lips touched again and the kiss continued for some time, both of them barely taking the time to breathe.

Consuela suddenly realised what was happening; she pushed at Lord Croft's chest, breaking contact; the standing somewhat unsteadily on her feet, she began,

"We cannot do this," she stammered, breathlessly. "You must go. I am sorry. I just do not know what came over me. It has been almost a year since my husband was killed, and I have never touched or let anyone touch me since that day. You must forgive me." She whispered hoarsely turning away from him.

"I understand, but you must realise that there is something we both feel." Roy said as he got up and moved behind her.

Roy placed his hands on her shoulders, moving them slowly down her arms; then, using his fingers, he brushed her hair aside and began kissing her neck. Instead of doing what she felt was right, and pushing pushed Lord Croft away, she felt herself carried away on a sea of rising sensuality, she moaned in delight; then turning her head as if surrendering to the inevitable outcome, she leaned back to kiss him once again. This time Roy let his hands drop to her buttocks, feeling her press her hips hard against him.

"No," she murmured. "We can't do this."

But Roy had already pulled the long zip at the back of her dress down, and as she pulled away, the dress slid down her body, pooling around her ankles and revealing her lacy underwear and her wonderfully sculptured body.

Consuela gasped at the suddenness of Lord Croft's move, and she could see the obvious signs of his arousal, and unable to resist the urge brought on by her increase in her hormone levels and having been denied such pleasures for so long, she instinctively stretched out her hand. Consuela was on a cloud, as incredulously she watched her fingers trace over Roy's body, enjoying the feeling of intimacy she had missed for so long.

"Oh God! I've missed him, and I've been so lonely for months," was all she could say.

Neither said much in the hour that followed, both surrendering to their own needs. It seemed unreal as their passions rose and their bodies moved together, Consuela felt herself carried away on an erotic journey culminating in one of the most intensive orgasms she had ever imagined and when it was over, both were fulfilled; in Consuela's case, more than she could ever remember.

Consuela lay there unable to move; what had come over her, she did not know; all she knew was that this stranger had fulfilled her desires more than she had ever known in her whole life. The other thing she knew was that she wanted to let it happen to her over and over again until, sadly but inevitably, he would leave the island. Roy fell forward onto Consuela's more than ample breasts; his whole being enthused with the feeling of euphoria at the release of his pent up emotions and the satisfaction that he had completed the seduction of yet another new conquest, one that he had not expected, especially after seeing young Madeleine getting seduced by the American captain. He had known in his own mind as he had watched her enthusiastic response to Chuck's lovemaking that Madeleine would probably not be available until they set sail once again. This meeting with Consuela had come from nowhere, and now that she had let him make love to her, it was more than a chance thought in his mind that she would in all probability be available to replace Madeleine for the time he remained on the island. Roy stood up and looked down at Consuela, who lay seemingly unabashed that Roy could see her naked. Roy smiled as he casually reached out and took a good gulp from the half-filled whisky glass before he helped Consuela to sit up. She looked at him with amazement as he calmly sat down on the chair in front of her desk, as if having sex with her was an everyday occurrence.

Roy watched as Consuela get to her feet; she was a little unsteady as she opened the office door and still naked, she made her way to the bathroom. She returned, having freshened herself up, and pointed the way to Roy, who, holding his trousers up, made his way to the same bathroom. When he returned, Consuela was once more dressed and sat behind the desk.

"Before I invite you into my home," she spoke remarkably calmly and said in a business like manner, "Let's get the business of the day over with, shall we? Which freight company has the engine been consigned through?"

Lord Croft had no idea which local firm would handle the cargo or which clearing agent would be involved.

"The consignment will have been sent via DHL," Roy said, quoting the consignment note number from memory.

"Oh, then, I know who will handle it this end," she muttered half to herself.

Consuela rang the freight company who confirmed that the consignment Roy had quoted as 1438871 would be arriving the following day.

"It will be here tomorrow," she said, looking at Roy for some kind of acknowledgement. "Is that OK?" she asked calmly and casually, as if nothing had happened between them.

Roy nodded in agreement. Consuela spoke into the phone again and arranged for the delivery to be sent to her boatyard as early as possible. Replacing the phone back into its cradle.

"Do you think you could show me this cruiser of yours, Lord Croft?" Consuela asked Roy in a tone that belied their earlier tryst. "Then I will be able to determine how long it will take to do the work and I can finalise the estimate for your approval?"

Rather taken aback by Consuela's sudden change of tactics, Lord Croft smiled and nodded his agreement.

"May I?" Lord Croft asked.

Then not waiting for a reply, he picked up the telephone and dialled the cab company which had brought him, and a few minutes later, they were heading back to the docks.

The journey was short, and soon they were set down near the wharf where the cruiser was moored. Madeleine was preparing herself for her date with Chuck as Roy climbed aboard with Consuela in tow. Roy explained that Madeleine was one of his crew, before introducing Madeleine to Consuela as the owner of the company he was considering being the one to carry out the refit of the engine. Leaving Madeleine to complete her preparations, Roy invited Consuela to sit in the main cabin and poured her a drink. Roy was only too aware that Chuck was keen on to get Madeleine to himself once again, for it was still only seven o'clock when he called for her. Madeleine, in the eagerness of youth, waved Roy goodnight.

"I don't know what time I'll be back, she said with a smile holding onto Chuck's arm, "only that it will in all probability, if the evening goes as planned, be late."

Consuela asked to see the engine room, and Roy showed her below. She was very business-like, noting how the access to the room could be gained to allow the new engine to be fitted. Then returning to the main cabin, she sat and, after making a few notes, looked up and gave Roy a figure for the work. Roy had a rough idea how long it would take to complete the task, from his engineering experience, and quickly working out her rate per hour, Roy felt the price was fair to both parties.

Once the price of the repair had been agreed; Roy poured Consuela another drink, and after he had poured one for himself, he sat down.

"Roy, I'm intrigued at the way you have converted this old MTB. Do you think you could show me over the rest of the boat?" Consuela asked.

The galley, the smaller cabins, came first, and as they entered the stateroom, Consuela turned and threw her arms around his Lordship's neck. Swiftly tilting his head down, Roy kissed her full lips, feeling them soft and rubbery against his own, her lips parted giving him free access. The intensity of the kiss increased in passion as Consuela pressed her body against Roy's, feeling the obvious sign of his arousal once again. Roy kissed down her throat as she moaned softly, and when she felt Roy's hand slid under her buttocks, cupping the soft flesh, she knew she was lost. She felt herself swept up off her feet, and surrendering to Lord Croft's expert touch, she let herself be lifted to new levels of pleasure, she had thought after the death of her husband she had lost forever.

It was sometime later when they got up, Roy showed Consuela the main shower, and he went into the small one in the stateroom; when they had dressed and once more looked respectable, Roy offered to take her out for supper. Consuela shook her head.

"Oh no, I want to cook you supper at my place tonight," she said emphatically. I don't want to let you out of my sight for a moment, and I hope your crew won't mind, but I insist you sleep in my bed tonight."

Roy arranged for a local watchman to keep an eye on the cruiser informing him that a lady member of his crew would be returning later and once she was on board, his duties for the night would be completed. The taxi dropped Lord Croft and Consuela Marias off at a large colonial-style house, not far from the boatyard. Roy's eyes quickly scanned the property and he was suitably impressed at what he could see in the half light of the moon.

Consuela and her husband had obviously done well; the house was enclosed by a high-security fence, and as Roy entered, he could see that it was furnished expensively. It looked as though he had chosen well, especially if she had retained her husband's engineering crew. Consuela walked through to the kitchen to reset the security, telling Roy to help himself from the liquor cabinet and requesting him to pour her large tequila. Carrying the drinks into the kitchen, Roy saw that Consuela was a serious cook; seafood was the order of the day. She was concocting one of the most interesting chowders he had ever seen; there was lobster, crabs, clams, oysters, prawns, langoustines, and every other shellfish caught in the area being prepared; the rich smell of cooking was almost as intoxicating as the whisky. Much later, they sat down and ate their fill with a couple of bottles of local wine; eventually, they were replete. The two of them climbed the stairs and fell into bed, both tired from their earlier sex and the magnificent supper; they soon fell into a deep, undisturbed sleep.

The couple woke early, and as if they had been used to waking beside one another, it seemed natural for them to make love. This time the desperate need she had felt before was replaced by the relaxed, easy enjoyment of sex between lovers used to one another. Consuela lay back, and when her breathing had returned to normal she looked up at him,

"That was the best yet." she said to Roy. "You seem to get better every time. I have never felt so satisfied. You truly are a remarkable lover. One day you must tell me who taught you how to please a woman."

Then grabbing her robe she walked into the bathroom, the white colour of her robe contrasting starkly against her dark thighs. Roy walked in to the shower when she had finished; his mind was willing to make love to her again, but the ache in his loins told him enough was enough. Lord Croft had a leisurely shower taking his time enjoying the relief from his ache as he let the water give wash away his cares and after drying himself with the fluffy towels he dressed before going through to where Consuela sat eating breakfast.

The meal finished and cleared away; Consuela asked Roy to bring the boat into the yard, and she would chase the delivery of the engine from the couriers. Roy called a taxi, and when he got back to the cruiser, he climbed the gangplank and went down the companionway into the lounge. There were clothes scattered everywhere, leading to Madeleine's cabin; Roy walked towards the door and could hear the sounds of them in the throes of making love. The door was slightly ajar, and Roy being curious gently eased it open further. The American captain was once again making passionate love to his newest conquest. He finally fell forward on to Madeleine's chest and lay there allowing his breathing to calm down; Roy, for some reason, could not move away as he watched as Chuck turned, lifted her up, and laid her face down on the bunk.

Roy was surprised when he heard Chuck speak to Madeleine; this time there was no softness in his voice, it was demanding, hard, and totally void of any tenderness,

"Now I want a piece of your ass, my girl." He demanded

Chuck ignored her plaintive cry; he had one thing in his mind and nothing was going to stop him from attaining his goal. He gripped her hips and began to push forward.

"No, Chuck, stop." Madeleine screamed, "I don't do that. Oh God, that's disgusting."

Chuck laughed; the thickness of his voice affected by his sexual arousal sounded coarse. The polite charm, which had influenced Madeleine, had now evaporated in his eagerness to obtain his objective.

"You do now, Madeleine my girl," he said gruffly, "and there's no one around to help you. Lord Croft is off with that black whore I saw with him last night. I know just what I want, and I'm going to take it with or without your consent."

Madeleine's scream of protest drove Roy into action; he grabbed the small box stool from the dressing table in the stateroom and quietly walked up behind Chuck, who by now had forced his way partially inside. Madeleine's struggles were all too obvious; she did not want him to do the odious, obnoxious act of defilement to her, and the scream of agonising protest tore at Roy's heart. Raising the stool up in the air, Roy brought the hard boxwood crashing down on the back of Chuck's head. Chuck half-turned his mouth open in surprise, as he crumpled forward on to Madeleine's back. Roy pulled the insensible Chuck up off the prone form below; he dragged him unconscious and naked up the companionway before throwing him down the gangplank on to the wharf. He went back inside where Madeleine lay weeping; then grabbing Chuck's clothes before walking back up on the deck; Roy had a certain amount of pleasure as he threw them overboard into the water. Then casting off the fore and after lines, Lord Croft climbed up on to the bridge and slowly maneuvered out of the mooring and headed for the 'Marias' boatyard.

On board, a tearful Madeleine, who had showered and dressed, came up on to the flying bridge full of apologies.

"Oh, Roy, thank you for saving me from that evil, crude, and depraved man. I had no idea he was like that. Up to that point, he had acted perfectly normal, but I abhor the thought of what he tried to do to me. I don't know how I would have ever faced myself if you had not arrived in time to stop him."

With that she burst into tears again; Roy pulled her towards him and put his arm around her shoulders.

"You should take things more slowly. He said quietly, "Don't rush into new relationships too fast."

His own mind reeled as he said the words, thinking to himself that he really should take his own advice; he had rushed into a stupid but exciting relationship with Consuela without any knowledge of her, other than she had been a lonely widow for almost a year. His mind reeled and he realised that even the information he had, only came from someone who knew her husband better than he knew Consuela herself. God, he thought, *she could well have infected me with any sort of venereal disease; she may have told me she had been without sex since the death of her husband, but I only had her word for that. Island women were notorious for their promiscuity.*

Roy nosed the craft into the boatyard, and Consuela stood in front of a large boat shed, with an overhead gantry, where she had arranged for her crew to do the repairs. She waved him forward, but she glowered at Madeleine as she threw the ropes to one of her crew to secure the moorings. Consuela said nothing as she walked back towards the office, and Roy thought she must have had bad news about the arrival of the engine and other spares. Switching off the engines, Lord Croft made his way down on to the catwalk and followed Consuela into the office, leaving Madeleine on board. The courier's truck was offloading Roy's engine and other spares as he entered. Consuela turned towards Roy as he entered the door, and she glowered at him, her face as dark as thunder.

"What relationship do you have with that young woman?" she demanded.

Roy was somewhat taken aback and spoke quietly and firmly,

"I do not think that my relationship with any of my crew has anything to do with you, Consuela. We have only just met, and just because you allowed me to get into your bed does not make us man and wife. If you wish, I can easily take my boat to another yard, and I can assure you that you will never see me or my boat again."

Consuela knew he was right, but she was a jealous woman, and if she took a man to her bed, she did not allow him to sleep with anyone else. She knew she needed the work, and so she said apologetically,

"I'm sorry, Lord Croft. I just took too much for granted. We should act in a purely business fashion from now on and no more sex between us, if that is OK with you."

Roy nodded curtly and turned away; without saying another word, he walked back to the boat.

Madeleine was waving at him excitedly; she was holding the radio mike in her hand; as he got closer, he could hear what she was saying,

"It's Elian and Fiona; they are at the harbour. I've told them to get a taxi and come to Consuela Marias's boatyard as soon as they can."

Roy's heart skipped a beat; he was looking forward to seeing his permanent crew members again. Soon life would be getting back to normal. Roy waited for the taxi to arrive, when it did so Elian and Fiona ran up to Roy; Elian was the first, she threw her arms around him and hugged him telling him how glad she was to be back as she kissed him. Fiona was next; her kiss was more passionate that Elian's and she whispered eagerly in Roy's ear,

"Oh, Roy, you have no idea how good it is to be back. I've missed your touch. I can't wait for you to make love to me."

Roy could feel her pressing against him, but for once he did not instantly respond; his loins still ached too much from the earlier session with Consuela. He knew, however, that he had the rest of the day to recover. That evening, as he lay in bed, it was Elian who joined him; after he had heard the low murmur of conversation and he guessed that she had pulled rank over the other two.

Roy had no idea if his casual relationship with Consuela, a woman he knew nothing about, could possibly have infected him. Did he dare have sex with his crew until he was sure he was clear of any infection? Roy lay naked on the bed; the thought of having the two of them back had aroused him. He was so worked up he selfishly decided he would get checked in the morning, and if he had been careless enough to catch something, he would ask Elian to go for a check-up as well. The following day, Roy suggested that they move into a hotel to allow the work on the boat to proceed without any more delay. Elian said she would join them later as she wanted to see that Consuela and her engineering crew did the work properly. Elian was funny about who fixed her boat, and into the bargain, the only lady engineer she trusted was herself. Whilst Elian busied herself at the yard, Roy went for a test and, later in the day, was very relieved to find he was clear of any sexually transmitted infection. The hospital informed him that as far as AID's was concerned, the clear report did not show any infection;

that they had informed him could be as long as six months to show up. Roy ignored the latter part of the report and was glad that as far as the tests went, his worries about Consuela had been misplaced.

The progress on the repair was slow; with all the various refitting the cruiser had undergone, it took a while to get the various hatches free from superstructure that had been overlaid, and a fair amount of dismantling was necessary before the engine room was fully exposed. Once this portion of the work was completed, things went smoothly. Consuela fitted the new engine, but she advised Elian to speak to Roy. The technology of the engines was old, Consuela explained, and when Lord Croft had the chance, she recommended that a complete refit with new sea-rated Penta diesels would make a world of difference to the fuel consumption and the power to weight ratio of the cruiser.

Whilst the crew were fitting the new engine and reconnecting it back into the complex transmission, Elian and Consuela stripped the ruined engine to find the cause of the trouble. It appeared that a bearing in the oil pump had worn; the shaft had been running out of true and had seized causing a catastrophic failure of the oil pressure in the engine. The oil supply to the turbo had been insufficient and the turbo had overheated, and the high-speed turbine shaft in the turbo itself had broken. It was the old story, and Consuela pointed out that if each engine had an oil pressure warning on the flying bridge, the oil pressure would have been spotted and the engine shut down. The pump could have been repaired before the engine had failed. Elian explained that when the boat had been designed, there had always been an engineer in the engine room and all the gauges were situated there. Elian took the decision herself and instructed Consuela to extend the pipe work so that repeater gauges could be installed in the lower control bridge and warning lights with audible warning fitted to the open bridge on the flying deck. She would OK the extra cost of the work and get Roy to agree to the extra charge. The two women worked well together, but neither of them discussed their relationship with Roy, and it appeared that the subject between them was taboo.

The days passed quickly with Roy enjoying the favours of Fiona during the day and Elian during the night. Madeleine seemed sullen and ashamed of her behaviour and avoided being alone with Roy during the week following her affair with Chuck. She insisted that if anyone was needed to stay aboard overnight, she should be the one to do it and no form of persuasion would make her change her mind. The day before the work was finished, Fiona complained of cramps, and that night, Elian also told Roy she was suffering from menstrual pains, both women suffered badly from the painful process each month. Although Roy and Elian slept in the same bed, there was no sex. Lying beside Roy, Elian explained that she had authorised some extra work to be done to the boat, and hearing what she had decided, Roy was pleased that the current problem would not occur again. The following morning, Roy went with Elian to the boatyard to see the upper superstructure being put back in place. Elian was fussing about like a mother hen, and Roy went down to the office to discuss payment with Consuela. Roy walked in and saw that Consuela had paid particular attention to her appearance that morning: her hair was tied up in a pleat, she wore make-up, and her blouse and skirt set off the dark colouring of her Afro-Spanish-Caribbean skin. In fact, Roy thought she looked in excellent shape, work obviously suited her. She smiled at Roy and said,

"I am so pleased you decided to come to me for the repairs on your boat, and it seems that work on your cruiser has set aside local fishermen's worries about my capabilities. Word has got around very quickly. If the harbour master had recommended my yard to the English Lord and the fact that a member of the British aristocracy has trusted her with his luxury cruiser, then to them my work had to be the best. As a result, I am suddenly flooded with enquiries, and orders for work to be done are coming in thick and fast."

Consuela walked up to Roy and put her arms around his neck and kissed him tenderly at first, but the lingering kiss became more passionate; Roy felt her press her body against his.

"Can you forgive me?" She whispered, "I'm so sorry that I upset you. It was my stupid Hispanic jealousy that caused us to stop our relationship; but is there anything I can do to make you reconsider making love to me, one more time, before you leave."

Roy had not had been able to make love to Elian the previous night; he had had a night of restful sleep; the closeness of Consuela's obviously aroused body and pressed against his own made him feel his own arousal begin. With Consuela pressed hard against him, Roy could not help but respond, and he pushed her back towards the couch, which caught her behind the knees, and she fell backwards with Roy lying between her thighs and his body resting on top of her.

"I am so desperate since you made love to me." she whispered to him, "I just need you to do it just one more time before you leave."

Consuela had been a widow for almost a year and had not taken any precautions against getting pregnant; she had been within her safe period when she had let Roy take her the first time, but she had not considered that time had moved on. Caution set aside, her needs took over, and for the next hour time stood still until finally the passion subsided. They lay there spent. Consuela said, when her breathing had returned to some semblance of normality.

"I hope no one heard me cry out. I have to admit I have never felt so content and satisfied as I do at this very moment."

They got off the couch and went through to clean up and get dressed. Roy was more aware of the ache that compared to the pain of toothache in his scrotum; he knew he had done too much and would need to ease up. Although Consuela would not realise it, until Roy had left the island, she would bear his child. The child would be a boy, and he would bring new meaning into her life. The young man would give her great pleasure as he grew into manhood, and he would take over the business as she grew too old to manage it. She would have no way of contacting his Lordship, or even know if he was really a Lord; she had not asked for his address as he had paid her in cash. The following day, Roy, with his crew of three, cast off and headed for Barbados; Elian was at the helm on the flying bridge and Fiona was in the galley.

Madeleine approached Roy and apologised for avoiding him for the last week.

"I was so afraid," she had said to him in hushed tones, "that if Chuck had been the kind of person to try and force me to do that odious and disgusting act. I was afraid he may have infected me with AID's or some other sexually transmitted disease. I went to a doctor and loads of various tests. The results showed that, please excuse my language, the bastard had given me a dose of syphilis. The doctor gave me antibiotics and only gave me the all-clear this morning, just before we left the island. I felt so ashamed, Roy. I just could not pluck up the courage to face you."

Roy hugged her, his mind going back to that night he had been with Consuela, and he knew he should have waited until he had been checked, but he had not been able to wait. His estimation of the girl in his arms rose as he said,

"I had no right to object, nor did I mind you having a relationship with Chuck. He was much nearer you age than I am. I'm just so sorry the relationship turned so sour."
Madeleine reached up and kissed Roy softly on the mouth.

"Thank you for helping me. You always seem to be the one to rescue me from one thing or another. I'm here for you whenever you want me."
She walked away, leaving him on the bridge; she wanted him badly, but up on the flying deck in the open air and the possibility of being caught by the others was not what she wanted at the moment. She wanted it to be more private and relaxed. She only hoped her parents would not object to her accompanying Roy on his next voyage. She could not wait for the news that they were sailing for distant places once again; she loved being aboard Roy's boat with the excitement, the sex, and the adventure.

The following day, Elian climbed up on to the flying bridge where Roy was in command; she checked their position and relieved him, taking over the controls.

"I'm going below for a rest, Elian. I think it would be wise to continue to take it steady with the new engine in situ. I think we should put into St Kitts for the night. I don't think it would be out of place for me to hope you would join me in the stateroom after dinner," he said with a wry grin.
Elian knew exactly what that meant as she smiled in anticipation and said,

"After what Fiona tells me you have been up to, I'm surprised you still feel you can cope with the demands I'm going to be making on you."

With a smile, Roy turned and walked down the companionway to the lower deck; he could still smell Elian's fragrance, hanging in the breeze, momentarily before the wind swept it away to be replaced by the salt air as it whipped around the windscreen. Roy loved it here in the Caribbean, and he loved the sexual freedom Janet allowed him with his crew; however, he was looking forward to being with his wife and family soon and hoped everything was well with them. He knew nothing of the wild week of sex his wife had spent with Michael on his boat; it was a fact he was to learn all too soon. That night after they had tied up just off the island of St Kitts, they ate the last supper of their voyage; they would be back in Barbados the following day, when Elian and Fiona would be able to clean and polish the cruiser until it shone like new once more. Madeleine would return to the residence of the High Commissioner to see her pregnant stepmother, whom she was fully aware that she was carrying Roy's child. She knew her father genuinely believed the child to be his; she would never disillusion him, but a pang of jealousy tore at her heart for she would love to be carrying Roy's child herself. Perhaps during the next voyage, she let the idea float through her mind, realising the impracticality of such a notion.

The night passed without incident, and the following morning, Roy went up on deck and watched the sun rise over the east, the red sky gradually changing to pink, and as the sun cleared the horizon, the reds and pinks faded to become a rich blue sky with patches of white clouds scudding across the blue. Roy stood waiting for the rest of the crew to come to life; it was Madeleine who came up and informed him that breakfast was served, and he went below to join the others. Breakfast over, Elian went up to the flying bridge instructing Fiona and Madeleine cast off from the moorings, then they headed south for Barbados and to their current base. Roy was looking forward to seeing his family again; little did he know just how soon he would be back at sea, this time working for the Colombian's who would not take 'no' for an answer.

Chapter 16

Elian radioed ahead to let Janet know they would be arriving later in the day. She did not want her to be caught with Michael when Roy arrived; she need not have worried Janet had done enough straying for the time being, and she knew it could become a habit that was hard to break. It was bad enough for Roy to have so much freedom, but she had come to the conclusion that if they both made it a habit, their marriage would break down and there were the children to think about. Sean was old enough now to know when his mother was away when Roy was not around, and she would not put it past him to say something to his daddy about his mommy's absences. Janet had her hair done and she took time with her make-up wanting to look her best as she accompanied Morag and the children down to the harbour to welcome Roy. The children busied themselves looking at all the craft as they came and went. Sean pointed out individual makes and styles demonstrating his burgeoning knowledge of boats. Sheenagh soon lost interest and became bored asking Morag to take her for a walk. It was well after lunch when Sean spotted Roy's cruiser through the new binoculars Lady Jayne had given him for his birthday.

He was very excited, jumping up and down pointing out the boat to Sheenagh, his younger sister, who was by now also very excited at the prospect of seeing her daddy. Janet waved as the boat entered the harbour entrance; the harbour officials together with customs and immigration stood by Janet as the large boat tied up alongside. The officials boarded but soon left when they saw Lady Jayne arrive to welcome Lord Croft and his crew. Lady Jayne was now looking every bit as pregnant as she felt; she was here not only to meet her stepdaughter but also Roy, the father of her unborn child. She had not realised just how much she would miss him when he had gone away; she could swear she missed him as much as Janet had done; but their reunion would have to wait a few days or risk losing Janet's friendship. She believed that Janet already suspected that it was Roy's child she was carrying, but Lady Jayne realised that Janet had not forced the issue as it would have been at the expense of their developing friendship.

Roy had hardly walked down the gangplank when young Sean threw himself into his daddy's arms and Sheenagh stood by miserably, waiting for her turn to be picked up and hugged. By the time Roy had picked Sheenagh up into his arms, huge tears were rolling down her face, but when her daddy kissed her, she was all smiles, and as soon as her daddy put her down, she ran towards Elian and gave her a big hug around the legs. Roy embraced Janet, who hugged him close to her and kissed him eagerly. Lady Jayne was next and gave him a friendly kiss on the cheek. Once all the greetings had been completed, Janet handed Roy the keys, and he drove them back to the house. Lady Jayne with Elian, Fiona, and Madeleine, followed in the chauffeur-driven embassy car. Once they had all arrived safely, Roy, much to the children's enthusiastic joy, gave the children the few presents he had picked up for them at the various places they had stopped. Then as packages were undone and the wrapping paper tossed aside, the excitement was followed by 'oohs' and 'aahs'. Much to Janet's pleasure, Roy gave her the new dress he had chosen for her, and she held it against herself and gave a swirl; delighted with his choice, her eyes widened as he opened the gift box containing jewellery he had selected when he had been shopping on some of the islands. They all had tea; afterwards, Lady Jayne and Madeleine left to go to the Residence; Roy was finally left alone with Janet after Morag had taken the children up for their bath. The children pulled long faces and had only agreed to go when Roy had said he would read them a bedtime story. Roy took Janet in his arms and kissed her passionately, feeling her mould her body against his, and it seemed so long since they had been in each other's arms, but Roy was aware something was not quite right; Janet seemed somehow uneasy.

Roy knew almost instinctively that she had been with Michael, her ex-lover from university, whilst he had been away. Although he felt a little concerned after she had told him it would not happen again, he knew he could not really complain since Janet gave him as much sexual freedom as he wanted and never objected to his philandering ways, even when she had caught him in the act, something she had done several times in the past. He could not help himself, and he still felt sad; after all, this time he had been away for quite a time, and he knew she had needs and desires as well as he did. He went up and read to the children and then when they were asleep, he went down and enjoyed a candlelit dinner alone with his wife. When they eventually went up to bed, Janet was surprised by the tenderness and passion that Roy showed her. She lay enjoying the lavish care he took over their lovemaking; she could almost believe he had been faithful to her during his recent voyage, but she knew that to be a wild illusionary dream. They finally fell asleep in each other's arms like lovers still early in their relationship. They woke to begin again with the tenderness of lovers on honeymoon; Janet knew then that she loved him more than ever, despite all his failings. They dressed and went down to breakfast, holding hands like a pair of young lovers who had consummated their romance for the first time. Even the children, as young as they were, sensed the mutual love their parents had for each other, and everyone was happy and ready to go on the beach like any other family as soon as breakfast was over.

Lady Jayne joined them around mid-morning; she wore a one-piece swimming costume with a robe around her shoulders, Roy could see that her waist had now become a definite lump rather than a thickening. After an hour on the beach with the children and their father splashing in the shallows, Janet suggested they go back inside as the children were feeling the heat, and it was getting towards their lunchtime. The two women changed before they joined Roy inside, and Janet took the children into the kitchen, but not before she had scolded Roy,

"Why don't you get Lady Jayne a drink," Janet said sharply, "instead of sitting there expecting everyone to wait on you, lazybones? I shall have to have a word with Elian; she and the crew have spoiled you aboard that floating harem you call a cruiser."

Roy nodded; not wishing to disturb the tranquillity between them poured Lady Jayne a large piña colada. Janet had hardly left the room when Lady Jayne turned to Roy and embracing him whispered,

"Oh, Roy, I have missed you. I hope you have behaved yourself with my stepdaughter. You should remember she has had a very sheltered upbringing."

Roy thought back to the time he had caught her with Chuck and how the bastard had given her a dose of syphilis; the picture faded as it was replaced by the memory of how he had enjoyed Madeleine's rich sensuality to the full, only the previous day. Lady Jayne's lust sprang up; she had been wired up all the way to the house, and when she saw Roy in person, it became so much more powerful. Lady Jayne knew she needed him to make love to her, she had to have him, anytime anywhere, whatever the risk, and she just could not resist him when he was so close. Roy could see how she felt, and he knew he would have difficulty holding back once they began. Moments later, he pulled her close to him and kissed her with a rising passion as his own arousal soared.

Lady Jayne felt the change in them both; despite her need, she knew they had to be cautious.

"Oh God, Roy, I do so want you, but No! Not now. We do not have time. When the house is quiet and everyone is asleep, I will creep out and come to you."

Roy knew he could not let her go as it had to be now. He moved quickly.

"Oh God, Roy, we can't have sex now. Oh God, but you make me feel so good. Oh God, we can't possibly do it now; Janet or one of the children might walk in any second."

Feeling that fate was against her, Lady Jayne gave up the struggle and let the tide of passion ride over her. Despite the risk of being caught, she knew she could not stop; already she could feel her first tingle of excitement as her orgasm began to build. The moment seemed to go on and on, their bodies not wanting the exquisite pleasure to stop.

Suddenly they heard footsteps crossing the courtyard. It was Janet calling out, "Roy, are you drinking Scotch or would either of you prefer coffee before it goes cold?"

The couple parted with a soft moan, both full of guilt. Minutes later, Janet entered the room and just looked at the two of them, both with a look of guilt on their flushed faces, and she guessed what had been going on. She smiled at her friend Jayne's discomfort but could not blame her; Janet had in the distant past taught Roy how to please any woman he was with; she knew only too well how good he had become, and she would tease him when they were in bed and tell him, if he enjoyed having sex with pregnant women so much, he had better get her pregnant again before he left on his next charter. Lady Jayne, on the other hand, was so frustrated by the sudden interruption to the mutual satisfaction she had been enjoying with Roy, but she was determined she would fulfil her needs later, if the opportunity arose. After lunch, Lady Jayne spoke to Janet,

"I feel faint. It must be something to do with my pregnancy. I get so tired these days. Could you call the Residency and ask the driver to come and pick me up?"

Janet would not hear of it saying that Roy would take her back.

Roy knew what was coming, and as they climbed into the car, he knew he would be only too pleased to fulfil her Ladyship's wildest fantasies. Roy drove to the Residency, knowing neither her husband nor Madeleine would be there; Lady Jayne pressed the remote to open the large doors to the underground garage, allowing Roy drove his car inside. Lady Jayne led the way; the couple hurried up the stairs to her marital bedroom. They could not get undressed quick enough, and once naked, they climbed onto the huge bed. It was much later when Lord Croft took his leave of Lady Jayne to drive back to Janet, his long-suffering wife. Arriving back home, Roy spent the rest of the afternoon with his wife and children as though nothing had taken place between Lady Jayne and himself. That night when Roy and Janet retired to their bedroom, they sat dressed in just their robes when Janet whispered to Roy,

"Darling, I want you to get me pregnant again. I am due to ovulate anytime, and I want the baby to be born before we return to Ireland."

Somewhat startled at her request,

"Why? Now of all times, "Roy asked her, "the children will be old enough for us all to travel back as a family on the boat, something I thought you wanted to do, so why the urgent desire to have another child now?"

Janet looked at him with doe-eyes.

"I know in my heart, and I have never discussed it with anyone, that Lady Jayne is carrying your child, and I'm jealous, it's not as if we cannot afford another child, and I feel I'm ready," she whispered in his ear and kissed the lobe delicately, something only she knew he loved.

Roy's heart seemed to pause, and his stomach churned in the anguish he felt at Janet's correct assumption of the status quo regarding Lady Jayne's pregnancy. Almost as if an automatic self-defence mechanism took over, Roy looked at her hard.

"What about this affair with Michael? What will he say about you being pregnant? Above all, how will I know it's my child I'll be bringing up?"

Janet burst into tears and punched Roy's chest with her fists balled up.

"Oh God, Roy, how could you even think such a thing? I have given you so much sexual freedom even before we got married. I have never objected to you getting involved with anyone. Heaven knows how many children you have fathered in the past, and you have never in your life taken any precautions to prevent you getting any other women pregnant. It's your child I want, not Michael's. Michael was and probably may well be in the future, who knows, just some kind of relief whilst you were away. There is no love in that relationship as well, you know. You are the love of my life. I just feel I need to have another of your children whilst I am young enough to cope."

Roy looked at her and scooped her in his arms.

"I'm sorry," he said. "That was a cruel thing to say. I know you love me, and I am fully aware that I have neglected you in the past and will, in all probability, have to do so again in the future, if more charters come along. We can have another child if that is really what you most desire," he whispered.

Smiling to himself at the thought of the pleasure, he was going to take from her right here and now.

Janet's moods were swinging wildly with her ovulation upsetting the balance of her hormones, and she was highly aroused at the thought of Roy agreeing to get her pregnant for the third time. She looked into his eyes and whispered,

"I don't want this to be a chore, darling; I want this time to be just for us, for our sexual enjoyment, and if I get pregnant, so much the better."

Roy had all but taken himself to the limit with Lady Jayne earlier that afternoon and not wanting to disappoint his wife; he remembered the hip flask in his pocket and walked into the dressing room and took a deep draught; the warm burning sensation flowed down his throat and into his stomach. He returned and stood before Janet, his renewed vigour evident. They made passionate love before falling asleep, and they made love yet again before breakfast. The next few weeks were idyllic with Roy making love to Janet whenever she asked; she knew she had missed her period and was overjoyed when the doctor confirmed that she was pregnant for the third time. She broke the news to Roy, who hugged her and his joy seemed genuine; when on hearing the news, he told her he could not be happier.

Later that day, Roy was sitting in the lounge when the telephone rang; it was a voice he did not recognise. Roy was asked to meet the caller at the Sandpiper hotel, if he was ready for his next charter; Roy, who was beginning to get bored with sitting around playing with his children, had achieved what Janet had wanted, she was pregnant with their third child. Roy could feel the urge to be on the move and have a change of sexual partner. A new charter would achieve all he wanted, and he knew Elian and Fiona would be ready to sail as well as the opportunity to have him back in their beds; Even Madeleine had only been to see him that very morning whilst Janet had been on the beach with Morag and the children.

"Roy, I'm getting so bored with life at the Residency. She confided to him.

"I long for some more excitement in my life. When are you likely to get your next charter?"

In response to her appeal, Roy took her into the small office adjoining the lounge whilst Janet was busy with the children, and Madeleine had looked to him with a renewed hope that her boredom would soon end. Roy had pulled her to his chest, kissing her passionately. Her reaction had been instantaneous, her eyes had opened wide, her lips parted, and the kiss had become more and more passionate. He remembered that she had gasped and said, just as her stepmother had done some days earlier,

"Roy, we shouldn't be doing this here. Janet could come back any minute."

Then as he had gone to pull away from her, she had drawn him close, saying, "But don't stop. I haven't had anyone make love to me since we got back, and I need you so much."

Roy simply took advantage of the opportunity, taking the young woman with ease, never hesitating for a moment, and it was sometime later when he went upstairs to wash and change before returning to find Madeleine chatting to Janet as if nothing had happened.

Roy excused himself and went to his meeting at the Sandpiper. He was surprised to see a swarthy man in a typical straw fedora hat sitting in the bar waiting for him. As soon as Roy had introduced himself, without any explanation, as to who he was or who he represented, the man took Roy by the arm and they went over to a table set aside at the back of the bar and said coolly and casually,

"Lord Croft, you have come very well recommended, and we wish you to convey certain goods from Colombia up as far as the coast of Miami. We know it is dangerous, but we are prepared to pay you a handsome reward if you are successful, if, however, you are not successful, I'm afraid the consequences for your family will be terminal. Now that we have met, you have no choice but to accept our offer. Or we shall have no alternative but to kill you and your family, and believe me, don't for a moment think this is some kind of veiled threat. We do not make those, believe me, the threat is for real. Do not think for a moment you could slip away and disappear, for no matter where you hide, we will find you."

Roy looked at the soft-spoken, open-mouthed; this was the first time they had met and a cold chill ran down his spine as he realised the man in front of him was deadly serious.

Not wishing to put his family in any more danger than they were in already, he was resigned to carry out the man's request, regardless as to where it would lead him. He quietly resolved that in order to protect those nearest and dearest to him; he had no choice but to accept the offer.

"When and where do I make the first rendezvous?" Roy enquired, trying to hide his loathing for the man before him, who had so readily threatened the lives of himself and his family.

"We will call you with the map references, but it will be within the next twenty-four hours, so you should get your crew together and prepare your boat. Your payment has already been paid into your offshore account even as we speak, so don't fail," the swarthy man whispered.

The tone of his voice leaving; no doubt that he meant every word he spoke. Roy picked up his drink, and the two men touched glasses, the act sealed the bargain; despite Roy's mistrust and hatred of the man, both parties understood each other implicitly.

The next twenty-four hours had flown by as Elian, Fiona, and Madeleine had fuelled and restocked the supplies aboard the cruiser. Janet had been shocked by the suddenness of Roy's departure. That night had been frenetic as Roy had seemed so desperate to please her in every way almost as if he expected it to be the last time they would ever make love to each other. All he would say as he kissed her as he prepared to leave was,

"I shall be away for several weeks, but after this trip, I should be able to retire, and we will be able to spend much more time together. Remember, I love you and the children with all my heart."

Then going into the children's bedrooms, he kissed each one as though he would never see them again; he knew this trip would be dangerous and could not afford to fail. Going back into the master bedroom, Roy hugged Janet, kissing her and telling her,

"I do not have all the details of this charter, but I will try and keep in contact as and when I can. Just trust me if you do not hear from me; don't worry even if it's several weeks before you hear, either one of the crew or I will be in touch."

Janet's heart sank as she watched him go; she had a feeling that he was not telling her the whole story; he had never been one for dramatic exits such as the one she had just witnessed, and she only hoped he knew what he was doing; but before she could offer any further words of caution, he was gone.

Elian started the motors as soon as she saw him walk towards the cruiser; Fiona and Madeleine cast off, and they all headed out to sea on a direct course for the island of Curaçao, a journey of some 600 miles, taking them north of the island of St Vincent. They would spend a day on the island of Curaçao refuel and wait for their final co-ordinates for the rendezvous would be communicated the following day. Roy had only been told the destination would be in Colombia. The fact that Roy was worried about his family did nothing to stop him enjoying the favours of his crew as they made their way towards their destination. On the second day, Elian took Roy's meal up on to the flying deck; she took over the controls whilst he sat and ate his food; looking at him, she could see that he was worried.

"Roy," she asked, "I can see you are worried, what's wrong?"
All she got out of him was that he hated doing these drug running jobs with new charter clients; he never really knew if he could trust them, and this job, he suspected, was more dangerous than usual. The amount of drugs they would be carrying was far the biggest amount yet. She nodded, instantly understanding his fears, not realising that he had not informed her of the threat to his family, he had kept that to himself. She was a little surprised but quite willing to leave him to his own thoughts when Roy said,

"Elian, thanks for bringing up my meal. Why don't you go down and just relax for a couple of hours longer? I want to stay at the wheel for a while. It will help take my mind off things."
Elian stayed and talked but still concerned for his well-being she went below; she poured Roy a stiff Irish whisky, then, taking it up to him, she kissed him gently on the back of his neck. Roy thanked her for her kind thoughts, and then he asked her if she would sleep with him when they had docked for the night. Elian nodded but was alarmed at his sudden change; he usually did not ask but just expected her to be there after he had retired. She realised that he was more worried about this job than any they had tackled before and she wondered why.

It was a bright moonlit night as they anchored in one of the bays on the west of Curaçao, and the sea was calm almost like a sea of glass. They ate a late supper agreeing to an early start the following morning to go on to Willemstad to refuel. Fiona and Madeleine lay listening to Roy and Elian, making love until well into the early morning. After the urgent need had been assuaged, Elian lay there beside Roy as he fell into an exhausted and fitful sleep; she was worried about him because this was not his usual behaviour. Elian lay hoping that he would be all right and that this trip would be no worse than any of the others; she knew that Roy for once was not the confident and self-assured man he usually was, and as a result, she lay awake for hours worrying about his strange state of mind. This time she was aware that he was worse than when the Mafia had kept Janet as a virtual prisoner. When Roy finally woke, he had fallen to one side of Elian, and she was in a deep sleep; he rose quietly so as not to disturb her; Roy showered and shook Elian awake and walked through to the galley where Fiona was preparing breakfast. It was just breaking dawn as Fiona and Madeleine cast off; they headed south to refuel and then for Colombia, and they were to head around the point of Gallinas; the co-ordinates indicated that their destination was a cove near Santa Marta.

The time of the rendezvous was set for midnight, so they had little time to spare; it would mean a hard trip and the supply ship, they were to meet, had offered to refuel them so that they would not have to go into a Colombian port for fuel. Their cover for the trip up to Miami was that Lord Croft and the three women were on a sightseeing trip calling in at Kingston, Jamaica; Port-du-Paix, Haiti; along the west coast of Cuba; and north to Miami. In actual fact, when they arrived, they were to rendezvous fifteen miles off the coast to hand over the precious cargo before returning to Barbados by whatever route they wanted to use. Cautious to say the least after their previous confrontations with the authorities, it was necessary for them to keep well away from the islands to avoid the Venezuelan patrol boats, so everyone was on full alert. Fiona was set to watch on the bow, Madeleine on the stern; Roy and Elian were up on the flying bridge. The constant staring out to the horizon was tiresome and Roy was getting bored; the sight of Elian wearing her short skirt and her skimpy tank top clearly indicating that she was not wearing a bra was what put the idea into his mind. He strode meaningfully up behind Elian as she held the wheel with both hands, his intentions obvious to anyone watching. The swell of the waves held Elian's concentration as she combined a careful lookout and a firm grip on the wheel to keep the pitching vessel on course. Stepping up behind her, Roy slid his arms around her waist and drew her back against him. Elian froze, and instantly she knew just what his intentions were. Half-turning her head towards him,

"No, Roy, we can't, she gasped as his hands explored further. "We have to keep watch," she whispered hoping deep within herself that he would not stop.

Roy cast his eyes over the horizon; apart from the smoke emanating from a tramp steamer heading west, all was clear. Roy persisted, and Elian finally gave in, but in the ensuing bout of passion, she had let the boat drift off course. Elian cried out for him to stop as she stood up quickly grabbing the wheel and checking the GPS position; they had strayed off course during their struggle and were heading towards one of the Venezuelan islands, well within Venezuelan waters. She quickly corrected the course, and checking their actual position against the map, she headed north to get back to their original line and then turned south-west once again on their projected course. The Venezuelan patrol boat lying in wait, in a cove along the coast of the nearest island, had seen them on radar, and thinking their intention was to make for the island, they pulled out and headed for the luxury craft. Madeleine called out as she spotted the patrol boat emerge, and Elian, looking over her shoulder, opened up the throttles. The cruiser leapt forward; it was the first time, since Consuela's crew had fitted the new engine and re-tuned the other two, that Elian had had the opportunity to open the throttles to the limit; the speed was noticeably better now that Consuela's crew had improved the performance. The patrol boat had no chance of catching them, and realising any attempt to catch the fleeing vessel was fruitless, they slowed down, watching the cruiser head north, and once out of their territorial control, they saw it turn south-west. They radioed in to their headquarters the details of the incursion, but there was little they could do but watch the woman, who appeared topless handle the boat, like she knew exactly what she was doing.

The patrol boat skipper salivated at the thought of what he and his crew could have done with her; he envied the man who he saw beside her. He thought of his two friends Rodriguez and Ferdinand, one boat had disappeared under mysterious circumstances and other boat had vanished when apparently one of their own aircraft had sunk it with all hands, before crashing into the sea. That was the official version, but he did not believe it, for a moment; both men had been excellent seamen capable of handling almost any situation, legal or not. He missed swapping stories with both of his friends, on the way they had raped women from the yachts and boats they stopped; it was just the three of them who acted that way. The three had been at training school together and had always been the same; they had always had their way with women, but now there was only him and the memories of what had once been fair game. He wondered if the other two had finally run into someone more skilled than they had been and suffered the consequences; in his own mind, he knew he would never really know the truth.

Roy had recovered from his disappointment brought on by the patrol boat's untimely appearance and watched with some satisfaction as the patrol boat fell away behind them. Elian commented on the improved performance of the engines and asked Roy to take the wheel whilst she went below to freshen up. When she returned, Roy had brought the speed down to around forty knots; he noticed that to dissuade him against a repeat performance, Elian had changed into a T-shirt and slacks.

"That was close, too close for comfort," she said. "We did not want to encounter any more of those bloody Venezuelan patrol boat captains, if they were anything like the ones we met on the last trip."

Roy remembered the incidents well and how they had ended with them having to sink two patrol boats and down an aircraft; he could do nothing but agree with her comment. They put the incident behind them and headed towards their destination. To get there on time, Elian had to increase their speed, and it was almost midnight when they spotted a fishing vessel at their final co-ordinates; it gave the correct signal, and the two vessels closed on one another.

It took almost an hour to transfer the drugs and put them in the secret storage places below; the final quantities were packed in the wall of the cabin where Roy had discovered the counterfeit money. Once all the white powder was secreted away, the crew of the fishing vessel began to pump fuel aboard the cruiser from a tank in the hold. There was no conversation between the crews, and no signature for the cargo was necessary. The two vessels parted, and whilst Elian headed north, finally turning west in the direction of Curaçao on their way to Jamaica, Roy and the other two washed the decks of all evidence that could have been left by the movement of the cargo. The boat was soon gleaming like new. After all, they were supposed to give the impression they were holidaying; not running illicit drugs.

On the way to Curaçao, Roy wondered if Doctor Helga would still be around after completing her work contract at the hospital at Willemstad. He was determined to go there and enquire about her whereabouts as soon as they arrived, thinking to himself he may even be lucky to spend the night with her once again. He smiled as he recalled the night they had spent together the last time; he had been completely unexpected, but the sex had been most enjoyable. Roy could hardly wait as he felt himself stir at the thought. Roy walked down into the lounge; Madeleine had retired to bed, exhausted after helping to transfer the cargo and sealing it in the hidden compartments. He could hear Fiona in the galley making a hot drink for Elian up on the bridge; Roy stuck his head inside the galley and asked Fiona to make him a hot coffee. Fiona turned and smiled and nodded her head and walked past him to take Elian her drink; when she returned, she immediately went to the galley to make Roy's drink, pushing open the door to the stateroom; with the mug in her hand, Roy could see the twinkle in her eye. Guessing her intentions, Roy groaned under his breath, but when she slipped of her skirt, he did not deny her what she obviously needed. It was considerably later when Roy went up to relieve Elian, for his stint at the wheel, as they continued on their run to Curaçao. It was their intention to spend the day in the harbour, refuel, and later, that night under cover of darkness, head out to their destination, Kingston, Jamaica, a 500-mile trip that would take them some twelve to fourteen hours. Elian thanked Roy and went below to grab a few hours' sleep, leaving Roy to do the rest of the journey using the powerful on-board radar allowing them to travel at night.

Dawn was breaking as Elian went up to the bridge where Roy stood heading in towards the harbour at Willemstad; he had radioed ahead, and they had arranged to refuel and anchor in the harbour as no jetty was available. Once the formalities had been completed, Roy was ferried ashore in the tender by Fiona, who returned to the cruiser; the three women were to re-provision the boat whilst Roy was away. Roy had already taken a drink of the sexually stimulating potcheen to give him more zest with Helga, before he had caught a taxi to the hospital, where he asked a very attractive young doctor with the name Samantha Hillier on her name tag,
"Excuse me, Doctor, for the intrusion, but do you think I could speak to Doctor Helga van der Westhausen? She was so helpful the last time I was here, and I just wanted to thank her personally."
Doctor Hillier shook her head, replying,
"I'm afraid, she is not available. She has left to take up a post at another hospital. Tell me who can I can, say called, if I contact her?"

Roy told her his name was Lord Croft and he was a friend of Helga's, the disappointment at not being able to see her clearly showing in his voice. Doctor Hillier's heart began to hammer in her chest, standing before her was the man she had fantasised over ever since her friend had told her of her wild night of sex she had enjoyed with the English Lord. Making a decision that would, in all probability, change her life forever, Doctor Hillier asked Lord Croft to follow her into a side ward where they could speak without being interrupted.

"I'm sorry, Lord Croft, but after her contract expired at this hospital, Helga took another job and has been transferred. She told me you may call in to see her, and if you did, I was to give you a message and Helga's telephone number at her new posting."

The young doctor stepped around his Lordship, who was surprised when she closed the door and slid the lock into place, isolating them from any disturbance and turning back to face the ruggedly handsome Lord Croft, who could see the flush in her face; she was about to speak when Roy asked,
"Is there a problem, Doctor Hillier?"
"Call me Samantha," she whispered huskily, trying to regain her self-confidence before she began to speak to him with a more determined tone of voice. "Helga confessed to me, in confidence, the lurid details of the wild and passionate night the two of you spent together. From what I was led to understand, from her description of you, you seem to be better equipped in the nether regions than the average man. I have to admit Helga was so impressed she could not seem to get over it."

Roy was understandably a little embarrassed that Helga should have discussed such details with her friend, but what followed was even more surprising. Samantha moved towards him with an air of expectancy as she whispered softly, the flush rising as she struggled to control vivid pictures from dreams she had had when fantasising over what Helga had told her about this man,
"Lord Croft, after hearing the way she described you, I am intrigued, and have to confess my disbelief. If you have no objection, I would like see for myself if what she said was the truth or some wild figment of her imagination."
She walked towards him and, without further hesitation, put her hand between Roy's thighs, her experienced hand seeking and finding what she had been told was correct.
"Oh my," she said, the flush deepening as her heart beat faster, "I need to see more."
As she unzipped Roy's fly, she unclipped his waistband and pulled his slacks and shorts down. She sat on the stool in front of the desk and, as if in some school environment, she studied Roy's potcheen-stimulated manhood as it stood fully erect, as she released it from its confinement.
"Helga was right. It certainly is one of the best specimens I've ever seen, and believe me; I've seen plenty in my time as a doctor."

Lord Croft had been disappointed to discover Helga was away, but if his intuition was correct, this attractive young doctor seemed just as keen to take her place. With just as much audacity as the doctor had shown, he pulled Samantha to her feet, intent on opening the front of her white uniform dress. It was a simple wrap over with two rows of snap studs; Roy's hand quickly pulled at the studs, designed for a quick change, if soiled by a patient's blood, they snapped open. Once they were undone, the white uniform dress fell to the floor, revealing the startled doctor's breasts encased in a simple white cotton bra. She made no sound or showed any signs of resistance other than attempting to control her breathing, and as Roy unclipped the front fastener of her bra allowing her unfettered breasts to spill out. Samantha was shocked, but before she could speak, Roy bent forward and took one of her nipples into his mouth; the young doctor moaned pushing her breast forward as her libido soared out of control. Her mind sensed rather than felt Roy pull her panties down to reveal her nakedness.

"Oh, Lord Croft, we really can't do this. I'm a happily married woman, and I have never let anyone other than my husband touch me, since I took my wedding vows. I know I was way out of order, but I was just so inquisitive to see if what Helga had told me was true. I am married to one of the other doctors here in the hospital," she said, her voice quaking with emotion.

Her heart was beating faster, blood pounding through her body, and her sonorous breathing was making her chest rise and fall as she felt Lord Croft's mouth on her breast. Lord Croft held her against him, and seemingly unable to move, she became alarmed at how aroused she was. This had never happened to her before, and she could not really explain how she was standing naked with an English Lord, a friend of Helga's, kissing her breasts, and she had her hand around his oversized, fully erect penis.

To try and take the heat out of what was happening, Samantha's voice, trembling with emotion,

"Please let me explain, Lord Croft," she said, her body trembling with her growing excitement.

"It's Roy," he murmured.

A soft long moan preceded the words as the doctor felt herself being carried away by the hands of Helga's lover; the vivid dreams she had experienced after Helga had given her explicit details of that night of lust flooded into her mind.

"It's like this," she stammered, feeling herself losing control. "I met my husband the day I arrived at the hospital; the two of us were instantly attracted to each other and became lovers. I have never, from that moment, allowed anyone to see me undressed, let alone touch me this way, but I can't seem to stop myself letting you to do this to me."

At this point, she gave a long moan as she surrendered to Lord Croft's deepening caress. She continued aimlessly, not understanding why she was babbling like a silly schoolgirl and not fighting for her honour.

"We were married soon after my appointment as a doctor was confirmed."

Roy vaguely heard her voice as it trailed off, and she looked startled as Roy lifted her off her feet and laid her on her back on the examining couch. She gasped, and her eyes opened wide as she reacted to Roy's soft and gentle touch.

"Lord Croft, your Grace, you must understand, my standing as a doctor in this hospital would be compromised if anyone caught us. Oh my God, I have never felt like this, but please we can't have intercourse. I cannot let you go all the way," she said trying to control her breathing. "I'm married, and I am going home to see my husband this afternoon; I just know as usual when we are off in an afternoon, he will want me to make love to him."

Unabashed, Lord Croft was in his element; if he were not mistaken, Samantha's arousal was betraying her denial; he continued to arouse this attractive woman whose words were in no way coinciding to her desire; his hands roamed her body, getting more intrusive, and her sharp intake of breath was followed by,

"No further, your Grace, Oh my God you have me so aroused. I just want you to relieve me. I'll do the same for you, I promise. Oh God! Why am I doing this? Please. Oh God!"

Roy continued to arouse her to a point where she moaned softly.

"No further," she reaffirmed her breathing now ragged and sonorous.

In reality, she had lost all control, her arousal and the vivid pictures in her mind were just too much for her to handle, and she no longer wanted the wonderful feeling, his Lordship was inducing, to stop. She just surrendered; feeling His Lordship move closer, the last vestige of resistance evaporated and lust moved into the act of wild sex, and with a deep moan, Doctor Hillier let him slide into her with no further objection. She began to respond almost immediately, and their lustful encounter was both prolonged and enjoyable. Samantha did not call for help and no one came to her aid. She could not understand why she had just let Helga's friend make passionate love to her with no thought of the consequences, other than she had acted out her wildest fantasy. Her act of contrition was replaced by a sudden guilt complex, but here was no denying, the act of adultery had been truly an unexpected pleasure.

"Oh my," she gasped, "what have I done? I have committed adultery, but you took me, without any protection. Only God knows why I let this happen. They say curiosity killed the cat, and I now know what they mean."

Roy whispered to the sweat-covered young doctor underneath him,

"Just what did Helga tell you about me? I'm curious to know."

Samantha answered breathlessly,

"Helga told me you had given her the best sex she had ever had; she told me you're not only well blessed, but that you pleasured her as no man had ever pleasured her before. She said that you were almost insatiable; she would let you make love to her at any time, and you pleasured her several times during the night you had been together. I have had such wild dreams and flights of fantasy about you ever since. Now I must confess I feel the same way. I just have a feeling that I'm not going to get home to my husband this afternoon."

Roy did not know how or why no one had come into the small side ward as he spent the rest of the afternoon having wild and unprotected sex with Samantha Hillier, Helga's young friend, until she looked at her watch and cried out,

"Lord Croft, Roy, enough! I'm due back on duty. I'm sorry. I must confess it's been pleasurable, but look at the time. You really will have to go now." Then she calmly sat down and put on her underwear, before allowing Lord Croft to help her on with her uniform; she sat somewhat dazed as she watched him walk to the handbasin and wash away any signs of their sexual interaction. He dressed and, turning, kissed her softly on the lips before leaving her, looking somewhat perplexed as to how this had happened at all. She could not understand it, and at this point in time, she was so overwhelmed by the feeling of sexual satisfaction that she did not care. She had to speak to him again, and running down the corridor after him ignoring the discomfort, she caught up with him in the car park and said breathlessly,

"If you are ever in Curaçao again, please don't hesitate to call me."

With that she handed him a card containing details of her home address and all of her contact telephone numbers, and still mesmerised at what had happened between them, she watched as he put it into his pocket and climbed into the taxi. As the taxi turned the corner, she realised that, apart from his name, she knew absolutely nothing about him other than that she would meet him again sometime in the future.

Chapter 17

Roy arrived back and saw the tender tied up by the jetty, and it was obvious his crew had not yet returned from shopping; he climbed into the boat, started the engine, and headed out to the cruiser to wait for their return. He lay on the deck and relaxed, his groins ached, but the pleasure young Samantha had given him was immeasurable; he was content and wondered if Helga would be available in Kingston when they arrived in Jamaica. With these pleasant thought running through his mind, he relaxed under the sun, feeling his tired body slowly recover the energy he had expended. It was some thirty minutes later when he saw the three members of his crew wave; he climbed into the tender and went to collect them with the supplies to restock the larder. After the stores had been loaded, Roy took them all out to a restaurant for dinner, and when they returned to the cruiser, they cast off and headed towards Jamaica. It was a journey of some 500 miles, and they would not arrive until well into the following day. Roy took the first watch, and the radar showed a clear route all the way. Apart from the odd coastal tramp steamer and a couple of cruise liners, Roy avoided each and continued to head north. Halfway through his shift, Elian came on deck, complaining that she could not sleep, and she handed him a mug of coffee laced with his favourite whisky. Elian was obviously in a playful mood, but after his session at the hospital, Roy was not in the mood. Elian pouted with disappointment but reconciled herself to spend some time with him alone. They discussed the voyage and the other members of the crew; both expressed their concern that they had still not heard any news from Gael.

It was just breaking dawn when they heard sounds of movement from below.

"Roy," Elian whispered, "I think I should go below and make sure breakfast is on the way, and then I will take over for the rest of the journey."

Roy nodded in agreement as Elian, with a broad grin, kissed him on the mouth, and she slipped below, leaving Roy to ponder over what they had discussed. Elian was a very level-headed person and one, he felt, he could trust with his life; it was not love he felt for her but a deep feeling of admiration for the way she could handle his boat in the worst conditions to which everything else about her was an added bonus. Some fifteen minutes later, Elian arrived, looking fresh and ready for the day ahead; she took over the wheel and kissed Roy gently on the cheek. In the time, he had relaxed waiting for Elian to come up and take over, many thoughts and subjects had raced through Roy's mind. For no particular reason, he had made the decision that sometime in the near future he would contact Consuela Marias and ask her to fit the engines and turbochargers she had recommended. At the same time he would get her to install an autopilot to allow him to enjoy the added benefits of his crew without worrying about a collision with some freighter, which was off the normal shipping channels for whatever reason. The rest of the voyage passed without any problems, and as they approached their destination, Roy radioed Kingston harbour master requesting an anchorage for refuelling and rest and recuperation.

The anchorage was designated, and less than two hours later, Fiona was dropping Roy off at the harbour where after going through the necessary formalities; he phoned the number he had been given for Helga. The soft, buoyant young voice answering the call announced the name of a hospital; Roy asked to be put through to Dr Helga Van der Westhausen; the voice asked who was calling.

"Lord Croft," Roy replied.

The answer disappointed Roy as he was told.

"I'm sorry, Lord Croft, but Doctor Helga Van der Westhausen is away. She is in a village in the interior operating at a clinic." He listened as the voice continued, "She is staying with my mother, and she was apparently expecting you, and I was informed that when you called, I was to give you every co-operation. I am off in thirty minutes, and if you pick me up, I am instructed to take you home so that you can ring Helga and speak to her."

Roy was disappointed and apologised,

"Thank you for the invitation, but I must take a rain check on your kind offer. We are on charter, and I just wanted to touch base with an old friend. Perhaps we can meet again in the not too distant future. Give Helga my fondest regards and tell her I'm sorry to have missed her."

Returning to the boat, Roy was obviously in a mood of depression, and to the consternation of his crew, he grabbed a bottle of whisky as consolation, and after requesting Elian to take the route through the Cayman Islands, south of Cuba, he retired to his stateroom. They heard no more from him until the following morning when a dishevelled Roy emerged, unshaven and hung-over. No one knew why he had behaved as he had, and from the scowl he gave, no one dared to ask. Only Roy knew the worry of this trip was beginning to tell on his usually steel-edged nerves. Elian had done as she had been requested: taken the route through the Cayman Islands. As Roy walked up to the flying bridge, they were passing through the Yucatán Channel before turning north-east and heading towards their first rendezvous point, just off Havana. He apologised for not being himself and went down to shower and shave, emerging later looking like his old self. He took over the wheel, and the sea breeze restored his usual hearty appetite.

It was early evening when they reached the first co-ordinates and Roy throttled down; the three women had placed the rocket launchers, automatic weapons, and assortment of handguns to hand. They were ready for any sign of trouble. To Roy's intense annoyance, the contact was late. Roy's instructions were to wait no longer than one hour. The time was almost up when Roy spotted the cigarette boat heading their way at high speed; Elian had supervised the retrieval of the packets from below, and they were in waterproof floater bags. The high-speed craft did a pass and turned back; the driver was pointing to the shoreline and indicating that the cruiser should follow. Roy gave the thumbs-down sign indicating that was not part of the arrangement; he had his hand on the throttle to open up at the first sign of trouble.

The flashy boat did one more circuit before slowing down and coming alongside. The Cuban driver lifted his hat and gave the required signal; his men moved as though to board, and the three women appeared out of the lower wheelhouse, armed with their automatic weapons. The crew of the boat alongside stopped dead in their tracks, their mouth open at the sight of the three beautiful women handling automatic weapons as if it were an everyday occurrence. Only women in the army and terrorist women did that in Cuba. Elian indicated that they should stay where they were; then as instructed, Fiona and Madeleine began to carry the precious cargo to the railings; they then began to pass the floater bags down to the rough-looking men on deck below. It took around ten minutes until the last parcel had been delivered; the men had not taken their eyes off the women, each one of them envying the owner of the supply boat, but none of them took any chances. The woman standing with the gun trained on them looked as though she meant business, not to mention the captain of the cruiser who stood watching from the flying deck, his eyes never leaving their moves for a moment. The transfer completed, Roy gave the signal to the driver of the speedboat that there was no more packets to be loaded. The women cast off the boat lines, and Roy eased the throttle forward, and as soon as he was clear, he pushed the controls fully forward; the cruiser rode up on to the plane and sped away, leaving the crew of the launch to continue to pack their cargo into the watertight compartments in the hull.

Roy, using the satellite phone, rang the first one-time number and sent the agreed text message to confirm delivery had taken place successfully. The tiny burst of data on the satellite uplink was designed to last a fraction of a second, and the connection was broken, making the tracing of the position of the receiver or the sender an almost impossible task. Using the powerful night-vision binoculars, Roy could see the Cuban coast as they headed north towards the Florida Keys, where the second delivery was to take place before dawn. The women got the parcels up into the deck lockers in readiness, and as they approached the co-ordinates, the signal from the fast launch indicated they were in position. Roy drew nearer and finally alongside. The floaters were passed down swiftly and efficiently, and in less than five minutes, the two craft separated; the short burst of data was sent again, confirming the second delivery.

Roy then headed up into the bay of Florida, where they would lay over for the day and relax before moving to a set of co-ordinates yet to be specified to make the third delivery. This was to be followed by a night run returning to Key Point to deliver the fourth load of cargo and then south to Andros Island for the final delivery before returning home. Roy had a bad feeling about this run, and he called the three women into the lounge and informed them of his concerns, asking them to be extra vigilant during the day, and especially when the deliveries were to be made. Elian, who knew Roy's instincts were rarely wrong, asked,
"If you are so concerned, Roy, do you want me to arm the torpedoes?"
Roy, nodding in affirmation, said with a grim tone to his voice,
"If I'm right, we need all the weapons checked in readiness for any emergency. This close to the American coast, with what we have on board it is way too dangerous to take any chances of us being caught red-handed. If we are, I, for one, have no intention of going down without a fight to the death if necessary."

They lay about a mile off the coast, and although it looked, to the casual observer, as though the cruiser was just a tourist craft with a couple of half-naked women sunbathing on the deck, both were fully alert with weapons hidden under the inflatable bedding and machine pistols and side arms hidden under the towels. Roy was on the flying bridge with Madeleine, who had brought up the Sam7 and a rocket launcher, which was stowed under a couple of blankets. They watched as a couple of coastguard vessels passed fairly close to them; the officer on watch of the second coastguard cutter had his binoculars pointed in their direction; he spoke quickly to the other officers, and they all began scanning the decks of Roy's cruise then after pausing from their normal duties they studied the half-naked bodies of Elian and Fiona. On the return pass, they came closer; concerned they may ask to board and search, Roy decided to create a diversion, and pulling the near-naked Madeleine towards him and bending her back over the map table, he began to kiss her passionately. The binoculars locked onto him as his hands roamed her body. Madeleine moaned as she played her part for the watchers to see. They simulated the act of lovemaking until Madeleine, fully enjoying the voyeuristic crew watching, cried out, the sound of her apparent satisfaction carrying across the open water.

The officer on the US naval cutter indicated that they should sound the horn in salute as they sped away. Roy, however, was so turned on by the thought that the crew of the cutter had watched him apparently making love to Madeleine, so blatantly for all to see, that he indicated that Elian should take the wheel. Sweeping Madeleine up into his arms, he carried her below, where they made love long after the US coastguard cutter had departed. The afternoon drew on, when Elian took the craft out to the co-ordinates she had received on Roy's satellite phone, as expected the high-speed launch was soon alongside. Elian stayed up on the bridge whilst Roy helped Fiona and Madeleine to toss the floaters down into the centre well of the speedboat; as soon as the last parcel had hit the deck, the speedboat was away, arcing in a large semicircle and headed for the shore. Roy sent the short burst of data, indicating the delivery was once more complete, and Elian headed south towards Key West; the rendezvous time was one thirty, and they did not want to be late. The next delivery went as smooth as the last, and Roy began to think his premonition of discovery were all a figment of his wild imagination.

The co-ordinates were received, and checking the location, this time the rendezvous was nearer to Nassau, Bahamas, and the Andros Island. The route was quite close to the one they had taken when they had been challenged by the US coastal patrol last time, captained by the now infamous Chuck. Roy instructed Elian to stick one of the pre-prepared stickers over the name of the vessel to change the name of the cruiser and the registration, as they had done so often in the past; he went to the radio and killed the transponder to prevent recognition. The cruiser was now, to all intents and purposes, an Argentinean-registered vessel with a corresponding registration number. It was shortly after these preparations had been completed, when Elian called down informing Roy and the others that they were being tailed by a boat, she could see it on the radar, but it was not yet visible to the naked eye.

Roy knew in his own mind it was a US coastguard cutter, and he was certain it was the one that had been there before, with Chuck in command. This time he would search the cruiser from stem to stern, if for no other reason than Roy had thrown him off the vessel when he had attempted to force Madeleine to allow him to sodomise her. If Roy was right, they would close on them shortly; he raced up the companionway and alerted the women to be ready for action. He spoke quietly to Elian, telling her to open the throttles wide when he gave the command, and then give him the controls in the wheelhouse where the twin torpedo launchers were situated. Roy told her he was banking on the fact that Chuck would be so incensed at retribution that he would not radio the contact in; it would therefore be an illegal search, as no authorisation to board the Argentinean vessel would have been received. Chuck and his crew would be acting on their own volition.

Roy trained his binoculars in the direction the coastguard cutter would approach from; it was midday and their rendezvous was not until six o'clock in the evening. Elian, situated up on the bridge, confirmed that a US coastguard cutter was approaching them fast; Roy looked carefully using his powerful binoculars; he could see Chuck's face, set with grim determination. The cutter began to close the gap, although the cruiser was in International waters and was not breaking any laws. Using a bullhorn, the cutter hailed the cruiser, the voice informing the crew of the Argentinean-registered boat that the US coastguards had reason to believe they were smugglers and they should hove to and allow them to board them and carry out a detailed search. Roy wanted to get closer to Andros Island as it was the least populated of the group of islands known as the Bahamas. He felt Elian give him the controls, and as the cutter closed, Roy opened the throttles fully and the cruiser leapt forward, and Roy sent a radio message to the cutter to the effect that they had no jurisdiction over them in Bahamian waters. The message was acknowledged, and the reply came a few minutes later that if the cruiser did not heave to, they would have no choice but to put a shot across her bows.

The distance between the two vessels was widening, and Chuck felt that he was losing his face in front of his crew. He gave the instruction to fire; the second in command looked at him in amazement.

"Shouldn't we radio in and confirm the action to fire?" he queried. "After all, we are in Bahamian waters."
Chuck was furious with his first officer.

"I have given a command, and I want it obeyed immediately," he snapped his face like thunder.
The watch looked at each other but gave the order to fire. The shell fell short, and Roy turned in towards the shore, watching the waters shallow towards the reef. The second shot came closer, and Roy signalled that if they continued, he would have to return their fire; he once again reiterated that they were not in US waters and the cutter had no jurisdiction.

A third shot was fired, which came close to the bow, as Roy turned and began to run towards the oncoming cutter; swinging wide, he ordered Elian to prepare to fire a grenade in the direction of the vessel as a warning that they were armed and prepared to defend themselves. Elian sighted the shot at some distance behind the cutter and fired; Chuck, far from being shaken or warned off, said to his crew,

"We are being subjected to a completely unprovoked attack, and I order you to defend yourselves and sink the stupid bastard."
The first officer and the crew looked at him open-mouthed; they had fired on another vessel under foreign registration, without any justification, and their skipper was ordering them now to sink the vessel, which had quite rightly chosen to defend itself against an unprovoked attack by a US vessel. The crew of the cutter had no idea what the hell the other boat had done to upset their skipper and make him so irrational, especially as the other boat had been in radio contact. Unperturbed, Chuck ordered the deck crew to fire at will, and Roy watched grim-faced as he lined up the cruiser to be in a position to fire a torpedo broadside on to the advancing cutter.

The cutter fired again, and this time the shot fell just astern, the cutter having underestimated the cruiser's speed. Roy fired the starboard torpedo and swung away to pass astern of the cutter. Not expecting the cruiser to be carrying torpedoes, the crew were taken completely by surprise; with general quarters being sounded, the crew sprung into battle mode and took evasive action, but it was too late. The torpedo struck the rudder and exploded as Roy raced away at full speed from the crippled cutter. The cruiser raced away from Andros Island towards Nassau; the crippled cutter lay still in the water; Roy could see that she was sinking, but that the crew were taking to the lifeboats. Roy sent an SOS with a message that they had seen an explosion from the direction of Andros Island, but they were unable to respond due to engine failure, and they gave the false name and registration as a reference.

Elian went down and removed the overlaid name and registration, and they headed towards the co-ordinates. Roy left the transponder off, and as soon as the last package had been delivered, he ordered Elian to head south towards Cuba. Roy knew that as soon as the captain of the navy cutter gave details of the cruiser, the satellite search for them would be on. Darkness descended as they approached the Old Bahama Channel, north of Cuba; in this channel, there were thousands of small islands and many fishing vessels to confuse any satellite search. Roy felt here they could lose themselves for a few days until the surveillance went quiet; they could island hop until it was safe for them to head for Haiti, then to Puerto Rico and the Virgin Islands. Once at the Virgin Islands, Roy planned to get Consuela and her crew to refit the engines to give them a faster initial response and almost double the vessel's range. In the meantime, they would leave off the radio transponder and virtually disappear during the cover of darkness and hide in the tiny islands.

Roy's intentions were that they would hopefully find a large cavern open to the sea where they could be out of sight of even satellite surveillance. The movement of the many fishing boats around the islands would be enough to confuse any searchers from the air, the sea, or satellite. The following morning, after running between several fishing vessels similar in size to the cruiser, they were lucky enough to find an open cavern under the high cliffs of one of the larger islands. It was partially hidden, and if it had not been for the depth finder, they would never have realised how deep the water was in the cavern. They edged under the stony overhang and the foliage swung back behind them, hiding them from any casual search. Elian switched off the motors, secured the lines, and dropped the anchor; the whole crew fell into an exhausted sleep, apart from Roy, who took the first watch, just in case. He poured himself a large Irish whisky and sat up on the bridge thinking to himself, *just how lucky they had been. If Chuck had boarded them and found the drugs and the armaments, they would have been taken for drug smuggling pirates and all of them could have been incarcerated for a long time.* As he sat with these thoughts running through his mind, Elian, who had been asleep for less than an hour, had woken up, her adrenalin still high from the efforts to evade both Chuck's attack and satellite surveillance with the fear of possible capture. She trusted Roy's intuition implicitly and had no doubt that his luck would hold yet again.

She carried a glass and sat beside him, after helping herself to a large measure of Roy's favourite whisky.

"Roy," she said, "we have had a very narrow escape, and I'm not sure we are out of the woods yet. We shall probably have to remain in these waters for at least a week before we dare venture out. The problem is, if the locals get to know we are here, we could be in trouble with the Cubans for not registering with the customs and immigration. Besides, this is getting a little too exciting for my piece of mind, and what about Janet and the children, what would they do if you were serving a long sentence in jail? After all, we're not too far from Guantanamo Bay, the terrorist holding prison of America, and from what we hear; it's not the place to spend a holiday."

Roy stared vacantly, only realising that Elian had sat beside him when she spoke; Roy nodded in agreement to her comments but made no real answer.

He was getting tired of the constant adrenalin surges they had in this drug running business; the rewards were excellent, but the risks were getting higher and higher. He had completed his obligations to the Colombians, and he did not want to be at their beck and call any longer. It was at that moment in time that he decided to call Janet at the earliest possible time and ask her to meet him with the children in the Virgin Islands. He turned and put his arm around Elian, and she nestled close to his chest. Roy felt the stirrings in his groin and knew he would relieve both of their stress induced adrenalin high. He kissed Elian softly and thanked her for her efforts; she looked at him hard and whispered,

"I hope I've earned more than a soft kiss on the cheek. I was hoping for a lot more than that."

Looking around, he could see no sign of any boats in the near vicinity. Roy looked Elian between the eyes and asked quietly,

"Where are the others?"

"Out for the count! The last time I looked in on them, before coming up on deck, they were in a deep sleep."

Roy took her in his arms, and, in minutes, they were in a lover's embrace, nothing else mattered for the moment. Her soft moans echoed back off the cavern roof. She let Roy take full command of the situation, her back arched up as spasm after spasm racked her slim body. She gasped as wave after wave of erotic pleasure washed over her shuddering frame. She lay back satisfied for the moment; her desires quenched, she felt alive and very satisfied.

After checking their situation, Elian was satisfied the cruiser was well hidden from all but the most determined search. She woke the others and informed them it was their turn to be on watch, and knowing they would warn of any impending danger, she went below into Roy's cabin, where they lay together until night had fallen. Roy climbed off the bed and showered and went back up on deck, wondering what had disturbed him; the knock on the door came, and as he opened it, a worried-looking Fiona asked him to come up on deck. As soon as he went up to the flying deck, Roy became aware of an increase in the activity in and around the islands, and there were glints of searchlights. Rousing Elian, Roy quickly beckoned the others to join him, and together, they pulled the camouflage nets out of the locker and draped them over the superstructure; when daylight arrived, the cruiser would now blend in perfectly with its surroundings, and unless someone was extremely lucky, they would remain hidden from almost any close inspection.

After a week, the activity died down, and the only thing the four of them had to occupy their minds and bodies was sex; Roy was feeling the strain of being penned up under the cavern roof, but he was cautious; he insisted that they give it another four days before he allowed Elian to take the tender and scout the surrounding islands to see if the coast was clear. She returned, saying all was quiet and there were no signs of anyone searching for them any longer. That night, using the echo sounder and the radar, they cast off and slipped quietly out of the cavern, leaving the camouflage netting in place and running without lights until they were in the Old Bermuda Channel once again, and then they headed down in the direction of Haiti. Elian suggested they keep the camouflage netting in place as it would disguise the shape of the cruiser from any infrared search; she went on to say,

"I feel we should continue to run without lights, using the radar, to avoid other vessels until we are clear of the Cuban coast."

Roy agreed, and they finally removed the covering nets just as dawn was breaking, and the cruiser, now under its own registration, headed into Port-de-Paix for fresh supplies and to refuel. Roy took the opportunity to contact Janet to let her know all was well, and he would tell her why he had been out of contact when he got back. Janet almost wept with relief at hearing his voice and asked if the crew were OK. Roy was pleased to hear that the children were well and asked Janet to book a flight to the Virgin Islands for herself, Morag, and the children and he would meet them there and spend a few days together whilst the new engines were fitted. Janet was thrilled that she and the children would be able to spend time with Roy and said, in a voice reflecting her relief, with her usual confidence restored,

"We will see you a week on Monday, my darling. I and the children have missed you so much. It will be wonderful to spend some time together."

Once they had refuelled and restocked the supplies, Roy took his crew for lunch; they had a wonderful seafood meal and a couple of glasses of wine before returning to the vessel for a well-earned rest prior to leaving that evening to head west past Puerto Rico and on to Tortola, British Virgin Islands. Roy was under no illusions; there was still the possibility of being stopped and searched; he did not want to go into a port under US jurisdiction just in case Chuck had given them whatever details he knew about Lord Croft's cruiser. Roy was not aware that the only death that had occurred when the torpedo had hit the cruiser had been the captain of the vessel, Chuck, or that was the official version, given by the first officer and the crew when they had been rescued. They had told the US navy that the captain had ordered them to open fire on a cruiser under an Argentinean flag for reasons of his own, and as far as they knew, he had done so for personal reasons and for no other cause. The search for the Argentinean cruiser had been extensive, and as the costs mounted, after a week, when no sign of the vessel could be found, the case had been closed and Roy was safe once again.

Roy radioed ahead and spoke to the harbour master who recognised Lord Croft's voice at once. He allocated a berth and alerted Consuela that Lord

Croft would be contacting her to fit new motors to his cruiser. Consuela was delighted at the chance to see Roy again; he was after all the father of her unborn infant. She was elated with the possibility that Lord Croft may make love to her again, but she had no intention of letting him know he had got her pregnant, and she was not that far into her trimesters that he would notice. When Roy contacted her, she informed him,

"The order for the engines has been placed, but delivery will take several days, and if it's convenient, I would like to see you to arrange for a deposit on the work and materials to be paid. I have had to commit myself for the cost of the motors, and as yet I have no written order for the work to be carried out."

Roy had a vague idea just what arrangement Consuela had in mind, and his mind immediately remembered her soft lips and her sensual caress.

Chapter 18

In the remaining time it took to complete the journey Roy stood up on the bridge with Elian and talked about the improvements, she thought, the new engines would have on the boat's performance. Elian told Roy that when she had discussed the changeover with Consuela, before they left, she had suggested four engines instead of three and the ability to close down two and run on the remaining two when cruising at lower speeds would conserve a great deal of fuel; besides, the advances in the development of the newest diesels meant they were far more fuel efficient than the older designs. As a result, the range of the cruiser would be greater and the pickup to maximum speed would be smoother and faster. She did not know whether the top speed would increase due to the shape of the hull, but there was not really much they could do to change that. The boat was already one of the fastest seventy-three-foot wooden boats she had ever seen. The only drawback was the cruiser consumed vast amounts of fuel: it was comparable to a camel drinking water after a long journey through the desert. They finally saw the island come into sight, and Roy went down to tell the others that they would be arriving in the harbour shortly, and seeing Madeleine topless, he asked her to get dressed; she sighed, for like the others she had become accustomed to wearing next to nothing when they were at sea. Everyone moved up onto the deck to prepare for securing the boat and once more stretching their legs on dry land, and they realised that with the refit they would be ashore for some time.

Using his satellite phone, Roy booked rooms, as Janet would be joining them with the children; he did not book them as usual into the Castle Maria hotel, for as it was out of the tourist season, he managed to book the Breeze Haven, which comprised two interconnected villas, each with three bedrooms, separated by a staircase leading from one to the other. He planned to put the three crew members into the upper 'Leeward House', which was screened off by lush vegetation and a short flight of steps, whilst he and Janet along with Morag and the children would stay in the lower 'Windward House'. They docked and took a taxi to the villas; the accommodation was exceptional, fully serviced with its own private pool sheltered from the direct rays of the sun. The three women immediately, after they had parked their bags in the upper bungalow, stripped off and plunged naked into the pool to cool off. Roy stood and watched inwardly admiring each for their individual characteristics, and he knew intimately what each one liked in the way of sexual stimulation. Then after he had rung Consuela to make an appointment for the following afternoon, he stripped of and joined the others in the pool, naked and relaxed.

They sat by the pool to eat that evening; it was still warm, and they all sat, totally unashamed of their nakedness, they were relaxed and drank the local cane spirits until it was time to go to bed. Elian joined Roy, and after they had made love, they lay in each other's arms, each knowing that in a few days Janet and the children would arrive and Roy would need to spend most of his time with them. The following morning, Roy showered; afterwards, and whilst the three women relaxed by the pool, Roy rang to find out when Janet would be arriving; once he had the date and time of her and the children's arrival, he called a taxi to take him to Consuela's home. The journey was longer than it had been from the town hotel, but the beauty of the islands was wonderful, and Roy sat back and enjoyed the journey.

He rang the bell, and Consuela herself came to the door; she looked good and smelled wonderful, her faint alluring perfume wafted under Roy's nose; she had prepared herself for Roy's arrival and had chosen her mode of attire to show her attributes at their best. Her long black hair shone with health as it cascaded down around her shoulders; she seemed to radiate with good health as the low-cut bodice of her white blouse embroidered at the edges with tiny red flowers accentuated her dark-skinned breasts without being too obvious; her short wrap around skirt showed off her sculptured legs to perfection. Consuela beckoned him to enter, and as he did so, she put her arms around Roy's neck and pressed her soft body against him, leaving no doubt in Roy's mind what she had planned. He allowed her to take him through to her bedroom where he let her have her way. After all, he wanted her to do a good job on the cruiser, and what better inducement but to complete the work for a lover? He knew the price of the work would be fair on both sides; it was the commitment for the job to be perfect he was endeavouring to get, and this was the best way he knew how to achieve that.

Afterwards the demanding and torrid sexual activity they lay still, both with their own thoughts; Roy eventually stood and walked into the shower and turned on the water. He stripped off the remainder of his clothes and climbed inside. He heard the door open behind him and in climbed Consuela. He had to admire her body; she was in excellent shape for her age. It was all he could do to stop himself from taking her once again there and then under the cascade of water, but resisting the need, he resigned himself to washing her and enjoying the feel of her dark textured skin. They dried themselves on the fluffy towels, and Roy put on his shirt, before making sure no one was about, and retrieved his undershorts and trousers from just inside the bedroom door. Then they both made themselves presentable and walked into the lounge. Consuela's flush and radiant smile told anyone, interested enough to look, that she was satiated and content. Roy sat down, and Consuela poured them both a drink before they discussed the cost of the conversion to the engine room. Roy thought the price was more than fair and agreed to deliver the cruiser to the yard the following morning. Consuela said that the work would take about two weeks, including having Elian take the boat out for sea trials. Roy nodded in agreement, and they sat talking until dinner time. Consuela gave Roy another superb seafood meal and the couple parted, Consuela needing to sleep off the excesses of their overzealous sex and the huge meal; Roy, sitting back in the taxi, reflected on how wonderful it was to have such a good sex life and be in a position to be able to afford the lifestyle to go with it.

When he got back to the villa, the crew had all retired, and Roy was glad of the chance to sit and reflect on where his life was at present. His wife and family were soon going to be with him, and he had three mistresses living in the same house. It would be difficult, but with his luck, he anticipated that something had to go wrong. He sat enjoying being alone as the whisky was excellent, and by the time he went to bed, it was already getting light. He rose late the following morning, and leaving Fiona and Madeleine at the villas to relax. Elian and Roy took the boat to Consuela's boatyard, where the crew could begin to strip the old engines out so that when the new ones arrived, the preparation work would be completed. Being satisfied that the work was underway, Elian and Roy then took a taxi back to the villa; the other two were down on the beach enjoying the sun. Elian stripped off and dived into the pool calling for Roy to join her. Roy stripped off his own clothes and dived into the water as requested. The water washed away his fatigue, and Elian had swum over to him and, diving below the surface, had come up, saying,

"I'm glad I've got you to myself for a change."
Without waiting for a response, she put her legs around him as she reached up and kissed him, and as he responded to her obvious need, their

consummate loving soon had the waves splashing against the side of the pool. She urged him on with her hips and said,

"Oh, Roy, I need you so much." The joy on her face was obvious as she enjoyed the moment.

"Elian, you are not being fair to the others. You know today should be Fiona's day," Roy whispered.

Elian's reply was a smile, and she said,

"By this evening, if I know you, you will have recovered and she will never know."

Roy shook his head and laughed; he took her in his arms and kissed her before getting out of the pool and dressing, leaving her to languish in the cool water. The next two days passed quickly for Roy, with Elian going to Consuela's boatyard to supervise the removal of the engines; Consuela had arranged the sale of the used engines to three fishermen and put the proceeds towards the new engines. The gearbox was removed and the engine mountings were put in place to receive the smaller new Penta diesels. Although smaller, the newer technology would enable them to develop much greater horse power when combined with the new turbochargers, intercoolers, and blowers. Consuela chased up the delivery and told Elian they would be delivered in the next few days and she would let Roy know the day they arrived.

Roy went to meet his wife and children; then as soon as they had cleared customs and immigration, Sheenagh ran to her daddy, her arms flung wide open, and she laughed when Roy swept the small child up into his arms. Sean, who also ran, put up his arms, and Roy lifted him up with his free arm and hugged them both. He put them down and hugged Janet, who he had not seen for quite some time; he asked if everything was all right with the growing foetus; she nodded, saying she had not suffered any morning sickness this time, and she was extremely aroused just by being with him, and with a playful smile she added,

"Roy, I hope you are up to what I have in mind, and you have saved enough energy for me and not spent it all on Elian, Fiona, and Madeleine."

"Oh, I don't know about that," he said with a wry grin. "You will just have to wait and see once the children have been put to bed."

Janet playfully punched him on the arm, but the look she gave him said a lot. Roy and Janet walked out of the airport to the taxi arm in arm, with Morag holding the two children's hands walking behind them, and a porter pushing the luggage on a trolley following up at the back. The taxi swiftly carried them to the twin villas, and as soon as she saw them, Janet fell in love with them. She loved the setting; when she saw the courtyard with the swimming pool, she put her arms around him and kissed him.

"Oh, Roy, what a lovely place!" She exclaimed. "How on earth did you find it?"

Roy admitted it was more by luck than judgement as it had been recommended by the harbour master, and he had booked it without seeing it and it was theirs for another three weeks.

That night Fiona excelled herself, the meal was wonderful, and once she had cooked the dinner, she handed over to the full-time cook that came with the villa announcing that she too was going to have a rest from her daily chores. Later in bed, after the children had finally settled down, Roy lay beside Janet discussing the forthcoming sea trip down the Lesser Antilles Islands finishing up at Trinidad and Tobago. Janet expressed her worries about having two young children on board as both would need constant watching to ensure their safety. She said there was no way she would contemplate the crossing to Europe and then up to Ireland with them on board; Roy would have to do that leg of the journey without them, adding she was sure the three crew members would see that his sex life did not suffer, despite the fact that she would not be on-board. She then turned to him and whispered softly,

"Now can you stop talking and let's have more action."

They made passionate love well into the night, and when they were sexually replete, they fell asleep in each other's arms. The next few weeks she would really begin to show her pregnant state' and Roy intended to make the most of their time together. Later that morning, Consuela rang and told Roy the equipment had arrived and would he see that Elian came to the boatyard if she wished to supervise the fitting. All three of the crew decided to go, leaving Roy and Janet together like a couple of newly-weds. The next two weeks passed so quickly, and it was time for the sea trials after the new engines had been fitted and bedded in. The new gearbox had been fitted and the controls altered to allow the engines to be used individually or in banks of two or four. The result, when tested, was remarkable; the response was much faster than before, and the consumption, which was now monitored by flow metres, meant the improvement in the vessel's range was astonishing. The sea trials took a week before Roy and Elian were finally satisfied with all the adjustments and the final result had proven to be very satisfactory.

Roy went to see Consuela the day before they were due to leave to settle the account for the repairs. It was obvious from the moment Roy arrived that the financial settlement was not all Consuela had in mind. The day was almost a repeat of the day he had arrived, with Consuela's sexual appetite claiming Roy for most of the day. Roy paid her the bill and thanked her for the wonderful work she and her crew had done on the boat. Consuela smiled and said she had all the thanks she needed; Roy had not even noticed that her waist had thickened or any of the other subtle changes that had occurred to her body; she had no intention of telling him she was carrying his child, apart from her doctor, she had told no one about her condition. It was with a heavy heart she watched him walk from the house to the boatyard, when Elian and Roy took the cruiser round to the main harbour where they would load the in readiness for the family trip the following morning, when they were due to depart the islands for the last time. All of them worked hard to get the supplies aboard, and once refuelled, Roy fetched the family, and the crew loaded the families' luggage and cast off; the children were so excited, that it took all of Morag's and Janet's attention to ensure they were not going to fall overboard.

At last, apart from keeping a wary eye on the children, every one relaxed as they made their way slowly through the Leeward Islands intending to stay at the many of the islands before finally spending a few days on the island of St Kitts and Antigua. Out of the blue Roy received an unexpected call on his satellite phone as they got nearer the island of St Kitts; it was from Lady Jayne, she passed pleasantries with Roy informing him that she wanted to speak to Madeleine urgently. Roy called Madeleine up onto the bridge where he was in control of the vessel. She took the phone, and Roy watched as the look on her face grew more concerned. They spoke for some time before she rang off; Madeleine looked at Roy and said,

"My stepmother is having problems with the baby. She is suffering from toxaemia, and the doctors are worried about her condition. Daddy is calling a scheduled conference of all the British Consular representatives in the Caribbean, and my stepmother is not able to act as hostess. It appears that daddy wants me to help him out as Jayne will be unable to carry out her duties as hostess. It looks as though we shall have to part in St Kitts. Daddy is sending someone to meet me, and we are to travel back to Barbados together."

Roy replied that he would be sorry to see her go, and in his own mind, he knew he would miss the vibrant body she possessed.

"Roy, can we make love one last time?" Madeleine whispered, looking around to ensure they were not being watched, and adding with a grin. "Completely impromptu; right here and now."

Roy looked down on the deck below; Janet and Morag were busy with the children's lessons in the lower lounge. Elian was sleeping after being in charge overnight, and he guessed Fiona was as usual in the galley preparing meals for them all. He smiled at the thought of making love to Madeleine for one last time before she left, and he pulled her into his arms.

Neither of them heard Janet climb the companionway; she stood and watched the couple in the throes of making love. Janet knew that over the last three weeks or so, she had started to show signs of her pregnancy, being only too aware that she had slowed down in her sexual responses and had asked Roy to be gentle with her. Janet watched as they moved in unison until they had both satisfied each other's carnal desires. Roy and Madeleine lay stunned by the passion that had overtaken and consumed them. Madeleine's thoughts raced through her mind in a semi-panic. It suddenly dawned on her that she was at her most fertile time of the month; she thought back to when she had had her contraceptive injection. *Was it three months already?* She knew what the consequences could be, but Roy had the ability to rouse her lust to a level she would never have believed possible before she met him. She slowly became more and more certain that the injection she had received from her doctor had expired; how would she react if the inevitable happened? What would her father say? It did not bear thinking about. Roy looked at Madeleine, whose attention was obviously miles away; he shook her, bringing her thoughts back to her current situation. He bent and kissed her with such tenderness. Perhaps that was one of the reasons she had begun to love him; his passion had been fulfilled, but he still showed her such tenderness, whereas most men, once they had been satisfied, did not respond to a woman's needs. Madeleine lay supine, relaxed, and happy as Roy held her in his arms.

Suddenly, and totally expectantly, Madeleine caught sight of Janet, and her mouth gaped open; Janet clapped and said,

"Roy, that was one of your better performances," Janet said and she added with a grin,

"I just hope you have saved some of that raw energy for me tonight."

Roy turned and looked sheepishly at his wife,

"Have I ever let you down?" He asked in a quiet voice,

Janet walked forward and gave him a gentle but firm slap on his back as she gave a chuckle,

"There's always a first time, you know." She quipped.

She turned, her face carrying a broad grin; she winked at the languishing but shocked Madeleine and walked back down the steps.

Madeleine was visibly shaken but said haltingly,

"Oh God, Roy, I'm sorry. I just didn't think. I only hope things will not be spoiled between you two because of me."

"Don't give it a second thought Madeleine," Roy replied turning to face her, "We have an understanding between us that provided I keep her happy. I am allowed to stray from the supposed path of monogamous marital bliss, whenever I want. We have an open marriage, so I stray, and in the past, she has done so too. Now you had better get dressed or I may take advantage of you again. We shall be in the harbour soon, and I'm sure you would not want to be met in the state you are in at the moment, whatever would your father say?"

Madeleine got up and pulled on her shorts; she pulled her top over her head and sashayed down the stairs. Roy dressed and released the autopilot and saw the island appear over the horizon. Elian came up onto the upper deck and whispered,

"I think everyone aboard could hear you with Madeleine. What was the occasion?"

Roy told her about her returning to Barbados and that she was being met when they docked. Elian nodded and said,

"I wondered, especially when I knew Janet had come up to see you. I hope she was not too shocked at what she saw."

Roy smiled and replied, informing Elian that Janet had seen her have sex with him, and even that had not shocked her.

"Oh my God, Roy, When?" Elian asked her mouth gaping open in astonishment.

"Oh, several times," Roy whispered, "Let's not go into details suffice it to be a fact the she has also seen us in the height of a sexual frenzy."

Elian took the wheel, still shocked that Janet had seen her and Roy together. She hoped that Roy and she could be together whilst they were in St Kitts, and she wondered if Roy knew about Michael or not.

They docked, and once the formalities were over, Madeleine, in a fitted sundress that showed her figure to the full and highlighted her glorious tan, walked ashore to be met by the British representative for the island. He was strikingly good looking, tall, and about Madeleine's age. He introduced himself as Conrad. He thanked Roy on behalf of Sir Martin for looking after his daughter and apologised on his behalf for having to call her away before the end of the voyage, but he added Sir Martin needed her during his wife's confinement. Roy put his arms around Madeleine and whispered

"Be careful, Madeleine. Conrad looks the sort of chap who would take advantage of an innocent young woman like you."

Madeleine laughed at his ribald joke, and she said goodbye to the children and everyone else, and she was whisked away by the handsome, debonair man. Madeleine put her arm through Conrad's, then smiling, she turned blowing a kiss to them all and, finally she gave a sly wink in Roy's direction.

They made a handsome couple; Roy knew instinctively that they would remain so. Sir Martin had felt it was time his daughter settled down and stopped this wild adventurous life she seemed to enjoy so much. Conrad had been his first choice, Sir Martin believed he knew his daughter's likes and dislikes; Conrad was from an 'old money' family back in the UK, and being the second born son, he had been sent to university and then into the diplomatic service. The family had several estates in England and Ireland, from information he had gleaned when making his choice, the family home was in County Wexford in Ireland. He had also learned that Conrad's elder brother had been killed in a road accident and Conrad would inherit everything when his father died. Sir Martin had a feeling that if he had chosen right, the relationship would develop quickly and with passion, but he could not have possibly know how true that was going to be when Madeleine found out she was carrying Lord Croft's child. Madeleine knew that her father would not want his daughter to have a child out of wedlock; after all, whatever would the family think.

Chapter 19

It was only about a week later that Madeleine realised she had missed her period; she had always been a regular as clockwork. She did a home pregnancy test, and it proved to be positive. Madeleine had been flirting with Conrad from the time she had met him, he was such a dear; he had kissed, and they had petted, but being a gentleman, he had not tried to take matters further without some encouragement from her. Madeleine knew it was time she got him into bed. He would, she thought, make a wonderfully tame husband who would not make too many demands on her and adore her forever. She resolved that she would tempt him that very night. She called him and asked if she could see him that evening. He willingly agreed and asked if he could take her to dinner. Madeleine prepared for the seduction of Conrad, so was dressed to thrill; her dress revealed her cleavage and showed her suntanned breasts off to perfection; the dress was short and her legs were tanned to the same intensity as her breasts, in all, she looked like a model about to go out onto the catwalk. Conrad could not take his eyes off her all night; they ate and drank two bottles of wine before he invited her back to his flat, one which he had rented for the month. Madeleine was ecstatic that she should have got him to the point where she thought he would seduce her. They went back to his flat, and after he had poured drinks, he sat in front of her; he felt that she was the most attractive woman he had ever met. It was a matter of ease that she used the charm and skills she had learned from Lord Croft to seduce the young man. Conrad realised that this was the moment he had been waiting for, he put his one arm around her and the other under her and stood up with her in his strong arms. Madeleine felt Conrad lift her, and he began carrying her towards his bedroom with her head cradled against his neck.

Conrad's knowledge of sex came from the erotic movies he had seen, and he fell an easy prey to Madeleine's wiles. He had not the will or skill to stop the inevitable, and Madeleine had made no protest when he had made love to her without any protection. Conrad smiled; he had pleased her as the feeling had been better than he had ever imagined. He watched as she got out of bed and into the bathroom before she returned and slipped into his bed once again. Conrad got up and washed himself clean before he climbed in beside her, and she curled up in his arms and fell into a deep post-coital sleep. She had somehow found someone who could please her sexually almost as much as Roy. The pleasure had been wonderful on both sides; both knew this would not be the last night they would spend together.

Conrad and Madeleine slept together for the rest of the week, and her father asked where she had been every night as he had gone to her room on several mornings to find that she had not slept in her bed. She confessed that she had been with Conrad; her father was of the old school, and he tackled the young man asking him if he intended to marry his daughter.

"I will if she will have me and be happy to do so," was Conrad's jaunty reply.

Conrad was due to return to St Kitts that weekend, and Sir Martin held a party in honour of their engagement. The wedding was set to be in two months' time. Madeleine was worried that she could well be showing at that time, but nature sometimes plays tricks, and the day after Conrad left, she had violent pains and she began her period. Madeleine was mortified that it had been a false alarm; she had wanted to have Roy's child so much now it seemed as though her dearest desire would never be fulfilled. She began to send out the invitations; one of them was to Roy, Janet, and the children. In their invitation, she asked Janet if Sheenagh would be bridesmaid and Sean, her pageboy. That invitation was hand-delivered by courier, who followed the cruiser from St Kitts, finally catching up with them at Guadeloupe. Roy was overjoyed at the chance of seeing Madeleine again but was surprised that she had agreed to marry the handsome Conrad so quickly. Sheenagh was jumping for joy at the opportunity to be dressed up and be a bridesmaid, but Sean was not so sure; all he knew was that he and his sister, accompanied by his mother and Morag, would fly from Dominica to Barbados to be fitted with their clothes, whilst his daddy would sail the cruiser back with Aunty Elian and Aunty Fiona. He wondered why his daddy seemed happy for them to leave him again; he hoped that the journey would be quick and they could be together once more. Roy knew he would enjoy the journey with two of his crew who would be more than happy to satisfy his every need.

Finally Roy arrived in Barbados, where Janet and the children were there to meet him; the children could hardly wait to tell him about their new clothes. Sheenagh was quite excited about her new pretty silk dress, but

Sean was not quite so sure about his new velvet suit with a lace collar. Janet was suffering with the heat, and she told Roy she was quite worried about Lady Jayne, as she was not her usual buoyant self. The toxaemia had taken a lot out of her, but she said that Lady Jayne had assured her that she would be at the wedding even if they had to carry her there. When they got back to the house, there was a message from the Residency; it simple stated that when Roy had chance, Lady Jayne would like to see him and there was a similar message from the bride-to-be, Madeleine. Roy rang to say that he would like to spend the evening with his family, but he would be happy to see Lady Jayne at lunchtime the following day and that afterwards he would hope to see Madeleine. Roy spent the evening playing with the kids until Morag carted them off to be bathed and get ready for bed. Roy and Janet sat talking and enjoying several drinks before they went up to bed. Janet said that she hoped Roy would not mind, but she was tired and needed to go to sleep. Roy put his arms around her and kissed her gently on the mouth and lay with his arm around her until they both fell asleep. Roy slept late the next morning, and the children woke him by jumping up and down on the bed, happy that their daddy was home with them again.

Roy left at around eleven for the High Commissioner's Residence, and when he arrived, he was redirected to the hospital and shown up to Lady Jayne's room. Roy was surprised at how swollen her face and hands were; she looked an unhealthy colour; it seemed that her Ladyship had retained a lot of amniotic fluid, and she looked enormous. Roy kissed her on the cheek; she informed him that they were going to deliver the baby the following week, after she had spent a few days in bed. Roy sat and talked with her about the forthcoming birth.

"The baby has stopped growing," She told him, "but the hospital staff are monitoring me constantly to ensure the baby is OK. The slightest suggestion that the baby is in trouble, they will do a caesarean." She added with a sigh, "I will be glad when it is all over."

The nurse came in and told Roy he should leave as Lady Jayne needed the rest. Roy rose and kissed her on the cheek once more and said he would try and keep in touch through Madeleine and that he would try to call in and see her the next day.

Madeleine was waiting for him when he got back to the Residency; she looked very inviting, and she had lost none of the deep tan she had acquired at sea, and Roy wondered which area in the Residency she lay to keep her all-over tan; he was soon to find out. Madeleine led Roy up the stairs oblivious to anyone who may have seen them together; they went along the corridor past her bedroom up another flight of stairs and out on to a flat roof. The sun shone on to the area and a blow-up bed lay in the centre.

"This is my place," she said. "I come up here to sunbathe when I want to be alone."

Madeleine hugged Roy and then kissed him on the mouth, their passion rising quickly. Roy groaned inwardly as he had suspected that she would want him to make love to her.

"I thought you would want to be with Conrad, now that you are engaged to be married," Roy said, pulling away from her embrace.

"Conrad is good, but nowhere as good as you are. Besides, he has been away back in St Kitts for almost three weeks. I just need you to make love to me again, with him being away I feel neglected." Madeleine said with a lustful gleam in her eye.

Roy, ever game to please, succumbed to her embrace and not long after they went down to her room, where the fun really began and when it was finally over, they lay back, still only partially dressed, beside each other, and Roy asked the inevitable question,

"Why did you need me to make love to you now?" Roy asked as his breathing slowly regained some semblance of normality, "after all you are getting married shortly. Why are you so eager to have me to make love to you now? The energy and effort you put into the last session I thought you were desperate for me to give you everything I had."

Madeleine's reply confirmed what he had suspected but had hoped her was wrong another illegitimate child was something he had not really wanted to contemplate. It was just that she seemed so determined that he should take no precautions and ride her as always with no regard for the consequences.

"Conrad's family expect me to produce an heir within the first year of our marriage. Madeleine replied, looking guilty, "When you made love to me that last time on the boat, my three-month cover from my contraceptive injection had expired, and I naturally thought I was pregnant. As a result, I took no precautions with Conrad for the rest of the month. With no result, I started my period bang on time. I want to have your child, and nothing would give me more pleasure than to walk down the aisle knowing it was you who had got me pregnant. I am just at the right time at this moment, so I hope you have done the trick. I hope you will come to see me again before the wedding. I want to be sure it's not a false alarm again this time."

Roy could only nod his head. With Janet not being keen on sex at present, it fitted in with his plans perfectly. But he thought if Madeleine's three months' cover was up, then so would be Elian's and Fiona's, and he knew how fertile both of them could be. He would contact them as soon as he left the residency.

Roy broke his train of thought as Madeleine continued,
"You know that when Conrad inherits the estate, we shall be living in County Wexford quite near to your castle in County Kerry."
"You will be on the other side of Ireland." Roy corrected her by saying, "It's hardly next door."
The reply came quickly,
"It's a lot closer than Barbados or St Kitts, and I shall want more than one child, so get yourself prepared for a few trips to see us, won't you?"
Roy could only shake his head at her blatant expectations, but he smiled and whispered,
"Any time you need me, I'll endeavour to be there."
"I think I should reluctantly let you go now before Janet phones to see where you are." She hugged him and whispered, "If you don't want to arouse her suspicions you had better use my shower before you leave."
They slipped inside the en suite bathroom, and Roy pulled off his shirt as Madeleine turned on the shower before pulling off her own remaining garments. They stepped into the spray of water and began to wash each other. Roy resisted the temptation to make love to her again, just in case Janet was feeling up to a frolic when he got back. They stepped out and towelled each other dry and dressed. Madeleine's next comment shook him.
"Oh God! Roy, why do I have to marry Conrad, when you are always there when I need you? Now what time can I expect you tomorrow? Tell me, it will be the same time as today."
Roy nodded, knowing he had promised to see her stepmother in hospital.
"OK," he said, "but you must keep me informed about any developments with Lady Jayne."

It was Janet who got a call the following morning from Madeleine saying they had decided to operate that Lady Jayne was in theatre having a Caesarean as she was speaking. Morag watched the children as Roy and Janet went to the hospital to see how she was faring; both of them knowing and understanding that Sir Martin was away and would not be able to get back before morning. The operation was a success, and Lady Jayne had given birth to a little boy; the new-born child was small but healthy. Lady Jayne was recovering, and Janet offered to stay with her until she was allowed to leave the recovery room and was feeling better. Roy slipped away with Madeleine, the opportunity was too good to miss, and going back to the Residency. Unobserved they engaged in the pre-arranged tryst to have unbridled and un-protected sex; after which they both returned to the hospital to find Lady Jayne sitting up holding her baby boy proudly. In the absence of Sir Martin, she handed him to Roy to hold, confirming in Janet's and Madeleine's mind that Roy was definitely the father, but neither said anything. Janet smiled knowing it was just another child; the man she had trained to pleasure women all those years ago was as skilful as she had made him. She loved him and would never let him go, whatever the reason, and she had accepted his infidelities from the very start of their marriage. Women just seemed to be attracted to him, like bees to a honey jar; they all seemed to love him and have his children; she knew he never took any precautions, and if the women he slept with wanted children, he was only too willing to oblige. Janet looked at Madeleine, she looked radiant, and it occurred to her that Roy and she had been missing most of the afternoon, the penny dropped; but she had no idea that Roy had impregnated the bride-to-be, only days before her wedding.

The wedding was a society affair with dignitaries coming from all over the Caribbean and Ireland. Sir Martin was proud to be giving his daughter away to such an influential family, and her security would be ensured when Conrad inherited the family estates and fortune; in the meantime, he would be able to see his daughter frequently. Lady Jayne was out of hospital in time for the wedding, but she apologised that she would not be doing much dancing. The wedding went well, and at the reception, Roy and Janet danced until Janet excused herself and went to sit with Lady Jayne to rest. Roy looked around and spotted the bride pointing to a door leading off the reception room. Roy made his way over and slipped unnoticed into the small room that had apparently been set aside for the bride and bridesmaids. The only bridesmaid had been Sheenagh, and she was unlikely to disturb them; Madeleine looked wonderful in her white wedding gown; her suit for going away on honeymoon lay folded over a table beside the couch. Madeleine had planned this last encounter with care; she needed Roy to make love to her once again before she went away with Conrad, her new and totally unsuspecting husband. The thought of having illicit sex whilst her husband was in the reception nearby sent Madeleine's heart racing; she stood up and bent forward over the couch and said,

"Oh, Roy, help me out of this dress, will you? I need you to take me one last time before I leave it, may be a long time, before we have the chance to be together again."

The sex, for that's what it was there was no denying that love had anything to do with the euphoric and lustful exchange that went on in the brides changing room. When it was over, they lay in each other's arms, both sexually replete, when they heard Conrad calling Madeleine's name. It seemed that it was nearing the time for the arrival of the car to take them to the airport. Madeleine called back that she would be out in a few moments before the guilty pair quickly dressed, they kissed once again before Madeleine looked into the mirror and touched the odd curl back in place; turning to face him, she blew him a kiss and walked out of the door, slightly flushed but acting as innocently as she could. Roy waited a few minutes for all attention to be focused on the couple as they were leaving; then he slipped out of the room to join the throng as they waved to the happy couple. The newly-weds waved every one goodbye and were whisked away to begin their honeymoon; Conrad was overjoyed with his new bride; unknowing to him, the deed had been done; his family would be so thrilled that he had done what generations before him had achieved and that was getting his bride pregnant during their first month of marriage. It was after all a family tradition.

Roy was feeling very smug with himself having believed no one had seen him enter the room or leave. It was Janet who later pulled him to one side and whispered,

"I hope the bride enjoyed the last-minute present you gave her."
Roy kissed his wife on the cheek and, with a look of complete innocence, whispered,

"I really don't know what you mean, darling. I just went in to wish her happiness in her new life. Whilst she was on the boat we grew very close."
Janet smiled and said to him,

"I think you are forgetting I know just how close she was to you. I watched you with her on the bridge that day. The two of you could not have got any closer. I'm surprised you did not get her pregnant."
Roy smiled and just looked at Janet.

"Oh my God, Roy," she gasped, "you haven't, have you? Does Conrad suspect?" she asked appalled at the possibility.

Roy shook his head and said,

"We shall just have to wait and see, shan't we, darling?"

They collected the children and went over to Lady Jayne, who still looked pale but said she was feeling much better, and she showed them her son who she said would be named Martin, Royston Claiborne; Janet turned to her husband and looked him sternly in the eyes before they left as a family to return home.

Chapter 20

The following day, the decision was made for them to consider returning to Ireland; the tenancy of the castle was due to run out in two months' time; Roy's solicitor had already been notified that the castle had been vacated and was available for Lord Croft and his family to move back into. It would be a busy time for everyone, and Janet, who would not be able to fly in the last six weeks of her pregnancy, had agreed with Roy that she should travel back to Ireland by air as soon as possible. It would be left up to Roy to arrange for everything to be shipped back and tidy up their affairs in Barbados. He would then bring the cruiser back to Ireland, accompanied by Elian and Fiona. Roy rang Sam, his IRA contact in Ireland, and told him they would be returning to Ireland and that the cruiser would once again be available to him for charters. Sam sounded so pleased he said he would consult the committee and ring him back later in the day as he may have some work for him sooner than later. The call came through later in the afternoon; when Sam asked Roy if he could collect a special cargo from a source to be given and bring it directly back to Ireland to avoid trans-shipment from one vessel to another. The price for the trip was generous, but the risks were once again high. Roy said he would only be leaving in about two months' time, and Sam said that the timing would be perfect as it would give him time to make all the necessary arrangements. Roy told Janet that he had a charter from the Caribbean to Ireland and that he would buy her a new car on his return. Janet hugged him and said she would book her ticket as soon as she knew Lady Jayne was feeling better. They went to visit later that evening, and the patient was looking much better and the baby was small, but from the amount he was taking from the breast, he would soon be eating like a horse. He would quickly gain enough weight to catch up on his low birth weight.

Lady Jayne was excited about Janet returning to Ireland and asked if she could visit as soon as the doctors gave her the all-clear to travel with the new baby.

"After all," she said, "that's where Conrad and Madeleine will be living eventually, and we shall probably move to Ireland when Martin retires in a couple of years' time. Unless he decides to stay in the Caribbean, and somehow I don't think he would want to do that and see a new man in his job. It would be too painful for him."

It was just before Janet left, a few weeks later, that Roy had a call from Madeleine in St Kitts to tell him that the doctor had confirmed she was pregnant. Roy called Janet and told her what Madeleine had said, and as Janet knew, Conrad had been delighted at the news; he had after all always claimed he wanted a child as soon as they were married. Janet rang Madeleine when she had finished speaking to Roy; she congratulated her and told her how pleased she was for her. Lady Jayne called shortly after to tell Janet the news, and she said Martin and she were so pleased that Madeleine seemed to have settled down and that Conrad's family were ecstatic with the news; of course, she said everyone was hoping it would be a boy. When Janet put down the phone, she turned to Roy and, smiling at him, said,

"If you are true to form, she will have a boy. You seem to be able to produce boys easier than girls, don't you agree, darling? You are getting to be quite a family man with offspring scattered everywhere. I shall be pleased to get back home and see how Cathleen and Bridget are getting along. If you're not careful, you will have a harem or we shall have to start a day nursery at the castle." Then she broke the news, "The doctor says I will have to leave soon or else the airlines won't let me fly, so I'll book my flight in the next couple of days."

Roy told her he would miss her, and in all probability, the baby would be born before he got home.

"I shall probably be crossing the Atlantic with the cruiser on the day he is born, so I'm sorry there's no way I can be with you this time, unless I delay my return for a few weeks and fly back for the birth. Then I would have to come back and sail back later,"

"I would rather you sail back as soon as possible," Janet said. "Then you will be at home with us soon after the birth of your new son, with the three of them I will need your support."

When Janet boarded the aircraft, Roy, together with Elian, Fiona, and Lady Jayne, saw her and the family off, and as soon as the aircraft was in the air, Lady Jayne was driven back to the residence by the official chauffer while Roy drove Elian and Fiona back to the house. That evening, Roy had a call from London; it was Gael; she informed him that she had finally been discharged from hospital and was longing to join him on his return trip on the cruiser; she would be arriving on the following Saturday, and she would be using her return ticket so there was no cost to Roy himself.

Gael as promised arrived late on Saturday; Roy was there to meet her flight. As soon as she saw him waiting for, her instinct was to rush into his arms, but even the thought of being touched by a man sent shudders down her spine and the memories of her rape and what she had done to her attacker was still too fresh in her mind. She did not know how she would handle sex again, even with his Lordship. She restrained herself and gave Roy a perfunctory kiss on the cheek as she told him all about her long haul back into the land of reality. She took his arm, and as he escorted her back to the car she drew him closer.

"I'm sorry, Roy," she whispered, "but I don't know when I'll be ready to let you into my bed. All I know is it will take time. The doctors told me to take it one day at a time. It may never be possible for me to have normal relationships with a man again. I just have to be patient, and I hope you will not expect too much of me."

Roy squeezed her arm in acknowledgement and pointed out the Range Rover to the porter, who was busy with her luggage. They were on their way back when she said,

"Sam came to see me before I left. I think he has something he wants you to do before we go back to Ireland. I guess it's another collection, but he would not tell me what it was. He did mention that this time the appointment would be off Curaçao."

Roy sighed inwardly; he could guess that it would be another trip near the coast of Colombia, running the risk of being challenged by the Venezuelans once again. He had not considered that he would need to do that, but he resigned himself to the fact that if that was what Sam wanted, he would do it.

Sam called later that morning, and as Roy had feared, he was informed that the arrangements had been made; Roy was to meet a trawler where the cargo would be transferred to the cruiser prior to Roy's return crossing.

"The co-ordinates will be forwarded, Roy Sam said, "The payment has already been arranged, so there is no need for you to worry over that." The Sam added, "Roy I cannot express the need for speed is essential. Send me details of the earliest date and time you can do the pickup and I will forward it on to the trawler captain. Be careful and good luck."

Roy had not planned to leave so soon, but at Sam's entreaty, he arranged to leave the following morning, and he rang Lady Jayne to say goodbye. She was dismayed that he would be leaving so soon, and she begged him to visit her one last time before he left. Roy was reluctant as there was so much to do and so little time to do it; however, her pleas finally won him over, and leaving the three women to finish loading the luggage and the supplies, he headed for the High Commission. Their meeting was short, but through her persistence, Lady Jayne as usual had her own way; despite the hurry, Roy agreed to stay one last meal. As Sir Martin was away visiting another island, the two of them sat and ate lunch and drank a bottle of wine before Roy left and returned to the cruiser. On his return, to his delight, the crew had been busy and most of the supplies had been loaded and stowed away for the journey; later accompanied by Elian, Fiona, and Gael, he sailed on the evening tide heading towards Curaçao.

Roy stood up on the bridge, and as they moved westwards, he wondered if he might get the chance to see Samantha again on this trip; he could only hope she would be around. The fairly long journey was untroubled; two days later, they anchored in the harbour, and Roy, having cleared immigration, went directly to the hospital to ask for either Dr's Helga Van der Westhausen or Samantha Hillier. It was Samantha who answered the Tannoy; as she approached, she formally shook his hand and invited him to accompany her to her office. No sooner had the door closed behind them, when all sense of formality fell away; she hugged him to her breast and whispered,
"I knew you would come back one day. Helga is still away, but I'm sure if last time we met was anything to go by, I can be of just as much assistance, but not here. I'm due off duty shortly, and I'll take you back to my place. I do not trust anyone around here not to give me away."
"What about your husband?" Roy asked concerned he might meet up with him at their home.
"He will not be back until later this evening, so we have plenty of time. I wish you could have let me know you were coming. I would have tried to get a couple of days off work." Samantha whispered.
"I'm sailing in the morning, so it's as well you didn't do anything which might have alerted your husband to the fact that you were being unfaithful to him."
"I don't give one iota. I found out he has a mistress, and I suspect that's where he will be this evening. So don't give him a second thought. Just enjoy what I'm offering."
Roy waited patiently, and the next few hours were spent in Samantha's marital bed. Samantha gave Roy everything she had and when it was over she was sorry to see him leave. Her last words to him were,

"Don't let it be too long before you come back to see me again."
Roy returned to the boat, and he took the crew out for a meal; after all, it would be some time before they would get another chance, as the pickup and long journey across the Atlantic would leave them no chance for meals ashore.

The three of them ate at the famous restaurant Kura Hulanda; the seafood choice was outstanding; they ate on the deck overlooking the beach and drank excellent champagne. During the meal, Roy's cell received an SMS. It simply stated *Trawler 'San Sebastian' 12.7° 46.06' N 68.47° 38.96' W at 0630 and the date.* Roy noted the location, and it was the other side of the island near St Joris Bay. He hurriedly spoke to the three women, and as it was already quite late, they cut their meal short. They would need to leave soon if they were to round the southerly part of the island and get to the rendezvous point on time. It was the early hours of the morning and was dark when Gael and Fiona stood waiting to cast off; once this was completed, the cruiser headed out towards their early assignation with the deep-sea trawler, at the prearranged co-ordinates, where the transfer would take place. Elian took the wheel on the first watch telling Roy to take over in three hours so that she could get some rest before the rendezvous. Sam had indicated that it would be a large delivery and they all wanted to be on hand to transfer the cargo of uncut heroine for delivery to the IRA in Ireland. Elian handled the cruiser well, and even in these strange waters, with the instruments on the bridge, there was little chance of going wrong. She had time to think, she knew both she and Fiona were in a similar situation, but how to break the news to Roy was another story. Elian was only too aware that their pregnancy was entirely her fault for not remembering the date that she was supposed to have administered the contraceptive injection. She had no idea what Janet would say when she had two pregnant members of Roy's crew to deal with when they got back to Ireland. Fiona had confirmed that she, as indeed Elian had, would choose not to have a termination, both would be determined to carry their children to full term. Both of them had previously terminated pregnancies and both had vowed not to do so ever again. Elian had ensured that Gael was fully covered despite the fact she had shuddered at the prospect of any form of sexual relationship during the voyage.

Roy came up to relieve Elian, and a couple of hours later, he called down to the lower control room that he could see the lights of the trawler at the set co-ordinates, searching the fishing boat with his night-vision glasses; the crew were apparently busy repairing the nets, and Roy gave the arranged signal with the lamp in the still predawn gloom; the answering signal was returned and the two vessels closed. Elian came up on deck, pulling her jumper down over her head; sleep was rubbed from her eyes as Roy pointed out the trawler's location. Elian swept the surrounding area with the night glasses Roy had handed to her whilst Fiona and Gael scanned the sea for any sign of movement. The two vessels slowly converged until, with a gentle bump, they touched and ropes secured the two vessels together. The skipper of the fishing boat gave a grunt of recognition, and the crew began to load the waterproof parcels of cargo. Fiona and Gael tossed the packets into the lounge for storage in the secure hold, and as soon as the last packet had been loaded, Roy gave the order to cast off; he had a feeling of impending problems. Elian also had a similar sense, and she slashed the ropes, securing the two vessels together and with a shout of,

"Boat cleared away."

She held onto the rail as Roy opened the throttles, and the two vessels separated and the cruiser was hurtling across the water; the distance separating the boats broadened rapidly.

Roy was the first to see the Venezuelan patrol boat as it seemed to appear almost from nowhere, and as it turned to follow, it hailed Roy to stop. Roy knew they were within the waters under the Nederland's control, and the patrol boat had no jurisdiction. The patrol boat captain saw that the cruiser had no intention of heaving too, and he gave the order to follow. The next call from the patrol boat was to stop or they would fire. Roy held the throttles fully open; the cruiser was, to the patrol boat captain's amazement, pulling away from them. He gave the order to fire; the shot fell astern of Roy's cruiser, but Roy knew the radio message would have been sent giving a description of the vessel to the Venezuelan air force. Roy headed north into international waters where theoretically the Venezuelan air force would have no authority to attack them. Roy was about fifty miles north of Curaçao when he heard the aircraft approach; Roy turned on the missile radar and gave Elian instructions to bring up both the Sam7 launchers, calling out for her to load a missile in one and one of the anti-missile chaff rockets in the other. The jet aircraft swept low over the water using the international band; he radioed the cruiser to heave-to as a patrol boat had requested them to stop, and they had ignored the request. The pilot informed the cruiser that the patrol boat had reason to believe that they were carrying a contraband cargo of drugs. Roy responded and informed the pilot that neither the patrol boat nor the aircraft had any jurisdiction in International waters and arrest of the vessel could only be made if they were within Venezuelan-controlled territorial waters, which clearly was not the case.

The pilot, ignoring the message once again, informed Roy that failure to heave to and wait for the patrol boat to catch up and then to allow the crew to board them would leave him no choice; he would have no alternative action but to fire on the vessel. Seeing that the vessel below had no intention of conforming with the request, the aircraft circled and began to bear down opening fire and strafing the water behind the cruiser. Gael, assisted by Fiona, armed the Sam7 and shouldered the weapon located the aircraft in her sights as it began to climb away. Roy acknowledged he had missile lock on the aircraft as Gael released the first missile. The pilot was shocked when his own radar emitted a shrill sound that he was being fired on by the cruiser below and that a missile had been launched against him. He took evasive action, releasing his chaff, drawing the missile away to explode some distance away. Roy heard the pilot radio the patrol boat asking what nationality the cruiser was, and asking if the patrol boat knew it was in all probability a military vessel belonging to a foreign government. The patrol boat captain was astounded at the news; this was not what he had expected; his information was that drugs had been passed from the trawler to the cruiser, and he wanted to get his hands on them, come what may. He responded telling the pilot he had his instructions that the vessel was carrying drugs and gave the order to sink the vessel before it could warn its own government of the unlawful action he and the pilot had already taken.

Roy listening to the two way conversation on the open channel heard the Patrol boat captain say,
"If we cannot get the drugs, then no one must. Sink the damned cruiser now. If they send out a message that we have attacked them in International waters, there will be hell to pay. We shall have to say, if anyone asks that the cruiser opened fire on us."
The aircraft climbed and turned; the pilot armed his missiles and began his final approach. Roy saw they had missile lock on the radar and gave the signal. Gael, with Fiona's help, fired two SAM7's in rapid succession at the oncoming aircraft, and Elian, aided by Roy, fired two chaff deployment

missiles as the aircraft released its own missiles. Elian reloaded her launcher, and Gael reloaded hers, and instantly another two missiles were deployed in rapid succession. The aircraft's missiles locked onto the chaff, drawing the missiles away from the cruiser, and the pilot realised that two missiles were locked on to him and another two had been fired. He made a valiant effort, but having deployed his chaff earlier, he could not evade four missiles, and his aircraft exploded in an explosion followed by a burst of fire as the fuel ignited; Roy watched with some relief as the pilot ejected. He viewed the pilot's descent through the binoculars and saw the pilot land between the cruiser and the rapidly approaching patrol boat. Roy radioed the position of the pilot on the frequency last used by the two Venezuelans, but got no reply. The patrol boat kept coming towards Roy's cruiser, narrowly missing the downed pilot.

Roy gave Elian the order to arm the last torpedo and began to circle towards the oncoming patrol boat. The oncoming vessel opened fire with its deck gun, the shot falling short; the second shot hit the bridge superstructure, fragmenting the wooden side of the bridge. Roy was hit in the shoulder by flying debris, but not before he had set the range on the torpedo and fired. The long and thin silver fish flashed in the sun's rays as it splashed down into the water heading for the oncoming patrol boat. The captain was overjoyed at the hit on the cruiser's superstructure intending to close in for the kill, until one of the crew pointed excitedly at the white line of bubbles as the torpedo headed towards them; the captain gave the order to take evasive action, but it was far too late. The crew started to jump over the side in an effort to avoid being killed, and the torpedo struck the patrol boat amidships resulting in explosion and sending smoke and debris high into the air. The patrol boat began to sink almost at once, and Roy saw two inflatable lifeboats bob up on the surface; the crew headed towards them. Roy circled until he could see the crew safely on board, then he headed in the direction of the pilot, and seeing him bobbing in a small one-man lifeboat, he sent out an SOS, giving the position of both the patrol boats crew and the downed pilot before heading away from the site as fast as possible. Roy listened to the commercial traffic; as it picked up the SOS, several ships headed in the direction of the co-ordinates sent by Roy.

Roy ordered Elian to bring out the camouflage nets in an effort to disguise the shape of the cruiser and hide the structural damage. The camouflage nets would disguise the outline of the damaged cruiser at least until nightfall, which was still several hours away. Roy took evasive action; he was grateful that there was less traffic north of the island, and he carefully avoided all the main shipping lanes and any contact with vessels heading to rescue the Venezuelan sailors. Then after they had travelled north for about a hundred or so miles, Elian was worried about Roy's injury, but he refused to go below. The speed was making the hull bang against the sea, and Elian could see he was in pain but he doggedly refused to go below until they were relatively safe. When Elian was sure they were far enough away, she shut down the engines to slow, and they cruised slowly, still heading north, into the open waters of the Caribbean Sea. No one gave chase, just as Roy had figured out, the patrol boat and the aircraft had been operating on their own initiative and had no authority. They had been on a rogue mission to take the drugs from the cruiser, probably in collusion with the trawler captain. As night fell, under Roy's instructions, Elian turned west and, once again, opened the throttles; they were now heading in the direction of the Virgin Islands at full speed. Thankfully the swell had decreased; Elian realised they needed to get to Consuela's boatyard before anyone could see the damage to the bridge and start asking questions. Just before dawn, still in pain, Roy rang Consuela using the satellite cell phone he usually reserved for emergencies only. A sleepy Consuela answered the call; when she recognised Roy's voice and detected the sense of urgency, she was fully awake in seconds. She listened to Roy as he asked if she would help him, as the story of the confrontation with the rogue Venezuelan patrol boat was slowly conveyed. Consuela told Roy to go directly to the yard and she would meet him there. Roy told her the ETA, and she agreed to have the doors of the boathouse opened in readiness, giving him instructions to drive the cruiser inside.

Gael took over whilst Elian went below; Roy told her what he had arranged and that the doors of the boathouse would be open in readiness for their arrival; she was to approach the island slowly under cover of darkness, then head directly to Consuela's boatyard and go straight into the boathouse. Elian went back up top and slowed down to a steady cruising speed, then just, before dawn, she could see the entrance to the yard and she headed in. She could see the main doors wide open, and with Gael's assistance, Elian guided the damaged cruiser slowly into the space cleared by Consuela. They tied up, and Roy slumped back on the couch in the lower lounge, finally giving in to the pain of his injuries; he had previously told Elian, Fiona, and Gael that his injuries were only superficial, refusing them permission to get near and he would not allow them to touch him. They rushed over to where he lay and tore open Roy's bloody shirt; several pieces of wood from the boat's superstructure had embedded themselves in his shoulder and back, all of which would need to be removed and treated, in addition to which his forearm was torn in several places by bits of shrapnel from the exploding shell. How he had held on, they never knew, or how he had managed to hide the amount of blood loss, for the couch was soaking wet.

Gael pushed the others away telling Fiona to get the medical kit and then assisted by Elian they managed to get him into the stateroom with some urgently. The loss of blood and shock were the most dangerous symptoms; the wounds themselves looked worse than they really were. She knew they had renewed the saline on board, from when she had been ill, but they had no cross-matched blood. After getting him on the bed and setting up a saline drip, Gael went to work. She cleaned the wounds using saline solution, irrigating and removing all foreign bodies. She then poured a weak solution of hydrogen peroxide, watching as the wounds fizzled and bubbled, and then she began suturing the wounds wherever necessary; finally she bound them up using field dressings from the field kit. A noticeably pregnant Consuela came aboard looking for Roy and was devastated seeing him looking so grey lying on the bed. She watched, and seeing that Gael was working fast and looked as though she knew what she was doing, she asked what had happened. Elian told her he had been injured during the confrontation, and what they really needed was some cross-matched blood for Roy. Consuela looked shocked but answered hurriedly, for she could see that something needed to be done urgently.

"I have a friend who is a paramedic. I'll contact him immediately. He was a close friend of my late husband, and I know he can be trusted to be discreet."

Without waiting another moment, she rushed ashore in the direction of the office.

Consuela went into the office and called her friend Sebastian, who arrived ten minutes later with two bottles of plasma; as he boarded the cruiser Elian met him with a hostile stare until Consuela assured her,

"Elian, I would not let anything happen to Lord Croft. Sebastian is a friend. I can guarantee he will keep quiet and not inform the authorities. I give you my word."

Sebastian went below and spoke to Gael; he could see she was doing an excellent job in patching Roy up.

"I can see you have everything in hand. Can I be of any assistance?" he asked,

Gael looked up and looked enquiringly at Elian, who had followed close behind him, Elian gave her the thumbs-up sign, inferring that he was a friend, and Gael nodded. Sebastian scrubbed his hands and began to assist; he put up a bottle of plasma, and half an hour later, the patient lay quiet, his wounds dressed and his colour, although still grey, had improved somewhat. Sebastian took a sample of Roy's blood and said to Gael,

"Don't worry. I'll get back to the station and see if I can get this cross matched. I have friends who can be trusted in the lab. If I can, I'll return with a pint of cross-matched and authenticated blood." Then hesitating for a few moments, he advised, "I should warn you, however, that it should only be given as a last resort, as although it will have been tested to ensure it is free from the AID's virus as no test could be one hundred per cent sure."

The three crew members and Consuela sat by the bed and waited for Roy to come too. It was quite a while later when Roy opened his eyes and, looking around,

"What had happened?" he asked blinking his eyes and shaking his head.

Gael scolded him for not letting them look at his wounds earlier, but she said that she had stitched where it had been necessary and dressed the other wounds and abrasions, informing him that he would be sore for several days, and she advised him to remain in bed for the rest of the day.

Consuela spoke next as she said,

"My foreman had made a preliminary inspection of the damage, and he estimates it will take two weeks at least to repair the structural damage. He also told me that from his initial inspection, it did not appear that any serious damage had been done to the steering mechanism or other controls, although he would have to thoroughly check it over as well as doing a full check on instrumentation and wiring."

Roy listened carefully and whispered softly to Elian, who was close by his side,

"Tell her to go ahead. I will pay whatever she feels is a fair price."

When Elian had passed on the message, she asked everyone to move back into the lounge, adding,

"You can all see that Roy is tired and needs some peace and quiet. Only one of us should be in here with the patient. Let's give him some room to recover."

To reassure him that everything was in hand before she left, Consuela said,

"Your Lordship knows I will only charge for work done, and I have already told the foreman to get on with it and order the materials."

Once everyone was back in the lounge, Fiona was already getting on with cleaning up the bloody mess, and Consuela informed them,

"I am fully aware you have not checked in with immigration and customs, so none of you must be seen outside the yard. As soon as his Lordship is well enough, I want him and the rest of you to move into my house, preferably under cover of darkness. You can all stay there until the repairs have been carried out, and I'll have no arguments from any of you."

Consuela left to return to the house to organise an evening meal for them all, saying that if Roy was still not well enough, she would have the meal brought aboard. Sebastian returned with the blood, and Gael put it in the fridge; she told him that she had put up the second bottle of plasma, and Roy seemed to be recovering very well without the need to use the cross matched blood. She thanked Sebastian for all his help and gave him a kiss on the cheek. Sebastian disappeared and went to see Consuela in the office; a short time later, he returned to inform them that he had organised one of his buddies to provide an ambulance to take Roy to Consuela's house and he would be back after dark. Dusk came quickly, as it usually does in that area of the world, and shortly after dark, the ambulance arrived; Sebastian and his buddy put his Lordship in the back along with the three crew members and took them to Consuela's house. Consuela had been busy, and she had prepared one of her seafood meals; they all tucked in; even Roy, who after protesting that he felt much better, managed to eat a fair portion of one of Consuela's seafood chowders. Consuela even gave up her bed for the invalid and slept in the next room with Gael, who insisted that she should be within hearing distance from her patient. Fiona and Elian shared the twin room along the corridor.

The following morning, Roy was feeling much better, but when he tried to get out of bed, the aches and pains from his injuries were quite severe, and the bruising over his entire body was extensive; he decided to stay in bed for the day, and the crew and Consuela agreed that that was the best place for him. Gael stayed behind with her patient whilst the others went to the boatyard to check on the progress of the repairs. The foreman pulled Consuela to one side and told her that the damage to the boat was from the result of a shell. He had found several fragments of the casing embedded in the superstructure. Consuela told him that Roy had been attacked by pirates and had been forced to return fire to get away; the foreman who had read about the sinking of a Venezuelan patrol boat gave a wry smile.

"If it was those blasted Venezuelan patrol boat pirates, they deserve all they got." He whispered, "It was those bastards who were responsible for the death of my half-brother. They attacked his boat for no reason other than he had been fishing in their waters and had caught a huge amount of fish. They killed him and took his boat for their own profit. They had no right to do that; arrest him, yes, but not kill him in cold blood and steal his catch and his boat. Don't worry. Neither I nor any of my crew shall say a word to anyone about repairing the English Lord's boat. I must say though that the on inspection the steering was quite badly damaged by pieces of shrapnel, and, to be safe, we shall need to replace almost all of the connecting knuckle joints and shafts."

Consuela thanked him for his silence and said in little more than a whisper, "I'm sure Lord Croft will see that you and the whole crew will get a good bonus when the work is completed."

The foreman left smiling; he was always happy when the word *bonus* was mentioned, and he knew from previous work he and his crew had done for him, Lord Croft would tip them generously.

The next day, Roy felt considerably better, Gael was fussing over him like a mother hen, begrudgingly allowed him to get out of bed and sit in the veranda overlooking the lawn in the garden. Consuela sat with him sipping a large mint julep, and when they were alone, he said in a half-whisper, "Consuela, I cannot help but notice your condition. I congratulate you. I thought your husband was dead, so who is the lucky man you are keeping hidden? Is it Sebastian?" he asked with a wink.

Consuela did all she could not to answer, but, under pressure, she finally capitulated confessing to him that she was bearing his child. Roy could not believe it and asked,

"Good God, Consuela, I had no idea. Why weren't you on the pill?"

"After my husband died, I had never let any man touch me other than you. Roy, I knew as soon as I saw you that you would make love to me. Don't ask me how I knew, but I did. I had not even considered taking the pill; after all, I had been celibate for over a year. I never gave it a though that I might get pregnant. It never happened when I made love with my husband. It must be you are far more potent than my husband. I am so pleased that my life will be fulfilled. I have always wanted a child, and the doctor has told me it is a little boy. I hope he will someday take over my business."

Roy sat silently listening to her, and she reached over and kissed him just before Gael walked in to see how Roy was feeling. The moment between Consuela and Roy passed, and the rest of the conversation was about the boat. Consuela and Roy never spoke about the child again.

When Roy had fully recovered and the cruiser was finished, Roy went to see the results when he saw the work they had done he congratulated the foreman and his crew.

"She looks as good as ever," Lord Croft told them, pointing to the paintwork gleaming and looking as good as new. "I shall see that you are all handsomely rewarded for your efforts." Roy added.

The foreman and his crew cheered, and Roy asked Consuela if they could have the rest of the day off so that he could take them all to the tavern for a few drinks. Consuela shook her head and suggested that the foreman arrange for the local tavern to set up a bar in the yard, pulling him to one side and reminding him he was on the island illegally, and when he agreed, she smiled and said,

"In that case, your Lordship, I will be only too pleased to join you."

The owners of the local tavern were obviously used to such requests, and in less than half an hour, they had set up a bar in the boathouse, and it was late in the evening when Consuela arranged for Sebastian to drive her car to take herself, Gael, Elian, Fiona, and Lord Croft himself back to the house, leaving the foreman and his crew to drink the rest of the night away. Consuela had secretly arranged for one of the best restaurants in town to provide a banquet complete with waiter at her house, and they all dined in style. The following day, Roy paid Consuela in cash; the bills recovered from the secret hiding place aboard the cruiser, Roy gave her a bonus for herself and one for the foreman and his crew. Roy, assisted by Consuela and the three members of his crew, restocked the ship's larder, refuelled, they were ready to sail on the evening tide.

To avoid and chance encounter with either US or Venezuelan patrol boats, they headed in a north-westerly direction out into the open sea for a hundred miles; approximately two hours after setting out, they turned west in the direction of St Lucia and Barbados. Roy knew it was risky putting into Barbados, but with the protection of Sir Martin and Lady Jayne, the High Commissioner and his wife, he felt it was worth the risk. Early the following morning, Roy phoned the High Commissioner's Residence and asked to speak to Lady Jayne to tell her they would be arriving for the day before setting out for Trinidad that evening. Lady Jayne was thrilled to know she would see him once again before he left and told him she and Sir Martin would meet them in the official car. This was just what Roy had hoped for because being met in such a manner meant that clearance of customs and immigration would be so much easier, a cursory inspection at the most. They pulled into the allocated space and the necessary formalities were completed; then they climbed into the car and were whisked away to the Official Residence for breakfast. Lady Jayne informed Roy, as luck would have it, that Madeleine was arriving after lunch to stay with them for a few days. Elian, Fiona, and Gael were driven back to the docks to make sure everything was in readiness for the long voyage home. Roy was to meet them later in the evening in time for them to have a meal together before they sailed.

Sir Martin asked to be excused as he had official business to do, and he hoped he would see Roy before his final departure. Lady Jayne invited Roy into her private lounge, and she sat beside him, pressing her hips against his, and said,

"Roy, this is such a wonderful surprise. I had no idea I would see you again before you were leaving for Ireland."

Roy had expected this, and he drew her into his arms and kissed her on the mouth, feeling her lips part in complete surrender.

"Oh, Roy," she murmured, "you know I just can't resist you."

When the moment of truth came almost an hour later, Roy whispered that it was really time for him to go. Lady Jayne looked disappointed, but putting a brave face on, she smiled.

"Oh, Roy, why do you have to go so soon? I would love you to stay a while."

Roy looked into her eyes and whispered,

"I have to go. I have business to attend to, and Janet is expecting me back in Ireland. I'm sorry, but I have to leave tonight. If you insist, I will stay for lunch, but I must leave immediately afterwards."

They went through to the dining room where a meal had been provided, and they sat down for lunch. They had not even finished the first course when Madeleine arrived, looking as fresh and lovely as ever. She smiled at Roy and kissed him on the cheek as she sat down, and the staff laid a place at the lunch table. Intimate touches by Madeleine below the table; as she smiled at her stepmother told Roy she wanted more than just a meet and greet session with him.

Lunch went on for an indeterminable time with several glasses of brandy. Lady Jayne knew that Madeleine would want some time with Roy, so she excused herself saying she was in need of a rest. She retired to her room for the afternoon. Madeleine did her utmost to get Roy to stay, but he was determined to get back to the boat. They had to get away by the evening tide, and no matter how she tried, she could not get him to change his mind. To Madeleine's disappointment, Roy finally bid her goodbye, telling her to apologise to her Lady Jayne, but he had to get back to the cruiser to set sail for Trinidad on the afternoon tide. Roy was driven in the official car to the docks where the crew of three awaited for his return. Boarding the boat, Roy gave the order to cast off; Gael and Fiona cast off using the windlasses to recover the ropes as Elian started the engines and eased the seventy-three-foot vessel away from the mooring out into the harbour, and exiting the harbour master's control, they slipped quietly out to sea. The 200-mile journey would be completed before dark, and they would lay off the Port of Spain, Trinidad and Tobago, until morning when they intended to refuel and re-provision before beginning the long haul towards the North African coast, on their way home. Roy took the opportunity to get an early night and left the crew to complete the short trip. He phoned Janet, giving her Lady Jayne's and Madeleine's greetings; informing her that they would be spending the night off Trinidad and Tobago before heading across the Atlantic. Janet told him to be careful; she then informed him that the castle had been left in immaculate condition by Stella and her partner. She told Roy that the castle seemed to give everyone who stayed there a need to produce a family. Stella had given birth to a boy during her stay; Roy said nothing, knowing full well that he had sired yet another son. They talked for some time about financial affairs and staff matters before Roy wished his wife goodnight, telling her he would call again in a few days' time.

Chapter 21

During the night, Elian went into the stateroom; seeing Roy fast asleep, she walked up to the bed and shook him, and he was instantly awake and alert. Elian was dressed in a robe that concealed nothing; Roy looked at her enquiringly.

"What's wrong, Elian?" he asked, half-expecting her to say nothing and climb in beside him.

"You had better come to the phone. It's Sam. He has bad news for you." She said her voice conveying her deep concern.

"Oh God! It's not Janet or one of the children?" he enquired.

"No, it's Fergus." Elian said, "It would appear he had been taken prisoner by pirates."

Roy leapt out of bed, uncaring that he was naked; Elian had seen him naked many times, and he rushed past her into the lounge to take the call.

"Hello, Sam, give me the worst." Roy said earnestly

"I don't know where to begin, Roy," Sam replied. "Fergus has performed brilliantly all the time you have been away. He has done numerous trips, and the inflow of cargo has been excellent. The drop this time was using a new merchant shipping group and a new courier. It would appear that the ship was diverted to Lagos. You know what these bloody container ships are like as well as I do, and if there's half a chance to pick up more cargo, they do it. Well, instead of waiting for the ship to pick up its extra containers and head back towards the Mediterranean, the stupid courier panicked. He gives Fergus the location which was 5.08° 18.83′ N 2.34° 09.11′ E, and Fergus, like the man he is, headed south to pick up the goods."

"He obviously located the cargo after a long delayed search because I had the message that the cargo had been recovered and safely stowed away. Then total silence. I heard nothing for three days. I did not worry. I was fully expecting him to contact me to say he was back in Cobh. Then I get this phone call on my normal telephone line; how they got hold of it, I do not know. I have to suspect that Fergus or one of his crew gave him my name, and they did the research. To cut a long story short, I was informed that Fergus and his cruiser had been captured off the coast of Benin and was being held for ransom. There was no mention of the cargo, so I suspect they had not discovered it. They want one and a half million dollars for the return of Fergus, his crew, and presumably the cruiser. If they had discovered the cargo, they would have wanted considerably more. Knowing you are about to set out across the Atlantic, I wanted to know how you want me to play this? It's not that we can't pay the ransom, but I was just wondering what you want me to do."

Roy was dumbfounded for a moment. All thoughts of the half-clad Elian beside him fled his mind. Fergus was in trouble and he needed help. Roy was well aware that those bloody Nigerian pirates, or any other group in the area, would have no hesitation in killing the hostages, whether the ransom was paid or not. They had no fear of any reprisals; the law and order in that part of Africa was very corrupt, and there was little chance of them ever being brought to book for any crimes they committed, in the name of freedom. He pondered over the problem.

"Are you still there, Roy?" asked Sam.

"Yes, give me a minute to think, will you?" snapped Roy.

Sam waited whilst Roy pulled up the co-ordinates of the drop; it was some seventy miles off the coast of Benin and about halfway between Lagos and Lomé in Togo.

"Do we know the nationality of the pirates or which port they are being held in?" Roy asked.

"No!" Sam answered.

"See if you can find out more. When are you expecting to be contacted again?" Roy enquired.

"Tomorrow at noon, GMT. Why, what do you want me to say?" Sam asked in reply.

"I want you to delay for as long as you can. I need time to get across to Africa, and it's going to take me at least three days. Get proof that Fergus and his crew are alive. A video on a disc will do. We may be able to pick something up from the accent or the background to give us an idea where they are being held. Tell them you are having difficulty in tracking down the boat's owner, as I am abroad. That should hold them for a while."

"OK, I'll do my best, but what if they won't play ball?" Sam asked, some concern creeping into his voice. "What do you want me to do then?"

"If they want the money and it's not small beer they're asking; they will agree to give proof of life. If the worst comes to the worst, you will have to pay the ransom in order to give Fergus a chance. But let me warn you that even if you pay, there's no guarantee they will let him go or return the boat. Call me when you have more information. I'll be on my way in a couple of hours. I just have to refuel and re-provision for the trip."

Roy hung up and told Elian to wake the others. Elian saw the concern on Roy's face and knew he was planning something, realising that as usual he wanted them all to know what they were in for. She hurried down below to wake Gael and Fiona before she went into her cabin to put some clothes on. She heard Roy come down and go into the stateroom to get dressed. She had wondered how he had planned to address the crew in the nude, and she smiled as the picture came into her mind. The three women gathered in the lounge; each had a mug of coffee in their hands when Roy reappeared, thankfully fully clothed. Fiona handed him a mug of coffee with a good shot of Irish to get his mind concentrated on whatever task he had in mind.

"I don't know if Elian has told you, but Fergus and his crew are in trouble. It would appear they have been taken by pirates off the coast of Benin or Nigeria. Either country is bad news. We have to prepare ourselves for the worst. We are going to try and find out where they are being held and try to rescue them and the boat if possible. It's going to be very dangerous, and we could find ourselves in the hands of pirates or be attacked or even be killed in the attempt. You know me, I will do anything to save any of you, and Fergus and his crew are no different. We had intended to go into Port of Spain and spend a few hours ashore in Trinidad and Tobago, but that will mean us waiting for morning, and there will be no time ashore now. I suggest we head south and refuel in Georgetown, Guyana. We can get fresh provisions from the market and be heading for Africa much sooner. If any of you want to jump ship and head back home tell me now. Once we have committed to this, there's no way back."

Roy waited to see what the reaction would be. Fiona was the weak link. She may be the one to cry off. No one said a word.

"Am I to take it you are all with me on this then?" Roy asked.

Gael stepped forward, after looking at the others, and said,

"Roy, we know if it were us in that predicament, you would not hesitate to come to our rescue. We realise the dangers and are ready to go with you come what may. Now let's stop the bloody chatter and get under way. We're losing valuable time."

Fiona and Elian nodded their agreement, and Roy said,

"OK, what are we waiting for? Let's head south. Gael, you and Fiona raise the anchors, and we will set the course and be off."

Gael and Fiona raised the anchors, and Roy took the wheel whilst Elian plotted the heading and the course for Georgetown. They all knew the risk and were willing to do anything Roy asked of them. Fortunately, the weather was good, but it took them almost nine hours with the boat almost flat out to get there. They pulled into the harbour and refuelled whilst Roy, Gael, and Fiona went ashore for fresh supplies. By five o'clock that afternoon, they were ready. The forecast was good, and they cleared the harbour and headed west; it was less than 3,000 miles to Guinea-Bissau, and from what Roy had said, they had to get there quickly. Thankfully, the new engines ran more efficiently, and there would be no need for them to tow extra fuel behind them this trip. Even so, if nothing went wrong at a steady cruising speed, it would take them at least ninety hours to reach the African coast, and that was without a stop. It would mean each of the three (Gael, Elian, and Roy) doing shifts of six hours with Fiona doing the food preparation.

The best laid plans where the sea was concerned did not materialise; it seemed the Atlantic was doing its best to delay them by throwing everything it could in their path. They had storms and squalls, all of which held their speed down, and when Sam called, Roy could hardly make out what he said. The storm was playing havoc with the satellite connection, and it was several hours before they could speak satisfactorily, Sam broke the news,

"The representative or that's what he calls himself, when he called, listened to what I wanted. I can assure you he was none too pleased when I told them there would be a delay, but when I asked for proof of life, he seemed more understanding and told me that a disc containing a video of the boat and the crew will be delivered tomorrow. I don't know how long I can delay them after that."

"I understand, Sam, but the bloody weather is not co-operating. We have been held up in some really bad weather. Whatever you do, stall them as long as you can. We hope to be off the coast of Guinea-Bissau tomorrow night at the latest. Have they told you how or where to deliver the ransom?"

"No, not yet." Sam said, "I expect they will give me that information after I get proof of life. I have an expert on the Nigerian pirate situation coming to see me from London tomorrow morning. He has told me if they send a video of the boat, he should be able to guess where they are holding the boat and the prisoners, from the photographs. He also told me that there was no guarantee that the crew and the boat would be held at the same locality."

"All right, Sam, let me know what you have, as soon as you can. We will keep going as fast as we are able. The weather seems to be clearing. That bloody storm was not forecast as it seemed to come out of nowhere. Hopefully, things will get better when it clears. The barometer seems to be rising which is a good sign."

"Rather you than me," Sam said. "In all honesty I don't know how you handle such unpredictability and be ruled by the whims of the weather. Good luck, I'll call again soon."

Roy broke the connection; as he went up on deck, the sky seemed to be clearing from the west, and he hoped they would be able to make better time.

Elian checked their position when the storm had died down and satellite connections were back up to normal. The storm had blown them south of their intended route, and they were north of Ascension Island. Roy decided they would go in to refuel before heading directly to Lagos, some 1,500 miles west. They headed towards the island and anchored in Clarence Bay, intending to refuel. Elian set off in the tender to locate the fuel supply point whilst Roy relaxed on deck with a stiff whisky. A high-speed fishing boat closed in on them with two bikini-clad women sunbathing on the foredeck. They waved, and Roy waved back. The boat pulled alongside; Fiona and Gael went over to talk. It appeared from the conversation that the two women were staying on the island and were glad to see new faces; their names were Rachael and Susanna; they were staying at the Farm Lodge Country House Hotel, having been disembarked from a cruise liner after having a disagreement with the purser. Roy kept his distance as he was just too tired to be interested, even though both women were undeniably very attractive. He was just too concerned about Fergus to be bothered to go and talk. It was Fiona who came back to tell him that the two women were sisters, from America, and that they were staying on the island for an indefinite time. She told Roy that they had been there for a month relaxing after being offloaded from a cruise liner.

Fiona seemed set to inform Roy that the two women were looking for a lift to Europe, and she had explained to them they were going to West Africa, and the two women had seemed interested in joining the cruiser as passengers and crew. Roy looked at Fiona and said,

"Fiona, we are not on a pleasure cruise. We are going into a situation that we may not come out of. This is no place for passengers. You will have to tell them that the answer is no!"

Fiona looked crestfallen.

"Perhaps we could come back for them or they could join us when we have done what we have to do. They seem so nice I hate to turn them away."

Roy smiled and said that they may be able to do something when they had finished rescuing Fergus, not really believing they would ever see the two women again.

Soon after Elian returned and gave Roy directions to the refuelling point, and Roy told her what Fiona had proposed and how he had answered her. The sport fishing boat pulled away, and Roy moved down towards the wharf where he was to refuel. Gael came up on deck began speaking to Roy and Elian about the two American women.

"They seem so nice, and they are very well off. I would have liked to have spent more time talking with them, but I know we have a mission to finish. I took their hotel number, just in case they are around after we have finished in Lagos. They seem very keen to join us and sail back to Ireland, and they will pay you very well, Roy."

"Fergus is our main worry at this moment." Roy shrugged. "Perhaps when we have finished in Lagos, by then I'm sure they will have long gone from here."

Elian gave the thumbs up; as the last of the fuel was pumped into the cruiser's tanks, she had paid using Roy's credit card.

They were about to leave when a messenger from the Governor's office arrived with a message requesting Lord Croft to go to his office. Elian looked at Roy questioningly and asked,

"I wonder what that's for. I hope it's not just social. We need to leave as soon as we can if we have any chance of getting to Lagos before they set a deadline for payment."

"I know Elian, but we daren't offend the Governor. In our line of business, we never know when we might need a friend. He may even be able to give us a clue as to the whereabouts of these bloody pirates. He is, after all, closer to them than Sam, and he may have information that could be vital. Let's go and see what the old boy wants."

The messenger took them to the awaiting car, and the messenger climbed into the front passenger seat, and they headed towards the town. They pulled up outside an impressive colonial-style building, and the messenger opened the rear doors and invited both of them to follow him. They went up the steps and past the liveried doorman who doffed his hat as they passed. They were shown up the staircase to the outer office of the Governor, and the secretary sitting at her desk outside the Governor's office stood as they approached.

"Good afternoon, Lord Croft. If you will take a seat for a moment, I'll see if the Governor is ready for you."

The secretary disappeared through the door into the Governor's office; she reappeared moments later to say,

"The Governor will see you now, your Lordship, and this young woman, is she Lady Croft?"

She looked over her glasses, somewhat disdainfully, at Elian, who was dressed in slacks and a woollen jumper.

"No, this is Elian, my skipper and confidante. Lady Croft has had to return to Ireland."

"Then follow me," the secretary said and walked back through the door.

The Governor stood and walked around his desk towards Roy; they shook hands, and Roy was surprised by the confident grip the Governor had. He motioned Roy and Elian to be seated in the old but very comfortable chairs around a coffee table on which stood a silver tray with pots of tea and coffee together with delicate china cups and saucers.

"It's so good of you to spare me some of your time, Lord Croft, and you, Elian, such a nice name. I presume it's Irish. I've not heard of it before. Would you prefer tea or coffee, my dear?"

"Coffee, please," Elian replied.

The secretary poured her a cup,

"Milk and sugar?" she asked

"I'll take it black with one sugar, please," Elian said.

"Lord Croft, and for you; or would you prefer something stronger? I know it's a little early, but I'm going to have a gin and tonic," the Governor said.

"I'm a Scotch man myself, Sir," Roy replied.

"Capital."

The Governor beamed as the secretary crossed to the drinks cabinet and poured the requested drinks, returning with the crystal glasses on a tray but looking a little disapprovingly as she handed the Governor and Lord Croft their drinks.

"That will be all for the moment, Millicent. I'll call you if we need you."

The Governor, Sir Stanley Hillary, waited until Millicent had left, and then he turned to Roy and asked,

"Well, Lord Croft, we don't get too many Lords visiting us in St Helena, and I understand from my sources that you are anxious to get under way, so I will come directly to the point. I have a problem. First of all, am I right in believing you are going back to Ireland?"

"Yes, but not directly, Sir Stanley. We have business in Lagos first and then we plan to head back to Ireland," Roy replied, wondering where this was all leading up to.

"Be careful around Lagos. Those pirates are very active. Unless your business is essential, I should keep well away from that den of iniquity," Sir Stanley murmured.

His face conveyed a look of worry, showing his alarm at the prospect of his guest going to such a place.

"Unfortunately, I have no choice, but what was it you wanted to ask me?" Roy asked, wanting to bring the matter to a quick ending.

"Well then," Sir Stanley said, "I have a bit of a problem. I have two young women from America staying on the island. They are the daughters of a Texas millionaire. I accepted them on the island to stay when the purser of their cruise liner requested them to disembark here. I understand they had been a bit of a problem on board. Some of these youngsters of the rich and famous can be a bit like that, can they not?"

Roy nodded, still wondering when the old boy was going to get to the point.

"Well, I have to confess if I had known what I know now, I may well have refused. They are young, very pretty, with unlimited amounts of money, and have caused havoc in our small community. The young men around here are usually very well behaved, but since the arrival of these two women, there have been more disturbances than I can ever remember. We have had young men fighting, late-night revelry, and civil unrest, to say the least. I have several of them in jail, waiting to see the magistrate, at this very moment, and a couple in a hospital with knife wounds, something unheard of in our small island."

Roy listened patiently and asked,

"I can understand your problem, Sir Stanley. I think I saw the two young women earlier on a sport fishing boat. They were American and very pretty. My crew spoke to me about them. It would appear they want a lift to Europe or something."

"Exactly, Lord Croft. I would be so grateful if you could help. I understand your crew is all female. They would not be able to wreak havoc with them. The young men in this town have never come across anything like them. They are wild and a little, if you will excuse the expression, promiscuous to say the least. I need to get the Island back to a state of normality. They have shown no wish to catch a plane or leave us until you arrived. I am pleading with you to help me in this matter. I can't pay you, as such, but the re-provisioning and refuelling will be at our expense."

Roy sat back somewhat amused; the Governor was being dragged into the modern world and he was not managing very well.

"Before I give you my reply, Sir Stanley, let me tell you why I'm going to Lagos, and then if you still want me to consider your request, I will do so. I own a small but successful charter company, and one of my cruisers and her crew have been kidnapped by those bloody pirates you have mentioned. The official line is we do not negotiate with terrorists, and that I understand includes pirates. It is my intention to try to effect a rescue of my boat and its crew. I fully realise the dangers of such an enterprise, but I and my crew are willing to take that risk."

At this point, Sir Stanley sat open-mouthed, his quiet respect fell away, and he looked grave.

"You could all be killed," he said quietly.

"Of that, Sir Stanley, I am all too aware. To locate and find my way in to wherever they are holding my crew is my biggest worry."

"Let me bring someone else into this conversation, will you, Lord Croft? I can assure you he will be of great benefit to you," Sir Stanley said, rising from his seat.

He crossed the room and picked up the telephone, looking at Roy to see if he would raise any objection. Far from objecting, Roy was looking for whatever help he could get and just nodded. Sir Stanley dialled a number and waited for it to be answered.

"Brigadier Castleton, come to my office immediately. I need your help." The governor said.

The Governor crossed the room and sat down. He looked directly at Roy and asked,

"Can I get you a refill?"

He waited for Roy to hand him his glass, then to Elian, and said,

"I have to revise my opinion of you and your crew, young lady. Can I get you something stronger than tea?"

"I'll have Scotch as well, Sir Stanley, if I may?" Elian replied.

They all sat drinking and making polite conversation when there was a tap on the door. It opened and a head poked its way around and a distinguished-looking man said,

"You wanted me, Sir Stanley?"

"Yes, Brigadier, come in. This is Lord Croft, the chap who owns that converted MTB in the harbour. Damned fine chap, he is too, but look here, he is going to gallivant off to Lagos to rescue one of his other boats and its crew from those damned pirates; he wants some advice. Can you help us, old chap?"

The brigadier shook hands with Roy and sat down.

"It's bloody risky, you know. They are a bloody, ruthless lot. They do not give a fig for law and order and will have no compunction about killing you all, you know," the Brigadier said, his face drawn and stern.

"I'm well aware of that, Brigadier, but I will do anything for my staff regardless as to the risk. I know only too well even if we pay the blood money, there is no guarantee that I will ever see my crew or the boat again. So I am determined to give it my best," Roy said.

"That's the spirit, your Lordship. If more people did that, there would be far less of these beggars around. Now tell me, how they contacted you and what was said?" the Brigadier retorted, bending forward so as not to miss a word of Lord Croft's reply.

Roy, with Elian joining in, told how the message had been conveyed and that it had been passed to his charterer because he, himself, had been in the West Indies at the time. The Brigadier wanted to know, as near as possible, the exact words used. Roy used his cell and called Sam; after he had told him where he was and that Brigadier Castleton wanted him to repeat word for word what the pirate connection had said when they had contacted him. The Brigadier listened carefully asking several questions during the conversation. When he had all he needed, he handed Roy the phone.

"Any sign of that proof of life yet?" Roy asked.

Then he switched off and turned back to face the Brigadier, who had been making notes.

"Lord Croft, I need you to keep in touch. When you leave, I need to know how the proof of life is delivered and in exactly what form. From what I can gather from Sam, is that his name? I think the group is from Benin, and they hold up in a cove near a disused wharf at Badagry Creek."

He pulled out a well-folded map and laid it on the table; opening it up, he said softly, almost as if he feared someone was listening,

"This is the breakwater at the entrance to Lagos Harbour, go north up towards Marine Bridge Road, take this turn. Here, this is Apapa Oworonshoki Way, and here is Badagry Creek. The disused wharf is here. They had a fire which destroyed the terminal, and things being what they are in Lagos, it's cheaper to build another than to repair the old. If it's the group—I think it is—your boat will be here."

He marked the spot with a cross and continued,

"Your crew will be somewhere around here," he said, pointing to a nearby township.

"I'll have my man try to pinpoint the exact spot, and I'll contact you again by the time you are getting close to your destination."

Then whispering to Roy whilst Elian kept the Governor in conversation about sailing,

"Have you all the weapons you need or can I help?" The Brigadier asked, "I can see if you are going into that nest, you have to have had some experience before or you would be stark raving mad."

"I could do with a couple of Sam7 missiles and a couple of RPGs, and we have all the light machine guns and side arms we need."

"I thought I could judge a mercenary when I saw one," the Brigadier whispered. "I'll see what I can do when I leave. If I can help, there will be a truck on the harbour by the time you get back. Good luck, you will need it. Here is my number to contact me. Give me your satellite contact number."

Roy wrote the number down and slipped it into his hand.

"Thanks," Roy whispered.

The Brigadier rose and bid them a safe journey and wished them luck again as he left. The Governor looked at Roy,

"Look, Governor," Roy said, "I will do my best, but I'm not taking them unless they are fully appraised of the risks and the fact that none of us may get away. That's all I can offer. Now get them to come to the boat in a hurry. If they are not there in an hour and a half, we shall leave without them."

The two men shook hands; then Elian and Roy walked down the stairs to where the messenger was waiting. They climbed into the official car and were driven back to the wharf. There stood a truck in camouflage with a couple of squaddies leaning against the front wing. Roy walked up, and they stood to attention.

"Lord Croft, we have a couple of boxes for you, sir. Where would you like them stowed?"

Roy showed them, and the two soldiers carried the boxes on board and stacked them by the rear hold. They made several journeys before they had loaded everything the Brigadier had sent. When they had finished, they saluted Roy again and whispered,

"Good luck, sir."

They climbed aboard the truck and drove off. Roy, assisted by the three women, carried the boxes below and unpacked the contents. The Brigadier had done them proud. Two boxes contained two Sam7 missiles in each, and the RPGs were in two other boxes, the third box contained an M15 with several bands of shells and a dozen hand grenades. The crew packed them away and put the boxes back on the quay where they would be collected later. Roy looked at his watch; the two proposed passengers were not going to make it. Gael and Fiona prepared to cast off when a Jeep Cherokee raced along the wharf and two women arrived, dressed, if you could call it that, as they wore the shortest shorts possible and a crop top which barely contained their breasts.

"You, Lord Croft?" they asked.

"Yes!" Roy responded.

"This is Susanna, and I'm Rachael. We are your passengers."

Roy went ashore and explained the situation to them. He did not mince his words, and he expected them to cry off. To his amazement, they both told him they were fully aware of what they were getting into, and as both had been used to handling guns since they could walk, they did not want to miss the action. They slung their knapsacks aboard.

"Where's the rest of your luggage?" Roy asked.

"We decided that if it was going to be that bad," Rachael answered, "we would forward the rest direct to Shannon and travel light. We may never need anything else. Right, Susanna!" she said in a broad southern drawl.

They jumped aboard, and Fiona showed them below and where to stow their gear. Roy eased the cruiser away from the wharf and headed out to sea. They had some 1,500 miles to cover, and he did not want to waste another second.

Roy was pleased that he had contacted Janet before they had set sail and told her they were safe and well but would be making a detour on the way home to give Fergus a hand as he seemed to have gotten himself into a little difficulty. He had wanted to tell her more, but at this stage, in her pregnancy, he did not want to worry her any more than necessary; if he survived, she need never know, and on the other hand, if he died, she would learn of it in due course. Then he knew she would worry, but by then it would be too late to do anything, and he knew he had left her very well provided for and the children. He had listened as she had told him to be careful, but he had noticed that the tone of her voice had been different, almost as if she had been distracted. He shrugged the feeling off and put it down to her pregnant state and the imminent birth of her third child.

Chapter 22

The sleeping arrangements aboard the cruiser had to be changed, with two extra passengers, or crew, as Elian referred to Rachael and Susanna, she had said to Roy when they were some distance from the island.

"I don't care what you say, Roy, and if they are going to be on this boat, then when we go into that cesspit of a harbour, they are going to have to be of more support than hindrance. I am going to find out if they can handle a gun, and if they can, so much the better, and if they can't, they will bloody well have to learn fast."

Roy had to agree as he knew that two inexperienced and frightened women aboard the boat, when he and the rest of the crew might have to fight for their lives, would be very dangerous. He knew in his own mind that between them, Gael and Elian would get them into shape somehow. That's why he had been reticent in the beginning about taking them. He knew they would have been a liability. He had agreed that Elian should go with Gael and find out just what experience they had. Texans, he knew, were people who had guns as part of their lives, as a rule, but whether their father, albeit he was a millionaire by all accounts, had taught them anything about shooting at targets that fired back was something that Elian and Gael would have to discover for themselves.

Sometime later, Elian came back up to the bridge, and the look on her face told Roy she was pleased about something.

"Problem solved," Elian said. "Daddy has a ranch, and seemingly they have ridden stock since they were old enough to ride. They can both handle a rifle and a pistol. Gael has agreed to train them on the Uzi and the Beretta as neither have been used to either weapon. It seems as though these two might be of use after all. I would not expect them to be with us when we go ashore, but they will be more than useful to hold the boat in case of trouble whilst we are away. The last thing we would need is to rescue Fergus and crew and come back to find the cruiser gone, stolen whilst we were away. They can stay aboard with Fiona. Three of them armed should be able to hold off any attack. What do you think, Roy?"

"What was their reaction when you asked them if they could handle a gun, and you broke the news of what we intended doing when we reached Lagos?"

"I could not believe it. They both seemed more than happy to be involved. Daddy had told them to get their privileged asses out into the world and get some experience before they settled down and got married. They are rearing to go, a bit too enthusiastic for my liking, but Gael will knock that out of them if she puts them through her training regime over the next couple of days; they will be too tired to be over enthusiastic. Don't you agree?"

Roy nodded his head in agreement; the sound of weapons being loaded came from below.

"You had better get down there before they use all the ammunition before we arrive. You know how keen Gael is to show off her own abilities."

Elian gave a chuckle and disappeared below, and the sounds of Gael instructing the newcomers on how to handle automatic weapons drifted up as Roy opened the throttles sending the cruiser up on the plane. They needed to close the distance between themselves and their adversaries quickly.

The next two days were hectic with Gael getting Rachael, Susanna and Fiona, when she was not too busy cooking, into shape and familiar with handling the weapons on board. Rachael and Susanna had been a little shaken when Gael had displayed the Sam7 rocket launchers and the RPGs, but she had emphasised that the people they would be dealing with were ruthless killers. Surprisingly enough, both women took to the training well and seemed eager to please. Roy had watched Gael put them through a keep-fit regime that would have made a trained athlete tired, but they had seemed to cope well. Roy had looked them over as they had trained in vest tops and skimpy shorts, and he had liked what he had seen, both women were more than just attractive; for Roy, they were very desirable, but whether he would get the opportunity to bed either or both would have to be seen.

Gael reported to Roy at the end of day two,

"The two new recruits are really shaping up. Thank God both of them were fairly fit to start with. All that time on horseback has kept their muscles well-toned, and they handled the weapons like a pair of pros. I think, with Fiona, they will be more than capable of holding the cruiser in case of attack and giving an excellent account of themselves. Both women are good shots. Both of them have told me they have hunted cougar, and both have trophies back home to prove it, if I believe what they tell me."

"Well done, Gael, you have done a really good job, but if we don't hear from Sam shortly, I think we may be too late to do anything about Fergus and his crew. It's been more than a week since they were taken captive. I don't know what condition they will be in after a week in that hellhole." Roy said, "Let's hope we hear soon. No news is good news. It means they still have to contact Sam about the payment and the proof of life."

Her face showed the same concern as Roy's as she turned and walked back down to the others. She turned at the top of the companionway and said, "Elian will be up to relieve you shortly. She was getting dressed when I came up. I'll get Fiona to get your food ready. It's best to eat whilst we can. Once we are into this mission, we may not get any time to eat."

Roy knew she was right, and he did feel peckish and was also feeling randy. There had been little time for sex during this voyage, and there was going to be even less time until Fergus, his crew, and the boat were safely back in their hands. The tension aboard was high, and everyone was strung out, not the most convivial atmosphere for wild sexual fantasies, which would have to wait.

That evening, the message came through from Sam. The proof of life had been received on a disc; it was a video showing Fergus and his crew in a filthy state, but all apparently alive. The voice on the tape had ordered Fergus to talk, when the video was being shot; from the content, it was obvious he had been alive a couple of days before. Roy told Sam to send a copy by email to the Brigadier on St Helena, and he gave Sam the email address.

"When have you got to pay the money and how?" Roy asked.

"The message that came with the disc said they would contact me with the method of payment. Oh yes, the package was delivered by courier, but it had been through several courier services, and we have not been able to find out where the parcel originated. I'm sorry about that, but I have tried my best," Sam said.

"Don't worry, Sam. The Brigadier seemed to think that the way the package was delivered, and how the information was presented would give him sufficient information to know which group had them captive."

Roy sat and waited, his agitation was obvious to everyone, and they left him alone. Two hours after he had spoken to Sam, the satellite phone rang again; this time it was the Brigadier.

"Lord Croft, I've seen the video, and from what I can make out, it's a group who operate from one of the townships behind the oil terminals in Lagos itself. It's a pretty hellish place and not the easiest to extract your men from. They will be hidden in a shack in the township, and I'll try and get you a guide. If I'm right, your boat will be tied up on the disused wharf nearby."

"This guide," the Brigadier continued, "if I can get him, won't come cheap, it's bloody dangerous, and he will know if he's caught, they will kill him and possibly his family. Those buggers have adopted the same method as they have in South Africa, the lethal punishment of 'necklacing' any traitor of their own. They put a car tyre round his neck after binding his hands and feet with wire, and then they pour petrol into the tyre and set it alight. It's not a nice way to die, I can assure you. You will need to give him a thousand US dollars in cash before he gets aboard. He will direct you to a place nearby, and then he will be gone. You will need to give him another thousand when he leaves."

"That's not too bad, Brigadier." Roy said, "I would have been prepared to pay more," Roy added.

"Don't, and my advice is, when you go in, keep the little bugger on board until it's over. I've known these weasels take money off both sides, so hang on to him until the deal is done one way or the other. I've never met the guy who will guide you, so there's no guarantee," The Brigadier explained.

"I'll be leaving three armed crew on board, so they will ensure he remains until we return. If there's trouble, we might just need him to get us back in a hurry. Where do I pick him up?" asked Roy.

"When you begin to enter the main waterway into Lagos, there is a beach on your left. You will see a building up on the headland with a path coming down to the beach. He will be there any time between six and ten o'clock tomorrow night. Your signal will be two long and three short flashes. He will reply with three short flashes. If you are late or he is not there, you will need to ring me, and I'll try to direct you on the satellite phone. That will make your mission ten times more difficult. Have a high-detail map available on your navigation system. Good luck, your Lordship. I will be thinking of you. Sorry, I can't be more help, old man. Ring me when it's all over. If I don't hear from you, I'll fear the worst."

"Thanks, Brigadier. You have been most helpful. I'll let you know when we're clear."

Roy broke the connection and went up top where Elian was at the wheel; she turned as he approached and asked,

"Was that the Brigadier on the line just now?" she asked

"Yes," Roy replied, "and our target for getting into Lagos is between six and ten tomorrow night. How are we fixed for time?"

"If the tide and shipping are not too bad, and we don't have any trouble with either the engines or pirates, we will be due to begin our move up the main waterway by seven o'clock," Elian said.

"That's what I imagined. We have to pick up a guide from the beach who it seems may not be too reliable."

"If he knows the waterway, he will be better than nothing," Elian muttered grimly.

Roy nodded in agreement, then he gave her the signal codes and the parameters as well as the location explaining.

"If, however, the guide is not there for any reason, we will need to bring up a detailed map on the navigation system and the Brigadier will try to guide us in remotely.

Gael and the others checked the weapons, cleaning and ensuring everything was in full working order; the last thing they wanted was a gun to jam or not having the right weapon to hand when they needed it. The atmosphere on the boat was tense, with everyone fully alert for trouble as they approached the wide waterway leading to the busy harbour. There were more tankers of every shape and size as well as container ships, tramp steamers, tugs, and many varied and smaller craft of all sizes were heading in and out of the busy harbour. Roy spotted the lights from the square building on the headland and looked at the detailed map for the path leading down from the building. They were in the right spot and gave the signal. No answering signal was received. They waited anchored close to the shore, giving the signal every fifteen minutes. At the fourth attempt, the answer came.

Roy gave the signal to the tender which was alongside, waiting for the right moment. When they saw Roy give them the thumbs-up sign, Gael with Elian and Fiona, all fully armed, went with the first payment of a thousand US dollars to pick up their guide. Roy watched their progress through his night glasses, with the sniper rifle beside him in case of trouble. He did not have to worry as a man and a boy came into the water, and Elian handed over the thousand US dollars; to everyone's surprise, the boy got into the boat and the man ran back up the beach. Roy watched as the tender approached, and the boy was older than he had looked at first sight. He was dressed in a dirty vest ripped in several places, a pair of ragged trousers that had seen better days, and he was barefoot. When he came on board, he gave a grin, his two front teeth were missing and his face was grimy. He looked to be in his late teens, and when he spoke, it was thankfully in fairly good English, but heavily accented.

"I'm Sonny," he said. "I am here to guide you: the man you saw was my father and has been sick. I know the place you are going to." He looked at the women around him and said quietly, "It's not a place for women. It's very dangerous for men, but for women . . ." He shook his head. "It's a very bad place. They will have no mercy if any of you are caught. It will be a very bad death. You will be raped by many bad men who have bad diseases."

Gael looked at the dishevelled young black figure and whispered,

"They would not be the first. I've killed a man for trying that, and the same goes for my friends. So don't stress too much on that score. We can take care of ourselves."

She reached under her skirt and drew the thin-bladed knife, and picking up a piece of rope, she cut a piece off with the ease of a hot knife cutting through butter. Sonny grinned, as the others put their weapons down and began to recover the tender.

"You may need every skill you have to survive tonight, boss, just be careful, and avoid conflict if you can. The township is a maze of ramshackle buildings all interconnected, and if there's trouble, you will be treated as the enemy by everyone, not just the gang holding the hostages. You are the wrong colour to expect any kind of friendship from anyone around. You will be fair game," Sonny said, his voice full of concern for the women.

Sonny's skills at navigating the busy waterways surprised Roy; they dodged in and out of large and small ships. Sonny had told Roy to switch off his running lights and keep close to the shore. Roy did so keeping a watchful eye on the depth gauge as they moved further up the wide waterway. Sonny pointed out the wide gap on the left and said,

"Keep to the right close to shore. There are two other channels you don't want to get into. Watch out for the tankers, they come and go without warning, and it takes them a long time to turn or stop. There are terminals all along here, so watch out."

They moved slowly; edging from one wharf to the next, they were challenged several times, and Sonny gave an answer each time that seemed to satisfy the challenger.

"I just told them we are holding hostages. They think we are from the group holding your men."

Gael, who was at the prow, jumped up and ran back, waving her finger pointing it in the direction of a deserted wharf. Roy eased back on the throttle, and there, half-covered with a large tarpaulin, was Fergus's cruiser. Sonny pointed to a wharf close by, with a flat pontoon anchored alongside, and there were no lights showing, and the whole place seemed deserted. Gael and Elian appeared from below with their faces blackened, and each had a Kevlar bulletproof vest with side arms, an Uzi machine gun and several grenades hanging from their belt, both looking like a pair of commandos about to go into battle. Roy rubbed the black polish over his own face, his own Kevlar vest and his dark shirt and shorts melded in with his blackened legs. Slipping on his belt with a Beretta in the holster, he put several more clips, each containing fifteen rounds into his side pockets; then after he hung several grenades from his vest and was ready to go. Sonny, far from wanting to disappear, insisted he accompany the landing party.

"I have to come with you," he insisted. "You will never find your way through the township. I will go first and keep watch, telling you when the coast is clear. When we get to their hideout, you are on your own. I'll hang about to guide you back, but if things go badly, I'm gone, give me my second payment just in case."

Roy toyed with the idea of telling him he would pay him when they got back, but that had not been the agreement.

"Here's your money, Sonny," Roy said, and to keep him onside, he added, "if all goes well, I will double your payment, and that's another two thousand dollars, my lad."

Sonny's face lit up; he looked incredulously at Roy; that was more money than he could hope to earn over several years. He smiled, his white teeth with the double gap glistened against the blackness of his lips and face.

"OK, boss," he said, "I'll stay by you. Don't worry."

Roy checked with Fiona; she stood by Rachael and Susanna, all armed with Uzis, and each had a couple of grenades; the M15 was mounted on the foredeck pointing ashore, and it was obvious that Gael had trained them well.

"Fiona, I suggest you lay off about four or five metres from the pontoon to prevent anyone boarding you from the shore. Get these two to keep watch fore and aft and you get up top and keep your eyes peeled. Be ready to make a quick getaway if necessary, and if all goes well, we will see you before dawn. If we are not back by then, abandon us and get the hell out of here. You will stand no chance once it gets light. These bastards will realise you are not with them. If you hear us coming, I'll whistle like this."

He gave a long low whistle followed by two short and sharp whistles using his fingers in his mouth, but much quieter than he would be doing on his return to get Fiona to get the cruiser alongside the pontoon ready for them to board.

"Let no one else board you for any reason. Do you all understand that? Not even if they appear to be the police."

Fiona nodded her head in agreement, and she gave Roy a kiss on the side of his face and made a grimace as she tasted the black polish and burnt cork.

"Good luck and come back safe. We will keep the boat safe for you, so don't worry and be assured; we won't fail even if we die, trying."

Not waiting another second, Roy, Gael, Elian, and Sonny slipped ashore.

Chapter 23

They had no sooner gained a foothold on the shore; when they began to move away from the waterfront towards the township, the first thing that struck them was the overpowering smell of crude oil mixed with the rancid smell of unwashed bodies and sewerage. Sonny held up his hand for them to wait, and he slipped from sight; he reappeared minutes later and beckoned them forward. They slowly edged around the ramshackle buildings constructed of wood, corrugated sheeting, flat metal sheets, and car body parts. The going underfoot was muddy and oily, and they had to tread slowly and carefully to avoid slipping. Gradually, they moved ever deeper into the tangled wreckage that served as homes for the poorest of the poor in the area. Sonny trod carefully and guided them towards their goal. Suddenly, he held up his hand as the sound of men's voices was close at hand. Roy and the two women froze; they stood, ready to defend themselves, knowing the odds would be stacked against them if it came to an affray. The voices moved away on the other side of the shanty shack separating them. Sonny waited a while, and when it was all quiet, he whispered,

"That was a gang of oil workers going to work on the docks. Thankfully they were no threat as they did not see us. Not far now to the compound where I believe they are holding your hostages. Be extra alert."

Then turning to the two women, he whispered,

"Use those knives if you have to, but don't fire a shot unless it's to return fire, or you will have them alerted to us being here."

The two women shouldered their Uzis and drew their knives; Sonny shuddered he had seen just how sharp those knives were. After another five minutes, during which they stopped several time to allow men, women, and children to clear their path. The shacks around the group were occupied and smoke from fires within the dirty shacks mixed with the smell of food, oil, stale sweat and human waste.

Sonny crouched behind an oil drum and pointed to a building larger than the rest, surrounded by a chicken wire fence supported by a stout wooden frame topped by a curling roll of barbed wire running around the top of the whole of the perimeter fence. There were two men guarding the gate, each looking dishevelled, dirty, and ill-disciplined; they both were carrying a weapon slung over their shoulder and were relaxed, drinking beer from a bottle and smoking. Neither of them looked as though they were expecting trouble. Roy nodded to Gael, who in turn gestured to Elian. The two women disappeared silently; Gael, moving as silently as a cat, went round the perimeter and reappeared at the far corner of the enclosed compound. Neither made a sound as they closed in on the two slovenly looking guards; they stood no chance, and it was doubtful if they even realised anyone was near them. Simultaneously, an arm went around a neck, a hand clamped over each mouth, and a knife as sharp as any razor was drawn smartly across each throat. Blood spurted, both men slumped silently to their knees; the women dragged the two bodies into the surrounding darkness and gave the signal for Roy to move forward. The gate was not locked, and the three of them slipped into the compound silently merging into the shadows. They split up and reconnoitred the building; Gael saw two more armed men in one room, and Roy discovered a windowless opening at the back with bars of steel preventing anyone entering or leaving the square aperture. He crept up and listened; there was only the muffled sound of men breathing and the occasional nasal sound of a snore.

Roy moved back to join the others; both women were covered in the thick dark blood of their victims. They looked as though they had been in a slaughterhouse.

"There are two guards in the room by the front door," Gael whispered, "I could not see anyone else."

"I listened at what would appear, from the stench, to be a latrine, and I could not hear anyone inside," Elian whispered,

"The room at the back appeared to contain men sleeping," Roy informed them. "I'll go back and use the torch to see if I can identify anyone. If the guards come out to see what is going on, you know what to do. I don't know if there are any more than two inside or if there is a guard on the cell. If Fergus is in there, I'll try and ask him to give me the information through the barred window."

The two women blended into the shadows on either side of the door, and Roy moved around to the rear of the building. He got to the window and took out his small torch. He reached up on tiptoes and looked into the window. He could not make anything out inside except a number of forms lying on the floor. If there was a door, he could not make it out. He risked the torch, pointing it through the window; with one hand, he held his side arm in the other with the safety off.

Roy pressed the small button on the side of the torch with his thumb. A sliver thread of light illuminated the blackness within, the white light penetrating the darkness in the cell. As far as Roy could ascertain there were five people lying on the floor, all of them, from what he could see, were of European extraction. At least none of the figures had the usual tight curly hair associated with an African. It appeared to Roy from his vantage point that there was no guard present in the cell.

"Fergus!" Roy called softly, "Fergus! Are you in there?" Roy heard one of the figures move slightly, and he called again, "Fergus, wake up man. It's Roy." One of the figures sat up and blinked as the beam of light played over his face; Roy did not recognise the grimy face. The figure reached across and shook a nearby form and whispered something Roy could not hear. The figure sat up, and Roy pointed the torch on to the face, it was barely recognisable, but there was something familiar about it. The voice confirmed it.

"Roy, is that you?" Fergus whispered unable to believe his ears.

"Yes, but for Christ's sake, keep your voice down. How many guards are there in the building?"

"Normally three, there's one asleep outside the door of the cell and two others in the building. During the day, there are many more, but they go away during the night. There's nowhere for them to sleep."

"Can you walk?" Roy asked.

"Yes." Fergus whispered in reply.

"How many of your crew are in there?" Roy asked tentatively.

"All three and a lone sailor they took off a yacht. He's been here a while; he tells me his ransom was paid weeks ago, but there is no sign of them letting him go or releasing his yacht."

This confirmed Roy's fears that even if the money was paid, there was no guarantee of release.

"Are you all able to walk?" Roy asked again.

"We are. However, the lone sailor is very sick, but we can carry him. He's as thin as a skeleton, and he's been here a long time."

"Don't talk. We will try and get to you from the front. Be ready to get out. When you hear the guard at the door, wake up."

Roy made his way back to the front of the building and moved to the gate. He called softly and Sonny emerged.

Roy beckoned him from where he was hidden in the shadows.

"You and I will be in the shadows by the gate with a bottle each. I'll sit on the floor as though I'm drunk. You call out to the guards. Tell them

I'm drunk, and be prepared to move quickly if they seem to raise their weapons. I will have a gun trained on them in case of an emergency."

Sonny was nervous, but he waited until Roy was in position, his gun pointing in the direction of the door, but the weapon was hidden in the dark shadow thrown by nearby buildings. The only real light apart from a dull glow coming from building around them was from the pale moonlight.

"Get up." Sonny called out, "You're not supposed to be asleep. Get up, or I'll call the others."

There were sounds of movement inside, and one of the guards appeared.

"Is that you, Abah? What's wrong?" he called.

"This stupid bugger won't get up," Sonny answered softly, making his voice sound as though he was the worse for drink.

One of the guards came to the door turned and called out,

"Nzube, come out here. It's Obari. He's drunk again. You'll have to come and take over."

"I'll kill that bastard. That's the third time this month," came a voice from within.

The second guard appeared at the door, and the two men walked casually towards the gate. They had not taken two steps when the women slid quietly behind them, and the first guard slumped down, his neck spurting a series of jetting arterial blood. Elian had not quite got hold of the second guard, and he gripped her arm and dragged her to the floor, the knife slipping from her grasp. Gael, who was kneeling beside the dying guard, spun round and, in an instance, had buried the knife into the side of the guard. He let out a yell and released Elian as he tried to pull the knife from his side. Elian rolled from under him and grabbed the knife. Roy, seeing what had happened, rose up and ran through the gate just as the third guard appeared at the door. He had a pistol in his hand and was about to fire when Roy knelt down and, taking aim, fired the silenced weapon at the guard, who had not quite been fully awake and alert. The guard went down clutching his chest and his finger clasped at the trigger firing a round into the dirt before dropping his gun on the floor.

Roy ran through the door, dragging the fallen guard who had been hit in the chest; as Roy put his fingers against his artery to see if he was still alive, the guard's heels beat a now familiar tattoo on the hard floor, and he lay still. Gael appeared behind Roy, and they moved through the hut, checking each shadow to ensure there was no one else. The door to the cell was locked with a thick chain and a padlock. Gael raced back to the cell guard's body and found the key on a piece of string around his neck. Retrieving it, she ran back and gave it to Roy, who opened the cell and released the hostages. Fergus and one of the others had the limp form of the stranger between them, and the other two followed.

"Before any of you speak, I don't want any questions. If you have anything to say, it can wait till we get back on board. Fergus, where is the key to your boat?"

"They took it, but the spare should be where I've hidden it in the same place as you hide yours, as you told me."

"OK, let's get out of here whilst we can. Those shots may have alerted somebody for sure."

"Don't be so sure about that, Roy. We hear gunshots on and off every night. It may not have aroused anyone's suspicions at all," Fergus said hurriedly.

"Let's move out. Everyone follow Gael. I'll bring up the rear," Roy said, ushering everyone forward.

Elian was outside, waiting, and Sonny beckoned them forward. The sound of a heavy vehicle could be heard moving in their direction, and they followed Sonny, who moved quicker on their return than he had when bringing them to this spot. Although they moved quickly, they met no one; Fergus's crew were making a fair amount of noise, and Roy knew the sound would alert anyone following behind. He kept watch constantly, expecting trouble.

They approached the wharf, and as Roy gave the signal, the cruiser moved closer to the pontoon just as they reached the water's edge. Fergus ran towards the other cruiser and climbed aboard. The sound of the heavy truck was getting closer; it was crashing through the shacks, scattering men, women, and children as it headed for the wharf. Roy called out,

"For Christ's sake, leave it, Fergus. We don't have time."

Elian gunned the cruiser's engine, impatient to be away, and Fergus tried to start the other cruiser; the engine turned over too slowly, sounding as though there was some extra drain on the battery. It must have been booby-trapped, because suddenly there was a violent explosion and the cruiser erupted, sending debris high into the air. Seconds later, there was no sign of Fergus or the lower control room, where he had been standing only moments before. Roy stared at the explosion, transfixed momentarily; he knew then he had failed; Fergus and the cruiser were gone forever. It was with a heavy heart that Roy called Fergus's name several times, but there was no response; the cruiser began to settle immediately, and with a deep feeling of regret, Roy gave Elian the signal to move out. She gunned the engine just as the truck crashed through the shack at the rear and out on to the wharf, scattering sheets of corrugated metal in all directions. Bullets started flying in their way seconds later; Roy heard two of them hit the woodwork while the rest threw up small splashes of water around the hull or went harmlessly overhead. Elian took evasive action as the vessel surged forward and swung the boat out heading further out into the waterway. Roy and Gael lobbed grenades out over the transom as the boat began to race away. The grenades exploded short of the mark, sending gouts of water up over the pontoon. Shots continued to be fired in their direction, but there was not order or concentration of firepower as the panicked rabble tumbled from the truck, and, to Roy's surprise, Fiona fired an RPG from the upper deck, scoring a direct hit on the front offside of the stationary vehicle. Gael and Fiona fired several bursts from the M15; Rachael and Susanna fired short bursts of fire from the Uzis in the direction of the pontoon, causing the remaining gang members to scatter and dodge for cover.

Elian was now out into the main channel, and she moved behind a huge tanker, which sounded its fog horn at the dark shadow that crossed in its path. Elian ignored the tanker and was soon well behind it, heading back towards the main channel that would take them out and away towards the sea. Several small boats were appearing behind them as the alarm was raised. Roy went up on to the bridge and stood beside a white-faced Elian.

"I think we may have a fight on our hands. Are you up to handling the boat under Sonny's guidance? There's no chance of an error."

"You keep that rabble off us, and I'll get us out to sea even if we have to come back tomorrow and drop Sonny off."

Racing to the back of the upper deck, Roy grabbed his Uzi and began to fire in the direction of the small flotilla that was beginning to form behind and on each side of them. It soon became obvious that if the flotilla of boats giving chase continued to grow in number, then Roy's cruiser would eventually be caught in crossfire and more of his crew would stand a chance of being killed. Leaving the others to keep up, the impetus Roy went back to where Elian stood at the wheel, and Sonny was directing her around the larger vessels, either entering the port or leaving fully loaded with oil.

Scanning the radar, Roy could see a large tanker apparently beached; turning and reaching out, Roy grabbed Sonny's arm and pointed to the vessel as it came into view in the dawn twilight.

"What's that tanker doing beached there?"

"Oh, boss, that tanker ran aground in last week's storm and began to break up. She is leaking oil, but most of it was pumped out only a couple of days ago. I heard people say they can't get any more out of her, and they are going to try to tow it off into deeper water or break it up before it causes more trouble. You can see the oil slick now," Sonny said, pointing his finger.

"Elian, I want you to slow down when we are past the hull of that stranded tanker there and be prepared to go full ahead when I give the order."

Elian slowed down, and she watched as Roy picked up the RPG and aimed it at the beached hulk. Roy fired a salvo of four shells at the wreck and shouted,

"Go! Go! Go!"

Elian had already got the message, and the cruiser lurched forward, throwing everyone off balance for a few seconds. The rocket grenades hit the steel hull, penetrating the outer and inner wall. The fireball, resulting from the trapped oil and gas being detonated by the heat, sent a huge blast of hot flames through the open vents, then the decks seemed to bulge upwards under the pressure of the explosion, and huge pieces of metal were hurled into the air. This spectacular explosion was followed shortly afterwards by columns of thick, acrid billowing smoke that reduced visibility behind Roy's cruiser to a minimum. The small flotilla of boats were enveloped in the thick black tendrils of oily smoke, obliterating any chance of continuing the chase, and as pieces of metal began to fall around them, several of them panicked colliding with one another in the resulting maelstrom. The oil slick ignited, sending flames across the open waterway and panic set in. Tankers going in both directions began to slow down in an attempt to avoid the flames, and pandemonium reigned. Elian, taking advantage of the turmoil, hurtled down towards the breakwater, keeping a close watch on the radar, easily avoiding the tankers, each desperately trying to turn away from the fire. Elian was forced to slacken speed; as she approached the head of the breakwater, using the radar and the depth finder, she negotiated the safe channel, and as the water deepened beneath and opened up before them, they were suddenly out into the South Atlantic.

This area was always busy, and Elian slowed down, keeping close to the shore; she tucked in passing as near as she could to the many tankers anchored, awaiting their turn to enter the port. Scattered amongst these, there were other vessels, container ships, and tramp steamers, with black smoke emerging from ancient boilers that went from one African port to another, adding to the heavy traffic. Roy glanced down at the radar; there seemed no sea craft chasing them, and he would have breathed a sigh of relief except he heard the distinctive whop, whop, whop, sound of helicopters approaching.

"Turn for the shore, boss." Sonny called out as he pulled at Roy's shoulder.

"There is nowhere to hide there. It's just beach or cliffs. They will spot us for sure!" Elian shouted.

"No, boss, trust me, head for the forested cliffs in front of you," Sonny urged.

Roy looked at him for a moment.

"What do you know that the maps don't know, Sonny? Tell me quickly. They are sure to spot us if they have our description," Roy asked urgently.

"It was the last rains that almost washed the village away and opened a crack in the cliffs. The entrance is wide enough for you to get this boat in, and the water is quite deep, and from the air, the trees hide it from view. I need that second payment, trust me," Sonny said with emphasis on the latter part of his hurried statement.

Elian used the nearby super-tankers; the bulk of their hulls seemed to blot out the sky, effectively hiding them from view above, and as she sped towards the shore, the mass of shipping would also confuse the radar of any airborne radar, making any attempt at tracking them. Aircraft appeared and helicopters hovered menacingly above the closely packed ships, but the search did not reveal the cruiser. The cliffs got closer, but no sign of any break appeared.

"He's tricked us, Roy," Elian said, and Roy caught the sound of panic in her voice for the first time ever. "There is no way we can escape the helicopters, and we will stand out like a boil on naked flesh if we try to make a run for it," Elian called out, her voice unsteady as she prepared to turn the boat around.

"No, boss, Croft, keep going, head for that bunch of cocoa trees. They were washed down from the cliffs when the storm came. Go right and keep going, and there is a way through," Sonny gasped as Roy gripped his shoulder.

"Best, keep going, Elian. We have to trust the little bugger, or we'll be caught for sure," Roy said, straining his eyes for a break in the foliage.

Suddenly, there was a gap, almost indiscernible from more than a few yards away. Roy pointed and Elian eased the bow into the tree-lined gap, and the cruiser was immediately enveloped in the thick foliage. Roy, although not relaxing for a moment, breathed a sigh of relief. He released his grip on the young African who smiled, his white teeth, complete with the space where he had lost the two front ones, glistening against the dark skin of his lips, making his face light up with pride, that he, Sonny, was the one who had saved them all. Elian, seeing they were hidden in the tree-lined gorge with thick foliage hiding them from observation from all sides as well as above, stopped the engines and eased the anchor winch, releasing the weight down into the water slowly.

They went below where Gael had begun to organise the passengers, and the main cabin looked like a dosshouse. There were clothes and weapons strewn everywhere. Gael was giving orders to two of the men of Fergus's crew, and Fiona was busy in the galley. Rachael and Susanna were dressing the wound of the third member of Fergus's crew. They looked sullen and unhappy.

"What's wrong with you?" Roy asked. "You are safe for the moment."

"You left Fergus. We should have gone back for him," one of them said.

"What!" Roy asked, looking askance. "Are you mad? We barely got out with our lives. I called Fergus to come before the explosion. As soon as I heard the sound of the starter under strain, as though the battery was flat, I knew they had rigged the boat to blow to prevent anyone taking her. The detonator took the power from the battery."

"Yes, but we should have checked. He may still have been alive," said the other.

"If I had thought there was any chance of him surviving that explosion, I would have done so; the force of the explosion would have sunk us, if it had not been for Elian's quick thinking."

The two men slunk away, obviously still not convinced of the validity of Roy's argument. Roy then went to look at the wounded man who had taken a bullet in the shoulder and one in the arm. The two women had cleaned the wound, and Gael appeared with a couple of field dressings to help. Fiona was busy with the lone sailor, who had lain on a bunk during the whole affray too weak to do anything to help; she knew, through careful nursing and slowly building up his strength, she would get him back on his feet.

Elian appeared at the door of the cabin,

"Roy, you had better come up here and see the damage," she said.

Roy went up on deck, and Elian went to the stern where the man had been injured. There were many holes in the stern, the transom, and the rear of the cabin, where bullets from men shooting from the small craft chasing them had hit the cruiser in many places.

"If we don't dig out those slugs and repair them before we leave, it will be obvious to anyone that we have been in a battle. You can see they are bullet marks just by having a casual glance at them. I did not realise how close they had got to us. If you had not fired those RPGs and made that tanker explode, we would never have got away."

"I knew it was a close call. I suggest you get the two men from Fergus's crew to give you a hand and make the stupid buggers realise how close we were to being caught. I get Sonny to help as well. We shall be here for a few days until things quieten down, I'm sure."

"I'll get the emergency repair kit. It contains wood filler, putty, and paint. It will hide the worst of the damage until we get back and can complete the repairs. Just be grateful as the shots did not hit anything vital. I'll get Sonny to check below the waterline and Gael to check the bilges below, just in case. I've not heard the auxiliary bilge pumps working, so I'm pretty sure they're dry below," Elian said, reassuringly.

They went below to organise the labour force and get things under way. They needed to get the vessel ready in case of a patrol stopping them, and even the most casual inspection would arouse suspicion and there would be no way out for them, in that event. The slightest suspicion would lead to them being taken into port, and Elian was not as sure as Roy that a close inspection by a trained team of customs officers would not discover either the weapons or the drugs.

Chapter 24

The next couple of weeks aboard the cruiser were wearing for everyone, and the boat was overcrowded, and the living space was cramped with the three male crew from Fergus's boat; Susanna and Rachael as passengers; and Roy's own crew, Gael, Elian, and Fiona. It was during this time that Roy was given the news by Fiona that they had disobeyed his orders and gone aboard the cruiser and recovered the drugs but had made no attempt to try and recover the boat itself. Roy, for once, did not chastise them; he simply acknowledged what they had done. Tempers were frayed as the boat was repaired all too slowly for Roy's liking, but Elian was insistent, the last thing she wanted was for them to be pulled over when they left the well-hidden creek, and obvious bullet marks in the hull would have them marked as the cause of the affray in Lagos harbour. Sonny, the local guide, left at the end of the first week to see if the search had quietened down. He was away for several days, and Roy began to wonder if he had been captured and interrogated by the Lagos police or, worse either, the gang of hijackers, or the oil companies' own police security, which, from what Sonny had told him, were worse than the hijackers themselves when it came to getting information from people. They used methods that were denied to any normal force and just as the mine security police in southern Africa seemed answerable to no one but themselves. Roy was considering sending a scout out to see what the position was when Sonny reappeared smiling as though he had only been away for a few hours.

"Where have you been? We were worried about you," Roy asked the once in a life time clean, shining face before him.
"I had to make sure you were safe. They believe the perpetrators were damaged in the explosion and suspect you may have made it to the sea, but that the boat was so badly damaged it must have sunk. They question every captain of every vessel as it gets into the harbour. So far, no one has admitted seeing anything," Sonny said.
"When will it be safe to go?" asked Roy.
"That's why I came back to warn you that someone will report seeing you in this area, and they will comb the area from the sea and from the land.

You have to leave tonight swiftly, and as silently as you can. If I can have my money, I will return to my village before I am missed."

"OK, but be careful and thank you for your help," Roy said. "I will give my thanks to the Brigadier for recommending you and inform him what an asset you have been."

Lord Croft went through to the stateroom and counted the promised amount and added a similar amount as a further bonus; then he returned and handed the envelope to the waiting young African. He weighed the envelope and looked enquiringly.

"It's too much, boss," he said. "I did what I did for a promised amount I . . ." was as far as he got.

"Then take the rest as a present from my crew. Without you, we would not have got away. Use it to get yourself an education if you can as a present for a job well done."

He watched as the young man left grinning, as he slid ashore and disappeared into the foliage; then he told Elian to be ready to sail as soon as it was dusk. Taking the opportunity, Roy sent a text message to the Brigadier, thanking him for his help, telling him they were safe for the moment. The next few hours were hectic as they tidied away everything and got the boat ready to sail.

As soon as they were clear of the foliage and out into the sea, they ran without lights, slipping silently between the huge hulls anchored, waiting to enter the harbour for collecting cargo mainly of oil. Roy now knew, that once they had made their move, as soon as they were clear of the ships bunched together, they had to make a run for it. Someone would report a large boat running fast without lights. Sonny had told Roy that was how the pirates moved at night and the patrols were supposed to track them down. The pirates, Roy had been informed, paid blood money to the patrols, that ensured that in return they turned a blind eye and let them run freely to and fro. Roy hoped he would be mistaken for one of their vessels as they raced towards the Cape Verde Islands. They saw several patrols, but fortunately, none challenged them. Shortly after they were out into the open sea, Roy sank into a deep depression from the constant murmurings by Fergus's crew that he had been the cause of Fergus's demise, and once the guilt had been established in his mind, it became a worm that grew, obliterating the fact that he had done everything possible to save Fergus and his crew. If Fergus had not been impetuous and tried to save the cruiser, he would have been saved like the rest. Roy firmly began to believe that he had, as usual, gone into a situation like a bull in a china shop without any thought of the consequences. As a result, he had lost a valuable cruiser and Fergus, his captain. Fiona had recovered the drugs, yes, but even that did nothing to ease the guilt from Roy's tormented state of mind, all the drugs in the world did not replace Fergus, who had been a loyal employee. Gael and Elian did their best to console him, but Roy seemed too depressed for them to make any impression; he blamed himself even though he knew he had told Fergus to leave the boat. Roy was aware that Fergus had only wanted to please him, not giving any thought for his own safety. Roy seemed listless for, seeming not to care, just doing his turn at the wheel, and when he was relieved, he went below into his cabin and spoke to no one.

Whilst Roy had been busy in Lagos, Janet had settled back into her normal family routine in Ireland, and the castle had been left immaculate by the tenant and had been easy to slip back into her old way of life. Sean and his sister, Sheenagh, were both attending the local nursery school, and Janet was aware that would change when Roy returned. He wanted the children to attend a private school. The baby was moving within her, and she knew it would not be long. The head had not yet engaged, but she knew the time for her delivery was getting close. She was relaxed and hoping that His Lordship might just make it back before the baby was born, but she knew it was a forlorn hope; she had heard nothing from him for some time, not that that was anything out of the ordinary. Janet was contemplating calling Kate Delaney, Sam's wife, to find out if she had heard anything when the telephone rang. She picked it up, half-hoping it would be Roy, but the voice, though familiar, was certainly not Roy.

"Hi, Janet, how are you? Is that husband of yours around or is it safe for me to visit. I'm in the area and would love to see you."

"Michael?" Janet asked incredulously, "Is that really you? What brings you to Ireland? I thought you were going to be busy in St Kitts for months yet?"

"Oh, I'm giving a series of lectures on my work to help fund my research. You haven't answered my question. Is your husband still away?"

"Yes, but why do you ask? Just come and see me. I'd love to see you."

"Then I'll be there later today, Janet." Michael replied, "I'll tell you all about the last time I saw Roy, when we met. If it's all right with you, I'd like to stay over for a few days?"

"Of course, you can stay. I'll see you later, Michael. I can't wait." Janet whispered still unable to believe he was so close.

Janet put down the phone and walked slowly into the lounge of the castle; this was a surprise as the last person she had expected to see was Michael. Her mind went back to the last time they had been together and she sighed. There would be no lovemaking this time; she knew he would not find her attractive at this stage of her pregnancy; she was well into her last trimester of her pregnancy. It was later that day when Morag had bathed the children, although Sean was becoming more and more independent, Morag was telling her, and thankfully shortly afterwards, both the children were in bed. Janet had ordered the supper to be set for two, and she had been waiting patiently when the doorbell rang; it was Michael. She had gone to the door herself, and when she saw him, she had hugged him for several minutes before inviting him inside. He had been somewhat surprised to see how far advanced Janet's pregnancy was, but to Janet's complete astonishment, he had stood back and looked at her with greedy eyes and had confessed that pregnant women were his greatest fantasy. Janet had asked Bridget to show Michael up to his room and serve the meal. They had sat down to eat, and Michael had told her how Roy had come to see him and asked all about Mark and what he had revealed to him. Michael had drank a bottle of Roy's red wine; she had refused alcohol because of her pregnant state; he seemed very relaxed when they sat in the lounge, and she was shocked when he took her into his arms and kissed her with such tenderness and care. Janet had not seen Roy for some time, and she allowed his amorous embrace to continue until finally, she said,

"Michael, you can see the way I am, but if you keep that up, I'm going to have to ask you to take me to bed."

Far from putting him off, Michael readily agreed, and they climbed the stairs and went into her bedroom. It was as though she was pregnant with his child, he cosseted her and cuddled her, making her feel so special. He whispered to her that she looked lovely; Janet smiled. If Michael kept giving her compliments, she knew he would soon be making love to her, no matter how pregnant she was.

Michael seemed enchanted by her, and finally she cried out,

"Enough, Michael, or I shall surly give birth to this baby tonight."

Michael understood and reluctantly stopped his tender administrations. They lay beside one another; as they held each other close, she kissed him.

"I can't see what you still see in me. I'm a married old woman who has already had two children and am close to having a third," Janet whispered.

Michael smiled and replied,

"You will always be the same woman I knew in college except at the moment in your present condition I think you are more attractive than ever."
Janet sighed; Michael could always find the right words to make her feel special; she felt him pull her close to him, and they fell asleep in that position. They woke early, and Michael slipped out of bed and returned to the guest room; after all, it would not do for the staff to know they had slept together whatever they would think. No doubt they would report it to Roy the moment he returned if they had the slightest inkling of the arrangement.

The following morning, at breakfast, Janet introduced Michael as an old friend of hers and Roy's, and she informed Cathleen, who had been off duty when he had arrived the previous evening, and that he would be staying a few days. Bridget, Morag, and Cathleen accepted Janet's explanation without turning a hair; after all, Lady Croft was very pregnant indeed; not one of them gave any sign that they thought she would be having any kind of relationship this late in her pregnancy. The arrangement whereby Michael joined Janet after the house had quietened for the night and him returning to his own room before anyone was awake, continued every night for several days; to Janet, it was like a fairy tale, but she knew it was too good to last. Michael finally announced he would have to leave as his short break was over and he had to return to the Caribbean. Janet was sorry to see him go, but knew if Roy had the slightest suspicion that Michael had slept with her in his marital bed, no matter how innocent due to her condition, he was likely to take drastic action; he might even kill the poor soul. She waved him off the following day after breakfast and settled back into her routine, waiting for Roy or the baby, not knowing which one would arrive first.

Meanwhile Roy was still in his state of deep depression, and nothing, any of his crew said to him, seemed to make any difference. He had rung Sam and broke the news of his failure to get the boat back in one piece, and that he had lost Fergus. He explained what had happened, and Sam was very supportive, telling him there would have been no guarantee that any of his crew would have survived if it had not been for his rescue attempt. Roy told him the cargo had been saved, and although it was of little solace to himself; he was sure the committee would be pleased that at least something had been salvaged from his abortive attempt. Having got the facts off his conscience, Roy seemed to brighten up, but the guilt persisted, and he made no attempt to invite any of his crew into his bed, preferring to sleep alone with his own thoughts.

Rachael and Susanna overheard Elian, Fiona, and Gael whispering that they were worried about Roy and wondered how they could get him to come out of his depressive state. They had only once before seen him go into such a state of mind, and that was when he had shot Kevan when he has found him raping Kerry. Susanna put on a brave smile and walked forward; she was the sort of woman who did not stand on the side-lines and watch. Lord Croft had done what she thought was a brave thing; he had gone into the very core of the hijackers to rescue his men with little thought for his own safety, and she was determined to try to help, no matter what it took. Elian was taken aback when she heard Susanna approach; she turned and listened with her mouth open as the attractive American spoke in her southern drawl.

"Am I'h to understand that Lord Croft is blaming himself for what happened back in that hellhole? Why I'h do believe it was a very brave thing to do, and there is no denying that he told us straight what we were up against. If it had not been for that man, Fergus, insisting he got the boat out. Why we might have been able to go back when things quietened down and got it out without destroying it or losing anybody in the attempt. I think we have to work together on one of the bravest and most honourable men I have ever met. We somehow have to get him to see the truth. Rachael and I'h will do anything we can to help, and that's a fact."
Rachael stood behind her, nodding her head vigorously.
"Do I'h understand that you all sleep with him from time to time?" Susanna continued.
The three crew members nodded their heads to indicate that Susanna's assumption was correct.
"I'h do declare. Rachael, this here is a love boat, and we have been on our best behaviour for nothing. Why if Rachael and I'h cannot bring that man round, then we are not the women we think we are. Where did you say we were heading?"
"The Cape Verde Islands," Elian said the incredulity of what she was hearing clearly showing in her face. "What do you have in mind?"
"Rachael and I'h will book rooms in one of the hotels, if they have such a thing on those islands, and leave the rest to us. If we can't help get him out of his depression, my name is not Susanna. Is that right, Rachael?"
"I'd have to agree with you there, Susanna. You three leave it to us. We will tell his Lordship we need to sleep in a bed for a couple of nights before we go on. It surely is very cramped on this boat; Why, I'h do declare it's very difficult with us all together, it is just too difficult to make a move on

Lord Croft. I'h have to admit those other three men have tried it on me a couple of times. I'h just looked at them and laughed till my hips ached," Rachael said, wriggling her hips and smiling.

No more was said about the matter, and the following day, Roy announced he would be heading for Praia on the island of Santiago.

"It's a small island. I don't want to be in the middle of a busy resort. I'll find a hotel and have a couple of days to think things through. I want to get 'Tony', the lone sailor, on a flight back to the States. He is now well enough to travel, and I'm sure he will be anxious to get back to his family. I will leave you to arrange the travel arrangement. Elian, just use my card to book him a ticket and give him enough cash to make sure he will not be short of funds."

Elian nodded her agreement, glad that at least one of the men aboard would be off their hands. Roy was almost taken aback when Susanna and Rachael, his two passengers, responded with,

"Why Lord Croft, We think that going ashore for a couple of days is a magnificent idea. We could do with a few days off this boat of yours, it's a bit cramped, and two days ashore will give us land-loving girls a bit of a break before the journey back to Ireland."

Roy knew he owed a lot to his two passengers; they had been a great help in Lagos, and he could not refuse to let them have a couple of days ashore. He had hoped to have a couple of days alone, but on reflection, it may prove interesting to have them along whilst the rest of his crew and Fergus's crew got the boat more shipshape for the run back to Ireland.

"OK, but I have no idea what the hotels in Praia are like. We will have to play it by ear when we arrive. It will give Elian, Fiona and Gael the chance to get Fergus's men to help get the boat in good order, and Fiona can restock the supplies. We have, no doubt, almost depleted her stocks. I think she has done well to make them stretch this far with all of us on board. That's settled then," Roy said.

On reflection, Elian had to admit he seemed brighter, either from the thought of a couple of days ashore or by the thought that he had two women in the same hotel that he had not yet had the chance to seduce. *It could be an interesting couple of days,* she thought to herself, *and not only for Lord Croft.*

Lord Croft made enquiries when they had cleared customs, and the best of a selection of hotels was the 'Pestana Tropico Hotel' as it had large rooms around a seawater pool, he was told. Roy and the two women took a taxi, and at first sight, the hotel was not very impressive with its flat slab front. Roy paid the cab, and the two women went into the hotel. They had already booked rooms when Roy got to the desk.

"Rachael and I have the room next to yours. They overlook the pool and are the two best rooms in the hotel. Lord Croft, I want no arguments as the stay in this hotel is on us. Show the desk clerk your passport and then follow us to the rooms."

Roy was still despondent and did not want an argument in the lobby. He went up to his room and found it surprisingly large, but although clean, it was not as luxurious as he would have wished. He dumped his bag and headed for the bathroom; a good hot shower was what he needed most before he went down to the bar for a drink. He was in the shower when he heard a voice say,

"Rachael and I'h will be in the bar, Roy. Join us when you are finished."

Roy pulled back the curtain and was surprised to see Susanna in his room; she was dressed in a summer dress, she had picked up from the hotel shop, and it showed her figure off to perfection. He could not wait to see what Rachael would look like, and he had not seen either of them in anything but cut-off jeans and a T-shirt since they boarded his boat.

Roy dressed in white slacks and an open-neck shirt, went down to the bar; Rachael was there, but there was no sign of Susanna; he took the bar stool beside her and ordered a large Irish whisky. Rachael was striking, and he had to look twice as he reappraised her. She looked better than he had imagined she would, from the tip of her toes up the shapely calves; her crossed legs revealed well-developed thighs, disappearing under the short skirt, and his eyes continued upwards taking in her slim waist, her well-developed breasts, and her face with its high aristocratic cheekbones, surrounded by the silky sheen of her long blonde hair which, until today, had always been under a turban or bandana. Revelling in his gaze, Rachael smiled and said, in her educated voice, but however hard she tried, she could not hide the thick trace of her southern drawl as she said with a broad smile of appreciation,

"Why, Lord Croft, Roy, I'h do declare, I'h do think those eyes of yours are giving me a full check over? I feel almost naked. Do you like what you see?"

Roy nodded guiltily, but he still tried hard to cover his embarrassment as he said appreciatively,

"It is really quite a change to see you out of those faded cut-off jeans, Rachael."

"Why, your Lordship? You only had to ask. I'h surely would have removed them any time you wanted," she replied with a wink.

Roy was somewhat taken aback by her answer, but he let it lie for a while.

"Where's Susanna?" he asked.

"I'h do believe she went to arrange dinner for the three of us. We are determined that you enjoy your short break at our expense," she replied, tossing back her drink.

Rachael stared up at him, and Roy began to see her in a completely new light; he began to think of the possibilities of getting her to go to his room. Sex was something he had not contemplated since they had left Ascension Island. He listened as she told him about her daddy and informed Roy, to his amazement, that he was one of the wealthiest men in Texas and had given them both gold and platinum credit cards and told the two of them to go on holiday and enjoy themselves.

"How come were you put off the cruise liner?" Roy asked casually. "I never did get to the bottom of that story."

"Well, we were just two girls having fun in the pool after a party. We did not go back to our rooms for our swimwear and shocked a lot of wealthy people in first class by swimming and running around in the buff. The stuffy old buggers complained, and when we did it for the second time, we were asked to leave the boat. One prim old lady almost had apoplexy when her husband had his arms around us. After that, the purser politely put us ashore. We enjoyed ourselves on the island, but I think we were a bit too much for the locals. Hence we joined you for the journey. I must admit it has been great fun."

She went on to tell him that she and her sister had been so terribly tired of the cruise liner and its stuffy passengers, then added looking around at the other guests,

"I'h suppose, I'h will have to change into something a bit more sophisticated to dine here. We don't want to be asked to leave. Would you be kind enough to walk me up to my room, Roy?"

Roy walked with his arm around her until they got to the grove of trees when she pulled him to one side and off the path, the foliage closed behind them, and leaning her back against a palm tree, she looked up at him and brought her hand up against Roy's chest; he stepped closer to her and kissed her full lips. Rachael's hands pulled at the buttons on Roy's shirt, sliding her hands around his bare back and pulled him against her letting him feel her breasts against his naked chest, and he was shaken a little by her eagerness. He looked around but could see that they were well hidden from the path by the dense foliage, and before he knew it, they were in a passionate embrace which just seemed to go on. Roy went along with the flow, his depression evaporated in a burst of unreserved sexual energy. He was swept along by her seemingly growing enthusiasm, all thought of his depression forgotten as his instincts took over, and moments later he was pleasuring the young woman beneath him as she had never been pleasured before. She gave her all as Roy used every trick he could to give them both the pleasure their frustrations desired. All too soon their consummate passion came to an end. Rachael lay back against the base of the tree and whispered softly, avoiding telling him of the arrangement they had made with Elian and the other two members of his crew.

"Why, Lord Croft, I'h do declare, I'h was only saying to Susanna that I'h imagined you looked like a ladies' man and that explains why you have those ladies as your crew? I'h am surely sorry if we cramped your style on board your boat, but now we know each other a bit better we don't have to be so formal. Now let's go up to my room and tell Susanna all about it, shall we? I'm sure the next couple of days will be very enjoyable for all of us, don't you?"

They quickly straightened their clothing; Rachael combed her hair into some semblance of order and tried to look presentable before returning to the path and making their way towards the stairs leading to the upper story where their rooms were situated.

The new-found lovers walked up the steps, and as they passed a waiter coming down, Roy ordered a bottle of champagne to be sent up to Rachael's room; they walked across the open balustrade-lined upper level entrance to the luxury rooms situated with their balconies overlooking the ocean. Rachael used her card to open the door, and they walked in. Susannah stood with a beach wrap tied around her, her auburn hair was hanging shoulder-length, and her face radiated health; the top of the wrap was loose, barely concealing her firm breasts; the tie belt accentuated her ultra-slim waist and the wide childbearing hips; her calves below the bottom of the wrap matched her elder sister's; they were shapely and well formed; her small, delicate feet spaced wide apart had pale-painted toenails. She looked good and very enticing even though, moments before, he had made love to her sister. Rachael was euphoric and could not contain herself as she told her sister what had happened in the garden below.

"My, that's some story," Susannah said. "Is there anything else I'h should know about this man? I'h always felt he had the passion bottled up inside of his chest."

"Well, honey," Rachael replied, "I'h do truly declare that his Lordship has just pleasured me more than I'h ever remember anyone I've ever had before, or is that too much information to share even with my own beloved sister?"

Susannah looked at Roy in a new light; she said, a broad grin running from ear to ear,

"That coming from Rachael is surely some complement. I'h am truly really jealous that she beat me to such a pleasure. I'm going in for a shower, and if you would like to join me, feel free. If what my sister says is true, why you are probably in need of a shower yourself, Lord Croft."

Pulling the tie of the wrap, she turned and the wrap fell to the floor, revealing her all, a sight to make any man eager to join her.

Roy looked at Rachael as if for approval; Rachael nodded to Roy, saying,

"Go ahead, your Lordship, she is a free agent, and I'h have no more claim on you than she has, apart from the fact that I'h had the pleasure of you first."

Roy followed the shapely Susanna into the bathroom; he was conscious that he would need some help with this, and feeling the weight of his hip flask in his trouser pocket, Roy pulled it out and took a deep draught of potcheen before unzipping his pants and unbuttoning his shirt; by the time he was naked, the water was on and the shower door closed. Opening the door, he looked the auburn-haired beauty, and his ardour, enhanced by the potent drink, was ready for whatever was to follow. Susannah looked down approvingly, her eyes wide open as she grinned,

"Oh my, Rachael was not telling me everything, was she, Roy? Why did you keep it to yourself whilst we were at sea? Come on in and help yourself to whatever you fancy."

Roy stepped into the cascade of water, and Susanna's arms went around Roy's waist pulling him towards her; their passions had no bounds as they clutched at each other without a thought for the future. Turning off the water, Roy stepped out of the shower and, despite having satisfied her urgent needs, knew he was not finished, the potent drink saw to that.

Rachael was nowhere to be seen; she had slipped from the room and he suspected she had gone down to the pool. Roy carried Susanna to the bed, and they continued to make passionate love until finally they were both replete. They lay entwined together, locked in a post-coital lover's grip, neither wanting the other to move. Susannah embraced her new lover; the knock on the door pulled them both from their thoughts.

"Are you two finished in there?" Rachael asked. " because I'h surely do need to get dry and change for dinner."

"Give us a minute or two," Susanna said, pushing Roy aside. "We'll be decent in a few minutes."

They hurriedly dressed and let Rachael into the room. Roy excused himself and went through the adjoining door to his own room to change for dinner. Roy had invited Elian, Fiona, and Gael to join them for the evening, and when he went down to the bar, they were already there.

The three of them were already on their second drink as he approached; it was Elian who spoke first, she could tell from his countenance that his depression had lifted.

"Was she as good as you expected?" she enquired.

"You mean our new crew members?" Roy replied. "Oh yes, she was good, but not quite as good as her younger sister."

"You mean you've had both of them already?" Fiona gasped. "Oh, my Lord, you are as bad as ever."

Roy was sure there would have been more ribald comments from the other two, but Rachael and Susanna joined them. Both women looked radiant, and to everyone present, it was obvious they had spent the afternoon in the hands of a lover of note. The three crew members whispered, but thankfully they were not overheard. It appeared they were worried about the arrangements for the rest of the journey. During the meal, Elian informed Roy that the remaining three members of Fergus's crew were eager to get back to Ireland, and it seemed as though they had had enough excitement and wanted to return to their fishing fleet. Without Fergus to keep them in check, they had lost their appetite for the wild life. Roy knew they would know better than to talk as all three of them were old members of the IRA and were aware of the implications if they told anyone what they had been doing off the coast of Africa other than picking up passengers for a charter.

When Roy heard what she had told him, he replied,

"Let them go I'll inform Sam and he will make sure there is someone to meet them when they land to remind them of their need to keep silent. As for me, I intend to get a couple of days rest and recuperation before we leave, so make arrangements to leave the day after tomorrow, and we'll head back. I'll find out how things are at home."

Roy was feeling guilty, realising that the birth of his third child was getting very near.

"I'll give Janet a ring after we have finished our meal."

Roy rang Janet, and she asked how long before he would be back; hearing how long he would be, she informed him that he had better get back soon as she would not be able to put the birth off for much longer. Roy assured her he would be home before the birth, but it would be a couple of days before they could leave. He did not inform her that, in the meantime, he would be enjoying the favours of his latest conquests nor did she inform him that she had been visited and overly cosseted by Michael. Both of them believed in their hearts, that it was better that way.

Chapter 25

All good things eventually had to come to an end, and Roy, Susanna, and Rachael left the hotel and made their way to the cruiser; the tender was stowed away, the anchors weighed and secured, and they headed north in the direction of Ireland. The weather forecast was good, and they were looking forward to a relatively smooth crossing. Roy, now fully back to being his old self, went into the stateroom and left the women to sort out who was sleeping where. Fiona and Gael were to share one cabin and Rachael and Susanna would share the second cabin. Elian, who would be taking the wheel on opposite shifts to Roy, would sleep in the stateroom whilst Roy took the wheel. The three men had opted to fly back to Ireland after Roy had paid them in full for the work they had done and a bonus to cover any effect their traumatic experience had left them with. The three of them thanked Roy for his generosity, and Roy drove with them in the cab to the airport. He had spoken to Sam, who had arranged for them to be met at Shannon where their allegiance to the IRA would be emphasised and their full co-operation and silence would be guaranteed. The gear stowed, and everyone settled in for the long voyage home.

Roy was happy and carefree on the homeward journey, but somewhat shaken when Elian broke the news that she and Fiona were in all probability both expecting, and neither had any doubts that in each case it was his child they were carrying. Elian confessed that it was all her fault she had simply forgotten when they were due to have their contraceptive injection when it had been due. She had said to him in an apologetic voice,

"I know it's my fault. I just forgot about the damned injection, and you know I told you last time after I had the operation to get rid of my growing foetus that if I ever got pregnant again, I would go through to the end."

"Oh my God!" Roy gasped. "What! Are you both sure? Is it confirmed?" he asked staggered by Elian's disclosure.

Roy understood how it had happened, but the thought of what Janet would say echoed through his mind.

"Yes," she muttered. "Are you very upset? Are you angry with me?" she asked.

"Upset, angry?" responded Roy. "Of course, I'm not. I'm overjoyed at the news, and I'm happy for you both if that's what you both want; but I'm worried what will Janet say when she finds out?"

Roy retired to the stateroom, leaving Elian to take her watch, and the time passed slowly over the next couple of days.

The following morning, Roy went up on to the bridge where Elian was at the wheel. They kissed, and Roy asked where they were. Elian's reply was that they were 150 miles from the Isla de la Palma, south of Madeira, off the coast of North Africa. Roy pulled the satellite phone out of the upper deck safe and sent a previously arranged message to Sam Delaney; the message gave no details of the position, just a blank SMS which as previously arranged would indicate he was off the coast of Portugal. A few minutes later, Roy received what at first glance looked like a reply; but no reply was scheduled and the message asked for the exact global position of the craft. Roy was concerned that their cell communications had been breached. Roy sent a set of co-ordinates 250 miles further south than their real position. He then switched off the phone, removing the SIM card; he went below and switched the radio transponder to that matching a tourism cruiser based at Tralee; he instructed Gael to change decals to that of the Rose of Tralee; this was a rouse he had used several times before. He then went up on to the bridge instructing Elian to proceed at full speed in an erratic course to Madeira. Several hours later, they were nearing the island of Madeira, and Roy had seen several coastguard patrols heading in the direction of the position he had given. Once the island lay behind them, Roy asked Elian to head at a normal speed in the direction of Lisbon. About an hour out of their destination, Roy heard a helicopter approach; it was a customs patrol; they called the boat on the radio, addressing the message to the tour cruiser *Rose of Tralee* to heave to for a routine search to be carried out by the European Union Customs and Excise. Roy knew that the cargo safely hidden aboard would easily pass a routine search of the cruiser; the cargo would only come to light if the boat were to be taken into dry dock and dismantled. Instructing Elian to heave to, Roy went down on to the foredeck to meet the customs officer being lowered from the helicopter. The officer released the cable, and the helicopter stood by hovering off the port bow. The visiting official was dressed in a one-piece jumpsuit and a full helmet. When the helmet was removed, Roy could see that the officer was none other than Catalina Cordoba. She put her fingers to her lips to stop him speaking to her as soon as she realised he had recognised her.

She showed no sign of recognition herself and formally introduced herself,

"I am Captain Cordoba. Señor, I apologise for the intrusion, but we are following up on information received that a vessel carrying drugs is in the area, and I have to carry out a routine search."

Catalina indicated the radio on her belt and stepped forward to shake his hand. Roy, taking the hint, shook her hand and formally invited her to carry out the search saying that his charter passengers would be excited at the prospect of being involved in a smuggling investigation. He went through the procedure of introducing Elian as his skipper, and then Fiona, Gael, Rachael, and Susanna as tourists viewing the coast of Spain, Portugal, and they had just been for a tour of the island of Madeira before returning to Tralee. It was Roy, presumed for the benefit of the operator listening to the radio on her belt that she introduced herself as Captain Cordoba; she asked to see the passports of the passengers and crew.

"They are kept below in the safe in the lower cabin, Captain," Roy replied. The officer apologised again, saying,

"Señor, as I will be left for a short time alone with you and your crew and passengers, it is necessary for me to check everyone for hidden weapons."

Still somewhat puzzled by her actions, Roy nodded his agreement, and she patted the women down and finally turned to Roy. Patting down, she ran her hands over his chest, hips, outer thighs, and then up inside towards his crotch; she smiled as she ran her hands over the familiar territory she had almost forgotten. They had been on a routine patrol when the tip off had come in, and she had recognised Lord Croft's cruiser from the description and had radioed in that she would do the search personally. The radio operator had insisted she left the channel open until she was satisfied that all was well aboard the craft and that no danger ensued. Using the short-wave radio on her belt, she reported that all was in order and that she felt confident that she could carry out the search whilst the helicopter picked up her opposite number, who was at present searching another large cruiser about fifty miles away.

Once the helicopter acknowledged her signal, it headed west; she turned to Roy and said,

"I recognised your cruiser as soon as I saw it. I just could not resist the opportunity to make your acquaintance once again, your Lordship. For the sake of expediency, tell your crew and passengers to remain on deck whilst we go below to carry out the inspection and view the necessary documents."

Roy could see she was slightly flushed as he stood back allowing her to go into the lower wheelhouse and down the inner companionway to the lounge below. As she descended she hesitated, letting Roy bump into her on the steps as her hand went behind her. She turned and, with a smile, said quietly,

"I'm sorry, Lord Croft," she said with a grin, "but I am not satisfied. I believe you have a hidden weapon on your person. I will have to search you a little more carefully now we are in the lower cabin."

"Catalina," Roy said, "you are bad. When did you change to helicopter patrol? I thought you had your own command last time we met?"

"I command a group now; consisting of both patrol boats and helicopters, but seeing your boat, I could not resist checking you out myself."

In seconds, she had thrown her arms around Roy's neck and whispered,

"It's been a long time since we slept together in Cadiz. Roy, I'm sorry if we parted company feeling somewhat aggrieved at my behaviour but today I don't have much time. I don't want to waste a minute more than necessary."

In minutes, her uniform lay on the floor with Roy's clothes, and they were in an embrace on the bed of his stateroom. Their passion rose, and as the time they had to be alone was short, both renewed their pleasurable need for each other until with a long, low moan of pleasure from Catalina, it was over. They quickly broke apart and dressed.

"Catalina," Roy whispered, "I am not complaining. I enjoyed that as much as you, but I thought you had married that army officer. What happened to him?"

"He was posted abroad on United Nations business for a year's tour, and I declined to go with him. I needed to have someone make me feel needed. It's been quite a while. I must say you are still as good as I remember, Lord Croft."

Smiling, Catalina swept her hair back over her shoulders; however, there was, no way she could hide the post-coital flush in her face. She made her way up the steps to the deck, pausing for a moment to turn and kiss Roy.

"I will, in all probability, never see you again," she whispered, "but I want you to know that I enjoyed the renewal of our acquaintance. Lord Croft, I can only wish you good luck with your charter business and bid you farewell."

She was smiling; her face flushed with pleasure as she stepped out on to the deck, putting on her full protective helmet as the wop, wop, wop of the helicopter blades could be heard approaching the cruiser. The lieutenant spoke into the radio and said,

"All clear, nothing suspicious here, you can pick me up."
The chopper hovered above the deck, lowering the recovery line, to pick up the officer, who was now fully satisfied in more ways than one. The now, once more, formal officer attached the hook to her harness; not knowing if Roy could see her face, she smiled and winked at him as she was winched up into the awaiting aircraft. The helicopter dipped its blades and moved away; Roy looked up, and he could see Catalina waving through the open door as the retreating helicopter moved away.

Roy turned and his crew and passengers gave a whistle of appreciation and in a chorus of
"Well, that's one way to avert suspicion," they all cried in unison.
"We could all hear her from up here. I would not be surprised if they had not been able to hear her in the helicopter," Elian said, laughing. "I thought I recognised her. It was Captain Cordoba, was it not? What was all the formality about?"
Roy just grinned and explained before he told Elian to head up towards Spain as they would spend the night off at A Coruña, their old stamping ground. Elian looked at him sternly and said,
"Roy, I feel you should make the effort to get back for Janet's sake. You certainly are not expecting to make love to any of us after that performance, and I think we should rather make it back to the castle and not run the risk of another customs examination."
Roy nodded, knowing that she was, as usual, right.

The weather forecast for the night crossing was not good, and the journey was rough; both of them spent the night on the bridge, dressed in weather-proof gear, and the others remained below in the cabin as the storm in the Bay of Biscay threw itself at the sturdy craft. Rachelle and Susanna, not being used to the bad weather, succumbed to seasickness. The storm eventually passed and dawn saw them moving up the west coast of Ireland. Roy, switching the satellite phone back on, rang home and informed Bridget, who answered the call, they would be arriving in the harbour in just about an hour's time. Bridget was delighted to hear Roy's voice again and ran upstairs to inform Lady Croft and the children of his Lordship's imminent return. As she went back down to the kitchen, she realised that she was quite excited even at the thought of Lord Croft being back; she smiled to herself as she thought of the possibility of his Lordship making love to her as she began preparing breakfast for a large party.

Chapter 26

The cruiser slowly entered the stonewalled harbour; Gael and Fiona jumped ashore to secure the lines to the wharf; Elian switched off the engines, and Roy stepped on to dry land for the first time in days. He turned to Elian and asked her to check the boathouse and prepare to get the boat winched up inside; he wanted to get the cargo securely stored in the underground store before anyone could make a surprise raid as it would appear that the European customs had been tipped off about their arrival and only fate had intervened. He knew how fortunate he had been that Captain Cordoba had been the one to inspect the cruiser, off the coast of Portugal and Spain. Roy was aware just how lucky they had been, and he had to admit to himself that it had also been much to his personal enjoyment. Roy rushed up to the house to be met by Janet, who looked as though she was going to have the baby at any moment; he put his arms around her and held her against him, careful not to squeeze her too tightly, kissing her tenderly on the lips.

"I'm so glad to see you home, safe, and that you could get back before the baby arrived," Janet said.

"By the looks of it, I was none too soon," Roy said, still kissing her and patting her bloated tummy.

"Oh, I'm not due for at least another week. I only wish it was over," she wearily replied.

Sean and Sheenagh ran towards their daddy; arms outstretched, Roy reached down, sweeping up one in each arm, and the children were overjoyed to see their daddy again, showering him with hugs and kisses. The door of the kitchen opened, and Elian, Fiona, and Gael entered; the children ran to greet them as the door opened again, and a still-green Rachael and Susanna entered. The rough crossing had not been kind to them even though Gael had given them both seasickness tablets. Roy introduced them to Janet, saying they would be staying for a couple of days until he could get them to Shannon to collect their belongings, before they continued their holiday in Europe. Janet smiled looking at how pretty the two American women were despite their grey-green faces; she was sure both of them would have received the close and unbridled attention of her husband somewhere or sometime during the voyage across the Atlantic. She was happy for him; in her state, he would get no sex from her for some time, and at her last examination, they had discovered a number of benign growths, and at the doctor's suggestion, she had decided, that if it was necessary, she would have a hysterectomy; there would be no more legitimate children for Roy. In Janet's mind, three was more than enough.

They all ate a hearty meal, and Janet asked Morag and Bridget to show the guests up to their rooms; Roy and his crew went down the quayside to winch the cruiser up the ramp into the boathouse. Once the boat was inside, Roy could see how barnacled the hull was, noting that Elian, Gael and Fiona would need to spend time cleaning the bottom before she was launched again to deliver the cargo after Sam Delaney had arranged the delivery co-ordinates and times. Arriving back, Roy rang Sam to inform him that they had arrived back safely; Sam was delighted and told him that there would be a council meeting in a couple of days; either he or Kate would ring and give him details. Then Roy rang the architect Gordon O'Leary to ask him to come and restore the entrance to the underground workshop; Gordon was away, but Megan, his wife, recognised Roy's voice at once; she said that she was delighted to hear that he was back and she would ask Gordon to ring him as soon as he returned to the house. Roy asked about her health and that of her brood of children. He remembered with some fondness just how fertile she was; each time he had had sex with her, she had become pregnant. She told him the children were fine, and the oldest two were now at nursery school. Roy hung up as he remembered how the first time he had taken her whilst her husband had been in the office at home looking over plans for changes at the castle. She had accompanied Gordon to the castle a week later, and Roy remembered that he had made love to her again aboard the MTB. He remembered her sister from the last time he visited their new home. Roy felt he should begin to quieten down now he was back, his mind reeled at the very thought of his extramarital sex and his brood of illegitimate children; he had always enjoyed sex with many women, thanks to his wife Janet who had taught him how to pleasure women in general, before they had been married, and she had never objected to his infidelity. She had always accepted his needs; after all, she had created them. He had been a virgin when she had met him, and she had taught him all he knew whilst she had been married to his boss and mentor.

Janet, who had kept Sean and Sheenagh back from school, went to get the gardener, to act as driver, to take them to school late; there was much to talk about, and after speaking to Kate, she wondered where Fergus was. She thought he may have gone back to his own base near Cork with his crew. She was so pleased to see Roy back safe and sound that she promptly forgot to ask.

At dinner that evening, Roy and Janet were joined by the two attractive visitors from America; they had recovered from their seasickness and ate well. Roy and the two women drank several bottles of wine during the meal, and the southern belles had gone to bed under the influence. Roy and Janet went up to bed; they kissed, and Roy lay behind her holding her, and they were soon asleep. Roy woke about four in the morning; he lay awake, tossing and turning; Janet was awake and sympathised with him; she turned and whispered,

"I'm sorry, lover, but I can't do anything for you like this. You had better go and speak to one of the American women. I'm sure they would be more than willing to help. I saw the way they were looking at you at dinner. They were practically begging for your attention."

Roy peeled back the clothes, put on his robe, went downstairs to the kitchen, opened the cupboard, and drank deeply from the supply of Cathleen's bottle of potcheen; he felt the warmth; as it went down his throat, he climbed the stairs to go up to Susanna's room. The look of joy on her face as Roy opened the door gave Roy all the encouragement he needed, and it was soon afterwards when hearing the noise coming from her sister's room, Rachael opened the door, as in a voice that sounded very sultry, and asked him to save some of his energy for her, as she was only in the next room. The two women were due to leave during the morning, and the influence of Cathleen's mixture ensured both visitors received his lasting and complete attention. It was getting light when Roy showered, the water washing all traces of his wild potcheen-induced sexual excesses off his aching body; once he was done, he dried himself and slid between the sheets and hugged his pregnant wife.

Later that morning, Roy delivered Rachael and her younger sister Susanna to the airport at Shannon, all of them completely unaware that Roy had impregnated both of the richest heiresses in America. They collected their baggage and boarded the aircraft that would take them to France; from there they would travel through Germany, Switzerland, until they reached

Italy, where they would meet their daddy's family from Sicily. The trip was designed to take several months by which time they would be well into the second trimester of their pregnancy. Roy drove from the airport directly to the Delaney's household; Kate had told Roy that Sam had left for an emergency trip to Dublin and would only be back for the committee meeting in two days' time. He had left strict instructions that she was to ask him to come to the house and get the envelope he had left for him; he anticipated that it held delivery instructions; his intuition had been wrong for once for the envelope contained a letter informing him he was once again a full member of the inner circle of the new IRA. Kate had, as usual, welcomed Roy at the door and took him into the large reception room and sat down beside him.

"I want you to see our son," she said, mouthing silently to him. "He is your son as well. He is asleep at the moment, but he will be awake in about an hour. I'm sure we can find something to occupy us during that time. The staff are all busy and have instructions not to disturb us."

She pointed towards the entrance to the old butler's pantry; Roy groaned inwardly would his dalliances never give him any respite; after taking a drink from the hip flask in his pocket, he followed her into the small room, and it was some time before they emerged. Roy knew he had done too much, the usual ache in his groin confirming the fact. He knew if he refused Kate, she would only have to tell Sam he had made advances to her and he would be in trouble.

Roy wished he had never started the affair on that fateful day of Sean's christening; his only excuse was that he did not know who she was at the time, but she was as exciting now as she had been that first time. They washed in the small hand basin and dressed before slipping into the reception room, where she poured Roy a large Irish whisky. She asked him to stay for lunch; Sam had insisted, she informed him. Lunch was as usual excellent, and he saw his son; if Sam even suspected, Roy knew he would be history, and when the meal was over, Roy left, much to Kate's disappointment as she had hoped for more of his attention.

Roy arrived home to be met by Bridget.

"It's time, sir. Lady Croft's in labour. You need to take her to the hospital now."

Roy was glad that he had resisted Kate and not stayed for more of her sexual delights. Helping Janet into the new Range Rover, he headed for the hospital. They had barely arrived and got Janet on to the trolley, or gurney as it would be called in America, when her waters broke; Roy looked up and thanked God it had not happened in his new car. The sister's name was according to the tag on her right breast was 'Leanne'; she was red-haired and her brogue was as Irish as could be.

"If you'll be taking her through to the labour ward, the midwife will be attending to her immediately," Sister Leanne said, fairly bristling with efficiency.

Roy looked her up and down; the starched uniform tried hard to hide her shape, but it failed miserably. Leanne was a stunner; Roy could feel himself attracted to her just by looking at her. The fiery redness of her hair intrigued him; she looked at him wondering why he was looking at her so intently; he looked almost the same age as her father; he looked so handsome and was, obviously, a seafaring man from his weather-beaten face and his deep tan, but something about him intrigued her; what it was she could not fathom out in her fuzzy brain, but he looked, how could she explain it, even to herself, the only word she could think of was sexy. Roy watched her as she moved about, even in her starchy uniform she oozed sex, her every movement indicated her high level of sexuality. Despite the reason he was at the hospital, with his wife about to give birth, his mind was already working out if there was any way to see more of the mysterious Leanne. Roy was ushered into the labour ward; he watched, as his wife pushed, when the midwife told her to and panted when pushing was not the answer. The actual birth was not the prettiest thing Roy had ever witnessed; but once it was over, he kissed his wife, thanking her for his new son. They had not even decided what to call him yet, and Janet suggested Darragh Michael Croft, and although Roy was surprised at her choice, he agreed and Darragh it was.

Leaving his exhausted wife to sleep, he went out of the maternity unit to see the attractive red-headed Leanne waiting in the car park.

"What's wrong?" he asked her.

"It's my husband," she said in her Irish brogue. "He is having to be working late and can't pick me up. I'm waiting for a taxi."

Never one to miss any opportunity, Roy said quickly,

"I'll give you a lift if you like."

Leanne's body shivered, it was late, cold, and it looked like rain was on its way; into the bargain she was stranded, and despite some misgivings, she heard herself agree. She gave Roy the number and rang and cancelled the cab. As gracefully as she could, Leanne climbed into the shiny new Range Rover; struck by the smell of new leather and the unusual comfort of the expensive vehicle, she lay back heady with the richness of the vehicle's interior; the warmth already coming from the vehicles preheat system softened any resistance she may have offered to Roy's intentions.

The drive to Leanne's house was fairly short through country lanes to an isolated house in its own grounds, it was not a huge house, but larger than most in the district; whatever her husband did, he obviously got well paid for it. Roy pulled into the drive, and she got out, asking him only out of politeness, she convinced herself,

"Would you like to come in for a drink? It's the least I can do after you were kind enough to give me a lift home, Lord Croft. It's a miserable night to be driving, to be sure."

Roy was surprised, but he accepted the invitation. Once inside, she closed the door behind them and asked him for his jacket, which she hung in a coat rack inside a small cloak room.

"I had not expected to be asked in," Roy said.

Leanne did not answer but gestured him to follow her, and taking a seat in the comfort of a large settee in the large lounge; the central heating was on and the room was very warm.

"I have to get out of this hospital garb. It smells so clinical," Leanne said. "Feel free to pour yourself a drink, and whatever you have, I'll have the same."

Roy found the drinks in a sideboard cupboard and poured two large Irish whiskies, one for him and one for Leanne.

When she came downstairs, she was dressed in a terry towelling robe and her hair was wrapped in a towel; she had obviously showered. She sat opposite him, and she took a drink. Quite unsuspecting the strength of the spirit, she downed a good half of the golden brown liquid Roy had poured for her; she spluttered and coughed.

"Oh, bejesus, that's strong," she stammered. "What is it?"

"Irish whisky," Roy responded.

"I don't normally take strong drink, the same as I usually don't ask strangers into my house. My husband won't be home until late again, and I just felt like company; knowing your wife was in hospital recovering from the birth and her scheduled hysterectomy, I knew you would be going home to an empty house, so let's keep each other's company," Leanne said with a sly smile.

With that, she tossed back the remaining whisky.

"You know, I think I'd like another one of those; it's something I could get used to."

Roy stood and picked up the two glasses and poured them both a second large measure. He handed it to her and sat back on the settee. Leanne picked up her glass and took a long gulp; as the fiery liquid burnt its way down, she smiled, and standing up, she walked towards Roy and sat beside him.

Leanne put her head on his shoulder and, to his surprise and horror, she began to cry; Roy put his arm around her to comfort her, and to her own amazement, she began to explain the reason for her being so upset.

"Oh, Mr Croft, forgive me. It's the time of the month I have these wild mood swings, but I have to tell someone my troubles, and I can't tell any of my friends at work. I think my husband has found someone else. He is often late from work at very short notice, and he hardly ever touches me feigning overtiredness. I feel so alone and uncared for."

The racking sobs shook her, and Roy felt himself transported back to the time he had comforted Janet when she had called him after her husband had drunk himself into a stupor. Roy let her cry the sadness out of her heart, and slowly the sobbing eased, but she made no attempt to remove Roy's arm from around her; instead, she turned her head to face him and said softly,

"Lord Croft, would you mind very much if I asked you to kiss me?"

Roy felt his fatigue fall away; his reflexes responded at the prospect of another conquest.

"The name is Roy," he whispered as their lips touched.

She was hungry for attention, and the kiss lingered, her breathing became almost sonorous, the kiss becoming more passionate. Leanne's arms went round Roy's neck, and she pulled him closer. She reached down, and taking one of Roy's hands, she placed it inside the terry towelling robe and placed it on her breast. Roy's palm touched the firm flesh, and she moaned softly; he squeezed gently, and his thumb and finger rolled the hardening nipple; it hardened to a firmness indicating that the neglected housewife was getting aroused and her need was growing. Roy kissed her neck and moved his lips kissing as he went until he kissed the hard-exposed nipple. She sighed,

"Oh God! Lord Croft, Roy, you'll think me a wanton. I don't know if I can go any further, but I'm so lonely, and you are so much older than my husband."

"Leanne, the fact is, that I may be older," Roy murmured, "but age can have its blessings. I am probably far more experienced than your husband. Just relax and let yourself go."

Leanne knew it was wrong, but Lord Croft had something about him she could not understand; she felt safe in his gentle touch, her body becoming more and more pliable. Roy felt her stiffness fall away as she relaxed. Roy the Lothario worked his magic on the very attractive but hapless and neglected housewife, and a low moan escaped from Leanne's lips. She was rapidly becoming beyond recall; her husband had been 'working late' and had been neglecting his duties towards his wife. Leanne, desperate for a man's attention, sighed, her body surrendered easily to the soft and caressing hands, and she was lost, she heard herself moan softly,

"Oh my God, I'd forgotten how good sex can feel."

Roy revelled at the feeling of satisfaction, knowing this seduction of women was too embedded in his very nature to consider slowing down. He was aware that whilst nature gave him the ability to carry on, he would never stop. He took Leanne to the edge and over, totally uncaring about the consequences of his actions, only heedful of the moment giving her what she wanted at that very moment in time and holding nothing back as he drove into her as she arched up taking all he had.

They lay still; their passions momentarily satiated, Leanne was deep in thought. She had never been unfaithful to her husband before; he had been her only lover. She felt sad that she had needed to let another man into her life, especially a married man who could have no long-term relationship, and she imagined that she would not want one. Her husband, she knew in her mind, was having an affair, the way he constantly worked late sometimes without any warning, paid her no attention either in bed or out of it feigning tiredness and falling asleep. She believed he was getting his sexual satisfaction with another; instead of facing up to her fears and discussing it with him, she resolved to do to him what she believed he was doing to her. She whispered, her voice still husky with a desire that had not yet been fully satisfied,

"My wayward husband won't be home much before midnight. Let's enjoy ourselves, shall we? I'll get two glasses, and follow me up to bed. If we are going to be lovers, let's be comfortable."

Roy watched as she grabbed two glasses from the sideboard, and he pulled the hip flask from his jacket, he took a drink, feeling the warmth flood down to his genitals; moments later, he followed her up to the master bedroom, and it seemed she was not only resolved in her intended revenge on her husband but was prepared to go one better and cuckold him in their marital bed.

The next two hours were both enjoyable and revealing as Leanne explained how, until the last six months, her husband had been the most attentive man she could ever have wanted. Money was good, but if not plentiful, it had always been regular. However, of late, he seemed hardly to notice her. She continued bemoaning her fate whilst taking everything Roy had to give; she seemed as though her neglect over the last six months made her almost insatiable. Finally, she broke away and whispered,

"I think we should call it a night. He will be home soon, and I don't want to end a wonderful evening with a violent argument."

Roy went through to the shower and quickly washed away any evidence of their infidelity and dressed; she followed him down the stairs and kissed him, as he left whispering,

"I'll see you at visiting time at the hospital tomorrow. Drive safely."

The door closed behind him, and he climbed into the Range Rover and drove away, and he did not see her watching him go through the upstairs window, the smile of satisfaction from her enjoyable evening and the fact she believed she had had her revenge for what she considered was her husband's betrayal.

Roy felt elated at his latest success. It had come out of the blue like so many of his sexual conquests; he had only been back home for a few days, and he was as bad as ever. He felt as though he was betraying Janet, but she had given him every opportunity, and he was only taking advantage; he drove back towards the castle, invigorated at the thought of what the next few days might bring. He could not remember when he last felt so good; the only time he could compare the feeling was when he had first made love to Kirsty whilst her husband Granville was out on the water with Elian on the cruiser for a test trip after the refit. The following day, Roy went to see Janet; he was met as he waited to enter the ward by Leanne.

"I want you to take me home again tonight," she whispered. "That no good husband of mine has told me he won't be home at all tonight. He apparently, or so he says, has to work to get his project completed. I just know in my own mind that the old devil is taking his mistress to some hotel. I'm off tomorrow, so you can sleepover, and we don't have to get up early in the morning."

Despite his concern that Leanne may become too demanding, he could not resist the thought of spending the whole night enjoying her favours; he replied,

"I'll see you in the car park after visiting is over."

He was about to move away when she caught his arm and pulled him into the sisters' office and locked the door behind him. She gave a soft moan and gasped,

"Oh God, I can't wait that long. Give me a kiss to tide me over."

The kiss was passionate, and as he pulled away from her grasp, she was breathing heavily, her face flushed with desire, and apart from releasing some of Leanne's pent-up tension, there was not much satisfaction in the hurried but very passionate kiss. Roy moved away, opened the door, and stepped out into the corridor, leaving Leanne to pull herself together and calm herself down.

Roy walked quickly towards to the ward where his wife was waiting with her new born son; she put her arms around him and, as she kissed him, whispered,

"Who is she, Roy?"

Roy endeavoured to look innocent, and injured by Janet's enquiry,

"What are you talking about?" he asked.

But the flush in his cheeks and the fine sheen coating his forehead were something she recognised and the excitement in his eyes had given him away.

"I have been married to you for a long time and know every inflection and mood you may try to hide from me. I can see in your eyes you have recently been with a woman or are planning to do so when you leave. It's someone in the hospital. I'll find out who it is, don't you worry. I hope she was good. You're late, and you have wasted ten minutes of visiting time. Now hold your new son. I hope he grows up like his father, but not with your sexual appetite. I just don't know how I put up with you, maybe it's because I could not imagine life without you?"

Roy held his son; he knew Janet would be in hospital longer this time, especially as the specialist had planned her hysterectomy to take place as soon as she had recovered. Roy had not told her, but the doctor had informed Roy that he was worried that the one of the biopsies he had sent following the delivery had looked very suspicious. Janet had just been informed that the doctor had thought it best to do the operation whilst she was in hospital, and she had told Roy that, as a result, she would be kept in for a week to ten days.

Roy's mind wondered as pictures of Leanne swam before his eyes; he felt elated at the prospect of spending a whole night with his latest conquest. To hide his thoughts and to take his mind off Leanne, he told Janet about the usual happenings at the castle, how the children were behaving, what the staff had been up to, and how the cruiser's keel was almost clean and they would be re-launching her in the next few days. Janet listened to his constant chatter, and when the bell for the end of visiting rang, the sister walked down the ward, and when she came level with Janet's bed,
"Oh, Lord Croft, I saw you were late, arriving. You can have a few minutes extra with your wife today," she said.
Janet's eyebrows rose up, and she looked closer at the sister. *Could she be the one?* she asked herself. *She is pretty enough*; but she dismissed the idea. She was so much younger than Roy, although that had never deterred him before. Janet dismissed the idea; the sister in question had always been so starchy and professional. There was no way Janet thought that even Roy could get into the iron maiden's panties.

Roy said goodnight to Janet and met Leanne on the car park; she climbed into the Range Rover, and they headed for her home. Leanne had prepared a meal for them; it only had to be warmed in the oven. The table was laid for two, and a good bottle of red wine was soon opened by Roy, whilst she went upstairs to change into, this time, a silky robe, and when she came down, the two of them sat drinking the rest of the bottle of her husband's good Irish whisky. They ate the meal, and she washed up whilst Roy, taking the hip flask from his pocket, drank some of the potcheen he had filled the flask with before leaving the castle. He felt the usual warmth spread through him, and he finished the last of the bottle of wine. Leanne came into the room, and they went up to bed; this time there was no rush. Although it had been in the early hours of the morning when they had finally fallen asleep, Roy woke early, and if Leanne had expected him to be there when she woke, she was disappointed. Roy was determined to get back to the castle before going to the hospital, and despite Leanne's entreaties Roy left and drove home.

Just before lunch, the phone rang, and it was Leanne.

"Roy," she said, sounding concerned, "I have to see you. Come for lunch. You can leave for the hospital from here."

Roy sighed; he hoped she was not going to become a serious problem as he had avoided such a thing all his life, and he prayed she was not going to be the first. When Roy arrived, Leanne opened the door; she looked grave and very worried.

"What's wrong?" he asked her.

"It's my husband," she replied. "He phoned a short while ago telling me he needed to see me urgently tonight, and he would be home at half past four. He hasn't been home that early for weeks. He told me he had something important to tell me. I just know he intends to leave me. I just know he's going to tell me he wants a divorce."

Roy put his arms around her, and she nestled her head into his chest; picking her up in his arms, Roy carried her upstairs to the bedroom and laid her on the bed. He sat and comforted her, but nothing he did seemed to help. She was in need and Roy was only too willing to oblige as their passions rose Roy felt her reach her climax several times before he finally slumped forward his own passion spent. They lay beside each other recovering from yet another reckless sexual tryst.

"Oh, Roy, that was wonderful, but what am I going to do?" she asked.

"You may be worrying over nothing. Don't be so pessimistic. He may have come to his senses and decided to give up his mistress and come back to you."

"Oh God, do you think so?" she asked.

"I find that it always pays to be optimistic at all times," Roy whispered, relieved that she had not given up on her husband.

"Oh, my Lord," she whispered, "I'll have tidy myself up. I would not want him to see I have been upset and crying. He might change his mind about coming back. He has always relied on my strength of character."

Roy gave her a kiss on the cheek and left glad that he had misjudged the situation and left hurriedly to go back to the castle to change; he thought he might be able to pick up Sean and take him to the afternoon visiting time to see his new baby brother. Janet was delighted with the surprise visit, and Sean asked what they were going to call his new brother. Janet and Roy looked at each other as it was something they had discussed but not yet announced.

"Oh, it's going to be Darragh Michael Croft," Janet said to him.

Her eyes looking at Roy, hoping he had not twigged that Michael had been the lover she had been so taken up with at college and in the Caribbean and she hoped Roy never got to know that Michael had been with her just before Roy arrived back after his Atlantic crossing.

"Oh, I like Darragh," said Sean. "I have a friend at school called Darragh, and he is such a nice friend. He shares everything with me."

Janet looked at Roy; she smiled at him, pleased at her son's response; his innocent comment had taken all the attention she had dreaded from the use of Michael as her new born son's middle name. She had dreaded any confrontation to spoil the new baby's arrival. It seemed that everything would be fine and her family was complete.

In the meantime, Leanne had dressed in her newest dress to make her husband realise what he was giving up and went downstairs to await his imminent arrival. She sat in the lounge and heard the key in the lock; she got up ready to respond in equal venom as she expected from her spouse. The lounge door opened, and Leanne gasped in surprise; in his hand were two dozen red roses. Leanne's first thought was that his mistress had thrown him over and he was looking for a way back into her affections, but just as she was about to speak, he began,

"Oh, Leanne, I'm so sorry. I've neglected you over the last few months, but I have completed the huge project I had been entrusted with at work, and last night, I made the finishing touches to this morning's presentation. I was so successful that at the board meeting I was offered the coveted directorship I had been working towards. My salary has almost doubled, and we can now try for that baby we both wanted but could not afford."

He dropped the roses on the table and swept Leanne, whose jaw had dropped open at his words, up into his arms and began smothering her with kisses. He carried her upstairs and made love to her in a way she had almost forgotten; he was tender, caring, and, above all, loving. It was a revelation as it was not as satisfying as Lord Croft but different and very, very enjoyable. When it was over, they lay together, embracing like newly-weds. Leanne was consumed with guilt as she heard him say,

"I've booked a table at an expensive restaurant in Dublin, and we are booked in at one of the best hotels at the expense of the company. Get ready. We have to leave almost at once."

Leanne was changing when she realised the enormity of what she had done. It was not her husband who had committed adultery, but it was herself. She had let another man make love to her, and she realised the consequences as they had not taken any precautions. She had checked her calendar that morning after Roy had left, and she was well past her safe period. As she opened the front door to leave for her evening out and to her surprise, she could see the new jaguar on the drive.

"Whose is that?" Leanne asked.

"It's my new company car. They delivered it just as the board meeting finished. Isn't she a beauty?" her husband replied.

Leanne lay back in the warm comfort, smelling the new leather just as she had done a couple of days before in Roy Croft's Range Rover.

The following afternoon, when her husband had dropped her back at the house, she rang Roy and asked him to come over on his way to the hospital. He did so, and she told him everything her husband had explained to her. He listened, impressed that she was able to tell him of her error of judgement about her husband's infidelity when Leanne put her arms around his neck and kissed him passionately pressing her body against him as she did so. Roy immediately found that he was responding. Leanne broke away, telling him she had needed to kiss him goodbye, but after what her husband had said, she could go no further. Roy understood he had never forced anyone to make love to him; he told her he was happy that she had got her life back together, and Leanne breathed a sigh of relief; she had wondered if he would make a fuss about her using him not realising Lord Croft was thinking the same thing. The affair was over. She was glad that Roy had gone, and she listened for the last time as the distinctive sound of his Range Rover's diesel engine fading in the distance.

Leanne had only just got back into the house when she heard the Jaguar pull on to the drive. She realised just how close she had been to being caught with another man in the house. In a way, she was sad she had enjoyed the flourish of sex Lord Croft had aroused in her, and in her mind, she wondered if he would call to see her again when it had all blown over. Leanne realised that her heart was racing with the thought of her infidelity; if it happened again, she would need to be more careful; she would have to be stronger, and in her own mind, she knew it would be hopeless; she was what her mother would have called a 'fallen woman', and helpless to stop, Lord Croft from taking her whenever he wanted her. She ran towards her husband with open arms as the door of the car opened; they embraced passionately; they made love again, this time in the lounge on the settee where Roy Croft had taken her the first time. Her husband was again more loving, and the euphoric feeling of her illicit sex with Lord Croft, would never be the same; her husband was so pleased that his wife had forgiven him for neglecting her. So pleased, they could now afford to try for that long-awaited child. In her frame of mind, Leanne's newly discovered wanton behaviour was both reckless and exciting, and she was sure she would miss her period; she hoped there would never be any reason for a DNA test of her firstborn child.

Chapter 27

Sometime later, when Roy visited, Janet was obviously feeling much better and was already asking when she could go home; she missed young Sean and Sheenagh, and when Roy arrived, she was bemoaning the fact that the doctor had refused to discharge her until he was satisfied that she was, in his opinion, ready for the demands her family would put on her when she arrived home. Roy stayed and listened to her complain, but eventually she became used to the idea she would have to stay for at least another two or three days. When Roy arrived back at the castle, there was a message on his IRA cellphone: it gave a number to ring; the short message gave date and time. The meeting was to be held the following day at the Delaney's house.

The following morning, Roy drove to the meeting, and he was met as usual by Sam. It was with a beaming smile, he said,

"Welcome back, Roy," as he pumped Roy's hand in greeting. "The meeting will only start in a couple of hours, and I still have to finalise the documentation, so you will have to excuse me. If you don't mind, I'll ask Kate to look after you."

Kate appeared from nowhere, and she smiled and kissed Roy lightly on the cheek.

"I'm pleased to see you again, Roy. How is Janet and her newest addition?"

"Oh, she's on the mend, and young Darragh has a good pair of lungs. I'm expecting her home in a couple of days. But it will take her some time to get over her operation," Roy replied.

Kate walked in front of Roy and said loud enough for Sam to hear.

"Come with me, I'll take you into the reception room, and you can bring me up-to-date developments with the family. From what Sam tells me, I understand you have had some modifications done to the cruiser, and you have had some wild adventures to say the least."

Roy replied, explaining that he had renewed the engines, and the craft now had a faster response and was very much more economical. He would have told her more, but they were now out of Sam's hearing and were entering the large reception room.

The moment the door closed behind them, Kate grabbed Roy's arm and guided him silently to the entrance to the butler's pantry. The door closed behind them, and seconds later, she was in Roy's arms. Kate pressed her soft, now slightly thicker, but still voluptuous body against him and whispered,

"Oh God, I have waited for you to arrive all morning. We have almost two hours to ourselves. Let's make the best of it."

Sometime later, they sat drinking and talking when Sam entered the room. His mood had changed as he was angry; one of the domestics had dropped a tray of food intended for the meeting, and he had been forced to get the cook to do something else. His anger was such that he overlooked the flush on his wife's face, and even if he had noticed, it he said nothing. To all outward appearances, he apparently had no inkling that his wife was having any form of relationship with the man who was destined, in the future, to become his second in command.

Roy and Sam walked to the meeting room; the meeting went well with everyone welcoming Roy back into the fold. All of them expressed their concern over the loss of Fergus and the other cruiser; they discussed the delivery of the drugs to the mainland. Roy wanted to deliver fewer numbers of larger loads, but the committee preferred to deliver smaller amounts on more trips; the risk of loss would be considerably smaller. If the police intercepted a delivery, the cost would be less in value; after all, they argued the value of the cargo was worth millions of US dollars, and they needed to make a profit as well as disrupt the development of the upcoming generation of the British. It was suggested at the meeting that Roy bought another cruiser to maintain the appearance of a successful charter company, and probably a third later in the year. They asked the price of a new or nearly new boat and agreed to sponsor half of the cost. They were delighted when Roy suggested that Gael take her master's ticket and they would supply another 'Fiona' to be mate on the second boat. They did not want Roy to be directly involved in the actual deliveries anymore; they felt he was far too valuable to them as the new director of operations.

Roy protested he loved the adrenalin rush of being personally involved. A vote was taken, and it was decided that Roy could be involved, but he should not be on board at the actual point of delivery. Roy drove back to the castle, thoughts of his new cruiser going through his mind; arriving back, he called Gael, Fiona, and Elian to a meeting. They sat in the small office in the boathouse when he informed them of his intention to replace the lost cruiser. He put it to them that if they were agreeable, Gael and Fiona would need to go to be trained and obtain their master's certificate; both were ecstatic at the news. Elian asked who would skipper the new boat, and when she learned, she would, she smiled with a degree of satisfaction.

Roy realised that another chapter in his life was opening; he was once again in the innermost circle of the IRA. He was a trusted member of the organisation. They had made him Director of Operations for the drug supply to the United Kingdom and insisted that he replace his lost cruiser with the possibility of even a third. He had three wonderful children by Janet, his wife, and countless children from his many mistresses, most of whom had managed to persuade their husbands that the children were theirs. This included some of his staff at the castle and his architect friend Gordon's wife, Megan; he numbered Kirsty, his boat re-fitter's wife as another of his conquests, and above all, the wife of Sam Delaney, the irascible head of the IRA, and some of her friends amongst others. In the future, he planned on calming down, hoping he would be given the opportunity to spend more time with his family in his home in Ireland.

It was sometime later when Roy rang Granville Williams, the owner of a boatyard, in the north of England; he had used several times before, and after giving him the specifications of the vessel he wanted, he asked him to find out what boats were on the market, either new or nearly new. Granville told him the Earls Court Boat Show was coming up and suggested that Roy and his skipper Elian come as his guests. Roy accepted the offer at once, and Granville said that he would send details as soon as he had booked the accommodation. Granville rang only about half an hour later and said he had booked two double rooms at a five-star hotel near Earls Court and would send the air tickets. Roy, always conscious of being compromised, would not accept the proffered tickets.

"Granville," he said somewhat sharply, "we'll make our own way to Earls Court. I really don't expect you to pay for our air tickets."

Granville was disappointed; he had felt happy to make the offer not for any other reason than he expected to make a handsome commission from the arrangement, but he reluctantly agreed to let Roy pay for his own air tickets and then told Roy that considering all the specs he had given him, he would recommend the Princess 25M power cruiser.

"The only problem I can see," he told Roy, "as with all the standard boats is its speed." He added, almost as an afterthought, "Are you going to operate this as a separate business like last time or will it operate from the castle?"

"From the castle, after losing the last one as we did, I want to be on top of all my operations. There will be no more remote companies from now on," Roy replied.

"In that case, it would be possible to reconfigure the engine room, but it would prove to be expensive on top of the cost of the actual cruiser." Granville continued, "Extra fuel tanks would need to be fitted in the base of the hull to give you your required range."

Roy listened intently; he took a personal interest in any alterations to his boats as, in his line of business, it paid to have all the information at his fingertips.

Granville knew that space would be very tight; cross-flow pumps would be needed as they had been in Roy's MTB. Roy was delighted at the prospect, and he could not wait, so he asked Granville to send the detailed specifications of the boats as they were, including cabin layouts, detailed hull drawings showing crawl spaces, and the estimated cost of re-engineering the engine room for greater speed. Granville, excited at the thought of being involved in the conversion of such a fine craft, agreed that he would get onto the manufacturers. About half an hour later, he rang to inform Roy that the required documents were being couriered directly to him and informed him that he had contacted a dealer who would pay excellent value for the Caterpillar diesels currently fitted. Roy asked the price of the cruiser and was pleasantly surprised as he had expected the figure to be much higher.

Later that day, Roy collected his wife from hospital and told her he had contacted Granville and he and Elian would be going to the boat show over the weekend to try to choose his new boat, and he also told her all about training Gael and Fiona for their skipper's license and confessed to her that both Elian and Fiona were carrying his children; she took a deep breath,

"Roy Croft," Janet retorted, "I'm not really surprised. The only thing that amazes me is that it has not happened sooner. I've warned you before to make sure any woman you are about to have sex with is safe, or keep your pecker in your trousers. You have to have more consideration and respect for me and the other women in your life."

Roy decided to change the subject, and he continued to talk about his new boat like an overexcited schoolboy expecting a new bicycle. Janet was glad when the time came for him to leave for Earls Court; she had heard enough about boats to last her a life time. Janet had her new baby to keep her happy, and she smiled as she waved him off, saying,

"If you don't start keeping that weapon of yours under control, we shall have a children's home of our own and all the children in it will have the same father."

She considered her own faults, and in her own mind, she felt she could not really criticise him, as she believed herself to be just as guilty; she had not or nor would not tell him about her affair with Michael; she knew she should never see her ex-college lover again, and if she did, she also knew that she would let Michael make love to her again if he wanted to, at any time in the future, as he made her feel so wanted.

Roy arrived, with Elian, at Earls Court. After all, she was going to be the skipper of the new boat. Granville met them, and they went around looking at many of the power cruisers from manufacturer's like Bayliner, Sunseeker, Princess, and many more, far too numerous to mention; the boats were magnificent as some were well over 100 feet long, fitted out in the utmost luxury. The common fault with all of them was the top speed; every one of them, even at best, would only manage thirty-five to forty knots, and this meant that none of them were fast enough to outrun the law, if and when necessary, as all would need serious changes to the engine room. After a long day, the three of them went back to the hotel for dinner; the discussions over, the meal were argumentative but in the end conclusive; Roy decided that if he was going to have to change the engines, he would be better taking a second-hand boat and doing a refit. Granville agreed and broke the news that he had anticipated Roy's decision. He had, as a result, done a considerable amount of research over the last couple of days and that he had found two Princess 25Ms, one sited in the south of France and the other in Kingston, Jamaica. They both sounded in excellent condition, both had portfolios available on the Internet.

Roy was delighted by the news, and after dinner, he went up to his room and, using Granville's laptop, accessed the hotel's Internet facilities and connected to the sales sites, and once he had seen both boats, he decided to view the one in Kingston, Jamaica, first. He rang home and told Janet the good news, and after asking about her own and the children's health, he requested that she tell Gael and Fiona to be ready to fly to Jamaica, if he decided to take the boat on offer. Janet's reply was somewhat disheartening, as she said,

"For your information, poor Fiona is suffering from very bad morning sickness, and I would not expect her to be well enough to make the flight or the journey back across the Atlantic." After a moment's pause, she continued, "Perhaps you can contact Shilpa whilst you're over there. She has helped on the boat before, and don't forget to see your mother. She looks forward to your visits, as I assume does Shilpa, but for different reasons. Now don't get yourself into anymore hot water, will you?" she said sharply.

Roy reeled from the sharpness in her voice, knowing only too well what she was referring to.

Roy and Elian left the next morning in a hire car to drive to his mother's; it was his intention to contact Shilpa in the hopes that she would be available for the forthcoming trip; to his surprise, he found her still staying with his frail-looking mother. He was shocked at his mother's appearance as her health had deteriorated considerably since he had seen her last. He rang Janet at the first opportunity and explained the position.

"You had better get her to come and stay here, Roy. I can arrange for her to be properly cared for with full nursing care over here," Janet said.

"I'll try, but you know how she is," Roy replied.

"Roy, listen to me. Don't take no for an answer. You seem to be able to persuade women to do almost anything for you. Just do it for her sake." Janet exclaimed.

Despite his mother's protests, Roy insisted on her coming to stay at the castle where she could be looked after properly; Roy told her he would get a private nurse, day and night, until she was fully recovered. That having been agreed, Roy pulled Shilpa to one side and asked if she would consider crewing in place of Fiona on the return trip from Jamaica. Shilpa was enthusiastic at any chance to spend time with Roy, and she readily agreed, and as Elian was talking to Roy's mother in the kitchen, Shilpa drew Roy into the lounge and, once the door closed behind them, embraced and kissed him open mouthed.

"Oh, Roy, I've missed you so much. I'm so glad you've come. I've been so worried. Your mother would not let me ring you."

Roy broke her passionate embrace and whispered,

"Later Shilpa, let me talk to my mother. There'll be time for that later."

Roy sat chatting to his mother and explained that he would need to leave the following day for Jamaica, but Shilpa and Elian would stay and escort her back to the castle in Ireland, where Roy felt he could arrange for her to get proper professional nursing help. His mother, who never wanted to be a burden to Roy or Janet, reluctantly agreed, realising that she was not getting any stronger. Elian understood what she had to do to get both Shilpa and Roy's mother safely to Ireland. Roy had given her carte blanche, and she was busy arranging an ambulance and a private aircraft to take her to the castle. She was taking no chances with her precious cargo. Elian knew Roy would never forgive her if anything happened to his mother; she was not quite so sure about Shilpa; she had not been able to avoid hearing the sound of them together the previous night. Roy, on the other hand, was trying to convince himself that he was becoming overburdened with all the women around him; although after leaving the West Indian Island's last lime, he swore he wanted nothing more than to get back to Ireland, now here he was, unable to wait to get back to the warmth and the wonderful Caribbean sun once again.

End of Book Two

=I=

To be continued

Lightning Source UK Ltd.
Milton Keynes UK
UKOW040647290313

208378UK00002B/51/P